I0681000

Praise for
LADY GRACE

Lady Grace holds its own with the best of today's sci-fi page-turners while accomplishing much more. Nathan's second book in the Tales from Earth's End is just as much a spiritual and psychological exploration as it is science fiction/fantasy thriller. Nathan has created a unique niche that leaves her without rival in the canon of contemporary fiction.

– Nathan Fisher, M.B.A., Stanford Graduate School of Business

A gripping original sci-fi tale that brings politics, spirituality and personal responsibility into the mix. As in all interesting tales of good versus evil, the path to outcome is not predictable but the trip is super enjoyable and will keep you clicking for the next page.

– Consuelo Saar Baehr, author of *Daughters*

I LOVED *Lady Grace!* From the first moments, I could not put it down. Sandy Nathan has done it again. Within her believable, gripping tale of people who have somehow survived a thousand years, Sandy explores instant telepathic teleportation, human-animal relationships, survivalism, personal relationships, social experimentation, dehumanization, and the most of these . . . Love. The twists of Jeremy's evolution with Eliana and his mother, Veronica Edgarton, are breathtaking.

– Ilene Dillon, M.S.W., Host, Full Power Living Internet Radio
www.emotionalpro.com

LADY GRACE

ALSO BY SANDY NATHAN

Stepping Off the Edge: Learning & Living Spiritual Practice

Numenon (Bloodsong Series I)

Tecolote: The Little Horse That Could

The Angel & the Brown-Eyed Boy
(Tales from Earth's End I)

Sam & Emily: A Love Story from the Underground
(Tales from Earth's End III)

LADY GRACE

TALES FROM EARTH'S END II

SANDY NATHAN

VILASA PRESS

SANTA YNEZ, CA 93460

Copyright © 2012 by Sandy Nathan
Vilasa Press
A Division of Vilasa Properties LLC
PO Box 1316
Santa Ynez, CA 93460
www.vilasapress.com / www.sandynathan.com / www.talesfromearthsend.com

First Edition

ISBN-13: 978-1-937927-00-4 (Trade Paperback)
ISBN-13: 978-1-937927-01-1 (eBook)
Library of Congress Control Number: 2011944248

Editor: Melanie Rigney
Cover and interior design: Lewis Agrell

Publisher's Cataloging-in-Publication Data

Nathan, Sandra Oddstad.
    Lady grace : tales from Earth's end II / Sandy Nathan.
        p. cm.
    ISBN: 978-1-937927-00-4
    1. Future life—Fiction. 2. Extraterrestrial beings—Fiction. 3. Nuclear warfare—Fiction.   I. Title.
PS3614.A864 L34 2012
813—dc22

                                        2011944248

First Printing: 2012
Printed in the United States of America

To my family: Barry, Andy, Zoë, & Lily

PART I

1

"Come on, Ellie! They'll let us go this time." Jeremy dashed out of the tiny place where he and Ellie lived. His waist-length dreadlocks flopped behind him and his bare feet slapped the smooth surface of the hallway.

The door's membrane tried to catch Eliana, but she slipped through. His wife was as agile and beautiful as the day they'd met.

He carried two bags of survival gear that he'd created from intergalactic junk. The goldies had swept the heavens to get him raw materials for construction projects. Before they'd given him something to do, Jeremy's boredom-induced screaming fits had traumatized the planet.

He and Ellie ran through a translucent passage in the planet's depths, bells booming all around them. Chimes always sounded on the planet, carrying messages. These bells were alarms.

Horrified faces wailed in the walls, pointing at them with luminous fingers. They were the souls of the departed elders and formed the elastic, semi-transparent substance of the golden planet. The whole world was some shade of amber—ranging from glowing yellow to almost black. Lights shone from the planet's depths, raking arcs like searchlights and then fading.

Jeremy galloped past Belarian's grand, bejeweled palace. "Bitch," he shouted and kept running. Belarian, the "mother" Eliana had missed so much when she was on Earth, was really her owner. She had tormented Jeremy.

He made a quick turn, going up another corridor. Jeremy thought living in their adopted home was like being inside someone's guts. Undulating, ribbed tubes ran everywhere. The tunnels moved and shifted. But Jeremy knew where he was. They were on a major thoroughfare that didn't change.

"Come on, guys! It's on!" Jeremy shouted as they ran past James and Mel's "place." That's all they had: places. No street names, no addresses, nothing but places. The natives didn't need anything more than knowledge of a place's existence to find it, but finding anything was hard for the humans.

"Come on, we've got to go!" Jeremy yelled to the guys.

A glass-like amber sheet locked Mel and James into their space. Mel kicked at it with the bottom of his foot. The wall retracted before he touched it. He and his partner, James, slipped through. They took off after Jeremy.

"Trouble?" Jeremy called.

"Nah. It's chicken. They're all chicken."

They jogged up the corridor. No real need to hurry at this point; the bells had tipped the golden world to their escape attempt. They couldn't get away anyway; they were on an unidentified planet without the technology to get off it. The goldies would capture them no matter what they did. Their objective was to get their message out.

"Henry! Lena! We're on!" Jeremy slapped the door of their tiny nook. She and Henry emerged and joined the others.

The hallway emptied into a huge lobby, the antechamber to the hall of the elders. Ribbed and folded like living tissue, the foyer's walls seemed permeable. They weren't, unless they wanted to be.

"Let us in," he shouted at the portal. "We have to talk to the elders." A face appeared in the wall. It scanned them carefully. The door did not open.

Jeremy didn't have the right mumbo jumbo to make it work. He'd seen Ellie's "mother," Belarian, unlock it. She had stood where he was and intoned in the goldies' wordless way, Open, portal, we are here at the will of the elders. She had held up her hand with authority and the barrier admitted them. Of course, Belarian was a big cheese in the golden world.

He held his hand up to the door and made various gestures, ending by flipping it off. "We know you're in there. What you're doing is illegal. You brought us here under false pretenses."

Jeremy *had* to leave, couldn't stay a moment longer. The golden planet had been unbearable since he discovered the real reason the goldies had granted them sanctuary.

Ellie's first pregnancy had been long and hard. After a difficult delivery, the golden people took their baby without letting them so much as hold it. He and Ellie had never seen any of the thousands of children she had borne since. Ellie was a pet; he was her mate. They had the same rights as dogs in a puppy mill. Once he realized that, every second on the planet was misery to him. Every *instant*.

He choked out his message to the elders. "We thought you had a free society. We thought we would be equal citizens. We didn't know you brought us here to experiment on!

"Let us in! You know what I'm saying is true!" He didn't feel afraid. The elders had confined or tranquilized him after his previous outbursts, but they'd never hurt him.

"We can't stay here any more!" Jeremy slammed the door with the flats of both hands. "We're United States citizens! This is unconstitutional!"

With that, he shot away from the portal, finding himself stuck to the wall on the far side of the foyer. The others were lined up next to him. They seemed unable to move.

The elders' faces appeared in the doorway. Eight of them, all different heights and shades of gold. Tall and elegant, they moved like dancers. The tallest one, a doctor, spoke. He'd helped Ellie with her pregnancies and births.

What do you want? Jeremy heard the doctor's silent message inside his head. The goldies didn't talk. What they wanted to say just appeared in his mind, not even in words, either. It was all intuition. The humans had to put words to the aliens' communications.

"We want to leave. We hate it here and you hate us. The experiment has failed. Let us go home. Earth must be free of radiation by now."

Shimmering bells indicated the elders' amusement. *The experiment has failed?* the doctor transmitted. *You don't know that. You don't even know how long you've been our guests.*

"Let us go back, please. We can't live this way."

The elders surveyed them, craning their necks, blinking with expressionless gold eyes.

Do you think you can live on Earth? The question came from all of them.

"Yes. With the survival packs I made. We'll have the tools we need as long as the radiation is gone."

The silent response: *The packs will become very hot as you enter Earth's atmosphere. They'll kill you if they travel with you.*

"You can put a protective coating on them . . . Or you can send them later."

You can survive?

"With the packs, yes."

We will send you now. We will send the others later, and your bags.

Jeremy found himself sitting in the middle of a wide grassy field. He looked around, amazed. Brilliant blue sky. Trees bordering a meadow. Something else: the crash of surf. He was on Earth! He took a deep breath. Good old air. The place looked gorgeous. The trees were huge. Obviously the danger from radiation had been over for hundreds of years.

He stood up and examined his surroundings. None of the buildings were left standing, but he was sure he was at the estate. His family had owned Piermont Manor for hundreds of years. His bones recognized the place; his blood felt at home. He had grown up here, as had his mom and countless ancestors.

The big house had stood in front of him. He could see it in his mind's eye, lacy stonework and tall parapets. A fifty-thousand-square-foot confection built in the eighteenth century. His mother's garden had sprawled on the mansion's other side. The village, where the staff and workers had lived, had been behind the house and to the west. Everything was gone.

His eyes returned to the place where he thought the main house's back door had been. He could almost see it. The door flying open and Ellie leaping out. Ellie and he had fallen in love on Earth's last night. He had played his clarinet in the ballroom while she danced. They had spent their wedding night in his room, loving for the first time, both of them. The glow they had created seemed to illuminate the air. Jeremy shivered.

The next morning, they'd walked out the back door. Sam Baahuhd, the headman of the village, waited for them. They hugged him and said good-bye. Jeremy had felt warmer toward Sam that morning than he had felt his whole life. Then they ran across the meadow to the huge blob of light the goldies had sent to carry them away. It hovered by the cliff above the ocean. All of them ran, he and Ellie, Lena and Henry, and James and Mel. They ran away from nuclear Armageddon and toward a brilliant future in an alien world.

A cynical snort escaped him. How many years had passed since they made that run for freedom? How many years had they been prisoners?

Jeremy turned toward the sound of the surf. That was the Atlantic Ocean. He knew the sound of it and the smell of it. This was the estate. He was home. Jubilation grew inside of him. His chest swelled and a smile stretched across his face.

He'd been returned to Piermont Manor. He was Jeremy Bentham Piermont Edgarton, heir to all he saw. He was in the good ol' USA, in the great state of Connecticut. They'd send the others and his stuff soon. Everything was A-OK.

2

Hours later, Jeremy stood at the cliff's edge, watching the sea throw itself at the rock face below. The surf roared and exploded. The jagged rocks and undertow would destroy anyone down there. If life got too bad, he could end it with one step.

He backed away quickly. No need to think like that. His stuff would come. The others would come.

Twigs and rocks threatened to puncture the soles of his feet. They hadn't touched anything but the smooth surfaces of the golden planet for how long? He had no idea. After dozens of prickly steps, Jeremy stood in the middle of a rough pasture, which he remembered as the manicured lawn behind his family's mansion. That's where he had landed when the elders dumped him earlier.

Jeremy had returned to this spot again and again, looking for what they'd promised. Nothing.

He'd arrived naked, the way they'd lived on the golden planet. He looked down at his long arms. Goosebumps decorated them. The late afternoon was chilly. His skin was café au lait, thanks to his African-American father and white mother. His arms looked like sticks with robotic joints and Halloween monster fingers. His legs and feet were the same.

All the humans were emaciated like him. Jeremy thought the goldies were trying to make them appear similar to themselves: tall, graceful forms gliding around. Or maybe the way the humans looked was simply the result of eating seeds and tasteless golden glop for a couple thousand years.

He was too nervous to be still, so he kept walking. He could feel his dreadlocks brushing his waist and back. He didn't have any body hair; the goldies didn't like it, so none of the humans had any. They really liked hair on the head, though. And on pets.

A snort of a giggle escaped Jeremy. When they first arrived, they had been blown away by the golden aliens lounging around like ballet dancers on downers, the lights undulating, and the faces looking out of the walls. But the alien life forms—the furry slugs, blue crows with four legs, Day-Glo lizards with eyeballs on stalks, and so many more—were the most bizarre. The goldies couldn't have children, so they sent pet hunters throughout the universe capturing anything cute by *anyone's* standards. The place swarmed with weird creatures.

The pets weren't the only surprising thing. For enlightened overlords, the people of Ellie's planet had a surprising appetite for the good life. They piled on jewelry and decorated their spaces like palaces. Before seeing the goldies, he had thought his mother was the universal champion of conspicuous consumption.

And entertainment freaks! They'd watch anything that moved. They loved to cluster outside their space when he and Ellie were making love.

That popped him out of his giggles. The goldies weren't funny. They weren't kind or good, either. Except to their own kind.

He felt something running down his cheek. He lifted his bony hand and wiped it. His hand came away wet. Don't worry, Jer, he said to himself. Ellie is coming. They'll send her and the others and the stuff.

He was standing in the middle of pasture so rough that Sam Baahuhd, the estate's headman in the old days, would have had a fit if he'd seen it. Jeremy looked around the weedy plot behind him, wondering where the back door of the shelter was. He'd built a huge bomb shelter under this field. The shelter was as big as a small town and as far below the surface as the sea was from the cliff top, hundreds of feet. It was equipped to last a couple thousand years, if its inhabitants were clever.

They should have been very clever. The shelter was built with the intention of housing an international community of scientists, scholars, and philosophers. One hundred of Earth's best and brightest were supposed to go down there, preparing to build a perfect society when the radiation cleared. But the disaster came so fast that the scientists and scholars couldn't get to the estate.

Jeremy had ended up giving the place to the people who lived and worked in the mansion's stables and fields. Ninety-three villagers plus Arthur, his driver and an undercover commando, locked themselves in after he and the others left for Ellie's home.

He could see no sign of the shelter or the estate. The stone mansion was gone. He looked for some evidence of a foundation. Nothing but grass. He couldn't find the rear exit of the bomb shelter, a concrete pipe that had stuck out of the ground a couple of feet.

Had the people down there survived? They could have died of hunger or disease. They could have left ages ago.

Massive trees spotted around wide grasslands had replaced the mansion's cultivated gardens. The huge trees were exactly like California's valley oaks. Some of the old giants he'd seen at his mom's Santa Barbara estate had trunks four feet across. Their leafy heads spanned a hundred feet. These trees were at least as large.

They were strange, too. The oaks that lived around there in the old days were skinny-trunked. They grew very close to each other. Bright green and leafy, the Hamptons' native oak forests were nothing like the wide-open savannahs surrounding him.

Jeremy poked around where he thought the back entrance to the shelter had been. A lump in the ground might be it, but he was shivering too much to explore. He'd have to look for the village tomorrow. The light was fading. He needed to find a place to spend the night. And then he heard a sound he recognized, even though he'd never heard it before. The drawn out wailing of many canine voices came from the forest to the west. Intertwining howls. Those were wolves, not dogs.

The wolves howled again, coming closer.

That's when the nerve block wore off. They weren't sending Ellie or anything else. He'd been a pain in the ass on Ellie's planet, so they spit him back.

They'd sentenced him to death.

3

Making his way across the meadow, Jeremy scanned the forest for a tree that forked low enough for him to climb. OK. There was one. Something was standing in the grass at its base. He stopped, staring.

It was a dog, a definite dog, not a wolf. A modified dog, heading in the direction of wolf, but not yet there. As he got closer, she wagged her tail. She was a bitch; her swollen teats said she had puppies. She raised one paw and dropped her head the way Sam's hound dogs had when he approached.

"Hi, sweetie," he said. She rolled over onto her back. She had the mottled coat of one of Sam Baahuhd's hunting dogs. Her ears were neither up nor down, not floppy hound dog ears, but not pointed jackal or wolf ears, either.

"Are you Flossie? Flossie's granddaughter?" That would have been many hundreds of generations in the past, he knew.

The bitch stood up and yipped, motioning him to follow with her head. She had a rabbit stashed by the oak's trunk and grabbed it as she trotted into the forest. He could barely keep up with her. Only the howling behind him kept him going. She led him deep into the forest, to a hill he'd never seen with a small clearing in front of it.

Flossie took him to a hole in the hillside and disappeared inside. He looked at it, not knowing if he could fit. A howl from the forest behind him had him clawing at the hole's dirt sides. He made his way in, leaving some of his skin on the walls. Inside, Flossie fed her babies while having her own dinner. She ripped the rabbit's guts open and devoured the contents. She made a handy job of it, also consuming one of the rabbit's hind legs. The rest, she prodded to him with her nose.

"Thankee, Flossie," he said, attempting to speak the brogue of the old village.

Jeremy's stomach growled. He didn't eat the rabbit for a long time. He kept thinking of parasites in raw flesh. He hadn't eaten meat in Ellie's world. They were too kind and nonviolent to consume flesh. Some of it had rubbed off. The real part, he hoped. What was she doing now, his beautiful wife? Crying. He could feel Ellie crying. They didn't tell her what they were going to do to him.

A bark of a laugh escaped him. The goldies didn't know how to lie before he and the others had come. Having five humans in their midst had corrupted them.

He devoured the meat and chewed the ends of the bones. He scraped the inside of the skin with his teeth, both for whatever flesh clung to it and to clean the skin for later use. Shoes?

Finally he slept, the worst sleep of his life. He was so traumatized that his body was stiff. When shock let go of him so that he might sleep, the fleas attacked. Flossie scratched and whined as she slept, never having known a life without fleas. Jeremy scratched and hoped they didn't carry diseases and that he'd live through the night.

"Well, Flossie, we're alive." The sun flooded into the den's opening. Flossie was reserved now, keeping her pups behind her. She still dropped her head when he moved. "Thankee, ma princess. Ah hope we never sleep together again." She tilted her head when he spoke and whined.

"Remember Sam, lass? Ah do." Jeremy said as he dragged himself out of the opening of her den and into the day.

"Whoa!" He found himself blinking in the sunlight, facing a snarling male dog. Around him were twenty or so of his mates. The pack leader and his lieutenants.

The snarls were low and deep, signaling that they meant business. What would Sam have done? Jeremy thought furiously. He had about three seconds to establish dominance before they tore him apart.

He stood to his full height. The dogs were ringed around him, with the big male closer than the rest. Jeremy didn't make eye contact, just looked at him out of the corners of his eyes. The animal had matted hair and was covered with scars. His ears were tattered. This guy had been around.

Jeremy took in a breath and let it out slowly and audibly. He relaxed his shoulders and settled into the earth and himself. He'd seen Sam do that working with rough horses and dogs. If they went for him, Sam knew what to do. Jeremy had seen him throw an attacking stallion on the ground with a flick of the wrist. Sam would have huge hounds groveling at his feet. All of it effortlessly and apparently without violence. But what did he *do*?

The leader looked at him, ears erect. The growl turned over in his throat. The other dogs' eyes darted between Jeremy and the leader. They would spring if their chief did. Jeremy took another breath and stood, doing nothing. The dogs seemed to settle down, still looking at the alpha male.

"Hey, lads. Ah got bit o' business this morning. So whadya say, ah'll scoot." He aped Sam's accent and whistled the way Sam did. The dogs looked startled. He balled up the rabbit skin and threw it as hard as he could out of the circle.

The big male charged after it, catching it. The others took corners and tore it to bits.

Maintaining his calm, Jeremy walked away silently. The leader looked up. His eyes followed Jeremy as he walked slowly out of the forest, but he didn't follow.

"Holy shit!" Jeremy whispered when he was a sufficient distance away. He had no intention of going near the dogs again until he had a better idea of how to control them. He scratched his arm. And he wasn't going to sleep with Flossie either.

He put his hands on each side of his head, thinking. Something had to be left of the estate. A huge mansion and sprawling outbuildings, barns, and equipment sheds could not be totally swallowed up. He was crossing what he thought was the field behind the main barn.

He turned around. The barn had to have been around here. Where? The oaks had infringed into the field, with denser trees in the distance. He wanted to scream. He was hungry and thirsty and his feet hurt.

He curtailed his search as a basic need asserted itself. He had to admit that one of the nicest things about planet Earth was that he could piss wherever he wanted. On Ellie's planet, the humans had to go through a whole rigmarole so the goldies didn't know what they were doing. They didn't have a process of elimination. That said a lot about them: They were so uptight they didn't even shit.

He did, though. His stomach roiled from his rabbit dinner. Jeremy walked to a likely tree. "Do bears shit in the woods?" he asked the tree as he squatted. "Not to be offensive, old boy."

Squatting was a bit of providence: Ten feet from him, a pipe stuck a couple of inches out of the earth. It was an exhaust pipe. From what? The machine barn? The machine barn had housed farm equipment and a small mechanics' shop. Plus everything that would be needed to set up a sawmill. Did that pipe lead to the barn? All he had to do was dig to find out.

Hours went by. No food, no water. No shovel. He dug with his lily-soft hands and a branch he found that was straight enough to pulverize the soil. After breaking up the dirt, he scooped it out with his hands. His atrophied muscles trembled with the exertion. He wasn't fit for this. He wasn't fit for anything.

Why couldn't they have given him a shovel? If they didn't want him to have his potentially-used-for-violence knife, how about at least a shovel?

He would have wept when he finally reached a roof, but he was too dehydrated. Was it the roof of the equipment storage? He had no idea. He had to find a place to sleep and something to eat. It was early afternoon by now. If whatever was below him was empty, and if he could get through the old tin roof without cutting himself up, it might make him a good place to hole up. He giggled at the possibility, and then couldn't stop laughing. Why did that seem funny?

Much later, he'd dug out around the vent far enough to stand on the roof. He pulled up a corner of the metal by the exhaust flue and it peeled back the way he'd hoped it would. He made a big enough hole to slip through. First he stuck his branch into the opening and felt around, then threw pebbles in at various angles to try to determine what was down there. It was a room with plenty of space for him. One of the pebbles bounced off something that resounded with a metallic ping! Tools? Something really useful like an ancient truck with no fuel? His laughter had a hysterical edge.

Jeremy shook with exhaustion. His lips were swollen and parched. But he had to get down there and back out. He had to get food or he'd die. He slipped through the opening and dropped to a dirt floor.

It *was* the machine room. He could see some of the inside with the light from the hole in the ceiling. The metal walls didn't look melted, just decayed. The walls on the northern and eastern sides were stone. That was the side that faced toward the nearby town of Jamayuh where the atomics would have originated. The framing was metal. Metal and stone didn't burn. It had survived. This was the barn he remembered!

Earth had covered it completely. It had to be three feet under the ground at its highest point. The peak would be about eighteen feet high. Fortunately, he'd dropped near the side wall or he could have broken a leg.

Tractors, a backhoe, a truck. Other farm vehicles. All sorts of equipment that he had no idea how to use. And tools. The walls held banks of tools, and shelves full of screws and hardware. It was a bonanza, except that it was deep underground and probably thousands of years old. He was sure that none of the engines worked. He had no way of getting them out, even if they did.

Jeremy found a shovel and a pickax. He picked up a steel canteen. There was more, but food and water came first. Jeremy moved some empty steel barrels so he could climb out of his new home. The full barrels he couldn't move at all.

Well, after he went out to dinner at the local bistro and had a latté, he'd find out what was in the barrels. Or maybe he'd just come back and crash in his new pad.

As he was heading toward the meadow, something came to him. Why were the wolves to the west and the dogs to the east of the estate? The wolves had to be dominant. They would have the best side. Water would be on the best side.

Jeremy put his tools and canteen's chain over his shoulder and marched into the forest, heading straight for the place he'd heard the wolves the night before. He stumbled up a small hill, struck by the moisture in the air and the greenery tracing along the bottom of the knoll. He heard running water and almost ran toward it.

It was a brook from a fairy tale. A babbling stream surrounded by ferns. A logjam had created a wonderful pond just downstream. He drank until he thought he'd burst. He filled his canteen and was going to plunge in for a swim, when he saw something move at the edge of the water. A rattler. Snakes drank at dusk. Jeremy shot backwards, bent on going back to the "lawn" where he had arrived. Maybe he'd catch a rabbit. Maybe his in-laws had sent his stuff. Maybe they'd sent Ellie.

He felt buoyant as he headed toward the sound of the surf.

The rabbit almost ran into him. A big jackrabbit. He swung out in reflex, breaking the rabbit's back with the shovel. He finished it off with a chop on the neck. Jeremy smiled widely. It was not an elegant kill, but it was his first.

He remembered reading that you should gut animals immediately. He did it with the shovel, practically tearing the creature in half. He pulled the hindquarters from the skin and ate them. He wanted to take the rest back to his hole and eat it quietly. He might find a camp stove in there.

But first Jeremy had to check to see if the goldies had sent anything. He walked behind what had been the mansion. He'd wrapped the rest of the rabbit in its skin and held its innards in his other hand. Flossie was over there somewhere. She was a working mother. He'd give her the guts.

He found her hunting on the dogs' side of the mansion. "Here, Flossie. Thankee for dinner last ni'. Much obliged." She devoured the intestines and licked his fingers. He smiled at her. His first friend in his new home.

"Ye're a good girl, Flossie. When ah get my place fixed up, ah'll come for ye and yer pups. We can go on huntin'." He gave up the pretense of speaking the village dialect. "Well, girl, time for bed." He was crossing the pasture, when he almost stepped into a big round hole. It was three feet across and about three feet deep. He dropped a pebble on the top. It was metal.

This was the tube for sending the canaries out! He'd told Sam and the others that if the instrumentation failed, they could test the level of radiation by putting a canary in a cage and passing it up through the seven levels of the shelter to see if it lived or died. He'd designed the system so that any dirt that accumulated on the top would be blown away by bellows inside, or would be cut away by a steel sheath that surrounded the vent. He bent down and touched the sides of the hole. Metal.

He'd stumbled upon one of three ways anyone could access the shelter. This and the front and rear exits were it. He assumed that debris had rendered the "front door," through the ballroom under the house, impassible. He looked around. He had been looking in the wrong place. The mansion wasn't where he thought it was; it had been farther east. The sea had shifted, carving out a new cliff.

Jeremy put down his rabbit and tools. He wondered who was in the underground shelter, if anyone. Sam Baahuhd had been a shrewd, intelligent, and very skilled man who had the best for his people in mind. He was a decent man. He had four wives, all of whom were his first cousins. His first wife, Mollie, had the hereditary disease the villagers carried. The disease caused the afflicted person to go berserk and attack. Mollie had killed people. She was protected by Sam's status, but the woman was a killer. All of the people in the village were at least as inbred as Sam's family.

No matter how bad Ellie's world had turned out to be, what was below his feet was likely to be far worse. What was down there? A hundred clones of Sam's wife? Genetic mutants? People with no brains at all?

As he wavered by the hole's edge, the cover began to move. It was unscrewing itself. Jeremy grabbed his stuff and stood up, ready to run. Then he almost laughed. A *canary* in a cage would be coming up. Nothing to worry about.

"*Get the fuck up, ye . . .*" A stream of profanity blasted out of the opening. The man speaking was a monster. The sadism and cruelty in his voice spoke louder than his curses.

He could see someone struggling in the cylinder.

"Ah need more rope. Ah cannot get all the way out," a cowed male voice replied.

"*Ye stinking,*" and more curses. The voice made Jeremy cringe. It sounded like the voice of a giant, or the devil.

A head poked over the rim, followed by two arms. A man pulled himself out so that he sat on the edge of the hole with his feet in the opening. He was naked.

"*Well, whadya see? C'n ye breathe?*" The guy below snarled like an animal.

The man sitting on the edge saw Jeremy and started to duck back in the hole.

Jeremy had a clear look at this face. He could have been Sam Baahuhd, leader of the village, but he was older than Sam had been. Jeremy grabbed the man's shoulder and put his hand over his mouth, shh-ing him. He could see that he was tied around the waist with a rope.

"Are ye alive, ye shit-eating . . ."

Jeremy pantomimed screaming and acting as though he were choking. He indicated that the new man should roll back way from the edge.

"Sam" did as directed and began gasping and shrieking as though he were dying.

As the man writhed in mock agony, Jeremy took the pick and struck the rope where it passed over the metal edge of the tube. It took two blows to sever it. The sound was covered by the other man's screams.

When "Sam" was free, Jeremy grabbed the guy's arm and his stuff and ran for his hideout. The voice from the hole continued.

"Wha's this? Th' rope's cut? Whadya do, ye bastard whoreson?" Screams and growls from more voices floated up. *"Are ye alive? C'n ye breathe?"*

The wolves' chorus resounded. The animals' baying was louder than the obscenities boiling up from the underground.

"Wha' the fuck is that? Shut 'er down, Rupert."

The metal lid clanked as the hatch was sealed.

4

Her eyelids fluttered. Something moved inside her. She had no thoughts and couldn't name what was happening in her body. She heard whispers of air entering and leaving. They became gasps as her eyes opened wide. She jerked, half sitting. She was dying; she knew that instinctively. Her finger pulled the trigger without conscious effort. Her eyes closed and she fell back.

A slender metal arm deployed from the side of her chamber. It positioned itself to the left of her breastbone, between two ribs. A hypodermic needle emerged from the arm and slipped through her flesh. It shot its payload into her heart and retracted quickly.

Her eyes shot open and she jolted, hands moving to her throat. She gasped and began to fight for her life. She could hear her heartbeat on the monitor. Erratic pulsations. Veronica Piermont Edgarton lay back and gave herself another shot of adrenalin.

She gasped and struggled. She would live. She would live. Her heartbeat settled down, hammering steadily. Her breathing became rhythmic and strong, though her body's responses to her will were sporadic. She couldn't remember how to open the vessel that held her. She lay back, resting. Sleeping. Jerking awake again. She didn't know how much time passed.

When she remembered where she was, Veronica sat up with a jolt, hitting her head on the glass dome covering her capsule. She clawed at the side panels. Panic almost took her. She had to get out of there.

Forcing herself to think, she found the controls. She pushed a couple of buttons and pulled a lever. The glass top opened like a casket and the right side swung out and down. She sat up for the first time in how many years? She didn't wonder, didn't look at the chronometer behind her.

Her bare feet found the slippers left for her, and the uniform. She wore the distinctive garb of the general's guard when she was clothed, except that her uniform had been tailored to accommodate her voluptuous figure. She didn't go to the wall to activate the solar heat in the frigid space; she went directly to her husband's vault and looked in.

His eyelids were fluttering. He'd awaken soon. She pushed the manual control to activate the adrenalin. The steel arm came out and positioned itself exactly where it belonged. She pushed the trigger.

The general jerked and his eyes opened wide. His head turned and his eyes locked on hers. She pulled back, below his range of sight. And then she pushed the arm's control again, and again, and again. The trigger kept pumping, loading and emptying the syringe. Each time she hit the control, she felt a wild terror. Each time she punched the button, her face contorted with rage. She couldn't kill him often enough.

She heard him struggling, attempting to rise, gasping. Trying to get out. Clawing at the glass, pawing the side of the chamber. But that wonderful Russian technology held. That thin arm of the steel syringe was designed to keep doing its job, even if the patient fought. It kept deploying the drug until all of it had been injected. Finally, he was quiet.

She slumped to the ground. Was he really dead? Panic arose inside her. What if he wasn't dead? He *saw* her. He'd know who did it.

She stood up and looked at him. Eyes bulging, tongue protruding, face and chest bright red, limbs rigid. He looked dead.

But was he? She groped her way to the wall and turned off his life support systems. He would get no oxygen and none of the circulating vapors that had kept them alive. She turned his chamber's temperature to its lowest setting, twenty degrees below zero.

Was that enough? Had she killed him? When the thermostat hit its lowest point, she felt safe enough to creep away from his vault and close the steel doors around it. He couldn't survive that, could he?

Her mind was functioning now. They had brought two storage units with everything people starting a new world would need. The first was full of medicines, supplies, tools, clothing—all sorts of necessities. The second was loaded with weapons. She went to the second container and pulled out an automatic rifle. She loaded it and took off the safety. He would never get her again.

She began to explore the bunker. Eight of them had made the trip. Their home was a compact room with vaults built into the walls of the cement bunker. She and the general had the biggest spaces, and the two most advanced cryogenic set-ups. They were the only units that had been able to go the distance, as she quickly discovered.

The people in the bunker were supposed to repopulate the Earth; of necessity, more women than men had been included. They had brought two physicians, both women. The doctors were dead. They and the others had been assigned older technology cryogenic units. The female computer/communications officer had died. As had the two munitions specialists. Warriors, the general called them. Murderers who didn't need any excuse to kill. A man and a woman. Both dead, thank God.

Veronica laughed at what she'd thought. God. She knew perfectly well that God did not exist. When she looked at the dead occupant of the last cubicle, her mouth tightened.

Beautiful Zhanna, as porcelain-skinned and delicate as a tsar's daughter. She was the Tsar's daughter, joining their happy family at the general's invitation.

"She is nothing to me, Veronica, Nothing. We're bringing her as a breeder, that's all. You are my favorite." She must have been his beloved; he gave her the best cryogenics. You'd never know it from how he acted. He and the eighteen-year-old Zhanna had flamed every night. Veronica had welcomed their intimacy. As long as he was besotted with the girl, he stayed away from her. Had Zhanna been anything but a vicious power-monger as trustworthy as a viper, Veronica would have welcomed her.

She and Zhanna married the general two days before the conflagration. No matter that two wives were illegal in the old world. The old world would soon be gone. They were wedded and bedded, then locked into the units that would save them forever a few days later when the bombs stopped exploding. She looked at Zhanna's peaceful face in frozen repose in its glass case and spit at it. She shut the doors of the vaults quickly. She turned off the automatic releases, locking them in forever.

Veronica leaned against the wall, shaking. She had to get out of there. As she moved around the lab, she kept thinking that she could hear him moving in his crypt. That he would get out. She wanted to level her gun at it and blow it to hell.

But she *was* in hell.

Hunger hit her with visceral force. She went to the first container and opened the door. Carefully engineered metal storage compartments filled it to the ceiling. Packs of military rations were crammed into the unit closest to the door. She pulled two packages out and made herself eat them slowly.

When she was finished, Veronica headed for the communications center. Their computers were programmed to communicate with every satellite in operation. Also with every country on the planet and every alien world that anyone had any notion might exist. Banks of computers filled the room, which formed a large L off the cryogenics lab.

The bunker had a digital periscope, a tiny thing that would insert itself through anything, from snow to bedrock. It could peek out and give a 360-degree view of whatever was up there. They didn't know how long they might be in cryogenic sleep, or what would be happening above when they came to life. She and the general had worked through all sorts of scenarios, from finding themselves under a city of the future to an icepack hundreds of feet deep. Veronica activated the device and it began to deploy its arm.

The periscope disclosed ice. She raised it higher. Ice as far as she could see. No sign of life. When she entered the bunker, the land above it had been the planet's most productive source of timber. The Ice Age had returned. Veronica's heart raced. She had food enough to last years. The temperature would be OK—they were far below the permafrost. But she couldn't stay in a cement hole with seven corpses.

Veronica turned on the computers and the satellite connection. She could feel the controls humming. Still working. Good old Russian technology. While her computer booted up, Veronica thought.

How long had they been there, frozen? She had looked at the chronometers over each body before folding the steel doors. They said different things, indicating that from 120 years to 2753 years had passed. Her own timepiece was shattered and hanging off the wall, as was the general's. They had the most reliable timepieces of the bunch, but they had *both* broken. Why had their cryogenic mechanisms worked, but their clocks failed?

She had an eerie feeling that someone had broken into the vault and changed the clocks and broken theirs. And turned off the others' cryogenic machines. The general and her machines were better than the others', but not that much better. At least one should have survived.

The idea that someone had broken in was crazy. The general had been obsessive in his security while they built the bunker. Who could get in? Who knew the codes? The general's son was the obvious answer. But why would he leave them alive? He hated his father. Who else could it be? She didn't know.

If someone was outside, their instrumentation would have registered the little periscope she'd raised. They'd notice the systems below starting up. She jumped up and turned off the heat. The satellite connection she couldn't shut down. She needed that.

Veronica looked around frantically. She had to get out of there and find her son.

She knew something about where he was. Veronica knew that Jeremy had gone off world to escape the atomics. Everyone in the bunker knew it—they had watched on computer screens as Jeremy and the others had left.

Jeremy's spectacular departure had filled the bunker with cries of dismay and amazement. The eastern sky around the estate had lit ultra-bright, and a huge, shimmering golden ball had docked against the cliff. Veronica had watched them leave: a lovely girl, a dancer, leading the way. Jeremy followed, yelling "Geronimo!" when he jumped into the ship. Mel Adams, Jeremy's teacher from the Hermitage Academy, and his partner were next, holding hands. And Henry and Lena. Her chest caught even thinking of them. Henry was her first husband Chaz Edgarton's half brother. He and Lena had watched out for Jeremy for most of his life.

The last time she'd seen him, Jeremy had bragged about his surveillance skills, saying he had "the village wired for sound—and sight." He would be surprised to know that he wasn't the only one. The entire estate was hooked into the general's system, including the interior of the underground shelter. Because of that, Veronica and the others had eavesdropped on the tour of the shelter Jeremy gave the night before everything blew up.

How could she contact the golden planet to get him back? Veronica had a few tricks of her own. She'd had Jeremy's room at the academy bugged for years—and had had the contents of his computer sent to her in Russia. It was the only way she could keep track of her reclusive son.

Veronica pulled a transparent cylinder from a hidden pocket of her uniform. Though tiny, the apparatus held the contents of Jeremy's personal computer and all of its internal settings. It essentially was Jeremy's computer. Jeremy's driver and guard, Arthur Romero, secretly had made the cylinder and had it smuggled to her before she went into cybersleep.

Inserting the tube into a port in one of the lab's computers, Veronica waited a few moments for it to download. An icon labeled "Jeremy's Computer" appeared on her screen. She double clicked it and read down the contents. Sure enough, he'd recorded the coordinates to which he'd broadcast and the number of times he'd sent messages to each.

Now all she had to do was contact outer space.

5

Veronica straightened her hair and put on the expression she wore for public appearances. Quickly adjusting the focus of her computer's camera, she broadcast to the top frequencies from Jeremy's list.

"Hello, people of the golden planet. This is Veronica Edgarton of the planet Earth," she said into the microphone. She used the famous Veronica Edgarton voice, which had conquered almost the entire male gender and made her a broker in world power. Her cultured, upper-class voice was something that only a thousand years of genetics and upbringing could create.

"I want to thank you so much for taking care of my son, Jeremy Edgarton, and his friends all these years. You were so good to respond to his pleas for help and lift him and his friends to your world.

"I'm afraid I have a request of my own. As you know, we've had a nuclear war here and have lost the planet that we knew. *I'm* in a desperate situation.

"I'm in a bunker close to the north pole with seven dead bodies. It's not very pleasant, I must tell you. I have enough supplies to last for a while, but my husband's son could break in at any time and make off with me.

"I ask you to look into your hearts and hear a mother's plea. Reunite me with my son . . . please."

She dropped her voice and leaned closer to the screen. "I need to be very frank with you. I'm terrified that the general's son will find me." Anguish crept into her voice and onto her face. "He's always fancied me. I don't want to spend the rest of my life as a concubine to a sexual pervert.

"So please, please, take me to my son. I have two storage containers here that are filled with things we'll need to start a new world. If you could transport them with me, I would be more grateful than I can say." Tears of desperation and fear sparkled in her blue eyes.

"Signing off,

"Veronica Edgarton."

She set the machine to rebroadcast her message every half hour. Then she went into the first storage container and made herself a nest just inside the door. She fell asleep and dreamed of Jeremy.

Veronica awakened in a panic and clawed her way out the container's door. The bunker's cement interior greeted her. The golden planet had either received her message and decided against helping her. Or they were still making up their minds. Or—they didn't get her message.

She stared at the screen, studying the frequencies Jeremy had used. Using a simple statistical program, she graphed their distribution. The graph was a bell-shaped curve, rising in the middle with the most popular addresses and tapering to tag ends on both sides. She'd sent her message to the middle range of coordinates, the ones Jeremy had used most. Why didn't it work?

Veronica sucked in a breath. What did she know about the way her son programmed? Jeremy never made anything easy. Everything he wrote was encoded and password protected. Had she used a password to enter his computer and download his data?

No. Had she used a password before using the data and sending her message? No again.

She'd opened "Jeremy's Computer" assuming that it was what it purported to be. Would her son ever put confidential information into something so obvious? No. She was lucky the file hadn't been booby-trapped, destroying all the data because of her unauthorized usage. She pulled away from the console, horrified. She might have ruined her only hope of escape.

Veronica also knew that if Jeremy didn't want someone to get into his files, they wouldn't be able to. He could create algorithms that only a genius could break. If he was being sloppy, he might write code that an intelligent person could crack if he or she was lucky.

She gasped as she remembered the worst. He built lockdowns into all of his work. Someone trying to break into one of his systems would find themselves locked out with three incorrect tries. Or fewer. When the machine locked down, only Jeremy would be able to open it.

Her heart pounded as though a frantic bird was trying to break out of her chest. Her hands grew icy. She looked around the cement bunker, eyes moving from the steel doors enclosing the corpses, to the computers, storage units, and weapons bays. Panic threatened to overwhelm her. She had one chance left. Veronica wanted to scream and throw herself on the floor.

Suck it up, soldier. The voice came from inside. She stiffened and pulled herself erect. Do the job you trained to do.

Veronica wasn't in the general's bunker because she was beautiful and a great lay. The general could have chosen thousands of women with those qualifications. It wasn't because he loved her so much. He didn't love anything.

She earned her place by working for it, by beating teenagers and women in their twenties and thirties. Beating the crap out of them on training courses and martial arts fields. She had been included in the cryogenic chamber with the general because she was the best.

Veronica walked to the cabinets at the far end of the computer lab. Eight superbly conditioned athletes had entered the bunker. Except for Zhanna, all were commandos. They expected to be confined to the bunker for an unknown time after awakening, and expected to use it for a home base for longer than that.

The cabinet doors swung open, revealing a recess jammed with gym equipment. She pulled out a long platform about seven inches high and set it in the aisle between the bays containing the frozen bodies. She selected two ten-pound dumbbells, gripping one in each hand.

Facing the wide part of the platform, Veronica stepped up with her left foot, following it with her right. Down with the left foot, then down with the right. She pumped the weights when her feet went up, lowered them when she stepped down.

Up left, up right; down left, down right. One, two, three, four, arms bending and straightening with each repetition. Two, two, three, four. Three, two, three, four. As time passed, she increased her speed, feet slapping the step.

Fifty, two, three, four. . . . *Eighty*, two, three, four.

Her pace slowed as her leaden legs rebelled. *Ninety-one,* two, three, four.

Ninety-two, two, three, four.

Her legs trembled and her biceps would barely straighten and contract. Sweat rolled between her breasts and ran down her face.

All she could do was a lousy ninety-two. She could hop up and down that step for hours before their cybersleep. She was in shape to do exactly nothing.

The voice kept giving orders. Working out curbs anxiety. Let your subconscious solve the problem. What would Jeremy do? Just hold that thought. Don't try to solve it. Move it. Move it, Veronica!

She pulled out the portable bench press, then hooked the pulleys to the wall for the lat pulls. Last to come out were the body bag and gloves. She'd work on target shooting later. They'd planned well, building a superbly engineered compact gym to keep killers busy.

Using the bench, she started out pressing one-quarter of the weight she'd been used to, then adjusted that down to one-tenth. She was useless. Worse than useless.

Work it, Edgarton. Keep going.

Veronica used the bench press and free weights until she fell to her knees. She crawled to the storage container and flopped inside. She'd managed her anxiety, but no answers had come. The golden planet hadn't responded to her message. She hurt everywhere, foreshadowing the pain that would come tomorrow.

The next day's muscle aches were exactly what she'd expected. Any movement exacted a price. Compared to how she'd felt in field training, it wasn't so bad, except that her workout barely would have counted as warm-up on any commando course. She forced herself to her feet and to the computer bay.

"I have no idea what to do," she said looking at the graph she'd generated the day before. Nice bell-shaped curve, fat in the middle and tapering out on both sides. So what? Where was the good data? She went through the computer, file by file. Found nothing using the amount of memory required to store a whole computer's contents.

Don't try so hard, soldier; let the answer float to the surface. The voice in her head gave orders as she ate her army rations and sipped purified water. Let all your faculties work.

Get back to work, Edgarton. Pick it up. She began again, stairstepping with free weights. The most effective cardio exercise for a small space. She did 120 before collapsing onto the floor.

Get up, Edgarton. Do you want to die down here? Pick up those feet! Move!

Then she was transported back to the training course in Russia, feeling the mud and sweat. She'd trained for a year, her last year on Earth. Knees pumping, feet hopping, she'd run across fields laced with live land mines. Sparred with killers. Rappelled down mountains. Parachuted in Siberia, Africa, and Guam.

She'd used every kind of weapon from hand-held missiles to garrotes. Learned more about computers than she thought possible. Piloted a ship and flown a plane.

And then she had put on a ball gown and brought the general to his knees with her loveliness. None of her competitors could do that.

She had one disadvantage.

"I know I'm forty-one," she'd told the general when she convinced him to take her into the bunker. "But women in my family have healthy babies into their fifties. Look." She had shown him the records. "I can repopulate the Earth better than those little girls."

She ended up frozen next to the general, the prototype female of the new age.

You won, Edgarton, but it's not over. Where did Jeremy store the data? She paced in front of the computer, kicking a trash container in frustration.

A trash container? She flew to the keyboard, double clicked on the trash and went through the items it contained. The contents of Jeremy's computer were in the trash, stored in a huge file labeled "Hermitage Academy." Simple but very effective. She never would have looked there. Where were the frequencies to which he'd broadcast? Under "Letters to Mom." The file had a mish-mash of numbers. That had to be it, but how could she interpret the mess?

She ran a couple of statistical programs, resulting in something interesting: another bell-shaped curve like the one she'd produced from the data she'd found originally. She compared the two diagrams.

Shit! Shit! Shit! They were the *same* diagram. All of her work had brought her no closer to a solution. Why was he so damn secretive?

Furious, Veronica stalked off to the gym locker and set up targets at the end of the bunker. She pulled out one of the air pistols.

She aimed the gun carefully and squeezed the trigger. Perfect. She'd been a markswoman since childhood. Her father liked to hunt. He taught her to shoot. She took another shot, and another. Another. Again.

When her fingers were so tired she could barely unwrap them from the pistol's grip, she collected the targets. Round concentric circles. She noticed the lower half of the circles. They formed smiley faces. Lower in the middle than each side. The opposite of the bell-shaped curve formed by Jeremy's frequencies. Inverted bell curves. Her eyes widened.

That was it! Jeremy had reversed the number of times he'd broadcast to each location. The frequencies he'd used most were not those stacked in the middle of the bell, they were the outliers! That was perfect Jeremy.

She went to the computer and flipped the distribution of the data she'd created. Another bell-shaped curve appeared, this one showing completely different most-used coordinates. That's why she hadn't heard from the golden planet. They didn't get her message.

Now all she needed was the password so she could broadcast. She had one try left before the computer locked up.

She sprawled in the opening to the storage container, defeated. What would Jeremy use as a password? He liked funny things, or enigmatic things. People. Friends. Places.

Would he use Hermitage Academy? His school. No. He hated it. Henry Henderson. Maybe. Henry and Lena had cared for him since birth. Would it be Henry and Lena? Or H. Henderson? What about Arthur? His driver/bodyguard Arthur Romero was a good friend. Jeremy might use his name. The estate? Piermont Manor? Would he use that?

Chaz Edgarton—his father? No. Jeremy hated him. How about the general? He *really* hated him.

Get up and move, Edgarton. Move. Work it. Jump. She pulled out a jump rope. Taggety, taggety, taggety. The rope ticked away the cycles. It flew over her head, under her feet. Taggety, taggety, taggety. She did tricks, crossing the rope before her. Behind her. Taggety, taggety. The sound echoed from the bunker's cement surfaces.

A smile came to Veronica's lips; she was really good at jump rope. She'd shown off in front of Jeremy a few times. His eyes had opened wide and he smiled, unable to believe that his mother could do anything athletic. He'd looked at her with love on those occasions, so different from his usual suspicion.

It came like a flash—*her* name was the password. She was the most enigmatic thing in Jeremy's universe. He loved her and hated her, wanted to be close to her and couldn't stand being around her. Veronica Piermont Edgarton.

Veronica took a deep breath and set the machine to broadcast her taped communication to the new coordinates. A password box came up.

"Veronica Piermont Edgarton," she typed, hitting *enter* decisively.

The screen indicated a message had been sent. Her broadcast was successful.

6

Sam seemed to be wounded. He held one arm wrapped around his belly and positioned the other arm over it, pushing down hard with both. He'd run a few steps and bend over, groaning.

"We can't stop, Sam. I don't know if they're following us." Jeremy felt sorry about pushing him, and worse the more he observed his condition. It was almost dark, but he could see that Sam's skin was gray-white, dusted with something like splotches of flour. Jeremy recoiled when he realized what it was: mold or a fungus. Jeremy couldn't slow down, no matter how hurt his companion was.

Sam's bare feet looked as tender as his own. He's never walked on anything but a cement or dirt floor, Jeremy thought. He walked as fast as he could, an arm around Sam's back, holding him up with a hand under the armpit. He could feel the other man's ribs. His shaved head and face were covered with stubbly hair. Jeremy thought he was in his fifties or sixties, though with his gray skin, it was hard to tell. Sam was very tall, probably as tall as Sam Baahuhd had been: 6' 8".

Jeremy had had the growth spurt that everyone told him would come while they were on the golden planet. He'd gotten used to being a big man, at least compared to the other humans in the golden world. But Sam was still half a head taller than him, maybe more.

Sam had some muscle. He didn't look like a concentration camp victim, quite. But he looked like he was in very bad shape. Another week in there and he would have been dead.

Shit. He realized why they'd put him up the canary-port. They must have run out of canaries. They threw Sam up the hole because he was going to die anyway.

Pissed, Jeremy made a final charge to his home in the machine shop. He deflated when he realized that his companion couldn't climb into the buried building. If he managed to get in, he'd never get out.

The wolves howled, coming closer.

"We may end up wolf-chow," Jeremy said to his new friend. Jeremy saw his face clearly by moonlight. Once again he was struck by the resemblance to Sam Baahuhd.

"Sam? Is that you? Sam Baahuhd? The headman of the village?"

"I'm Sam, but not Sam Baahuhd."

"Which Sam, then?" Jeremy remembered that Sam seemed to be the favored name of the village.

"I'm Sam of the line of Sam and Emily, and I have Arthur in me, too."

"Who is Sam Baahuhd?"

"He who threw me out."

The raging degenerate. A chill went through Jeremy. "How is he related to Sam Baahuhd?"

"He is straight bred to Sam and Mollie."

"Sam's wife who had the disease?"

"Aye. He has the disease and more." Sam leaned over and groaned, his lips pulling back from gray teeth. He swayed.

"We can rest if you want."

"No. They will find us."

How he made the last few hundred yards, Jeremy didn't know. He kept looking for the pipe sticking up under the trees, but he couldn't find it. He found something much easier to spot: a light with a huge black mass next to it.

"Oh, Jeremy! I've been so worried about you!" His mother was standing in front of a storage container like they put on ships and trains. It sat on railroad ties, raised a bit off the ground. She wore black pants, a parka, and combat boots. Next to her were a plastic table and chairs. An electric lantern sat on the table. Night bugs dive-bombed it.

Jeremy stopped dead, digging his fingers into Sam. "*Mom*! What are you doing here?" He stood, open-mouthed and rigid.

"I came to be with you, Jeremy."

His head moved from side to side, denying her silently. "How did you get here?"

"It wasn't easy. I had to get through the security measures on your computer."

"My computer? Which one?"

"The one from your room at the Hermitage Academy."

"What were you doing with my *computer*?" His sense of being violated merged with his shock at seeing her.

"Arthur put it on a cylinder and had it smuggled to me just before the meltdown. I hid it in my uniform in the bunker before we were frozen. When I woke up, I downloaded it and hacked into it."

"You saw everything on my computer?"

"Yes. From the cylinder. Getting it wasn't easy, either. A half dozen people put their lives on the line to get it to me."

"I can't believe you'd do that . . . And you got Arthur to help you. He was my friend."

"He was my friend, too, Jeremy." She stepped closer, holding her hands out to him. "Why are we arguing? Aren't you glad to see me?" She smiled tremulously. "I contacted the people on the golden planet and asked them to reunite us. I asked them to bring that," she nodded her head in the direction of the storage container, "so we'd have what we needed to survive. There was one with weapons, too, but they didn't send it."

"They sent *you*, but kept Ellie?"

"Yes, Jeremy. They came to me before they sent me. I could feel them floating around in the bunker. Then they put me here."

"They didn't say anything about Ellie and the others?"

"No. I knew they had sent you back to Earth alone, but I'm not quite sure how."

"That's how they are. No words."

"I'm truly sorry about Ellie." She looked at him tenderly. He regarded her without saying a word. Her mouth tightened.

"It's nice to see you, too, dear." She held her head high, but her lips quivered. "I rather hoped for a warmer welcome." She turned to Sam, who was slipping out of Jeremy's grip. "Your friend seems to need help." The wounded man fell on the ground, groaning. "Who is this? My goodness, he looks like Sam Baahuhd."

"He's from the underground shelter, Mom. They were using him like a canary to see if the air's safe."

"*What?*"

"They had him tied by the waist and threw him out the chute for the canary cage."

Sam made a choking sound, the sort of noise someone who was determined not to show pain would make before completely losing control. He held his arms over his belly.

"Are *you* hurt?" Veronica asked. Jeremy shook his head. "Let me see what's wrong with him. Hold up the lantern, Jeremy."

"No! No light!" Sam gasped and passed out.

Veronica bent over him and untwined his arms. She looked, and quickly wrapped his arms back again.

"What was that, Mom?" Jeremy asked. "It looked like an eye sticking out of his stomach."

"That's exactly what it is: an eye like the ones they used to have in public places to spy on us. This type hooks up to the victim's belly and looks out from there. I've seen them in the general's camps."

"Shit. I've never heard of anything like that. Does it know we're here?"

"Maybe. Depends on its range. Did he keep it covered like that all the time?"

"Yes."

"Good for him. Whoever was on the other end was undoubtedly hurting him to make him uncover it. Did he show pain?"

"Yeah."

"We need to get it out of him. I'll get some things from the container." She disappeared and came back with a tarp and medical supplies. "You take his shoulders, I'll take his feet."

They lifted Sam on the tarp and got ready. Sam awakened during the process, looking at them with wild eyes.

"Sam, we're going to get this thing out of you, and we're going to do it without killing you. I'm going to give you a shot to dull the pain around the implant. You'll feel a stick or two." Veronica injected spots around the eye. "It won't hurt as much in thirty seconds." She looked at her watch and flicked his belly with her fingers. "Hurt?" He shook his head.

"OK, let's go." Veronica took a scalpel from a sterilized packet and made a neat incision around the eye's head, revealing the casing, a cylindrical sheath about two inches wide and a half-inch deep. The eye was on the front of the head, the side that had been exposed. They could see a snakelike tail sticking out the other side, tunneling under Sam's skin.

"Look at this, Jeremy. This is why the people who try to remove this themselves die." Her fingers wrapped around the circular head of the device, below the eye. Three long, slender protuberances sat below a rim. "Retractable knives are positioned at the end of the cord. They withdraw into the cord to allow it to be inserted or removed by people who know what they're doing. If someone tries to pull it out of the carrier's belly without depressing those, the knives will spin and cut a three-inch swath inside the carrier. Who then dies.

"When you remove this from Sam, you need to press all three buttons flat and totally under the rim. That will pull the knives back in. Then yank that thing out as hard as you can. I'll be ready with the gauze pads to stop the bleeding. Whoever put this in him will know that it's being removed. They'll try to kill him. The eye is electric; it's still hot." She turned to Sam.

"Sam, I'm going to count to three. While I do that, breathe in as much air as you can. Take big breaths, starting now. On the count of three, blow out hard. Do you understand that?" He nodded. "OK, Jeremy. On three, you pull. One . . . two . . . *three!*"

Sam blew out and Jeremy pulled. The thing ripped out, with small chunks of Sam attached. It was a monster; they'd seen the top of the head, but it looked bigger pulled out. The tail was a segmented metal line a foot long and a quarter of an inch thick. The minute Jeremy let go of the three buttons, something like a propeller burst out on the end and started spinning, outside of Sam.

"Jesus!" Jeremy exclaimed.

Sam passed out again. Veronica bent over him with heavy sterile pads.

"I'm going to take care of him while you disarm *that*. See the tool kit in the bucket? You need to pop the eye out of the casing, turn the device inside off, and disarm it. It can explode."

Jeremy picked up the toolbox.

"Pop the head off it by keeping those little buttons pushed in and twisting the eye. Careful, it will try to shock you."

The tail turned and twisted as though it were trying to find Jeremy's skin. He did what she said and the tail went limp.

"What a nasty bastard," Veronica said. "It's an all-purpose device: You can torture or track or eavesdrop with one, or use it as a mine. They can't have one of these on everyone down below. They'd lose too much population. Sam must have tried to escape or done something they really didn't like, so they put it on him."

She appraised her patient's condition. "He'd have been crow bait in a couple of days."

"No crows down there. Now what do I do?" Jeremy had the top of the eye open. The lens looked around balefully.

"Don't let it see you. It will remember you if it sees your face. Remove the battery from the unit underneath and separate the eye from the holder. Then it's disarmed. Don't smash it. We may be able to do interesting things with it tomorrow."

"What about him?"

"He's stopped bleeding. I'll bandage the wound. Most of those who take them out themselves die of infection, if they're not cut to ribbons by the blades.

"We have the means to keep him alive." She filled a syringe from a glass ampule. "Penicillin. With this, all of us have a better chance. Hope he's not allergic. We've got the equivalent of a hospital in there," she jerked her head toward the container. "The medical supplies are set up right inside the door so we could get them in emergencies. Like now."

She injected the antibiotic into Sam's buttock and dropped the needle in a vial filled with clear liquid. "Bleach. Another lifesaver. We'll have to reuse needles. We don't know how long we'll have to nurse our supply." She filled another syringe with something else. "I don't like to give people this, but he's going to need it."

"What is it?"

"Morphine. That wound is going to hurt very badly, very soon. Stow those pieces of the eye where animals won't get to them, Jeremy. I don't want it inside with us tonight, even if it is disarmed."

"OK. Mom, where did you learn all this?"

"In the general's camps and his commando training programs. You'd be surprised what I know, Jeremy. I've been busy the last few years. Now please stow that thing."

After doing as she asked, Jeremy was ready to lift Sam into the crate and go to sleep. He was exhausted. He turned to see his mother examining their naked visitor with gloved hands. She was peering at his genitals when Jeremy looked. She lifted his balls and looked under them very carefully.

"What are you *doing*, Mother?" he cried.

"What did you think, Jeremy? I'm jumping the first man I see, even if he is unconscious and almost dead."

Jeremy ducked his head, an admission that what she had said was exactly what he thought.

"I'm checking him for parasites. If you recall, the village crawled with them. Can you imagine what it's like underground now? Our friend has crabs, body lice, head lice, and funguses. I do not want to have them, too, and I'm sure you don't either. Understand?"

"Yes, Mom."

"We'll discuss your feelings about me later. Right now, I need to treat him for those. I'm not putting him in the crate with me while he's infested." She applied a parasiticide cream to Sam, covering him entirely. "Help me push him to the side."

They rolled him to his side. Veronica parted his buttocks and looked. Her face registered distaste, and then bounced back to its professional expression.

"What's that, Mom?"

"Something I've seen in the camps. Someone's been hurting him for a very long time." She read the label on the tube of parasiticide. "You're supposed to leave this on for twenty minutes, then wash it off. Is there water around here, Jeremy?"

"Yeah, there's a stream with a pond over there." Howling wolves indicated the direction. "There was a rattler by the water."

"Oh, dear. Well, I'm not up to braving wolves and snakes to wash him off tonight. Let's just wrap him up with the tarp and go to bed."

After a pause, Veronica added, "I couldn't help but notice that you and Sam aren't wearing any clothes. I've got Russian army uniforms."

Jeremy blushed. "You sort of get used to it on the golden planet. No one wears clothes."

"You're very thin, dear."

"They did this to all of us. Trying to make us look like them."

"I'll get you a uniform."

They ate packets of military rations and bottled water before calling it a night. Jeremy watched the insects bouncing off the lantern. He didn't recognize any of them.

"We're going to have to ration everything," Veronica said. "We have to get set up permanently somewhere. Where they don't know where we are."

"Yeah. Hey, Mom?"

"Yes."

"I'm sorry about what I said."

She turned away from him. "I understand, dear. I have given you great cause for embarrassment. What you thought of me might have been true once. But not any more. I've changed. Now let's wrap up our friend, put him inside, and go to bed."

The storage unit was filled with huge metal cases. They reached to the ceiling and from wall to wall, with a narrow aisle down the center. Each box was labeled in Russian and secured by tracks in the ceiling and floor. Other than the corridor and four-foot open areas in the front and rear, every inch was jammed. Cabinets on the left wall in the front held emergency medical supplies.

Veronica made a nest for herself in the open space at the far end. "There's a sleeping bag in that box in front. We can put Sam by the door. Easier to get him out tomorrow."

"Mom," Jeremy didn't know how much time had passed when he whispered. "Are you asleep?"

"No, dear."

"Mom, could I sleep with you? I'm feeling weird."

"I am, too, dear. Yes, let's cuddle."

Jeremy wormed his way forward and lodged himself next to his mother. He'd never done that, even when he was a child. She always had to pursue him, looking for a hug. She put her arms around him, "What's the matter, darling?"

"They took Ellie, Mom. They took her away and there's nothing I can do."

"I know, dear. It's terrible. But the fact that they brought me here with the crate is an atonement, I think. Perhaps we can do more."

"Do you think so, Mom?"

"It's not over until we're dead." She looked at him earnestly. "We're here together, and tomorrow is another day."

Jeremy relaxed against his mother. He felt like she was someone he hadn't known, and yet she was. He was drifting off when she said something.

"Jeremy, are you sure the people in the underground will stay there?"

"I think so. Sam made noises like he was dying. When they heard wolves howling, they slammed the hatch. I think that should keep them in. I hope. Sam was worried about them following us, though."

"Once they figure out they can live outside, we're in trouble. How far was it to the shelter?"

"A twenty-minute walk."

"Not long enough. If they did what they did to him, what would they do to us?"

7

Jeremy untangled his arms from his mother's and crawled out of the tunnel between the boxes. He stood up next to the crate's door and pulled the lever opening it. Light flooded in. He looked down at Sam.

"Mom! Mom! There's something wrong with Sam."

Sam was wrapped in the plastic tarp, face bloated and red, and eyes swollen shut. He struggled to cry out, but could barely breathe.

"Mom! Come quick! He's dying!" He threw the doors wide and saw that Sam's body was swollen and discolored. "What happened to him?"

Veronica clawed her way out and stood over Sam. "He must be allergic to that stuff for lice! Or it could have been the morphine, or the penicillin. Oh, my God." She turned to the medical cabinet just inside the container's door, rattling through medications. Filling a syringe, she put a tourniquet around his arm, popped a vein out and gave him an injection.

"Adrenalin," she said. "I'm sorry, Sam. We bring you here and almost kill you. I've got cortisone, too, but I don't know how much to use.

"Jeremy, can you check in the encyclopedia on the computer?"

"Computer?"

"Yes. I brought almost everything from the general's lab. I couldn't get all the big stuff, but I got the computers. They're so miniaturized that a child could lift them. There's a generator, but the computers were charged when I left the bunker. They're right over there." She pointed and then studied Sam carefully. "How much do you think he weighs?"

"Holy shit, Mom!" Jeremy saw the heaps of computers and peripherals where she'd indicated. "I didn't see this stuff last night. This is a whole lab. I'll be able to do everything but fly."

"You may have to, dear. Now get me that dosage, please."

Sam got his cortisone shot. Minutes later, he was less swollen and breathing better. They had pulled the parasiticide-soaked tarp out from under him and replaced it with a clean one. Veronica checked his wound and changed the dressing.

"Since we don't know exactly what he's allergic to, we've got to eliminate everything I gave him. And we've got to wash the guck off him." She looked at Sam. "Sam, does your wound hurt terribly? I can give you something for pain that won't make you sick, along with an antibiotic that will be safe."

He took the medication, choking on the pills.

"You'll feel better in a while." She turned to Jeremy. "Sam can't go anywhere and he can't get that wound wet. He'll have to have a sponge bath." She went to one of the compartments and pulled out towels and buckets. "Can you go to that pond and get some water? I'll sit with Sam." She squatted next to him as he lay in the open area in the container's front.

Sam was able to study her for the first time. She was more beautiful than the stories they told about her. She had huge, dark blue eyes that seemed to glint. He'd never seen eyes that color. Her nose was fine and straight, her lips soft and full, framing her wide mouth. Her skin was silken and pale. Her black hair hung to her shoulders. All of her was lovely. She had some tiny lines around her eyes that he scarcely noticed; she didn't seem old enough to be Jeremy's mother.

He also saw what those of the line of Emily knew to look for: fine scars along her jaw. A tiny depression in one cheek where a broken bone couldn't be fixed perfectly. The lady had said goodbye to Sam Baahuhd just before the world blew up. She did it by making a cylinder and having someone get it to him secretly. The way that she moved and her gestures said that she was being watched when she recorded it. The lady had turned her face so that he could see her scars and know what her life was like. The general had beaten her viciously.

Being near her made it harder to breathe than it already was. When she picked up his hand and stroked it, he started to shake.

"Oh, Sam, you're in pain. I can give you one more of those pills." She gave him a pill and made him drink the entire glass of water. She gave him more water than he'd get in a day in the underground. The lady sat next to him, holding his hand.

Sam drifted into and out of consciousness. The medicine she gave him made him sleepy, but his stomach hurt less. He couldn't believe he was free. He couldn't believe that Jeremy the Tek and the lady, Mrs. Edgarton, had saved him. The Tek was worshiped as God in the underground. His mother was a legend. He heard her talking to Jeremy.

"Thanks for getting the water, Jeremy. I'll give him a sponge bath now, unless you want to," her voice said.

"Sorry, Mom. That's not my thing. I'm going to take a dip in the pond and then scout around."

"Don't go in near the shelter."

"Don't worry. I heard the guy that threw Sam out."

Sam must have fallen asleep, because he was surprised when something touched him.

"Sam, I'm going to wash you with a soapy rag, and then I'll rinse you off. I'm going to wash you all over, but I'm not getting fresh. Can you hear me, Sam? Are you asleep?"

He drifted off again, and then awakened when he felt something on his face. It was soft and gentle and slippery. He pretended to be asleep. The cloth went all over his face and head, and behind his neck.

"I'm going to rinse you off, Sam." Another cloth stroked him, this one dripping with water. She rinsed him carefully, taking her time. Her touch electrified him. He lay as though he was asleep, but his body strained toward her, drinking in the contact. When she was finished with an area, she dried him with another cloth, one that was a little rougher.

"You look so much like your grandfather. Or whatever he was." The cloth caressed him across his forehead and then over his cheekbones. She spoke to him as though she was sure he couldn't hear.

"Sam Baahuhd was the most beautiful man I've ever seen." She stroked his nose with the wet cloth. She paused, as though she was taking a good look at him.

"Are you in your fifties?" He wanted to shake his head and say, "No, I'm not that old," but he didn't. "Your skin probably makes you look older. You look like an alligator from dead skin building up. You could soak for a month."

She ran the wet rag around his neck and then over his chest, moving it slowly and softly. Her gentleness shocked Sam. She kept the cloth moving, across his chest and down his torso, being careful not to get near his bandage.

The rag kept moving. Sometimes she was silent, concentrating, wiping a spot two or three times. He expected her to do something to hurt him, or shame him, but she didn't. She kept the rag moving, stroking him over and over. She touched him everywhere, places that no one had. The contact felt OK, not like it dirtied him.

"I was in love with Sam Baahuhd." Her voice was low.

He knew that and listened very attentively. The Bigs and those from the lineage of Sam Baahuhd's first wife said she was his whore. That he'd taken her all over the village, in front of everyone. In the old days, photos of the lady were prized. As time passed, those who had never seen her had pumped their seed on her image and cursed her as a witch for making them do it. When the photographs were ruined by all the men who'd used them, the stories remained. "A picture of her is better than any cunnie," they'd joke.

Only those of the line of Emily knew the truth. Mrs. Edgarton wasn't Sam Baahuhd's woman, and never had been. After Sam died, what he had been to the lady changed and shifted, being soiled by every mouth repeating it. Only those of Emily kept the truth.

Sam knew what they would do with her underground. They wouldn't kill her. They'd keep her alive. He had to protect her from that, no matter what it cost him.

"I only touched him once," she was saying. The cloth continued its progress as her voice whispered. "I put my hand on the front of his pants when we were thirteen. I don't know what I was thinking. Well, I do, actually.

"But it was impossible."

She carefully rolled him over on his side. Her touch moved up and down his spine. He wanted to cry out in pleasure, but kept still. She'd stop talking if she knew he was awake.

She rolled him over on the other side and kept washing. "I was awful to him. I'd go out to the estate with any silly boy I could find and make out in front of Sam." Her touches stopped.

"I'm not a very nice person." Her voice dropped to a whisper.

"I got what was coming to me." She finished washing his back and gently laid him down the way he'd been. "I got the general." A teardrop splashed on his chest. She wiped it off.

She knelt next to him, his hand resting on her thigh. Bending forward, she held up his arm and carefully cleansed his armpit. He heard the intake of her breath when she saw the scar there. "Oh, you poor thing." She wrapped the cloth around his arm and pulled it down to his hand, wiping each finger and then the palm of his hand. She saw what was there, too. She kissed the palm of his hand. "You and I know, don't we? What the rest of the world doesn't know."

She got up. "You need some moisturizer." She went into the container and came back. He felt a cold liquid and then her hands touching him again. She smoothed the liquid all over him, releasing a wonderful fragrance. He couldn't move. He couldn't imagine anything like what was happening to him. His body trembled.

"Oh, you're cold." She covered him with something soft. He felt her lips on his forehead. Her breast brushed his shoulder. "Live, Sam. I want you to live."

She walked away. He felt like his soul followed her. He wanted to be as close as he could get to her, to hold her, and touch her. He wanted to do something he had never done with her.

And he was terrified. He knew what Sam Baahuhd had told Emily. Emily was his only wife in the underground and the true love of his life. He had carried her into the shelter naked on Earth's last day. Sam Baahuhd gave her the name Emily, but she was really named Valerie. She was a federal agent from New York City, a killer and torturer that Sam healed. She loved Sam and taught him to read and many other things. He told her things he never said to anyone else.

He told Emily that the lady had hurt him for years and years. She had tormented and tortured him, almost breaking his heart. She was bad. Only after he met Emily was Sam Baahuhd happy.

8

"Oh, hello, dear! Where have you been all this time?" the lady's voice said. Sam heard Jeremy walking up. He continued to pretend to be asleep.

"I jumped in the pond and then reconnoitered." Jeremy sounded disturbed. "We're sitting ducks here. This area is totally indefensible. The land just rolls on, almost flat, with no underbrush, not even a creek for cover. Arthur would have a fit if he saw it. We've got to get out of here. If any of those monsters from the underground get out, we're dead meat."

Sam almost opened his eyes at the mention of Arthur. He was one of Sam's ancestors, a commando who went into the shelter instead of up into the angel Eliana's world. He was the only one who could run the computerized life-support systems of the underground, so he made the sacrifice of staying.

"Getting out of here will be a good trick," the lady said. "I don't know how we'll move this container. But I'm going to take a bath. Who knows how many years it's been. Where was that pond?"

"Over there." He shrugged in its direction. "I'm going to see if I can find any functional satellites. I want to get a look inside the shelter."

"If anyone can do it, you can. Sam's been sleeping all morning. I gave him some pain pills and they knocked him out. There's a uniform for him when he wakes up. He hasn't eaten, either."

"Don't worry, Mom. I'm on it."

The lady left. Sam heard Jeremy moving things. He dragged something to the front of the container and sat down noisily.

"OK, you motherfuckers, I'm back." Sam opened his eyes to see Jeremy seated before a computer. The screen shone brightly. He cracked his knuckles, and then shook out his hands. "We'll see how bad the goldies fucked me up." He began typing and talking to himself. "Most of the satellites are probably dead, but there should be some that work." Sam heard a whirring noise from the computer. "I'll run a search algorithm. If I can get a hot bird, I *know* the hardware in the underground will work. I designed it to take *anything*. I'll bounce a signal off one of the tin cans, restart the surveillance systems inside, and it will be show-and-tell time down below."

Sam couldn't resist studying the Great Tek. Jeremy had his back to him, absorbed in the computer. The screen's light shone on his hair, making it glow. He looked like Jer the Tek that Sam Baahuhd and all the headmen since him had described in the meetings.

Jeremy's hair hung in a tangled mass down to his waist. He was tall, not a little shrimp, as Sam Baahuhd had portrayed him. Sam had never seen anyone with Jeremy's skin color. "Café au lait" it was called, which he also knew from the legends. His mother was the lady and his father had been a famous Afroman. Chaz Edgarton was a musician beloved by the village. Whenever he had visited the estate, he came out to the barn to play for the villagers, though sometimes he was so loaded he fell off the bench.

Sam worked himself up to a semi-sitting position so he could watch the Great Tek. Awe filled him. The Great Tek was God. He had given them the Commands and the Book, which ruled their lives.

"I live by the Commands," Sam whispered.

"What?" Jeremy turned to face him, eyes piercing. Sam could see his cocoa skin. His lips were wide and his nose broader than those of the villagers. Sam recoiled from his intensity.

"I live by the Commands, O Great Tek," Sam stammered.

"You mean the Commandments?"

"No, the Commands."

"What are those?"

"On the night before the end of the world, the Great Tek stood before Sam Baahuhd and gave us the Commands. He gave us the Commands so that we might survive and live to take over the world," Sam spoke with the dramatic cadence of the Book Readers, who were the only ones allowed to read the book.

"You sound like a snake man," Jeremy said, wrinkling his face.

"No snake men!" Sam invoked one of the Commands.

"You're damned right. Those guys were poison, going around scaring everyone to death. But what are the Commands?"

"They're from you, O Great Tek." Sam touched his heart with his hand and bowed. "Your gift to us. They are the law in the underground."

"What? My name is Jeremy. Who's this Great Tek?"

"Sam Baahuhd told us you were the Great Tek. You could do anything with your powers." Sam looked at Jeremy, disbelief on his face. Didn't the Tek know this? "He told us how you gave us the Commands on the last night of the Earth."

"What are you talking about? I'm a pretty good tech, but I'm not magic."

Sam was shaken. "The Commands are written in The Book, a magic book of light that the angel Eliana gave you. The Commands were written in it when you spoke."

"Oh, I remember that now. The notebook's no big deal. That's how they write in Ellie's world. With light. There's light everywhere—walls, billboards, across the sky. After a while, you start praying for an eclipse. El's no angel. She's my wife."

"Did you give us the Commands?"

Jeremy wiped his face with his hand. "Jeez. What happened that night? It's been so long. I remember being really upset. I tossed out some ideas that I thought would make the underground work. What are the Commands?"

"The first Command is to take over the world when we get out of the shelter."

"Why?"

"Because the general is out there waiting for us and will kill us and take over the world if we don't."

"I'm not so sure about that. What were the other commands?"

"The headman has total power. He can kill all of us if he wants. Sam Baahuhd was the first headman. His oldest son would be the next headman, and his oldest, forever."

"Well, Sam would do a good job. I don't know about Rupert and those who came later. What about individual rights? The Constitution, checks and balances?"

"You took all Constitutional rights away. I don't know what the other things are."

"Oh, boy. What else?"

"We had to learn to read in six months," Sam ducked his head. "O Tek, I tried to learn to read, but the Bigs closed the library. They took the Book from us so that only the Readers can see it. I tried . . ."

"They closed the library! They had no right to do that. I set that up for the people. What were the rest of the commands?"

"We were to exercise and come out warriors ready to fight the general. But they closed the gym."

"The gym! I used to work out there with Arthur every day. You have to stay in shape or you end up like this." He indicated his emaciated form. "What are the rest of the Commands?"

"Only one husband and one wife, fidelity. No boingy boingy with your cousins. No weed, mushrooms, or hooch. We had to speak regular English."

"Those are pretty good. Do people follow them?"

Sam blinked and lowered his head. "I do, Great . . ."

"I'm Jeremy! Stop that Great business."

"Jeremy. I follow them. Some others do." He was silent.

"The leaders don't."

Sam shook his head. "No. They make hooch. Mushrooms and weed grow in the fields. The headmen have had many wives for a long time. When the Bigs came, it was different. The Bigs don't have wives."

"What do they do?"

"They have the Pit. The women go into the Pit."

"What! What are you saying?"

"The headman can do anything he wants. That's what he wanted."

"What a disaster. OK, I'll give you a COMMAND right now. Follow the Commands all you want, but if they're bullshit or make life worse, don't follow them. Do something that works."

"Yes, Great . . ."

"Jeremy. That's my name. I want to get a 360-degree view inside that shelter. I want to know what's happening down there." He looked at Sam as though remembering something. "Oh, yeah. You want anything to eat? We've got Russian army rations. It's slop, but edible. My mom put some clothes out for you. She'll be mad at me if I don't take care of you. Now *she's* someone whose commands you should pay attention to."

Sam was sitting up eating the most delicious food he'd ever tasted when the lady came back. Jeremy had helped him put on the uniform's shirt and pants. He'd seen that Sam had no idea of how to put them on.

Sam looked up when the lady came.

"Jeremy, did you notice anything about this area when you were walking?" the lady said. She was dressed in a black uniform with her hair wrapped in a white fuzzy cloth. The uniform showed her body's form. She was small around her waist and swelled at her chest. He could have wrapped his hands around her waist easily. Not around the top of her. Her hips were curved, but not big.

"I noticed lots of things, Mom."

"This place looks like the West Coast. Remember our ranch near Santa Barbara? The oaks grew far apart like these. I saw magpies with the yellow trim on their beaks—those only live in Central California. And those trees in the distance look like redwoods. Do you have any idea where we are? Or how long it's been since everything blew up?"

"No. But with one of the computers, I'll be able to take some measurements off the stars and figure it out."

"This doesn't feel like Connecticut. Could the skin of the planet slip over time?"

"So the West Coast ended up the East Coast? And the East Coast became . . ."

"Europe? But where would Europe and Asia go? To the West Coast? That's impossible . . . How much time would have to pass for the upper layers of earth to move thousands of miles? And for the polar ice caps to reform? I was under glaciers in the bunker. That area was forest when we were sealed in."

"It would take ages for that much change, if it happened at all."

"You know what else? I don't know what year it was when I woke up. The chronometers in the bunker were broken. I don't know if it was the same time there as it is here. Could the goldies have lifted me from one time and place into another time and place to be with you?"

"Probably. They could do pretty near anything."

"And what's the date here? Sam, do you know how long your people have been in the shelter?"

He jumped when she spoke to him. "The singers of songs say 105 generations."

"So at nineteen years a generation, that's five years short of 2,000 years." Sam was amazed at how fast Jeremy made the calculation.

"We do not have nineteen years a generation."

"How many then?"

"Fourteen."

Jeremy's jaw dropped. "OK. That's 1,470 years. That's still a long time. I built the underground to last that long. Do you think it really could be that long?"

"Sam, tell us about the underground. What's its history?"

Sam hesitated before speaking. He was not supposed to talk about this. He knew the history as remembered by the line of Emily—the true history. What the Speakers would say about their history would be different. He knew the Tek wanted the truth. "For a time after Jer the Tek made the shelter, things were good. Everyone followed the Commands and the Book. Everyone learned to read. There was enough food. The babies were all good and not too many were born.

"But then things changed. Sam's descendants from Mollie, his first wife, were the rightful rulers, according to the Commands. They took the Book away. They had the disease and hurt people, killing them, sometimes. Their babies were often sick or missing arms or legs.

"They killed those that weren't of Sam from Mollie, except for the Arthurs and Emilies and those with their blood. They needed us. We ran the computers and the shelter's systems. We were smarter than the others. The Sams by the line from Mollie divided the shelter. They locked the others up and stopped following the Commands. The air became bad. We didn't have enough food or water.

"The Bigs came. The Bigs are very bad." Sam hadn't talked so much in his life. But he needed to tell them. "If they catch you, kill yourself. Especially you, lady." She had to understand the danger. "They know you. You canna go down there." The brogue of the village crept into his speech.

"I don't want to, Sam, believe me."

That's all he could say. He wanted to tell them about the rest of it, but it was forbidden and too horrible to talk about. Sam sat leaning forward, eyes down, head bowed.

"Jeremy, does that sound like 2,000 years of history to you?" The lady's voice was soft.

"It could be anything from fifty years up. What about the furniture they took from mom's house, Sam? Does it look old?"

"There is no furniture. Only pieces of wood and bits of fur. And some metal things. Spoons and candle holders and dishes."

"Everything else has disintegrated?"

"In the old days, they say the underground was like the big house. Beautiful. All that is gone."

"How long would it take for furniture to fall apart like that?" Jeremy mused.

"A long time. Sam, where did they get that thing they put in you? Do they have more of them?" the lady asked.

"I don't know where they got it. They knew how to put it in me, but I don't think they have more. They would have used them before. They didn't make it."

"You're sure?"

"Yes. They don't make anything. They just fight."

"Where did they get it?"

"I don't know."

"Well, sooner or later, they're going to figure out that they can live outside the shelter and come out. We need to be ready," Jeremy said.

They'd been sitting in the opening of the container. The lady's eyes landed on a spot on the ground some distance from them.

"Jeremy, where did you put the box with the parts of the eye in it?"

"Under the container in the back."

"Well, it's over there now." She pointed at the open space in front of them. "I just saw it move."

The box with the eye in it moved a foot while they watched, heading in the direction from which Sam and Jeremy had come.

"It's going back."

"Yeah, it must have a recall function."

"Its track will lead them straight to us."

"Yes, eventually. But it's not fast." At the rate it was going, the box would take a couple of days to get back to the big meadow.

"Where will it go?"

"To the canary chute? The back door? I don't know." Jeremy's eyes narrowed. "Did they destroy all the computers, Sam?"

"Computers were in the library and in Arthur's room. The Bigs closed those. I don't know what is there now. I was not allowed near."

"Jeremy, could you take a picture of the inside of the shelter?" the lady said.

"Ninety percent probability that I can. The audio and video surveillance devices should be operational. If I can find a live satellite, I can activate them from here. What are you thinking?"

"Remember the way they used to market real estate using holograms in the old days? It was like being inside the house, a 3D view of the room. If we had one of those of the interior of the shelter, we'd know how bad it is."

"Doesn't the way Sam looks tell you?" Jeremy asked.

"Yes, very clearly, but it isn't a complete view or something we could broadcast. And I have an idea that could solve some of our problems. It's a long shot, but it may work."

Sam could barely hear them. He sat paralyzed, watching the box move.

9

They moved the metal box back under the storage container and surrounded it with large stones. That halted its homeward progress and gave them a limited sense of security.

"Let's get down to business. We have to figure out what to do with that nasty thing." Veronica moved the plastic table and chairs to the other side of the container, as far from the box as possible. "We've got to get to safety. We need the weapons in the other container. We need Eliana and the others. We're likely to perish without those things, and very soon. I'm going to call the golden planet again."

"You're going to call Eliana's people for *help*?" Jeremy said.

"That's how I got here," she said.

"But you don't know them. They're really bad."

"They weren't to me."

"You don't know the goldies like I do. They sneak and lie. You can't trust them." She could see Jeremy's hackles rise. He looked like a cat who'd run into a killer dog and was going to have to fight for his life. Veronica could feel their old patterns rearing up. "But maybe you *do* understand the goldies, Mom. You got Arthur to hack into my computer. Did you have him do anything else?" She could see a screaming fit on its way. Might as well tell him the rest.

"Yes. I had him monitor your room at the Hermitage, Jeremy."

"You had my room *bugged?* You spied on me?" he snarled. "I can't believe it. But maybe I can. That is so *you.* Did you get an earful?"

"Yes . . . but you did the same thing to the village, Jeremy. Maybe you should have thought about how they . . ."

"You *steal* my laptop, *bug* my room, *and* turn my friend Arthur against me. Now you want to contact the assholes who stole Ellie and tried to kill me. Really swell, Mom."

"I didn't turn anyone against you. Arthur was my friend, too. He knew how things were for me." Jeremy opened his mouth to start shouting. "*Listen to me, Jeremy!* I was alone in a foreign country, watched twenty-four hours a day. I couldn't go anywhere or talk to anyone who wasn't in the general's pocket. Your voice was all I had.

"They were trying to rescue me, Arthur and our military, but they couldn't. You knew that, didn't you?"

"Yes." His face was unreadable.

"I know how you feel about me, Jeremy. You've made it very clear in person, and over those transmissions. You swore at whatever you were programming and me in equal measure. But that's all I had to keep myself sane. Your curses were the best part of my life."

"Yeah, right."

She turned the side of her face to him and lifted her hair. Fine white lines ran along her jaw and hairline. "Do you know what those are?"

"He *hit* you?" Jeremy's mouth opened a bit.

"The beatings weren't the worst. He did things to me that were so bad that I will *never*, ever tell another soul about them." She lost her poise, struggling to explain. "Please, Jeremy. Try to understand."

"But I saw you on TV and in magazines, at fancy parties. On yachts. Smiling and laughing."

"Oh, yes. When the bruises faded, I'd get all done up and make a show of being the fabulously happy paramour of the worst mass murderer in history. It was staged, Jeremy. I was acting."

"But you married him. He took you with him in the bunker."

"I put myself there, Jeremy. He picked me over thousands of others, because I was the best. I went through a military training that made whatever Arthur did with you look like kindergarten. I did that in the hope that I would live—and one day get free, so I could be with you. And I did it. I'm here." She felt like whatever had held her together for all those years was blowing to smithereens.

"Why don't I feel triumphant?" She raised her head proudly, ignoring the way she trembled. "Oh, I forgot. You hate me." Her eyes misted. "Shit. I can't deal with this." She dashed away from the container.

Jeremy hesitated, then went after her.

He caught up with his mother within a hundred yards. She was bending down with her hands on her knees, panting. She looked up at him.

"I can't run for beans. I haven't recovered from being frozen."

"Mom, I'm sorry. I didn't know."

"I'm sorry, too, Jeremy. I hoped that this homecoming would be very different. In all my dreaming about the future, I forgot that I don't know how to be with you." Her shoulders dropped and her hands turned toward him beseechingly.

"I don't know how to be with you, either, Mom. But let's try. Please tell me how things were for you. OK? I don't really know you."

"Yes, let's try. And I want to hear what you're feeling, too."

"Right now?"

"Yes."

"It blows my mind that you want to contact the goldies for help. They pretend to be all peaceful and kind, but they're not. They use other species, and they'll use you. Don't trust them at all."

"I'll keep that in mind. But I don't see that we have much choice. Any time now, those monsters in the underground are going to figure out that they can live outside. When they do, they'll come straight for us. We have no weapons. We're outnumbered. We saw what they did to Sam. What else can we do but contact the golden planet? We have no options."

"Sorry, Sam. A little old business between Jeremy and me," Veronica said when they got back to the container. "I propose to broadcast to Ellie's people again and ask for help.

"If you can get images of the inside of that place showing exactly what's going on, Jeremy, I'd like to send them to Ellie's world and show them what we're up against. Maybe I can persuade them to give us the munitions crate."

"Mom, do you think they give a shit? They tossed me out to die."

"There's got to be something good in them. They kept you and the rest all those years. They came for you before the conflagration. They helped me. And maybe they'll fear what those monsters could do . . ."

"Why? They're up there, and we're down here. It won't affect them one bit."

"Oh, Jeremy. We're helpless. And what can they do to us if we ask?"

"You'd be surprised. They're so far ahead of us, you can't believe it. But, yeah, you're right. What choice do we have?"

She turned to Sam. "Did you see any weapons down there? There's an absolute arsenal. Terrible weapons that the general gave Jeremy. Did they show them to anyone?"

Sam shook his head. "They talk about them. They said they'd kill us with them if we did not obey. But they never showed 'em."

"That means they can't get to them. Or they don't know how to use them," she said.

"Or they're smart enough to know that if they used them down there, they'd blow the shelter to bits and kill everyone in it." Jeremy looked concerned. "Did you ever hear anything about really big guns?"

"No. But they scream about using them to take over the world. It's the first Command."

"You said that before, but I don't remember saying it."

Sam held himself erect and struck a theatrical pose. His voice boomed, "And the great *Tek* stood before his Lab, *lightning* blazing from his hair. His eyes shot *fire*. Light surrounded him and the computers in the Lab. And he said, '*Nay* to the snake men! *Nay* to the hooch! *Nay* to…'" Sam paused; he couldn't say "no boingy boingy with your cousins" in front of the lady.

He resumed with, "The great Tek *rose* into the sky in the yellow light, becoming one with the *heavens*. 'I *will* return, Sam of the village. When you get out, *take over the world*.'" Sam mimicked the voices of the Book Readers. "That's how the Readers speak it. That's what we believe, down below."

Jeremy raised his hands over his head. "I was just a screwed up kid. The planet was about to be destroyed. Sam would never let what I said turn into a religion. It wasn't a religion."

Sam spoke with the booming, syncopated voice of a Reader. "The great golden light took the Angel and the Tek. 'I will come again, Sam,' the Tek promised. 'And we will take over the world.'" Sam imitated the cadence and the worshipful fervor of the Readers. "That's how they say it, and that's what they believe."

"Do you believe that, Sam?" Jeremy asked.

Sam looked at him guardedly. When he spoke, it was in the dialect of the village. Jeremy's commands had forbidden its use, but everyone underground spoke it anyway, as well as regular English. "Ye have done more good to me than any in ma life. Ye took that out of me," he jerked his head toward the box with the eye. "Ye washed me an' gave me food. Ah'd be dead but for you."

"But I'm just a guy, Sam, like you. I've had some education. My mom had learned how to take out the eye. What we did was stuff anyone would do."

"But ye an' th' lady did it."

Veronica cut in. "Sam, whatever you think or believe is fine. Please know that I'm an ordinary woman. I'm not supernatural. We need to make a plan, not discuss theology."

"It is different than it was, down there. They *say* they keep the Commands, but they don't. They have hooch and mushrooms, and they hurt people."

"We saw that," Jeremy responded.

"Worse than w' me," he said.

"Let's get some pictures of it so we'll know what's going on," the lady said. "Jeremy, can you get the cameras on the computers going so we can photograph inside and see it here, as well as broadcasting images remotely?"

"Yeah, if I can find a live satellite. There are some huge Russian ones that are nuclear powered. They'll work forever."

"If you could find one that wasn't Russian, that would be good. The general's son . . ."

"Say no more, Mom. I'll find one that he can't trace."

"Can you photograph the interior without light?"

"I've got night vision on some of the surveillance cameras, but not all. Do the lights work, Sam?"

"They work in the main room, where Sam Big stays. And in the pit where the women are. The rest of us are kept dark, unless Sam wants someone. We are kept in rooms and canna leave."

"The women's *pit*? *Kept* in rooms? He wants them for *what*?" Veronica was appalled.

Sam looked down. "The women are kept for the Bigs."

Veronica stopped the conversation. "I don't know why I'm surprised. I saw it in the general's camps. The worst element, the sadistic goons, take over and terrorize the camp. They do whatever they want to the rest. They get the food, entertainment. Sex. Clothes. Keeping people in the dark is a good way to terrorize them.

"I want some really nasty pictures to shock your in-laws, Jeremy." She paused a moment. "I thought of something else. A visit from the soon-to-return Great Tek might be a nice touch, if you can broadcast into the shelter."

"On the screens?"

"Yes. I was also thinking of a hologram in the middle of the main hall. Weren't you working on holograms before everything blew up? Could you create something that would look real? I could do some wonderful things with makeup and your hair. We've got lights. What do you think?"

"Well, I could do a flash from the computers and the overhead lights at once. One blast of light and we'd get the pictures of what we want. The computers would send them to the satellite, then relay them here, and to Ellie's world. If I get any lasers up, I can broadcast a hologram. What should I say with the hologram?"

"Something on the order of 'I'm coming and I'm mad.' We'll work on that once we know if we can do it."

"I'll get to work right now. What about the eye?"

"Can you reverse it so we can broadcast through it? We could program it with some message."

"I can do that. Probably."

Jeremy settled into his computers. They brought the eye and its box inside. Being blocked in its homeward journey seemed to irritate the thing. It rattled against the inside of the box.

As Jeremy disappeared into the tech world, Veronica approached Sam. "Sam, I want to change your bandage." After doing so, she patted his shoulder. "OK. Let's eat and go to sleep. I'm exhausted."

He had something to say and felt so self-conscious that he could barely open his mouth.

"What is it, Sam? Think of me as your mother. You can talk to me."

Sam had almost no memory of his mother, but he could never think of the lady as his mother. "Ah . . . If ah could . . ." How could he ask? "Underground, we sleep together. Could ah . . .?"

"Sleep with Jeremy and me? Certainly. We can have a nice slumber party."

They put mats and sleeping bags down for three people. She put her fur coat over them. Sam had never slept in a nicer bed. He could hear Jeremy on the computer and see the light from beyond their corridor of boxes.

"He's wired in, Sam. That's computer wizard talk. He's concentrating so hard he doesn't know we're here. He won't stop until he's done. We might as well go to sleep."

He could barely lie near her. He knew that she was utterly forbidden to him, above him in every way.

Something kept coming out of him, feelings, and energy. Images of her face and lips haunted him. The way her chest protruded and her waist tucked in. He couldn't stop thinking of her. Sleeping next to her was impossible, and leaving her was impossible. He heard Jeremy talking to himself as he worked.

"Yes! Yes! Take that, you motherfucker!" Sam smiled. Jeremy was Jer the Tek.

Jer the Tek and his mother were utterly different from what they said underground. They were people, and they were nice. Not so much greater than him, and yet much greater, too. He wanted them to like him. He wanted to be part of their family. He had a family, once. Vague memories of faces flitted through his mind. He had had a sister. He finally relaxed and drifted away.

"Don't! Don't!" The lady cried out in her sleep. "No!"

He woke up and pulled closer to her. "Lady, I'll keep you safe," he had said the same thing to his sister before they dragged her from his arms. He put his arm around the lady and held her close.

"Oh!" she said, eyes popping open. "Oh, Sam, it's you. I was having a horrible dream. The general was chasing me." She clutched his hand. "He would kill both of us if he found us like this."

"Aye," Sam said.

"Hold me, Sam." He held her, almost paralyzed by what was happening inside him.

Veronica awakened when Jeremy touched her. Sam was sleeping. The sky was dark.

"I did it, Mom. It's ready. What I did with the eye is going to blow their minds. If you're going to broadcast to Ellie's people, you should do it now. I don't know how much time we've got before the eye hits the shelter. I sped it up."

10

"I want to thank you with all my heart. Being with my son means more than I can say." Veronica knew her words meant their lives and she let her feelings show.

"We have a third person with us now: Sam. My son rescued him when they threw him out of the underground shelter to die. They attached a tracking device to him, a vicious thing. Fortunately, we were able to remove it."

As she spoke, Jeremy broadcast photos of the eye. He'd labeled them with what the parts did and a drawing of how the thing fit into a person.

"Because of the medical supplies in the container you delivered to us, our Sam will live. Conditions in the shelter are more heinous than we imagined, and there may be other good people like Sam there. We'd like to rescue them if we can.

"Of course, we can't, because we are no match for them in numbers or in weaponry.

"I need to ask you for help. Jeremy was able to photograph the interior of the shelter. He will broadcast these images while I'm speaking so that you have a clear idea of what we're up against.

"I haven't seen the pictures yet. I was afraid I wouldn't be able to speak if I did. There are a hundred of them, versus three of us, one of whom is gravely injured. They have two caches of missiles and hand-held armaments that I hope you'll be able to see, in addition to biological and chemical weapons.

"We have garden tools.

"They'll kill us, or take us for sexual slaves. That is what our future will be, without your help.

"You have no reason to help us, I realize. Your experience with my son and the others was problematic. I believe that we can work together, despite our past differences. I know that doing the right thing carries a satisfaction of its own."

The images of the underground went out, unseen by either Jeremy or his mother. Jeremy was busy loading and sending.

"We need a safe place. We need land for growing crops and good water. We need a place where we can defend ourselves.

"I ask you with all the love in my heart, please help us. Move us somewhere safe. Give us the container of weapons. Send Eliana home to her husband, and send Henry and Lena and James and Mel home to Earth. They belong here. And as you deliberate this decision, I ask you to review the photos my son is sending. This is what we face.

"This is Veronica Edgarton on the planet Earth, speaking from Piermont Manor, my family's home."

She closed her eyes. If those words and the images didn't work, they were dead. Jeremy was on a screen watching the input he'd captured in the burst of light.

"Did you hear what I said, Jeremy? Did it sound OK?"

"Should be OK. They'll twist whatever you say to whatever they want. But what you said doesn't sound too dangerous."

"What about the latest photos?"

"I'm sending them continuous play." Jeremy stared at the screen as room after room of the shelter was revealed. "Mom, don't look."

"I need to look, Jeremy. I need to know Sam's world and we need him to identify these people and who might be saved."

"They don't look like people. They're huge, and so ugly." He turned away, then looked back. "Mom, don't look! Really."

She peered at the chaos of the underground. Misshapen bodies and bulging foreheads, massive muscles. A half-dozen fistfights dotted the hall. Two men held a screaming woman while a third stood between her legs. Howling figures were chained to the walls. A huge man raped a child.

"I want still shots of everything, and I want them printed out, here, now." She studied the images. "I want to kill them, Jeremy. I want to kill every one of them. Son of a bitch! I never dreamed anything could be that bad."

Jeremy had never heard his mother swear. He did as she asked.

"And they're doing it on *my* property. Did you get shots of the munitions?"

"Yeah, right here." There were computer monitors with cameras on them in the armament vaults. Jeremy had gotten a thorough inventory.

"It looks like they got into the first vault at some time, but long ago. Is that a skeleton?"

"Yeah."

"I wonder what happened. The other vault is untouched."

"Do you remember the security system, Jeremy?"

He thought for a moment. "Password protected. Face imprint and vocal password. My voice and my face."

"That's good. They can't fake those. But I wonder how they got into the first vault? Oh, Jeremy, what are we going to do?"

The images kept scrolling over. He got every face and room of the shelter, a flash freeze of hell.

"I think I should give them my I'm-the-Great-Tek-and-I'm-mad speech."

"YOU FUCKING ASSHOLES! WHAT DO YOU THINK YOU'RE DOING?" Jeremy screamed into the mike. His image was broadcast as a hologram in the middle of the shelter's main hall. "YOU THOUGHT I WOULDN'T *KNOW*, DIDN'T YOU? YOU THOUGHT I WOULDN'T *SEE*, DIDN'T YOU?"

His mother had made up his face to look as scary as possible, emphasizing shadows and lights. She used gels to make his dreads stand up straight. She arranged their two spotlights so that one hit him from the back, and the other underneath his chin. He stood before the computer's camera, dancing in anger.

"I LEFT YOU A GOOD PLACE AND WHAT DO YOU DO? *FUCK IT UP.*

"I SEE YOU, YOU FAT SON OF A BITCH, BEATING THAT KID. I SEE ALL OF YOU!" Jeremy could see the images of what he was talking about as he spoke, which made him roar in rage.

"I GAVE YOU MY *COMMANDS*. I GAVE YOU THE *BOOK*. I GAVE YOU THE LIBRARY. AND WHAT DO YOU DO? WHAT YOU'RE DOING." He described a few scenes. The participants stopped and looked around in wonder, then terror.

"YOU DON'T DESERVE TO RUN THE WORLD.

"SO YOU WON'T. I TAKE BACK WHAT I SAID TO SAM BAA-HUHD. THE *REAL* SAM OF THE VILLAGE. YOU ARE WORMS COMPARED TO HIM. YOU ARE NOT OF THE VILLAGE.

"I AM JEREMY THE TEK. I AM COMING. CLEAN UP YOUR MESS OR I'LL KILL *ALL* OF YOU."

His mother seamlessly took the stage. "This is Veronica Piermont Edgarton, owner of the estate and the property you currently occupy. I've just had a peek at your lifestyle. What I saw simply revolts me. I will not have it on my property or anywhere.

"I'd like to correct a misconception. My son Jeremy told my old friend Sam Baahuhd that his lineage could have the village when the lot of you came out from underground.

"You can't. He didn't own the village, *I* do. I wouldn't sell it to you," she unleashed a tirade of Russian swear words, "*vermin* if it were the end of the world. And I certainly won't *give* it to you.

"We are coming very soon. Clean up your mess.

"This is Veronica Edgarton, broadcasting from Mount Kailash, in Tibet."

The sound wasn't great, but the visuals were. A commotion started in the main hall. A misshapen monster of a man came in, bearing the eye that had been attached to Sam with its cord hanging limp. It had made its way home and they had retrieved it. The man grunted something as an even bigger monster grabbed it from him. Close up images of the larger man filled the screens. He was raving, spewing saliva. He swung the device by its tail, swinging it as though he intended to smash it.

"Oh, no," Jeremy cried. "Don't break it."

The creature tossed the eye on the floor. "We'll use it on someone else," was the gist of his garbled speech. A group milled around, huge brutes with heavy jaws and foreheads, eyes sunken into cheekbones that looked like they belonged on primitive men. They wore belts and bits of fur, but were otherwise naked.

"They're mutants," Jeremy said.

The monsters jumped as the tail of the eye began moving. It coiled like a snake, making a base that allowed the eye to rise and point upward. Murmurs of disbelief came through the speakers. Guttural sounds. The eye began to rock back and forth.

Golden mist rose from it, then sparkles. Eliana's lovely form appeared in space, hovering like an angel. She spun and danced while the beasts exclaimed in awe. One put his hand through the hologram, and pulled it out, more mystified than before.

"Watch," said Jeremy. They did, and the hologram of Ellie dancing began to spin faster and wilder, finally disappearing into the room at large.

The eye exploded. The monsters screamed and ran.

"I AM THE TEK. I AM WATCHING YOU." Jeremy screamed into the mike. "KEEP THE COMMANDS OR YOU WILL DIE."

"You didn't tell me I could kill anyone, Mom, so the explosion was mostly just light." Images of the shelter's interior continued to play. The largest of the monsters mouthed words, but the sound wasn't good.

"Lovely, Jeremy. Fantastic." She grabbed his face with her hands and kissed him. "I must meet your Eliana. She's exquisite."

Sam crept closer, wild-eyed. Jeremy turned to him. Sam stood rigid and spoke fervently. "You must stop! You do not know what you do."

Jeremy cut the power on the cameras.

"Sam Big has the Voice and he has the Power." Sam trembled.

"Like Sam Baahuhd? Sam could make people do what he wanted with the Voice. And he healed people with the Power," Jeremy said.

"Not like Sam Baahuhd. Much stronger. You cannot resist the Voice of Sam Big. If I heard him say, 'Sam, come back,' from that machine, I would go. I could not resist."

"You'd go back?"

"I couldn't resist. All the Bigs have the Voice and the Power. They use them to make people do what they want. They use them to hurt people. Sam Big is the worst."

"They're mutants. Did the powers Sam Baahuhd had mutate, too?"

"I don't know what that means." Sam looked like he wanted to run. "What you did will make them angry. No one can stop them. Even if the rest of us use our Voices together, we cannot stop them."

"You have powers?"

"Everyone in the underground has powers. We are not allowed to use them."

"But you have powers?"

"I have the Voice, and I have the Power, but not like the Bigs."

"Well, maybe what we did wasn't such a good idea," Jeremy said.

"And maybe it was," Veronica answered. "It's still dark. I think we should go back to bed. They'll either kill us as we sleep or something wonderful will happen."

11

"Mom, where's Mt. Kailash?" They'd eaten their K rations and were relaxing after dinner.

"It's in Tibet, Jeremy," Veronica said.

"Why did you tell them you were there?"

"I didn't want to say, 'We're right around the corner, just look!'" She laughed.

"Have you been there?"

"Yes I have. Tibet is one of the highest altitude countries in the world, and Mt. Kailash is high even for there."

"What were you doing there?"

"I went there with the general. We were there for two months."

"Why did *he* go there?"

"He was searching for a site for our cryogenic bunker. He built several bunkers around the world to fool anyone who might want to break in after we were inside. The general probably figured that no one would look for him in the holiest spot on the planet. I went to Tibet for a different reason. I didn't know what it was until I got there. Are you sure you want to know about this, Jeremy? It's not a very nice story."

Jeremy nodded at Sam. "Yeah, we're interested."

She smiled with a sadness he'd never seen in her eyes. "I got it into my head that I wanted to circumambulate Mount Kailash. Walk around it. That's what everyone does there, if they are up to it. The general opposed it, so I wanted to do it. He wanted me to take a military escort, which I refused. I was gone a month. I decided to do the tour 'the right way.' The basic trip around the mountain takes about fifteen hours, if you're in really good shape. Pilgrims try for 13 circuits. Those trying for enlightenment do 108. I thought I'd go for that. I didn't make it. Mount Kailash is 22,000 feet high; no one sets foot on it, of course. It's too sacred. We traveled the pilgrim's path, between 15,000 and 18,000 feet. Even with the best yaks and guides, I couldn't do it.

"But I did walk around Lake Manasarovar, a sacred lake near the mountain. I read the Buddhist and Hindu texts—in English, of course—and walked around the lake and mountain with the other pilgrims. I wanted to meet a real lama, a spiritual teacher. I wanted a teacher of my own.

"Mt. Kailash was the most intoxicating place I've ever been. The altitude intensified everything: the colors of the pilgrims' clothing, the prayer flags, the piety of the people praying everywhere. The monasteries, candles. The incense and chanting. The monks calling us to prayer with conch shells. Statues of the Buddha, Shiva. When I was there, I actually believed that peace could prevail on earth. I believed in the power of love. I believed in God for a while.

"I could have stayed there forever. Because I didn't have a military escort, the monks were gracious and open. I found one who captivated me. He was the head of one of the monasteries. I stayed for a week at his sanctuary, charmed by an ancient Asian man. They called him Shri Rinpoche. Rinpoche means 'precious one,' and 'shri' is a term of respect." She smiled.

"I've loved two men in my life, Jeremy. Three, counting you. I loved your father until I thought my heart would break. And I loved Shri Rinpoche, and my heart did break. Meditating in the presence of a true master is heaven, nothing less. The love that flows . . .

"I fell into ecstasies at the monastery. I didn't know that I could feel such joy. I swooned with it. I was in love with everything, especially with him—and he was an 80-year-old monk. Don't get any ideas. He was the most perfect man I have ever met. I will never forget him, or his country. He initiated me into his school of meditation. That was the happiest time of my life. Only when your father was well and our family was together came close to it. But this was just bliss, with no strain or worries. I could have been a nun."

"*You*, Mom?"

"Yes, Jeremy, me. The whore of Babylon." Tears rimmed her eyes. Her lips trembled.

"What happened to the monk?"

"A few days later, when we were back in Russia, the general had my dear Rinpoche flogged to death outside my rooms. I don't know how many of the monks he killed. A little payback for my disobedience. I was his prisoner from then on. That's when I stopped believing in God."

Her voice dropped to the faintest whisper. She repeated a phrase that he didn't understand.

"What's that, Mom?"

"It's my mantra. It's why I'm alive. It's why I changed. I'm not the person I was, Jeremy. I want you to believe that so much. I'm different."

He put his arms around her. "I'm trying to be different, too. I'm sorry about the monk."

She wiped her face with a handkerchief Jeremy offered her. "He died without crying out. He repeated his mantra until they slit his throat. They didn't break him. He died a perfect death."

12

"Mom?" Jeremy whispered. "Are you asleep?"

"No. I can't sleep."

"Me, neither."

The events of the day and talking about Shri Rinpoche had shaken her up. Veronica could hear Sam's gurgling snores and steady inhalations of breath.

"Mom, we've been saying all this stuff about being friends and trusting each other. I need to get straight with you. We can't just go 'Nicey-nicey, everything's fine.' Because it's not. A lot of stuff happened. *You* did a lot of stuff." His voice was low, but very intense. He turned up the electric lantern so they could see each other.

She dreaded what he had to say.

He glared at her. "Did you and Dr. Tambourg set me up?"

"What do you mean?"

"He diagnosed me as a high-functioning autistic. He told everybody at the school and *everywhere* about it. I spent my life with everyone thinking I was nuts. Did you tell him lies about me?"

She sat up. "We concocted that diagnosis, yes. You aren't autistic. You have a genius-level IQ. I took you to Dr. Tambourg because I needed to protect you. Do you remember all the tests Dr. Tambourg gave you? For days?"

"How could I forget?"

"He needed to know what you are, and he found out. Dr. Tambourg came up with that diagnosis because it protected you. Your 'disability' allowed me to supply you with the materials you needed for your work. Computers, satellite hook ups. Things that were illegal for everyone else. You were able to build the shelter because of that diagnosis. *Sam* is alive because of it. Mark Tambourg was the most respected psychiatrist in the country. He covered for you with the military, the FBI, and with Special Forces. He put his life in jeopardy for you."

"Why?"

"Because he was a good man. And because he knew you could save our world if you were given enough time and the materials to do it. He was a revolutionary, Jeremy. I became active in the resistance because of him. You knew revolution was coming."

"Yeah. And I knew you were working with us. But . . ."

"You were still lonely. And afraid."

"You left me, Mom. You stuck me in my 'basement pad' at the school and took off with . . . Well, who was the first after daddy died? Do you even remember?" Jeremy rubbed his eyes with the back of his hand. "Fuck!"

Her stomach lurched. This was it: what really held them apart. "I don't remember who it was."

"Dicks! Just dicks, weren't they?" He glared at her, hands forming fists. "You left me for a bunch of dicks!"

"Yes, that's all they were, for years. Dicks that I used and dicks that used me. But it wasn't quite so simple." Her eyes locked on his. She had to make him understand. "Jeremy, did you ever wonder how I knew Mark Tambourg?"

"You knew everyone."

"I knew many people, but people in society, and politicians and industrialists. I stayed away from intellectuals. They ended up in camps. But I knew Mark. Why?"

Jeremy shook his head.

"Why would anyone know a psychiatrist?"

"You were seeing a *shrink*?" He looked incredulous.

"Yes. I suffered terribly in my years of entertaining dicks. I felt like something was devouring me inside. I couldn't stop what I was doing. So I went to a psychiatrist."

Jeremy's eyes widened and he turned away.

"I don't want to talk about this, either, but I think we need to. And I think clearing it up is the only way we'll be a real family."

He turned back to her, looking guarded.

"The way I acted was a disease. But Mark said he could cure me."

"Really?"

"Yes. I met with him four days a week when I was in New York and talked to him on the phone when I was traveling. I did it for more than two years."

"Did it work?"

"Not at all. Same anguish, same desire." She made a bitter little snort.

"Why didn't it work?"

"Mark told me that whatever made me act the way I did was so buried that I hadn't gotten desperate enough or shook up enough to make it surface. Whatever it was didn't matter—once the general fell for me, I was his prisoner. What a fool I was, Jeremy, to think that I could tame a monster. Or get away from him.

"That's when I really abandoned you, darling. Not only was I the general's prisoner, I stayed away so that he didn't find out how smart you are. You would have ended up in a bunker in Siberia, designing things for him.

"I was a rotten mother and a terrible person. I didn't want to be bad, Jeremy. I tried as hard as I could to stop." She felt a million years old, her face drawn. Jeremy stared at her. She couldn't read his expression.

"I'm not like that anymore, I swear to you." She knew he would never forgive her. Trying to work things out with Jeremy was as useless as going to that shrink.

Veronica pulled herself out of bed and into a crouching position, as though she were going to run down the corridor and leap out the container's door. But she couldn't move, Sam was in the way. She looked around wildly. When she saw no way out, Veronica fell on her side, sobbing. The brave front she'd kept up crumpled.

Her hands covered her face and tiny cries escaped her. She felt Jeremy put his arms around her, trying to make her calm down, but the black despair she'd known with the general consumed her. Hope didn't exist; her life was ruined and she couldn't fix it. Veronica felt herself spiral downward, scarcely registering Jeremy's pleas. Her body stiffened and her hands became claws. She wasn't aware of anything.

"Mom! Mom! Wake up." Jeremy shook her. "Sam! There's something wrong with my mom!"

Sam moved so fast he was a blur. He lay next to her, cupping her with his body. One arm curved over her head, and the other stroked her rigid limbs. He whispered in her ear.

Her arms relaxed. Sam lay them down softly and kept his arm around her, stroking her with the other hand. He kept whispering to her. She felt very sleepy, almost drugged.

"Sam, is that you?" She opened her eyes. "Is that you, Sam?"

"Aye," he said.

"Oh, I'm so glad. I thought you were gone. Is it another time, Sam?"

"Yes, lady. I'm here. Sleep."

Jeremy couldn't get the way she had looked at Sam out of his mind. So soft and sweet, unlike the way she was with other men. He knew his mother had thought he was their old headman, Sam

Baahuhd. People wondered if she and old Sam had ever been lovers. Jeremy knew they hadn't been.

It was a new time, a new world. But was it one that permitted love?

13

Jeremy found himself standing on a flat rock shelf high above a rolling plain. The shelf was hundreds of feet deep and a thousand feet long, cut out of a much larger cliff face. They were in a broad cave stuck into a rock mountain. A stone arch curved above them, sheltering them from the elements. Some ancient adobe buildings were on the end of the shelf, down from their container.

He ran to the edge of the ledge. A river meandered in the valley below. Big bright green trees followed the river, and the banks along both sides were lush and green. They could grow things down there. They had water. He ran back to the container to tell the others when he saw it: Another crate stood behind theirs. They'd sent the one with the weapons.

"Mom! Mom!" he dashed inside and stopped dead. His mother and Sam were cuddled together, their arms around each other. The sight brought him up short. They looked so tender, like they belonged together. It shocked him. It was like seeing his mom with Sam Baahuhd, if everything in their world had been different.

He shook his mother's foot. "Mom! Mom! They did it."

She raised her head sleepily. "What?"

"They moved us, and they sent the other container!"

She scrambled out of bed and to the open door. "Oh, my God, Sam. Look at where we are!" She stepped onto the shelf's stone floor and looked around. They could see back to where the estate and bomb shelter were to the east. It was a long way. They could see any enemy coming for days.

"Oh, thank you, golden people." She threw her arms over her head and danced in a circle. "Sam, look! They moved us! They gave us what we wanted." She ran to him and hugged him as he emerged from inside. He stood blinking in the sun.

"I don't hurt," he said, unbuttoning his shirt so he could see the bandage on his belly. Veronica pulled aside the dressing and examined the wound.

"It's healed, Sam. Not even a scar." She removed the bandage. He walked into the sunlight and she gasped. "You look . . ."

Sam stared at his forearms and stomach. Jeremy also gawked. Sam wasn't gray any more. His skin was flesh-colored like his own, a different color than Jeremy's, but a regular human color. Sam's skin tone was very fair with a pink/ivory cast. He had a redhead's complexion. He looked up and Jeremy could see his face. Wide cheekbones, straight nose. Huge green eyes. The girls in his high school would have gone crazy over him.

"Sam, smile!" Jeremy called.

Sam did. His teeth were perfect and white.

His mother had put her hand to her throat and stood staring. Sam's closely cut reddish hair sparkled in the light, as did his nubby beard. His chest and belly were exposed by the open shirt. Muscles covered his stomach, which was brushed with dark red hair.

"Oh . . ." Sam had noticed the river valley below. He staggered back, covering his eyes. Then he was doubled up on his knees. He put his hands over his head and groveled on the ledge.

"Oh, shit! He's freaking out. He's never really been outside like this. He just saw the area around the container before." Jeremy rushed to him. "This is the outdoors, Sam. It's beautiful. We're on a ledge. That's a river down there. There's lots of space."

Sam remained curled up.

"It's OK. You'll get used to it." Jeremy couldn't get Sam to respond.

"Sam, dear. Try these," his mom placed a pair of sunglasses on his face. "The general's own magic glasses. Guaranteed to cure fear of open spaces and everything else. I know it's a shock, dear, but it will get easier." She put an arm around Sam and rubbed his back. "See. That's better, isn't it? Just take it slow and easy." She hugged him gently and helped him stand. "It's a river valley, a very beautiful one. Don't look until you feel up to it."

"What on earth is that?" They were having a breakfast of K rations and bottled water when Veronica pointed to something in the sky. Sam and Jeremy looked up.

"It looks like junk," Jeremy said. "Intergalactic junk." He explained to Sam, "Before Earth blew up, we made so much shit—garbage—that some places got rid of it by shooting it out into space. Not to mention us putting up tons of satellites and space stations. Junk's all over out there. On Ellie's world, they did big sweeps to clean it up." He whistled, looking at the approaching object. "It looks like a mountain of crap heading straight at us."

The thing veered toward them, moving fast and aiming at the space between the containers and the ancient structures. It jerked a few times and sat down in the empty space. Dust and debris flew around; they had to turn their backs to avoid getting it in their eyes.

Once the mess settled, they approached the heap cautiously.

"Man! That's more junk than I've ever seen," Jeremy chortled. "Maybe it's a present to go with the container. The only thing that kept me sane on Ellie's world was the garbage. You can find lots of interesting things in it. I made some good . . ."

"Jeremy? Jeremy?" A high-pitched voice came out of the top.

"Ellie? Are you up there?" He craned his neck and stood on tiptoe, trying to see her.

She flew off the mound with one of her prodigious leaps and ran toward him. "Jeremy." He leapt toward her, hugging her to his chest. He held her for the longest time, rocking from side to side, his face buried in her hair.

"Oh, baby. Let me look at you." He held her at arm's length and joyfully examined her. She was as lovely and sprightly as ever. Her silver curls bounced and her eyes gleamed. "You look great! They let you go!"

She nodded vigorously, clinging and wide-eyed. "I here." But she didn't look happy. "Jeremy. Bad happen," she whispered.

"Don't be scared, baby. You're here now."

Her eyes filled with moisture. "Jeremy. They take you away."

"But we're together now, Ellie. You're safe." He held her closely, stroking her tenderly. "I missed you so much. I love you."

He bent down to kiss her, but she continued to clutch him, making the little chittering noise as she did when very upset. "Jeremy. Bad happen. Mother say bad thing."

"What did Belarian say?" Jeremy was ready to fight. He hated that bitch.

Ellie looked at the mound of junk. They could hear noises of people moving on top. "No here, Jeremy. Is *bad*." Her shoulders were hunched and her head bowed.

"OK. Let's go over here behind the storage bin." He led her behind the first container. "What did she say, Ellie?"

Her eyes brimmed with tears. "Mother say I stupid."

"You're not stupid, Ellie. You're as smart as anyone and braver, too."

"No. I stupid. Mother say I no speak lots and no write many words. I stupid. She say I only good for making babies."

"What! That is not true. You're wonderful. You're sweet and kind and you understand people's feelings. You dance and you're musical. You're beautiful. And you love me. More than anyone, ever. How could she say that?"

Ellie clung to his hands. "She say you no there, I have to make babies with . . ." She looked in the direction of the pile of junk.

"What! Did she make you do it with the other guys? Which one?" He spun toward the junk pile, fists clenched.

"No make me. I say no. She go to Henry and Mel and James. They say no and get mad and see elders. They send us here. Oh, Jeremy, no go away. No leave me. Please."

"Baby, I didn't leave you, they kicked me out. I promise that I will never let them get you. I will never let anything hurt you again. And I'll never leave you."

They clung to each other, painfully aware that such promises sometimes can't be kept. He held her, petting and kissing her until she calmed down. "I'll always love you, Ellie."

"I love Jeremy, too. So much."

He could hear the others and wanted to check out what she'd said with them. "Let's go see what's going on." She clung to him like his soul.

"Hello, down there," Henry's baritone boomed out. "How the hell are we supposed to get down?"

"We'll help you." Veronica headed for the mountain of refuse. She couldn't see him over the top of the garbage. "Why did they send you like this? They moved our containers very nicely."

"Well, you're prettier than we are, Veronica. I take our mode of transportation as a statement of their feelings. They are peeved at us, but not as peeved as we are with them." He looked over the top, trying to find a way down. "I think we can climb down that satellite and slide down the jet wing. Yes, here I come." He slid down and turned back to help Lena. "Take my hand, Mother."

Mel and James stood up. James was wearing his Dog Master outfit from Earth's last day. He'd made quite a stir when he had arrived posing as the famous dog trainer. The rest of them wore nothing except for extravagant hairstyles. "Hey you guys, we bought our way out of heaven!"

Veronica looked at the newly arrived group, flabbergasted by their appearances. "Henry, you don't look a day over thirty. And Lena, you look like a girl. Mel, James, you look fabulous. All of you look thin, but fabulous. What did they do to you? And what's with your hair?"

"The hair part's the easiest. They loved James's styling abilities. He kept us at the height of fashion, along with half the pets on the planet." Henry patted his huge 'fro. "The first thing I want to do is shave this thing. For the other part, they were working us into their breeding program. We had to be young to do that. Then they intended to exploit us, just like they did Eliana."

Jeremy and Eliana came out from behind the storage container and walked toward the group. Ellie held back a little, clinging to Jeremy's hand and pulling behind him.

"Mom, I'd like you to meet Eliana, my wife." Jeremy scowled, as though he thought his mother wouldn't like his choice. "Ellie, this is my mom."

Veronica stood, transfixed by her daughter-in-law. Eliana was exquisite. She had a dancer's long-legged, perfect proportions. Beautiful features. Entrancing silver eyes, silver ringlets spilling down her forehead. The way she stood and moved couldn't be more graceful.

Veronica's eyes widened when she saw Eliana's hooves. "Oh." She hadn't noticed Eliana's hooves in the video. Jeremy hadn't said anything about them. When the girl clattered down the pile of junk, the noise they made had caught her attention. Seeing them up close was a shock. If your daughter-in-law had hooves, was it rude to comment on them? She decided not to.

"Oh, darling. You're breathtaking." She opened her arms to Ellie, who slowly let go of Jeremy and accepted a small hug. "Jeremy, what you said about Eliana didn't come close to capturing her beauty."

Sam stepped forward, looking composed behind his sunglasses.

"Sam Baahuhd, you rascal" Henry cried. "I never thought I'd see you again. Come over her and give your fishing buddy a hug." Henry embraced Sam, who stood stiffly, looking like he might shatter into pieces.

"He just got out of the underground shelter, Henry. He's a little shook up. He's Sam's five millionth grandson," Jeremy said.

"From the line of Emily. And I have Arthur, too."

"As I live and breathe, you could *be* your grandfather. Lord have mercy." He kept pumping Sam's hand. "Oh, we had some times. I'll tell you all about them, bit by bit."

"Let's get you settled in and fed, and then we can talk," Veronica said.

Jeremy looked over the valley below. "Mom! Look at that—those are *horses*. A whole herd of them."

A bunch of horses, perhaps fifty, galloped to the river and waded in. They squealed and kicked, enjoying the water. They came in every color. Little ones trotted by their mothers. A few rolled on the sandy bank.

"Mom, you're a great rider. All you need to do is catch them and train them."

"Jeremy, I can ride, but I've never saddled a horse in my life. Sam Baahuhd did that. And I don't have the faintest idea how to train one, much less catch them."

"Lena knows how to train horses," Henry said. They turned and looked at her. "She can shoot, too."

"What are you talking about, Henry?" Lena exclaimed.

"You are always telling me about your life on the farm and how you and your granddad trained horses. And how you had to shoot if you wanted meat."

"I was raised on a farm, that's true. And I can shoot. We had to know how to handle guns to feed and protect ourselves. But I didn't *train* horses." She looked at the quizzical expressions on the faces around her. "After my daddy disappeared, my mama took me back home to the farm where she was raised. I grew up there with my grandpa and grandma and her. I didn't move back to New York City until after I finished high school."

"But you rode horses and helped train them?" Veronica asked.

"Well, yes, we had to ride if we wanted to go anywhere. It was that or walk. We didn't have hover cars out there, not even regular cars. Everyone was poor, but we could feed ourselves and didn't have to worry about the feds so much."

"But you know how to ride?" Veronica said.

"Yes, I do. I also helped my grandpa train horses and mules."

"Really?" they all said.

"Well, I wasn't so much training them as acting as ballast. My grandpa couldn't be the first to get on. He said he was so old that he'd go 'splat' if he fell off, plus he had a bad knee. He put me on the first few times a horse was ridden because 'I was young and would bounce.'"

"You've *broken* horses?" Jeremy was wide-eyed.

"More mules than horses, and they broke me more often than not. I've been tossed so many times I can't count. My grandpa did most of the work, but yeah, I helped break horses about a million years ago. I haven't been on one since I left for the city."

"Well, Veronica," Henry said, "I think this situation calls for us to expand our job descriptions. Lena is the horse trainer and you and I are the assistants. Is that what they call them? Wranglers? We could be cowpokes, if we had cows."

Henry walked over to the edge of the cliff and studied the topography below. Then he looked back at the ancient adobe dwellings. "This looks like the Wild West. All we need is Indians." He put the palm of his hand to his mouth and made a few war whoops.

"Fat chance of that, Henry," Jeremy smirked.

14

Sam listened to the lady and Jeremy bickering. At first, he didn't understand what Jeremy was doing, but then it became horribly clear.

"Dear, you don't have to do all that work. I've got fire starters," Veronica said.

"I want to, Mom. This is fun. We'll have a bonfire tonight." The adobe dwellings' ceilings had fallen in. Jeremy had pulled some of the old beams out on the ledge and piled them up. He focused a lens he'd found in the junk heap on one of them.

A thin white stream arose. Sam stiffened. He smelled something acrid. Was that smoke? More of it rose. Its color changed from pale gray to black as Jeremy kept adding fuel. "We've got a fire!" Jeremy shouted as shoots of orange and yellow burst from the wood.

Sam restrained a gasp and pulled away. Jeremy kept at it until the flames danced and popped. Sam stared, transfixed. Fire was absolutely forbidden in the world underground. In all 105 generations that the village had occupied the shelter, no one had built a fire. It would consume the air supply.

Sam moved away from the dancing tongues of light. The day had been a nightmare. He couldn't imagine a space as vast as that around them. He couldn't comprehend the brilliant sunlight and overwhelming colors of the sky and trees. The river and its gurgling sound. The wind beating on him. The sun burning his face. And now Jeremy had made fire, the deadliest menace.

"Campfire tonight! Bring your marshmallows and hot dogs," Jeremy yelled. "Get your chow and sit around the fire!"

Dinner consisted of the usual army rations, colored glops of stuff in a segmented tray with a peel-off top. Ellie looked at her meal with something close to horror.

"Everybody, Ellie's a vegetarian," Jeremy called. "I think the green stuff in the trays is supposed to be vegetables. Do you think some of you could trade her for her meat stuff?" When they'd traded, he asked, "Is that OK, babe?"

She nodded, but ate almost nothing.

The others gathered around the fire with their packets. Sam tried to escape toward the back of the cave and greater darkness, but Henry called for him.

"Come on, Sam. We need to get to know each other," Henry said. So he joined them sitting around the bonfire. Everyone talked, except him.

Jeremy scowled and spoke loudly to the other men. "Before we talk about *anything*, I've got to find out about what Ellie said. She told me that Belarian . . ."

"We'll talk about that in a while, Jeremy," Henry nodded at Ellie. Her eyes were impossibly wide and she was practically sitting in Jeremy's lap. She'd been that way since they landed. "We'll talk to you about that later."

"But is it true?"

"Oh, yes. It got us off our butts. No way we'd go along with that. We got mad enough to make them an offer they couldn't refuse." Henry grinned.

"We got here by giving them extremely generous amounts of our genetic material," Henry explained their escape from the golden planet. "They have enough essence de Henry to populate their planet twice."

"Not to mention *our* input," Mel said. He had his arm around James, who hadn't made the trip too well. "We're good for a few more planets."

"They told me they left me enough eggs for me to raise another family. I hope so." Lena rubbed her tummy. "The whole thing was so degrading. And then sending us off on a garbage heap. We failed to adapt to their ways, but a garbage heap . . ."

Sam listened. He understood what the goldies had planned for Ellie, but didn't know what the others were talking about. Maybe he'd figure it out if he listened carefully.

"At least they didn't dump you next to a shelter full of maniacs with *nothing*," Jeremy said. "If I hadn't found Flossie that night, the wolves would have gotten me."

"Well, we're here now," Veronica added. "Now we have to make a new world. That's what we started out to do."

"That's what you and Jeremy started out to do," said Henry. "Mother and I didn't want to get fried by atomic bombs.

"Now, Sam," Henry turned toward him, "I'm interested in how my old friend Sam Baahuhd made out after the conflagration. Do you have any stories about him?"

"Yes, sir," Sam bowed his head as he would for one of the Bigs.

"Don't you be calling me *sir*, Sam. I've done enough shuffling and jiving for a lifetime, and my people have done it way longer than that. I'm Henry. Henry Henderson, if you want to be formal. I don't want anyone bowing to anyone here."

Sam had never met so many new people. The new arrivals weren't just people, they were legendary. Eliana, the golden Angel. Henry Who Could Drink the Leg Off an Ox. His wife, Lena, Who Got so Pissed at Him, He Almost Didn't Get to Come Back to the Village. But Henry made talking easy.

"Well, young man, are you going to tell me about my friend, Sam Baahuhd?"

"Yes, Henry." The word came thickly off his tongue. The wrong form of address down below could see a man flogged. That would mean death, because the rot would set in, or the flour disease would eat the skin.

"Sam Baahuhd lived to be a very old man and had many children," Sam took up the rhythmic cadence used by the singers of songs when speaking of their history.

"I'm glad that he lived a long time," Henry replied. "And of course he had many children. I've seldom seen a man who could attract the ladies like Sam." He looked at the others and smiled knowingly. "What did his wives think of the underground? And how did he do with the hooch? The only thing he liked more than the ladies was that home-made whisky."

Sam inhaled sharply and straightened up. "Sam Baahuhd lived by the Commands. 'One man, one wife, fidelity.' He was faithful to his only wife, Emily. He never touched the hooch from the moment he went underground."

"He couldn't have any of his old wives, anyway," Jeremy cut in. "They were all his first cousins. I dissolved those marriages. Who was Emily? I don't remember any Emily in the village."

Sam's eyes darted to the side before he spoke. "Emily was not of the village. Sam Baahuhd found her in the meadow and brought her to the shelter before the explosions. She was naked, except for boots made in Jamayuh. No one ever knew who Emily was." Sam shut his mouth tightly, not intending to say a word more than the official explanation.

"Sam showed up in the underground with a naked stranger before the nukes went off? That doesn't make any sense." Jeremy scowled. "She had to be a fed. The only people in the Hamptons in those days were villagers and federal agents." His mouth opened as he realized what had happened. "Sam dragged a federal agent into the shelter so he could have a wife who wasn't his first cousin!" Jeremy grinned. "That's right, isn't it, Sam?"

Sam choked. No one of Emily's lineage talked about their matriarch's origins outside the family. The villagers would have killed Emily if they knew for sure what she had been. Sam didn't like Jeremy's knowing smile.

"Yeah. She was a fed. She loved Sam Baahuhd mor'n any ever had, an' he loved her th' same way." Sam wanted to get up and leave. He wouldn't let a stranger mock a love like Sam and Emily's, even if the stranger was the Great Tek.

"Sam Baahuhd married a *fed*?" Jeremy sat back and guffawed. "That is *so* Sam!" The others tittered.

"I have to tell you guys something hysterical." Jeremy pulled himself out of his laughing jag long enough to talk. "Remember the last night on Earth, when we were down in the underground and I threw out a bunch of ideas about how to run the shelter?" Jeremy looked around. "They made them into *Commands*, like they were in the Bible. And they *live* by them."

"You're kidding me!" "Those were bullshit!" "You were raving when you said all that." "Nobody could keep those rules, they didn't make sense." The response was uproarious.

"Guess who's *God* in this system? *Me*, the Great Tek!"

"They've never seen you have a screaming fit, Jeremy!"

"Maybe they have!"

Sam stiffened, flushing. They were laughing at what he held sacred.

"What are things like down there now, Sam?" It was Mel again.

"I took pictures inside the underground yesterday," Jeremy said. "It's worse than my worst-case scenario. The villagers have mutated into monsters."

"Monsters?"

"Tell them about them, Sam."

Sam couldn't refuse a command from the Great Tek. "The Bigs come from the line of Sam from his wife Mollie. I'm a Little."

"*You're* a little? How big are they?" Mel asked incredulously.

"A little Big is this much bigger than me." He held his hands apart about six inches. "A big Big is this much." His hands were two feet apart. The people stared at him.

"How many Bigs are there?" Mel asked.

"When I was allowed in the hall, I counted," he signaled twenty-four with his hands, "Bigs. And," he signaled ten, "Big Bigs. That was ten winters ago. They could have many more children today. Bigs grow very fast. A Big of this many years," he signaled ten, "is as big as him." Sam pointed at Jeremy. They gasped.

"*Kids* that big?" Mel asked. "How can people grow that fast?"

"Not everyone grows, just the Bigs. They run everything, because they are so strong. They grow big very fast." Sam hunched over, the way he did when the Bigs were around. This talk was forbidden. He hoped the others didn't notice him cringing.

"What's it like down there, Sam?" Mel said, his brows knitted in concern as he peered at Sam sharply. "I saw the shelter before it was closed up. It seemed like it was set up to support a decent way of life. How did that change? I mean the Bigs can be big, but why should they be bad? What goes on down there?"

Sam struggled to explain life in the shelter. "I don't know how it changed, just that it did. Everything is dark now, except where the Bigs allow light. We can't count days and nights in the dark. Not knowing if it is day or night, or summer or winter, makes people more frightened. They don't ask questions if the Bigs come. They don't talk.

"Before the Bigs took over, we could look up at the windows in the ceiling when we were working in the fields. In winter, snow fell and we could see frost around the glass. The days were short. The crops didn't grow as much. Winter to winter measured a year. I marked the years on a wall. When the Bigs took over and made things dark, I still got to go to the fields to work. I was the strongest one. So I could keep track of the years.

"The Bigs always ran the underground, but the others, like me, had some say. Two winters ago, the Bigs took over everything. Before that, men who were not Bigs could have children. Their babies lived in the nursery with their mothers for a time; after that, a mama stayed with them. The mothers worked or went to the pit.

"When the Bigs put all the women in the pit, they were supposed to have babies in the nursery, but they didn't. They had them in the hall and raised them there. I know, because I became the mama in the nursery. I took care of the babies. Not many babies came to me after the Bigs took over.

"I kept the children safe." Sam could hardly go on, but he needed to. They had to rescue his people, the ones he'd saved. "The Bigs take the ones with the disease and the Big babies. I kept the others safe."

No one said anything. Sam didn't know what that meant.

"You're not the same bloodlines as the Bigs?" Mel asked.

"I am Sam and Emily, with some Arthur. I am straight from Sam Baahuhd's son Chad from his second wife, Sally. That was from the old days before we went underground, when he had four wives. And I'm from Sam Baahuhd's daughter Shira from Emily. I have no Mollie in me. I am the last like me."

"Like you?"

Sam looked down. "The last who can stand and talk and think. Many of my people . . ." His face worked as he attempted to say it. "Many have no," he indicated his arms and legs. "Some cannot see or talk." He looked down.

"How many are like that, Sam? And how many of your people are there, aside from the Bigs?" Mel's voice was gentle.

"I don't know. The women are in the pit, but they die or disappear. Maybe this many, once." He opened and closed his hands three times. "But t'was long ago."

"The others, who can't walk and so on?"

Sam opened and closed his hands again, indicating fourteen people.

Mel sighed and ran his hand through his hair. "Thirty-four Bigs, maybe thirty women, fourteen handicapped people, and Sam. That's seventy-nine people."

Sam looked ragged, like every word had taken something from him. "I don't know for sure."

"Do you know how old you are?"

"I know how many years I have. My mama counted the years when I was little, then I counted after. I am," he held his spread fingers up, opening and closing his hands twice and ending with nine fingers open. "I carved marks on the wall. One mark for every winter. I follow the Commands. I can read some. I was learning to do numbers, but they took away the lights."

"You're twenty-nine years old, son," Henry said, "I'd be happy to teach you numbers as far as I go. And you've got a numbers expert here in Jeremy."

"Sure, I'll teach you what I know—and Mel was my history teacher. He knows everything."

Mel laughed. "Not everything, Sam, but I'd be glad to tutor you."

Sam could barely breathe. He'd told them almost everything. Everything but what he dare not share. They would hate him if they knew that. *She* would hate him.

"Who takes care of the disabled people?" Lena asked.

"I do." Sam was shaking. "The Bigs wanted to have sport with them and kill them, but I hid them. I take them food. We have tunnels and secret places that the Bigs don't know. The diggers made them—I am a digger. Sam Baahuhd was the first digger. I hid the children, too."

"Children?"

"The children of the lines of Arthur and Winnie and Sam but not Mollie. The Bigs kill them. I took them from the nursery and hid them in a secret place. I fed them." He could hardly breathe.

"How many of them are there, Sam?" Lena asked.

"Eleven children. Good children. They will die with me gone."

Ellie held her hands to her cheeks, silver eyes wide and gleaming. She grabbed at Jeremy. He pulled her close and shot Sam a dirty look.

"Help babies, Jeremy," she whispered. "Help them."

"Sweetie, don't worry. We'll get it fixed." He turned to his mother. "Mom, Ellie and I are going to sleep in the container tonight. She's had a hard time."

"Certainly, dear. Just put Sam's and my things outside the door."

Jeremy carried Ellie to the container, shooting Sam another look. Sam was shaken by it, but the conversation continued after Ellie and Jeremy left.

"Do you want us to help save your people, son?" Henry asked.

"Yes! But I dinna know how many can live out here. It's hard for me. Those who canna walk or talk . . . The children could live here. They should be saved."

"And the Bigs?"

"They should all be killed. If they come here, they will kill the men and take the women."

"What about the women in the shelter?"

Sam looked down again. "They're in the pit. Some are crazy, and some have become like the Bigs. They like to hurt and torture the weak ones. All the women have the smell."

"The smell?"

"Yes, between the legs. They are sick. And they are bad, too."

The group looked at each other.

"We need to take a good look at those pictures tomorrow," Mel said.

"You're right," Henry agreed. "First thing in the morning."

James had been very quiet. "We just got out of someplace bad. This sounds a thousand times worse. What can we possibly do? I think we should . . ." He made a hopeless gesture. "We should forget the whole thing. It's not our problem."

"It is our problem, James. You should have seen Sam when we found him. In addition to being emaciated and covered with funguses, they put an eye in his belly. Like those we had in the ceilings before the war so the government could spy on us. Russian techs developed a portable form that was surgically inserted under the carrier's skin. It was used for surveillance or as a bomb. They almost always kill the carrier." Veronica turned to Sam. "Why did they put that thing in you? Why did they throw you out the canary hole?" she asked softly.

Sam's voice dropped to a murmur. "I am a digger." He spoke as though the others should know what that meant, as though it was a badge of distinction. "We are kept in different rooms so we cannot talk. I make tunnels to go from one room to another.

I bring messages and food. I hide things. They caught me. The first time, they didn't kill me." His body trembled. "When they caught me again, they took my sister. The last time, they put the eye on me."

"They killed your sister?" Henry gasped.

"After they were done," he said, looking down. "I didn't stop digging, so they put the eye on me to see where I was going. If I stopped, they hurt me to make me go. I was going to die, so they put me out the hole."

The people around the circle stared at him.

"OK, everyone," Henry broke the silence. "We just got a reality check on our neighbors. We've had a short honeymoon back on Earth. Tomorrow, we'll begin to deal with it. Right now, though, I want something that I haven't had for a very long time. Veronica, did the general put any of that good Russian vodka in his things?"

"He certainly did, Henry. I wouldn't mind a bit myself." She got up and went to the storage unit, returning with a bottle of clear liquid and some glasses. "See, only the best." She held the bottle out so they could see the imperial crest. "The Tsar's own."

Henry stood up to help her pour. "Anyone? Did what Sam had to say give anyone a thirst?" The others raised their hands.

"Me, too!"

"Me, three."

Sam sat, jaws clenched, hands curled into fists. He couldn't believe what they were going to do. As the lady began to pour, he shot to his feet, grabbed the bottle and threw it over the edge of the cliff. He heard it shatter on the rocks below.

"It is against the Commands!" He turned to them. "Ye don' understand!

"I keep the Commands. Without the Commands, I would be the same as the Bigs!" he shouted, anguished.

He ran to the farthest corner of the cave and slid down the wall. He sat with his arms wrapped around his knees, shivering.

They would come for him now and beat him. Or perhaps throw him off the cliff. He could hear them talking about him.

"Sam, I want to apologize to you," Henry was the only one who approached him. "I've never been a slave, but my people have. I know in my bones what it's like to have no rights, to have the man beat you or rape you or do anything he wants to you, any time. We disrespected something that means everything to you—the Commands and your beliefs. The United States Constitution gave everyone freedom of religion, but we didn't allow you that back at that campfire. We won't do that again. You have my friendship, Sam."

Henry bent down and embraced him. Sam watched him go to where he and Lena were sleeping. What had happened was more shocking than if Henry had taken a stick to him.

Everyone had walked away from the fire, going to separate sleeping places. Panic overtook Sam. His people lived in the darkness in tiny rooms. They touched each other. They couldn't see, so they oriented themselves with touch. Touch kept them from going crazy. Touch became sight.

His skin cried out for contact. They would have touched him underground, because they knew how hard talking about what he had was. All of it was punishable with death.

If he could have slept with her, it would have been all right. They'd slept together the nights before. But she had gone. He picked up his pad and looked for a place to spend the night.

Veronica remembered Sam's earnest face over the campfire. Jeremy had sat near Sam. They looked like they were about the same age. What had she been thinking?

She thrashed in her bed, unable to get comfortable. If she missed Sam's warm strength of the night before, tough. The aching inside would subside and the longing would go away. She was in control.

Her mantra went around in her mind, not quite obscuring the image of his beautiful face.

15

Sam's face felt wooden and his eyes ached. He'd spent the night exploring the cave and ancient dwellings. Night was his time; he could see very well in the dark, and he could feel and sense better than that. He knew their entire domain by the morning, moving past sleeping bodies without being detected.

He paused at her spot. She didn't sleep, either. She had chosen a shallow cave in the back of the main cavern for her sleeping place. It wasn't a good place—it gave no privacy or protection. He stood by it and listened, then moved past. She didn't know that he had heard her weeping.

The cave had many smaller grottos carved into the rear walls. Some were smoothly sculpted. He didn't know how to explain them; they were unlike the underground with its angular surfaces of poured concrete or the dirt burrows made by diggers.

The walls of the smaller caves were smooth and hard, made so by wind and rain, not people. He had little experience of natural forces. Sam had heard rain on the glass above the solar growing fields and seen it roll down the panes. He hadn't felt wind until he was outside. He still hadn't felt rain. Touching the walls soothed him.

People had carved some grottos deeper into the cliff. He could tell by the angular cuts and straight surfaces. Diggers had once lived here. Something rattled when he entered one alcove. He backed out.

Close to dawn, he found a series of joined caves on the side closest to where the sun had gone down, away from the others. A large chamber merged with the main cave. It had several smaller rooms in back where a person or two could sleep. He put his bedding in the largest of the spaces, claiming the entire cluster as his own. He had never known better quarters or so much room. It was a place where a man could have a family.

Sam had spent the dregs of the night touching the stone walls of his new abode. He took off his clothes and rubbed every bit of his skin on the rock. Shoulders, arms, back. All of himself. Then he rolled into a ball on the floor. Sleep claimed him for an hour.

When he came out of his cave onto the ledge, the lady was standing in front of the first container, talking to Jeremy and Ellie. He couldn't hear their voices, but they stood close together. They didn't smile. Jeremy put his arm around Ellie and drew her toward the adobe houses. The lady whirled and headed toward the edge of the ledge. His eyes followed her, but he was afraid to approach her. She looked furious.

"Well, are you ready, Sam?" Henry's voice startled him. The others were standing in a huddle where the fire had been the night before. Henry had approached from that direction. "Today's the day we go through the container and see what we're going to wear for the rest of our lives."

Sam turned to look for the lady. She had stormed as far away as she could. She stood with her back to them, hands clenched.

16

Damn! Damn! Damn! How could they think of doing that to that lovely girl? Jeremy had told her the goldies' plans for Eliana and the human men.

Is there anywhere in the universe where women aren't targets of abuse? she thought. She felt like opening the munitions container and blasting everything she saw. But that wouldn't be enough. Her chest rose and fell. Girls were always the target. Pretty girls.

Forcing herself to breathe deeply, Veronica managed to control her rage enough to see the sparkling scene spreading out below her. The golden meadow, curving river, wide-open oak savannah, and the thick forest to the east. Far away, she could see the depression in the trees that indicated the ocean was beyond.

Look at it, Veronica, she thought. What do you see?

A brittle snort escaped her. Once, her family's estate had covered half the basin. The mansion had been right over there, out of sight in the trees. Fifty thousand square feet under one roof. If that wasn't enough, she had her other ranches and homes. And factories, plants, and facilities around the globe.

All of it was gone.

She'd had her ownership records copied and carried them with her on a cylinder, hoping that she'd be able to claim what was hers, one day. Another choked snort escaped. Where? How? No legal system existed. No laws, government. No place to record ownership.

Hilarity swept her. She'd forgotten something: She was bankrupt. She'd mortgaged everything she had to fund bomb shelters for people all over the world.

As it turned out, only the shelter on the estate survived. The mega-shelter created with federal funds, the general's money, and her own. And look what happened there. Mutants and monsters. She choked back biting laughter.

She laughed so hard that tears came. It was just so funny . . . Her hands went to her face. She felt like someone had cast it in plaster. She hadn't slept at all the night before.

Suck it up, Edgarton! Kick it! Fight it! Her spine yanked her erect. Fight or you'll die. She heard a noise behind her. They were all waiting, thinking the container could be unpacked like a suitcase. Idiots. Kick it, Edgarton. Move it.

She spun and headed for the group with a stride straight from boot camp. The others pulled away.

"Well, Veronica? Do you need our help unloading boxes?" Henry smiled at her.

"This was a military operation, Henry, not a bunch of kids going camping," she spit the words at him, voice full of scorn. "Do you think we packed things in cardboard boxes?"

She opened the container's outer doors. Metallic cabinets reached from ceiling to floor. The only free space was the narrow aisle down the middle and a four-foot space in the container's front and rear.

"We packed both units 'last in, first out,' so that what we needed the most when we got out would be the first thing we got to." Waving at the cabinet of medical supplies to the left of the door, she said, "Those are just the basics. We have more supplies and a surgical theater stored farther in. Unfortunately, the doctors are dead." She repressed the urge to laugh.

Veronica opened a recessed cabinet on the container's right side and pulled out a thick binder. "This is the printed manifest. It's printed on fireproof plastic—virtually indestructible. The printout can't be corrupted or become obsolete. But I'm going to bet that the electronic version is good." She pulled a tablet computer with a metallic cover from the niche.

"There's a track on the ceiling and the floor. The storage units move around the track electronically. We can also muscle them, if the power's dead. They're all labeled," a wave at the writing down the front of the big chests, "in Russian, of course. Anybody read Russian beside me?" She looked at them haughtily.

"I'm fluent in Russian," Mel said sharply. "The rest of us can speak some."

"Good. You'll need it. Jeremy? Is Jeremy here?"

He jogged up. "I'm here, Mom. Ellie's not feeling well. I'm not going to stay long."

"What do we need most, Jeremy?"

"Solar panels. Almost all the computers are out of juice. If we don't get them recharged, we're screwed. Then I'd say some way of getting off this cliff."

"OK." Veronica powered up the tablet computer, checking its readings. "Bingo. Solar panels are in the second container on the right. Jeremy, you'll have to move all the computers."

"It's like a drycleaner," Henry said, looking at the track on the ceiling.

"Yes, exactly like a drycleaner's overhead track for storing and delivering garments. Except that our track packs a payload that our lives depend upon."

Jeremy and the others carefully moved the computers out of the way.

She pointed the electronic tablet at a control on the wall. A light went on. She pushed a button. The hanging containers jerked, then settled into place. She tried it again. They didn't move.

"Dead. We'll have to muscle the units around so we can get at the solar panels. Just grab the outside edge and pull. I'm going to see if I can find some ladders." She concentrated on the manifest while the others grabbed the first unit and tried to drag it along the tracks.

"Let me try," Sam said. She glanced at him and then looked back at the monitor. When she looked up, he had the first hanging box moving around the track, heading to the other side of the container. He pulled the second box forward.

"Yes, there they are," Veronica indicated the Russian script on the front of the box. "Solar panels. The box opens like this. Here they are: enough panels to power a community of eight. Now we have to set them up and get them going."

Jeremy ran to the storage container that held the weapons and opened it. He'd wanted to do what he was doing since the unit had arrived. He was sick of feeling scared of the Bigs and looking at the others' frightened faces. Jeremy returned, carrying an automatic rifle.

"OK, you guys. This is how we'll handle the Bigs." Pointing the gun at a tree by the river, Jeremy opened fire. The top of the tree cracked and toppled.

"Give that to me, Jeremy." Veronica snatched the gun, looking like she'd like to slap him. "You don't treat firearms like that. Or trees. You should see the camps, Jeremy, and what that monster did. You would never get excited about a gun."

With that, she whirled, took the rifle out of automatic and fired three shots. The entire tree fell. "We have enough firepower to blow ourselves to eternity. Let's just unload the crate, OK? We can go through the manifest and see what would make our lives better right now. There's coffee, spices, and foodstuffs. Lots of things."

They began to work furiously, Veronica searching the manifest and the others helping Sam move the containers along the tracks and open them.

"Here it is—what I was looking for." Veronica exclaimed, holding up the monitor. "The ladders! They're in the sixth box back. There should be a couple hundred feet of chain ladders and I don't know how much chain. All we have to do is figure out some way of anchoring them, and we'll be able to go up and down and to the river. Could everyone keep your eyes out for a wooden box? It's about this big," she indicated its size. "There's a book in it with roses on the cover that I especially want."

Veronica was going through the foodstuffs when Jeremy ran to her, anguish on his face.

"Mom, it's Ellie. She looks like she's dying."

17

Veronica and Jeremy ran to one of the old adobes, followed by the rest of the community. Ellie lay on one of the pads, hands drawn to her chest, convulsing.

"Oh, no," Jeremy cried.

"Was she bitten by anything? A scorpion? A snake?"

He shook his head. "Oh, Ellie, don't die." Jeremy put his arms around her and spoke to his mother. "She was sick to her stomach last night. She said she was OK today and wanted to rest, but when I came back, she was really sick."

"Henry, can you get my medical bag? It's in the container."

Jeremy huddled next to his mother and whispered. "I think she's pregnant again, Mom. On her planet, they gave her special stuff when she was pregnant, but they didn't send any with her."

"What do you mean, they didn't send any?"

"They didn't send anything with them on the pile of junk. She ate some of the army food last night. It made her sick. But we don't have anything else for her to eat."

"They sent her here without medicine or food?" Veronica stared at Ellie's little hooves. "She's a different species than you. There must be complications when your blood factors come in contact, like the Rh factor in people."

"They did tests on us when we first got there. That's when Ellie got the medicine."

"And they sent you here with nothing?"

"Yeah."

"Goddamit! I don't have anything in my medical supplies that can help her. Jeremy, get that satellite up now. I need to talk to your in-laws again." As he dashed out, Ellie became waxen and unmoving. "Jeremy! Something's happened to her."

He came back and looked at her. "She does that when she's really scared, Mom. Like a possum. She'll come out of it."

"OK. Go. Contact the golden world." Veronica began looking under Ellie's clothes. She turned to the others. "Can you let me look at her privately? I want to be sure that she wasn't bitten by something."

The others left, but Sam stayed.

"I can heal, lady. I have the Power."

"You can heal her?"

"Maybe."

Veronica spread Ellie's legs and looked between them. There was only one opening. For conceiving and bearing children, she assumed. How did she go to the bathroom? Or did that opening work for all functions? Rage erupted inside Veronica. "She bore thousands of babies for them and they sent her off to die?"

"Lady, let me try." Sam looked at Ellie. His expression said that he saw an emergency that Veronica couldn't.

"Yes, certainly."

He lay down next to her and wrapped her in his arms. He whispered in her ear, words Veronica couldn't understand but she recognized as the cadence of the village's old speech. She could see that whatever he was doing was helping; Ellie relaxed and brightened a bit.

"Mom, I'm ready to transmit."

"Stay with her and Sam, Jeremy. Sam's helping her." Veronica ran to the storage container. Jeremy had it brightly lit inside. She sat at the computer and began.

"Elders of Ellie's planet: Ellie is dying. You sent her here knowing that she would die." Veronica was so angry that she set the broadcast on a broad band, so that her signal went all over the universe. She did make sure, however, that the Russian satellites were excluded. She was angry, not stupid. "I want a doctor *now*. I want him to bring whatever he needs to make her well and keep her well the rest of her time on Earth.

"WHAT *ARE* YOU? YOU FEEL SUPERIOR TO US, YET YOU DO THINGS THAT THE WORST PERSON ON EARTH WOULDN'T DO."

"I have a few other things to say. I was *appalled* by the way you sent my friends home. *On a floating garbage pile?* You were saying that we are garbage, right? This wasn't an intergalactic communication snafu where you were trying to say, 'We come in peace and bring gifts?'

"How dare you treat my people like that? You got what you wanted from my son and his wife and my friends. Have you no gratitude?

"My son is a nicer person than I am in many ways. He said you sent all that junk as a gift, because you knew he'd make unbelievable things out of it.

"Well, if that were so, you should have giftwrapped it. Or sent a note.

"I want that doctor *now*.

"Oh, the last time we chatted, I told you that I was broadcasting just to you. Not this time. The *whole universe* can hear this." She raised her voice and spoke into the mike.

From over by the ancient dwellings, Jeremy shouted, "They're here, Mom. Three doctors."

"Thank you very much. I can't help but notice that the doctors didn't come until you knew all the galaxies could hear me.

"Thank you for your assistance.

"This is Veronica Edgarton."

Sam stood pressed against the adobe wall of the hut, staring at three tall golden visitors. They stood by Ellie, apparently talking to each other silently. Jeremy knelt by her side, holding her hand.

"Hello, I'm Veronica Edgarton." She walked into the hut, extending her hand to the tallest. "I'm glad to meet you at last."

The golden creatures pulled away. They were nine or ten feet high, with long arms and legs. Huge eyes and slender bodies, which were slightly see-through and very luminous. They were naked and had no physical signs of any gender.

"In my country, it's customary to shake hands when greeting a friend or potential friend," she said. "Though of course, you may have other customs."

The tallest extended his hand and lightly touched Veronica's.

"That wasn't so bad, was it?" she said, wanting to wipe her hand. It was like touching warm fish. "All right. What's the problem with Eliana?"

They looked at each other.

"We need her healed and able to live on Earth for the rest of her life. And we need whatever special food or medicine she requires." She withdrew and stood next to Sam, who was shaking.

One put his hands on Ellie's temples, another held her feet. The tallest had his hands between her legs, palpating her inside. He pulled out something that looked like a deflated seedpod, ruined and dead. He lay it on the pad and put his hand over it. The pod disappeared.

"Oh, no," Veronica exclaimed. "She lost her baby."

The tall one looked at her. It was a piercing look, but understanding. He turned his back to her and began doing something to Ellie that she couldn't see. His body blocked her view. Whatever it was didn't take very long.

He stepped away from Ellie, who lay peacefully in her bed. The three of them stood with their hands over her, humming. Veronica felt at bit dizzy. The sound of the monks chanting at Shri Rinpoche's monastery was the only thing she could compare to the aliens' song.

She lost awareness for a moment, but when she returned, the tall alien stood in front of her. The others had gone. He was saying something to her, silently. He was telling her that they had made Ellie well and that she should remain healthy. She should be a vegetarian, but if there was no other food, she could eat—and the concept cost him something to articulate, she could tell—flesh for a short time. He pointed in the corner. Sacks of food for her were stacked there, along with seeds so they could grow more.

He looked at Veronica, imparting an apology and a warning. The apology came from him, and was why he'd stayed to communicate with her. He was sorry for what had happened to Ellie and the way things had been handled. The warning came from the other elders. She was not to talk to them in that way again. She was not to call again. He started to fade.

"No!" Veronica called out. His fading stopped. "I will do whatever I must to help my people. And I will tell my truth. I have seen great evil done when people—and your people, too—hide the truth. If peace is to prevail, we must speak the truth."

She held out her hand again, and this time he took it. Her hand wrapped around a translucent glow. He had a body and substance. "I hope we can be friends, and I thank you with all my heart." She felt more than saw a flicker of a smile and then he disappeared. "Wait. What is your name?" But he was gone.

She turned to her son. "Is she OK, Jeremy?"

"She looks fine, Mom." He knelt next to Ellie, holding her hand. She looked at him with brimming eyes.

"I'll give you two some privacy." Veronica backed through the doorway.

"What's the matter, Ellie?" Jeremy said, lying down next to her. His wife's rigid body said that something was terribly wrong. "What happened?"

"Oh, Jeremy. Is bad. Doctor."

"Did he do something to you?" Jeremy grabbed her shoulder.

"He make me better. But one thing he no can make better."

"What, baby?" He stroked her shoulder and arm. "What is it?"

"He say I no have more babies." The tears rolled over her lower lids and down her cheeks.

"Why? What happened?"

"I have too many babies. Hurt body. Is why I get sick. Is why baby die." She rubbed her tummy. "We *never* have baby." Her stifled sobs ripped through Jeremy. "Never baby for *us*." He clutched her.

"Those bastards. They did that to you." Jeremy wanted to scream at the goldies, but his anger ricocheted through Ellie. She cried harder, trembling. He stroked her. "Baby. Calm down. We've got each other. We'll be OK. We don't have to have kids."

She looked at him, catching him in his lie. "I want babies. You want babies. Is *not* OK."

He caressed her and whispered. "I love you, Ellie. I love you more than anything. When I was down here by myself, I thought I'd go crazy. I'll die without you. Please, please don't cry. I can't stand it." His chest heaved. "Please, baby. Just don't cry."

He had to keep quiet. Their house didn't have a ceiling or doors; everyone could hear. He choked down his grief. "We'll be OK, you'll see. We'll do something." He cast around for any solution. "We can adopt!"

"What *adopt*?"

"It's what your people did with our babies. It's when you take someone else's child and raise it as your own."

"No babies here."

He hadn't thought of that. There weren't any babies needing parents. Except . . . "Sam said he has babies."

Ellie pushed up on one elbow and gazed at him. Tears glistened on her cheeks, but she looked hopeful.

"We can adopt one of Sam's babies. Or a bunch of them, if you want. It will be all right, baby," Jeremy's face showed how much he adored her. "Don't cry, Ellie. Let me hold you. I'll make it better."

He cupped her body with his and stroked her, kissing her face and neck, running his hands over her thighs and hips. "I love you, Ellie. I don't care about anything but you. I'll do anything to make you happy." He kissed her more deeply, his hands becoming insistent. "I love touching you, Ellie. Let's love each other."

But they didn't. Both of them realized that Ellie needed to heal, in her body and her soul. And they realized that the goldies hadn't forced them to produce so many babies. They had a part in what happened. Jeremy choked up, trying to hide his face from her. She knew exactly what he was thinking.

"No cry, Jeremy. I like it," she said, petting his head. "You like it. So we do it lots. Make lots babies." The corners of her mouth turned down. "Not know hurt me." Her hand rubbed her abdomen.

"Oh, sweetie. It's all my fault. If I hadn't been so . . ."

"Not just you, Jeremy. *Me*, too. No *fault*." She put her arms around his neck. "I love you, Jeremy. Love you like crazy."

Jeremy whispered, "I love you. Nothing matters if we're together."

"We together, Jeremy. Together all time." The ghost of a smile brushed her lips. "And we adopt Sam's babies."

When Veronica turned to leave Jeremy and Ellie's adobe, Sam was right in front of her. The cave was dark. Voices of the others bedding down murmured from various corners.

"Oh, Sam, I was so afraid." She fell into his arms, leaning against him, wrapping her arms around him. His embrace was like none she'd known. Powerful, comforting, loving. He was so big. She let herself fall into him. She never wanted to leave his arms.

She heard Jeremy talking to Ellie behind her and remembered Sam's age. She pushed herself away, looking up into his face. "I'm sorry, Sam, I didn't mean . . ." She mumbled a bit more. "I'll see you tomorrow, dear."

In her little cubbyhole, she tossed and turned. I'm an immoral woman, she thought. She needed to get control of herself. She thrashed about, lost in the falling sensation she'd had in his arms. "That's absolutely wrong. He's the same age as your son."

Sleep eluded her. She tried to repeat her mantra, but it wouldn't stick. All she could concentrate on was Shri Rinpoche's face. Help me, please help me, she prayed.

18

Sam was so excited that he didn't try to sleep. All that she'd done ran through his mind, over and over. She was a queen, and a mighty warrior. She made the gold creatures come and save Ellie's life. He'd heard her scream at them on the computer. He'd never heard anyone scream at leaders like that. She was unafraid of the gold things. She touched one twice. He saw her shoot the gun better than the stories said she could. She saw Ellie's deformity and said, "Poor thing." She didn't shun her.

Maybe she could save his people. Maybe she could care for the women in the pen and heal them. Help them get past what happened. Some of them. Maybe she could see his people as he saw them, as beautiful, not deformed and mentally disabled.

Hope flamed inside him. That and something else. When Ellie was all right, the lady had hugged him. She clung to him. He could feel her softness against him. She went to her own bed, but maybe she felt something for him. He thought she did at first, before he threw the bottle.

Sleep wouldn't come. He did what he had done the night before, took off his clothes and pressed against the walls, touching the stones with his flesh. It wasn't enough.

Sam lay face down on the floor of his cave and extended his arms. He thought about her being under him. He remembered how she felt, soft and yielding. He opened and released, opened, and let go. He did that once, and again. He finally slept.

Dropping into a black emptiness, he felt Sam Big turn toward him. It felt like the eye he'd once worn was searching for him. Sam Big knew he was alive because of what he'd done. He lived in a world of darkness and touch. Sensation and odor. Silence and intuition. Everyone in the shelter developed powers that wouldn't have appeared in the outside world. He could feel everyone he cared for, people full of throbbing, breathing life. Souls. They could feel him.

And so could the Bigs. He was Sam Big's pretty. He belonged to Sam Baahuhd, the legitimate leader of the underground according to the Commands. They had to obey the headman on pain of death. He had belonged to Sam Big since he was a boy. He had been able to fight him off when they were young, but when Sam grew Big, fighting him off became impossible.

He had hoped to be free when he left the underground. He had hoped to join these people and leave his shame behind. What Sam Big did to him wasn't what he wanted. He wasn't one of the jolly boys.

Fortunately for him, neither was Sam Big. He rutted in the women's pen, siring children without care. He only called for Sam when he wanted to humiliate and hurt him.

Sam Big could feel what he'd done, lying on the floor and thinking of her. When his body released, his soul entered another reality, the reality of spirit, of talking and knowing without words, of love. Sam Big had felt him. He knew he was alive. Sam's eyes flew open.

The Bigs could find him if he slept. If he dreamed. If he strayed from absolute alertness, he was in danger. Sam Big already knew he was alive. Soon he would know where he was.

He would come for him as fast as he could. For if his pretty, Sam of Emily, was alive outside, anyone in the underground could survive there. He would hone into his essence and come straight to this place. He would kill him and take her and all the rest and begin a new underground.

Sam shuddered. He'd seen her shoot, but she hadn't seen how fast Sam Big could move, or how he could use the Voice to call in prey. To trick them into thinking someone else was calling. Someone they loved.

Rocking back and forth, Sam tried to plan. They had found chain ladders and were going to put them out the next day. He could climb down when no one was looking. He could head away from the underground. Or he could look for a new land and people up the river.

That was stupid. He would die in a week. He didn't know how to live in the world above ground. He needed people. He needed touch. He needed love. His people loved him; the deformed and feeble people that he cared for loved him.

The Bigs would kill him if he went back. They kept only one of the Commands: "The Angel said that bad people should be loved until they were good." The Bigs exchanged the word love for another word, fuck. Bad people should be fucked until they were good. They disciplined people by raping them. They executed people by raping them.

Calm yourself, he thought. He won't find you if you're calm. Think of what to do.

Throw yourself off the cliff, he thought. Kill yourself. Do it fast. These people cannot survive an attack by the Bigs. Kill yourself and stop it.

19

The group was out on the ledge when Sam emerged, all of them but her. They'd made a fire and put a grill over it. A tantalizing aroma came from a metal container on the grill.

"Come over here, Sam, and have some coffee," James said.

"What is *coffee*?"

"It's the elixir of the gods," James said, pulling out a metal cup from the stash of kitchen stuff. "We've got the Russian Army's finest coffee. We found it yesterday. I figured we deserve a cup. We even have sugar and creamer." He handed Sam a big cup with creamer and sugar. "Allow me to introduce you to the joy of caffeine . . ."

"Go easy, Sam, if you've never had coffee," Mel warned. "It has a stimulant in it called caffeine. It can keep you up all night if you're not used to it. It can also be addictive—not a hard addiction, but you can get a bad headache if you stop drinking it."

"Come on, Mel, he's not going to become a caffeine fiend on one cup," James said.

Sam took a sip. It was delicious. He liked the sweetness. Nothing in the underworld was sweet.

Henry and Lena also sat by the fire, drinking coffee. When Sam got his cup, they went back to the previous topic of conversation, the nightmares they'd had. Everyone had had the same dream: A monster was searching for him or her.

He knew it was Sam Big, penetrating their unguarded minds. He would catch them so easily. He had to leave so they could live. If he wasn't there, Sam Big would leave them alone. If he wasn't there, they'd never find out what he had been to Sam Big.

"I want to take a look at those pictures Jeremy took inside the shelter," Henry said. "I dreamed of a monster. Terrible looking creature. I wonder if it's something in the shelter searching for us. Jeremy, can you bring us those pictures?"

"Yeah. I'll do that, but we have to get the solar panels up today or we won't be doing anything. Almost everything needs charging. I don't know how we're going to anchor them on solid rock. I've got tools, but I don't know how to use them."

"We need to get the ladder down, too," Henry said. "I intend to take a bath." He rubbed his face. "And shave. And I want to cut off all this excess hair." He indicated his unkempt 'fro. "I'm sick of looking the way the goldies wanted me to look."

"Yeah, James. Help me get rid of this Mohawk," Mel begged.

Henry had one more desire, "I want to catch a fish. I found some fishing gear yesterday. I'm sick of these K rations."

As they talked, all Sam could think of was how to get out of there and keep Sam Big away from them.

20

Veronica awakened but didn't move or make a sound. She listened carefully, trying to figure out where she was. She lay on her side with her knees drawn up to her chest. Her hands clutched each other. She felt like she was back in the bunker with the general and all those dead bodies.

After thrashing for hours the night before trying to get to sleep, she had a nightmare. A huge brute was chasing her. He'd almost get her, and then she'd get away.

Then the dream came.

She was in her bed at her family's house in Manhattan. She had given the building to the Hermitage Academy, Jeremy's high school, but it had been her family home. She was herself, an adult woman, lying on her back in her childhood bed.

She could see the invisible outlines of a child's body over her own. Short torso, chubby round thighs, knees pulled up and parted, little feet and calves. The outlines were *her* body as a child. The door to her room opened. Someone entered and came toward her, and then the dream dissolved.

The little girl was still there as she lay in her bed. She could see her, a clear outline like a painting made of water on water. She could hear the child thinking, I've got to get away. She didn't hear the thoughts in words, because the little girl was too young to think in words.

Veronica lay still and searched the camp with terrified eyes. What was happening to her? The sun was well up and everyone was gathered around a campfire. She could smell coffee. The others were talking as though everything was fine.

Her breasts rubbed together. They made her sick. Her belly disgusted her. She felt the way she had in her wild days when she had awakened next to some stranger and he looked at her like he'd scored the best lay in the world. Sometimes the loathing she felt for herself lasted an instant. Sometimes her self-hatred lasted for hours. But she'd never felt it like now, hard in her body, jabbing her the way they had.

What she had done wasn't the way people thought of it. She wasn't liberated, free, and powerfully sensual. "She takes men like men take women." "She's the modern Cleopatra." What she did wasn't sporting or boinking or boffing or a thousand foolish words.

It was physical. It happened inside *her*. They touched her in that deep place where *she* was. In those days, she didn't care. She'd be fucking some man and feel him ramming her like he was beating her. She liked that, the drubbing, shoving something down. How many times did it have to be shoved down until it stayed down?

She felt her eyes fill and saw tears spreading on her mat. She'd climax and scream, the famous scream that said, "Veronica Edgarton, the most liberated woman in the world, has come again."

How many times did she have to scream to feel satisfied? How many orgasms until she was full? She'd never felt full. Fury drove her to seek out one after another after another. It wasn't great sex and she wasn't liberated. The general had shown her exactly what she was.

Veronica smoothed her rumpled black jumpsuit under her blanket. She'd chosen a bad cave. It offered no privacy. A lady couldn't have a bad morning without everyone knowing. She'd pick another sleeping spot today. Everyone looked toward her when they saw her move. Time to be Mrs. Edgarton again.

"Hello, everyone," she said. "I know I look like hell. I haven't been sleeping. I think Ellie being sick last night got me stirred up. And I had nightmares. A monster was chasing me." She shook her head.

"Well, join us, Veronica," Henry said. "Everyone had that dream. And what a brute he was. Have a cup of coffee." A metal percolator sat on top of a grill someone had pulled off the junk heap. Henry fixed her a cup, "One sugar, and a bit of creamer, is that right?"

"Yes, Henry. You remembered." She took the cup and sipped. "This is the general's private stash. The best you can get." She smiled.

"We're going to get the ladder set up today and go down to the river. We found fishing gear yesterday. I propose a fish dinner."

"Mom, Ellie's fine now," Jeremy said. Don't worry."

She looked at him, shivering. She couldn't get the image of that young girl to go away. But Ellie was OK? "That's wonderful, dear."

Henry approached her. "Veronica, I found your wooden box under the coffee. I hope you don't mind that I opened it—I thought it was more coffee. It's a box of books. This was in it." He handed her a large book with roses on the cover.

She snatched it. "Oh, thank you, Henry." She pulled the dust jacket off to reveal a plain cover with a circular emblem embossed on the front. "This is only thing I've got left of him. Is there a knife or scissors around?"

She slit along the top cover of the book and opened it, revealing a hidden compartment. Some brown beads and an ochre-colored shawl made of silk were inside, along with a recorded disk. She took the disk out, wrapped the shawl around her shoulders and looped the beads on her hand. "Oh, thank, God, they didn't find this." She looked at Jeremy, but addressed all of them.

"Would you like to see Shri Rinpoche? He's the monk I met on Mount Kailash. He's my teacher." She opened the volume, which was a regular hardback book except for the secret compartment. Veronica flipped through a number of pages showing a spectacular mountain with a pointed, snow-covered top. "Jeremy, do we have any players for disks? I'd like to play this. It's bulletproofing against nightmares."

"Yes, let's listen to it," Henry said. The rest of them nodded in agreement.

"I found a player inside," Jeremy went into the storage container to get it while she continued.

She leafed through the pages, searching for ones that were slightly thicker. She cut a sliver off the outer edge of each. The pages proved to be folders. A photograph was hidden in each. She gathered them as though they were jewels.

"See, here we are," she showed pictures of an elderly man in muted orange robes. Some images had snowy mountains in the background, while others were indoors. The old monk posed with the other monks in a couple of shots. She was in one shot, wearing an orange outfit. "I'm so lucky he let me photograph him. I don't think he'd ever been photographed before. I'm wearing the garb of a novice."

Jeremy returned and put the disk on. The sound was unearthly. Human sounds, deep, guttural, rising and falling. Tone upon tone. Unreal. The half dome of the cavern was a perfect concert venue. Its acoustics magnified the haunting and piercing sound.

Veronica let it wash through her. It penetrated, driving her unease away for the moment. "It's throat singing, Buddhist throat singing. It's a blessing and a cleansing." She could see the others were repelled by it. They pulled away, cringing at the sound. "It's strange when you first hear it. I didn't like it either, but the droning and vibration gets addictive. You can feel it clean you out spiritually." She turned off the player. "I'll spare you. I'll listen on the headphones."

The others moved off to get on with the day's activities. She sat by the fire listening to the disk, entranced. Finally, something gave her relief. Veronica looked at the photos time and again, finally replacing them in the book's compartment. She felt serene and sleepy. Her haunting fears disappeared in the chant's guttural sounds.

She went to her little cave and lay down, placing the disk player and book next to her.

21

Sam was shocked when he saw the lady. Sam Big had found her in her dreams. But something else found her, too.

Henry brought her a book. She held the hidden pictures so they could see, but she didn't pass them around. He wanted to look carefully at the holy man and everything in the book and pictures.

And then she put the singing on.

The music! It was like the music of the underground. *They* sang like that. All of his people sang in their burrows and holes, even in the main rooms. The only ones that didn't sing like that, deep in their throats, were the Bigs. The singing is what kept the underground whole. It healed his people, and it calmed the Bigs, sometimes.

He relaxed. If he could hear that music, he could stay there. If they could *make* that music, they would be safe. The Bigs couldn't penetrate it. Sam Big would not be able to find them. Things would be all right. He could feel himself relaxing, but for one thing.

A buzz of energy played with his insides. He trembled a bit, feeling like he needed to do something. Work. Dig. He wanted to dig. But this was solid rock, how could he dig here? He watched the cup jiggle in his hands. Coffee! He'd never had coffee before. He poured what was left on the fire. He'd never drink it again.

"Sam?" Jeremy stood beside him. "Can you help me set up the solar panels? I do electronics, but I'm no good at mechanical stuff."

"No, the ladder should go over here." Sam took over the installation of the chain ladder and solar panels. He did it naturally and easily; he was the one who did the maintenance in the underground.

The group had wanted to set the ladder up on the side of the cliff closest to the east, the side where the underground shelter was located. "They will see you going up and down over there, if they're coming." He showed them where it should go on the other edge of the cliff, close to his rooms. He didn't like that, but if he wanted to leave in a hurry, it would be good.

"We have to get the solar panels going. We're running out of juice." Jeremy was insistent.

Sam had seen solar panels from the bottom in the underground. The shelter had many of them, sealed in glass and metal. They had worked for the 105 generations. He looked at the solar panels that had been in the container carefully, admiring their workmanship. Tools were arrayed around them. He loved tools. What was here was so much better than what he had underground.

Sam took out the instructions. He could not read any of the words. He could follow the pictorial instructions, but he wanted to make sure he was doing the right thing.

Jeremy was watching him and moved closer, whispering, "I can help you read that. Most of this is in Russian, but there's an English translation." He leafed through the booklet and found the English part.

Sam flushed. Jer the Tek was offering to help him. The Great Tek, whom he had worshipped as a god and now saw was a man. A very skilled man, a brilliant man, but just a man. He was also a nice man, who had a wife what many might shun, and who understood that Sam was embarrassed because he couldn't read.

They worked together most of the day. Sam figured out a way to get the solar panels to work without being mounted permanently. Once the solar was functioning, they had power to charge up all the computers and equipment, especially the drill.

Jeremy looked at the big drill bit and said, "They must have intended on using it to cut through the ice."

It worked fine on rock, as they found out in the early afternoon when it was charged. He drilled the holes for the anchors for the solar system, set the anchors and grouted them. Then he drilled holes for the anchors for the ladder, setting a second set. They had enough chain ladder for two stepladders, which might be useful in an emergency. The grout had to set before they could use any of it.

"This is great, but we want to get down today," Henry said. "Isn't there a temporary way to set up a ladder?"

"Yes," Sam said. He looped a chain around a boulder near the edge of the ledge and bolted the ends to the ladder. "This will be good for today. Tomorrow, I will fix the ladders right. And the solar panels."

Sam had never had such a good time. He could barely comprehend the overwhelming plenty of tools and things around him. Working with them was a joy.

He and Jeremy were putting the tools inside the computer/medical container when Jeremy said, "Sam, what's going on with you and my mom?" Sam froze. "Don't tell me 'Nothing,' because I know there is. You were friendly when we first got here, and now you don't even talk."

"She does not like me," Sam managed to say.

"Why?"

"Because I threw her bottle."

"I don't think that's it." Jeremy thought a moment. "I'll ask her what the deal is." He stumbled over his words. "I wanted to tell you that I'm glad you're here. I couldn't do what you did today. None of us could. Uh. I wanted you to know that I wanted to tell you, like . . . Well, you and my mom. You know, if . . . Like . . . Well . . .

Sam wondered what Jeremy was talking about. Was he saying that he approved of his mother and him, if they were friends? Or more than friends?

"Are you going to the river, Sam?" Jeremy seemed relieved to change the subject.

"Yes."

"Tell the rest of them that I'll be right down. I need to print some stuff."

When he came out of the container, the group was climbing down the ladder for a picnic by the river. They let the fishing gear down with a rope.

"Hey, Sam, good job!" said Mel and showed him how to do the "high five" salute.

Sam smiled. "I will finish tomorrow, when the grout is dry." Earlier that day, he didn't know what grout was. Now he could high five and talk about grout.

Sam intended to go down to the river, but when he looked over the edge of the cliff, everything seemed to move. He stepped back fast. Such height was unimaginable. He couldn't go down the ladder. His feelings about leaving were changing. He didn't want to leave.

He'd had an idea about something for his rooms. He'd found chisels and rock carving tools in the container. He thought of something that would make him feel safe. Perhaps he could rough it out by that night. He picked up the tools, and looked around for the lady.

She was sleeping in her cubby. He felt the atmosphere around her. Not good. Her book and music-playing thing were lying next to her, as were the beads and scarf. He took them as silently as only a digger from the underground could. He'd have them back to her before she awakened.

He took a piece of charred wood from the fire and went to his room.

22

Jeremy stowed the printouts in his backpack and headed for the ladder. "Come on, Ellie, I'll go down with you now." He'd wanted her to stay up top because of her illness the night before. Also, he was concerned about her getting down the ladder with hooves instead of feet. But what he'd printed out made it imperative that he join the others by the river right away.

"Go meeting," she said, skipping to the edge and hopping over before he could stop her. He looked down, and she was on the ground waving at him. He turned and carefully stepped onto the ladder. He could hear Sam hammering away at something in his room.

Jeremy made his way down the swaying ladder, wishing there was some other way to reach the river. An escalator, maybe. What he had in his backpack proved the need for their cliff-top defenses. It proved the need for much more than that. They needed water up there. They needed to be able to withhold a siege.

They needed a community meeting right now.

'Hey, everybody!" Jeremy called, wading through the sand. The river curved just beyond their cliff. Years of spring floods had deposited sand and boulders along the curve. The shaded inlet formed a first-class waterside resort, and the group had taken advantage of it. James and Mel were having a water fight a bit downstream while Henry cast into deeper waters upstream.

"Hey, everyone! I have the printouts from the shelter, plus some infrared pictures I just took. They couldn't tell what I was doing underground." Jeremy sat in the shade and spread out the images around them, anchoring them with rocks.

They gathered around him. "Just take a look. It's self-explanatory. I've taped the images together to show the floor plan of the shelter."

Mel said. "Dante would have a good time with this. It's hell."

"That's the one that I saw in my nightmares," Lena pointed.

Sam Big. Jeremy had blown up a face shot of him.

"They're mutants," he said. "Giants by their size, but also with the exaggerated musculature. And those growths on their faces."

Mel took a close look. "It looks like bone."

"That's not even Neanderthal," James commented. "They're like monsters."

"They are monsters." Jeremy also brought 360-degree panoramas that he had taped together. That gave a full view of each room. He'd taken down shots from the ceilings to give an overview of what was going on in each area. He drew the floor plan of the shelter as he remembered it and superimposed it on the photos. And he'd produced some new infrared photos that showed what lurked in the darkness.

Sam Big was raping a man much smaller than himself in the main hall. Bigs wrestled nearby. Three Bigs were chained to the walls. They looked like they were roaring. Several Bigs were attacking women in the pit. Women were tied or chained to the walls.

"Here are the solar fields. They look pretty good. Sam's doing, I bet." Jeremy gave them a tour of the site. "The Bigs have the main hall and most of the space. There are other halls; here, you see one. These are for the less favored bloodlines." None of the people looked as normal or healthy as Sam. "And in these outer rooms, you'll see forms that seem to be just lying there. Those must be Sam's people. He takes care of them. Many of them can't take care of themselves. They have no defenses against the Bigs.

"OK, we all got the scene down there. The Bigs are monsters and the others are very handicapped. You can see all the tunnels here; they just look like black spots with lighter areas inside of them? Those are infrared shots. People are in those holes. I think Sam and people like him—diggers—made them trying to get away from the Bigs, or to get more room.

"This burrow is very close to this munitions storage." Jeremy pointed to a square he'd drawn on the printout. "There's a solid cement wall here, with extra rebar and support, but it doesn't have the security setup that the main entrances to the munitions bays have. Those are impregnable.

"If they get through here somehow, they can get into both weapons caches." He pointed to the area.

"What's in them, Jeremy?" Henry asked.

"The most heavy-duty shit they made before the war—lightweight versions. Formidable. I don't know what we've got in the other storage container. I assume that we've got the equivalent. But ours is here, and theirs is there."

"That's good," Mel said.

"Not necessarily. They can shoot a rocket at us and we'll be toast. If they know how to use what they've got."

"They probably don't, do they?"

"No. Not now. But it's all on the computers. If they can get my lab up and running, they can figure it out. They're smart—I can feel it, can't you?"

"I almost feel like they know what we're doing now," Lena said. "Of course, part of it is how I feel looking at those pictures."

"And part of it is the nightmares." He pointed at Sam Big. "He's after us because of Sam. He wants him back."

"And he's crawling all over us trying to find him."

"Sam isn't the point any more. He knows about *us*. He wants us. He's entered our minds and we're already scared shitless. We have to get up to speed to fight them right away."

James broke in. "You're talking as though we have no choice but to go to war. We just got out of one terrible place. Why can't we just set up here and let them live over there?"

"Why do you even ask that, James?" Mel scowled. "You saw the pictures. Jeremy says they've got super weapons a few feet away. And look at what they're doing. Don't you think they'll do that to us?"

"Why do we have to deal with this? I'm sick of all this."

"We all are, James," Lena said. "But I don't think we can do anything but face the problem."

"But how? March off to war? None of us knows a *thing* about that. You're going to go running after those monsters with what? We have weapons, Jeremy says, but no one knows how to use them." James shook his head. "I don't want to do this."

"None of us wants it," said Jeremy. "We do have one person with military training. My mom knows how to use everything in the container. And she's a commando—the general made her do their training. She could lead us, but there's something wrong with her.

"Yeah. What's going on with her, Jeremy?"

"I don't know, Mel. She's not sleeping. Did you see her standing by the ledge laughing yesterday? Then she was pissed off, and *then* she fell apart. I've never seen her like this, even when my dad died. The other thing is, I'm afraid Sam's going to leave. I was working next to him all day, and I felt like he'd be out of here the minute he could slip away."

"I felt that, too," Henry said. "It's almost like he knows what all of us are thinking, and them in the bomb shelter, too."

"Sam said that's how it is down there. They know everything without talking."

"That is like Ellie's world."

"But not quite. Ellie's people weren't like *that*," Henry pointed to the printouts.

"Well, I don't want Sam to go. I don't want Sam Big to get him," Jeremy continued.

"He wouldn't go back there, would he?"

"Maybe. To spare us. Give himself up so they'll leave us alone."

"But they will never leave us alone if they know we exist." They looked at the images again.

"I think they already know where we are," Lena said. The others were silent.

"We need to stop Sam from running away," Jeremy said. "Tie him up if we have to." They nodded.

"And I think one of us should talk to him about how much we want him to be with us. He needs to know we're with him," Henry said. "I think that person should be me. I'm older."

"You don't look that much older than him, Henry. But I agree. You're good at fatherly talks." Jeremy said.

"So we're agreed. Henry talks to Sam. We find out what's wrong with my mom. And then we get ready to go to war."

Ellie pointed at the diagram. "Where babies?"

"Sam would know, El. They're outside the underground's walls, so they don't show on the pictures."

"We fight for babies," she said in her tiny cricket's voice. Jeremy looked at his wife. Her posture was almost militant. He'd never seen her like that.

23

Veronica's eyes opened. The terror she'd been feeling came back full force. Jumping out of bed, she looked around for something to help her. She remembered her book and the disk of the monks singing.

She searched around her cubby, but the book and disk player weren't there. Neither were her prayer beads and shawl. Who would take her precious things? Someone in the group was a thief.

She stood by the stone supporting the ladder when she heard a sound in a nearby cave. The sound of metal striking metal. She walked into the cave.

"Hello? Is anyone here? Hello?" The cave had several rooms opening off it. Seeing a movement in one, she investigated. Sam was inside, wearing the headphones and hammering away at the wall with a chisel. Her book was propped open, with a picture of Rinpoche lying on the page. He had the shawl draped around his shoulders.

"What are you doing?" she shouted.

He jumped and turned around, removing the headset. She could hear the monks' voices coming from it.

"Those are *mine*." She grabbed the photo and put it in its pocket, slammed the book shut, and seized the disk player. "Give me that shawl. That's *mine*. You took my things! You're a thief. *Thief*!" Her fist struck his chest. "I thought you were so nice, but you're not." She pushed him out of his cave, shrieking, "Get out. Thief!"

Going down the ladder was the most terrifying thing he had ever done. He grabbed the chains and stepped on the rungs, sure that he would drop to his death. But if that happened, it would be better. This terrible time of trying to live outside would be over.

He reached the bottom and stood on the soft earth. Smells of grass and wild flowers and the river came to him. He could hear the water moving and feel the wind on his skin. He saw and heard it rustling the trees. He had never seen such beauty. He couldn't see any of it. All he could hear was her screaming, "Thief!"

Should he go back to the underground? Should he travel along the river until he found other people or died? Should he jump into the river? That would end it.

He decided to throw himself in the river. He was heading toward it when he met the others heading back to the cliff.

"What happened?" Henry asked. "We heard Veronica screaming."

His shoulders curled over as though he'd been beaten. "What is a thief?"

"You don't know what a thief is?" Mel asked.

"No."

"It means someone who takes things from someone without asking and doesn't give them back."

"I took the book and music thing. I did not mean to keep them. Underground, only the Bigs have things. I wouldn't take something from a Big."

'You don't have private property?"

"I don't know what that is."

Jeremy came forward, "Hey, Sam, I'll go talk to my mom. It will be OK. Come on, everyone, let's go up and let Henry talk to him."

They sat on logs by the river. Sam looked everywhere but at Henry. He wiped his eyes. His shoulders shook.

"She hates me."

"I don't think so, Sam. I think she loves you."

"Why? She called me *thief*. She talks to me like I am a boy."

"Yeah, I've seen her do that. And she loves you. Just like you love her."

Sam looked down. "I love her. She hates me."

"No, she's in a bad way, Sam. She's got her whole life sitting on her now and she can't make it better by running off to a party or going home with some asshole she doesn't give a shit about. That's eating her, in addition to what she feels about you."

"She talks to me like I was Jeremy."

"Ah. Now you're getting somewhere. What's the problem with that?"

"He's her son."

"That's right. She looks at you, a young man."

"I'm twenty-nine."

"Yes, a young man."

"I am the oldest man in the underground. Sam Big is younger than me, they all are."

Henry's mouth fell open. "You're *old* for your world?"

"Yes. People die before," he flashed his ten digits twice. "Most of them."

"Veronica doesn't know that. To her, you look like one of Jeremy's friends visiting from school."

"Like her son?"

"Yes. You get the problem, Sam?"

Sam got the problem. If boingy boingy between cousins was not allowed, between mother and son was *really* not allowed. "What do I do?"

"Nothing. She's going to have to see that you're lifetimes older than Jeremy for herself. And you need to learn some things about women. First off, do you think she was mad at you?"

"Yes."

"Women have feelings, son, lots of them. Veronica is more woman in many ways, and she has more feelings. With your being younger than her, she'll automatically feel old. And ugly, even though in Veronica's case that's nuts. Look, she's run around *more* than they said in the village, Sam. She and my brother were in love with each other, but they were never happy. They had a few good holidays together and made Jeremy. That isn't happiness.

"So, now she sees you, a handsome young man, and what does she think? That loving you is wrong. That you'll leave her, even though there's no one to leave her for. She's probably ashamed of things she did, and she's determined not to make the same mistakes. It's churning around inside her, making her act nuts. Just like you were thinking crazy, about to head back to that place where they'd kill you."

"You knew?"

"We all knew. We'll tie you up if we have to, Sam. We will not allow you to go back to that *thing*."

Henry sat up and waved both of his arms over his head.

"What are you doing?"

"It's a signal we worked out. Lena's going to talk to Veronica about you wanting to leave. I don't think she's aware of anything but her own pain right now."

"No."

"Yes. She needs to know what's she's doing to you. And she needs to know what a fix we're in. We will not allow that monster to have you or any of us. We know what that nightmare was about. It was him, searching for you."

Sam flushed. They knew about Sam Big and him. He jumped toward the river. Henry grabbed him.

"You're bigger than me, Sam, and can probably outfight me. So you can go drown yourself if you want to. I don't want you to, and neither does anyone else. And I won't make it easy."

Sam looked at him, wanting to hit him, wanting to leap into the water. Wanting to hug him. Wanting to cry again.

"*Oh, no! Sam, I'm sorry!*" Veronica's cries came down from the cliff. "*Sam, don't go. Please. I'm sorry.*" And then she was screaming. Not just screaming, erupting with the uncontrolled shrieks of a terrified child.

Sam darted up the ladder like a gymnast.

24

Her door opened and someone came in. The dark outline of a man approached her bed. She screamed and her body jerked as though something was shaking it. She kept screaming and thrashing until a child's voice came out of her mouth.

"Daddy, Daddy, don't hurt me anymore."

The cave's acoustics were so keen that everyone could hear her.

"I've never heard such terror in my life," Henry said. "I don't doubt it was him for a minute. I knew that puffed up F. Bentham Piermont was a stinking SOB."

"Her father?" Mel asked. "He was the richest man in the country."

"Rich don't mean good, Mel."

"Remember when you told me that someone got her started the way she was, Henry?" Jeremy said.

"Yeah."

"I wish I could kill him."

"He's already dead, Jeremy. Roasting in hell."

She screamed, out of control and unable to stop. And then Sam was there. He picked her up and carried her to his room. "Oh, Sam," she cried. "Help me."

"Ah will, lady." He laid her down on a bed and held her to him. The terror came again and she started to scream, but he took it. He was like a tide pulling out, an irresistible force taking everything with it. The terror, pain, memories, physical sensations, all the evil she'd done, all torn away.

Sam tore off his clothes and pulled at the neck of her uniform, trying to remove it. She held on, "No. No."

"Lady, ah need to get closer. Let me."

They lay together naked, wrapped around each other. His body was very hot, burning. Her eyes rolled back in her head. Something came off of him. She saw blue halos at the edges of her vision. An indigo sea. He kept pulling the pain from her, defeating the monster. Images came up. Her wedding night with the general.

The cement bunker with the cryogenic machines appeared in her mind. He could see it. He was inside her mind, seeing the computer lab and storage containers filled with what they'd need for a new life. The open space with a table and chairs. The sculpted bays containing the coffin-like devices in which each of them would be frozen to live until a better time.

"Forget about me, Sam. I'm no good, and I'll never be any good. I'll ruin your life." She wanted to jump off the edge of the cliff, but Sam held her.

He kept holding her, body burning, pulling off whatever arose inside her. "Run, Sam. Get away from me ..."

She lay empty, deserted as a beach with the tide run out. She felt nothing, no pain, no terror. Only the freedom of emptiness.

He twined around her, arms around her, leg draped over her. It was like being in him, breathing him in and breathing him out. As though he entered her with each breath and she entered him. In that way, she knew all of his world and what had happened to him underground and how he knew what she knew and the pain and terror of it. She knew the thread of similarity between his life and hers.

When she slept, she dropped into black unconsciousness. It was his world, the dark world of no light. The dark, deep, glowing world.

The cave was black when she awoke. He was next to her, pulled away a bit, staring at her intently. He trembled. She could feel his need. "Please, lady, let me. It's my Power. Ah canna stop it w' ye." He spoke the dialect of the village. "Let me, lady."

She lay back, powerless to stop it and wanting it to happen.

He knelt next to her and rubbed his face on hers, running his cheeks along hers, moving his face along her forehead. He rubbed his face along her torso and over her shoulders, touching her with the insides of his wrists and forearms. Moving constantly, silently. He touched all of her, but not with his hands.

Something arose inside of her, a light. It rose and exploded into bliss. She wanted to scream and swear, but he said to her, "No, lady. This is for thee and me. No one else."

She bit back the sounds and let pleasure pulse through her, again, and again. And again. Sweat covered her body.

Sam still knelt next to her. He sat back on his heels, swept his arm over her legs and then ran his fingers up the bottoms of her feet. Her knees sprang apart and outward. He moved between her legs, fumbled for a moment, and entered her.

She gasped when she felt him so deep, and he pulled out a bit, then started rocking forward and back. He didn't lie on top of her. He held himself up on his hands, elbows straight, so that they only touched where they were joined.

The sea rose again, moving toward her this time. Flowing in, inundating her with richness. The tide covered her, drowning her. Blue lights played in the corners of her mind. She struggled, but it was no use. The light inside her flared and flared again. Her hips moved.

"Oh, please, Sam. Please." When she could stand it no more, she reached for him. "Please."

He lowered his whipcord body onto hers, grasped her around the shoulders, and buried his face in her shoulder. He surged and then joined her in bliss.

"Was that your first time, Sam?"

"Aye. Like that." He caressed her cheek. "Ah couldna, y'see. They were all ma cousins."

"The Commands."

"Aye. The Commands. We touch each other in the underground, lady. We do that."

She wanted to ask him if his lover had had hands, but couldn't do it.

"Kiss me, Sam."

"Show me how, lady."

She reached up and showed him, and then the cycle of the tide began again.

When they awakened, dawn was barely tinting the cave walls. He looked at her with his green eyes and wide cheekbones and beautiful earnestness. He was disturbed.

He said, "Ah am a man."

He took her hand and put it on his chest. "Ah have a heart." She could feel its pulsation and his energy flowing from it.

"Ah have lain with thee and loved thee.

"Ah love thee.

"Ye can hurt me, lady."

She couldn't speak for a moment, but managed to stammer, "I won't hurt you, Sam. I'll *never* hurt you. I love you."

She wrapped herself around him and caressed him until he dropped into sleep.

Veronica sat up, moving carefully so he didn't awaken. This was the man she wanted, that she'd been searching for her entire life. Who knew everything about her and loved her anyway. Who was a lover beyond imagination. Who was good and kind.

Oh, God. She would betray him. She rocked back and forth, seeking something to help her. Some anchor. Some power greater than her insanity.

She cast about for something. The image of her teacher came to her. Sam had sketched a Buddha on the wall by their bed. He'd been carving a bas relief of the Buddha when she had called him a thief.

She dropped her forehead to the cave's stone floor. "Shri. Shri Rinpoche. Help me." He was there as powerfully as he had been when he was alive.

"Oh, Shri. Help me." She lay at his feet. "Help me."

He's dead because of me, she thought. Oh, God. I betrayed him like all of them. He got close to me and died. She felt herself spinning off an edge, entering freefall.

Do you think you are so powerful? His silent voice sounded as if he were there. I was destined to die at the hands of the general, just as he was destined to kill me. Nothing you could have done would have stopped it. No person can stop the death of another, or change its place or time even an instant. You must understand that, my beauty.

What do I do, Shri? How do I keep from wrecking this?

He laughed. His voice sounded deeper than it had in life. It felt as though it was coming from the stone walls. You need to learn discipline, beauty, his voice said. You need to learn control. You need to apply your warrior skills to your mind. You need to clean out your soul. His voice was kind and gentle, yet a steel sword.

Shri continued: You must renounce who you were. Renounce every part of your life that caused you pain. Walk away from it. Do not go back and pick it up again.

And you must obey him as though he were I. He is your teacher in life, and your husband. Obey his commands. Please him as you would please me.

Now, meditate.

She sat up in the cross-legged position he had shown her, plummeting into blue-black darkness. No sound, no visions, nothing. The light between her eyes came, a four-pointed star pulsating light. The lights up her spine began spinning. Her breath softly moved in and out of her relaxed mouth. All these, she had felt before.

The intensity of this meditation, she hadn't felt. The substance. The being. She boiled in it, cooked in it. It was Satchitananda: Existence. Awareness. Bliss. God.

She disappeared into it.

When she returned from the void, she began what she had to do. Sam slept deeply. The tools he had used to carve lay on the floor. A sharp knife was among them.

She picked up the knife and raised it.

25

When she was finished, she put the knife down and picked up Sam's shirt from the floor. She put it on, then slipped into the main part of the cave. Everyone was still asleep. She walked across the cave and opened the storage bin. Its track system had been recharged the day before. She used the control and spun the canisters until the one with her belongings in it was in the front. She began pulling out everything she owned.

Everyday clothes, ball gowns, furs, and jewels. A service of imperial china taken from the Tsar's palace, sterling silver for forty with all the extra pieces. Linens and candelabras to set up a new empire. When she was done, everything, down to her underwear and shoes, was arrayed before the container.

She stood apart from it, free.

"Veronica," Henry's deep voice announced his presence. He was the first to wake up. He gawked when he saw her. "What happened to your hair? You've cut it off."

"Mom! What did you do? What's all this stuff?" Jeremy was up next.

"I'll answer your questions. Wait until everyone's here."

They came out of their caves and the adobe buildings, one by one, registering surprise at her hair and her things laid all around.

Sam appeared, wearing the pants to his uniform and looking puzzled.

"I want to thank all of you for being my friends. I went through a trial last night and came through whole, with the assistance of . . ." she faltered.

"Sam of Emily, your husband," Sam stepped in. "She is ma wife. Ah take the lady as ma wife."

She fought back tears. He'd accepted her. "And I take you for my husband, Sam.

"He helped me a great deal last night. But I had an experience of my meditation teacher this morning. What I'm doing now came from him, not from Sam. Sam isn't telling me to do this.

"To be who I want to be, I need to separate myself from the person I was. I need to give up vanity and pride in my looks and possessions. I need to be a different person. The only way I can do it is like this." She indicated her hair.

She'd cut it off with the knife. It was very short and a rough job at best. She stood wearing only Sam's shirt. Veronica indicated all the things arrayed around the camp. "This is everything I've got in the world. I'm giving it to you. I'm giving you the weapons, as well. To be held jointly. They're very dangerous; you need to be careful. So, you can take whatever you want. And there's a whole lot of gold in the container. We brought it to back a new currency."

"Wait," Sam said. "Ah am your husband. By the law of the village, all you own is mine. Ah will say what you give away." He said it with a tinge of the Voice, just a suggestion of power, not a command.

She agreed immediately. "All right, Sam. Pick what you want, and the others can have what's left."

"Ah will keep all the gold." Sam took things she'd never expect. Like a palace-sized sterling candelabra. Two of her fur coats. Ball gowns. The jewelry. Place settings for ten of the sterling flatware and china. And all her everyday clothes and shoes. Plus her lingerie. He examined the lacy under things with great interest.

"You should not give away the weapons. You should hold them, and teach us how to use them. You will be their caretaker, for all of us."

She agreed and then spoke to Jeremy. "We owned a lot of property all over the world. I don't know if we can ever get it back, but I'm giving it to you, Jeremy."

Sam interrupted again. "Nay, lady. Share it with the three of us, you, me and Jeremy. You don't know how many children we will have. We may need it one day."

"All right, Sam. The last thing is—I am no longer Veronica Piermont Edgarton. I sever all ties with that person. She is not me and her past is not my past.

"I was trying to think of what I'd like to be called. I love it when Sam calls me 'lady.' And I have a name that no one knows. I always thought it too . . . sweet, or nice to fit me. But I am sweet and nice."

She smiled, eyes glistening. "I'm going to go by my middle name. It's always been part of me, Grace. I'd like to be called Lady Grace. Or just Grace, if you want. I don't want to be a Lady, like royalty. I want to be a lady, a good woman that you can trust.

"So that's it, please help yourselves."

After some balking, they did. Lena never had had good china and silver. The remaining Imperial Russian tableware did the trick. "But everyone can borrow it if you're having a formal affair."

James made off with a couple of ball gowns and a spectacular feather boa. "I've always wanted a Dior."

"Feel free to wear it whenever you wish, James. It's time that people were who they really are," Grace said.

Sam watched her, proud and relieved. What she did was part of the tradition of the village. When a person needed to be free of a bad past, he or she gave away everything and took a new name.

His ancestor Sam Baahuhd brought Emily into the shelter naked, with nothing of her old life, not even her name. When he healed her, she became the love of his life.

What wasn't told outside the line of Emily was that she had been with many men before Sam, using them. Nor was it told that she was a killer and torturer for the feds. She had been very dangerous. When Sam Baahuhd healed her, everything changed.

The lady came to him, smiling. "Did I do the right thing?"

"Yes, lady. Lady Grace." He kissed her.

PART TWO

26

The group sat in a circle on the cliff. Jeremy's printouts of the underground shelter's interior were laid out before them.

"I would like nothing better than going over there and wasting those bastards," Grace said. "But the bottom line is: We don't have what it takes to mount an assault on the shelter and liberate those who can be saved. We're not soldiers. I'm the only one who's trained, and I've just been frozen for who knows how long. The rest of you are emaciated. We'll have to march many miles, fully armed, carrying food, water, and medical supplies for ourselves and the people we hope to rescue.

"Or let's say we somehow win the battle and get them out. And who are 'them'? All of Sam's people, the disabled ones? Or just the children? Or both? Some are going to be sick. Some dying. We'll have to care for them. Where? Here? How do we get them back here? If we can't get them back here, we'll have to care for them near the shelter. Where?"

"Grace, I need to say something," James said. "Why do we have to save them? Most of the people we saw in those pictures will never be able to take care of themselves." He shot a glance at Sam. "Sorry, Sam. But that's the truth."

Sam opened his mouth as though he were going to speak, but Mel beat him to it. "James, you saw the photos. Don't you think that we have a moral obligation to try to rescue whoever we can? Sam Big raping that guy did it for me. That's *wrong*."

"Yeah, it's wrong. But it's not like he hasn't done it before. What good does it do if we end up getting fucked over ourselves?"

"James, you're just like you were on the golden planet. Figuring out ways to suck up and avoid fighting for what's right."

Henry raised his hand. "Stop it, boys. There's something to be said for trying to get along, and there's something to be said for fighting when you have to."

"We don't have to, is what I'm saying," James replied. "We can stay here and lie low."

"And act like chickens the rest of our lives," Mel retorted.

"Maybe it's not cowardice, Mel," said Grace. "Maybe it's facing the facts. Let's talk about inside the shelter. We saw the photos of the Bigs. They're horrible. So's the shelter. It's going to be crawling with parasites, bacteria, you name it. Does the sanitation work, Sam?"

"The part that works is good."

"But not all of it works. It's a swamp of filth and disease. What was that growing on you when we found you?"

"It was the flour, lady. The white disease."

"Fungus and mildew. He had big patches of it. That's what the people we rescue will have. The underground shelter is too filthy to use as a field hospital. We'll have to bring tents—but we have those. And cots. And penicillin and drugs. Our antibiotics are all that's between us and the germs and microbes of this world. We may need those supplies ourselves. I know this is hard to hear, Sam. Can we afford to take in the people in the shelter? Assuming we can rescue them. Can we feed and clothe and rehabilitate them when we don't have food for ourselves?" She looked around the group. "Anybody have anything to add?"

"OK. What you and James say is true. Rescuing Sam's people is a stretch. But if we don't go, that doesn't make the Bigs go away," Mel said. "We all had that nightmare of that monster searching for us. If we wait, they'll come out and find us. When they find us, they'll sit under our cliff until we run out of supplies."

"How do you feel, Henry? Lena?" Grace stepped in.

Lena looked torn. "I don't know, Grace. I was for marching over there and saving Sam's people—the children, at least. But when you lay it out logically, I can't see how we can do it. Those Bigs . . . How can we fight them?"

"And how do we not fight them?" Henry said.

"We're damned if we go and damned if we don't," Grace replied. "If I had six weeks, I could turn myself back into a soldier. Maybe I could do something with you, too. But we don't. Sam's been here for," she counted on her fingers, "four nights?" Can that be true, she thought. Only four nights? Her life had totally changed in those nights. "But that also means that his people, the disabled ones, haven't been fed for four days and nights. Right, Sam?"

"Aye." He looked down.

"Do they have any supplies?"

"Some water and food."

"That's still cutting it close. It will take us a day to get there, at least. If we had vehicles or trained horses, we could do it. But we don't. We have lightweight automatic rifles and machine guns. We can carry those. Have any of you shot automatic weapons?" Jeremy raised his hand. "Two of us. Not good. It's not target shooting. Do the Bigs know how to shoot, Sam?"

"No."

"They don't shoot that you know. By the time we get there, they might have broken into the general's stores. They may have the heaviest firepower you can imagine out on the front lawn where they can practice with it. Has anyone noticed smoke over there?"

They turned and looked. Jeremy got up with some field glasses and peered at the eastern horizon carefully. "Nothing, Mom."

"Things look bleak," Mel said.

"Very bleak, Mel. Do you know what the general would do?" Grace made eye contact with everyone again.

"What?"

"He'd shoot a missile or three over there and blow up the shelter and everyone in it. The problem would be solved in minutes. We have missiles. I can have them ready in an hour. No one will suffer any more and the Bigs will be neutralized."

Blank faces looked back at her.

"I didn't talk about the possibility that we might lose if we fight. We have to consider that."

"What do *you* want to do, Grace?" Henry asked.

"I think we should shoot the missiles and be done with it."

Sam pulled away as though she'd struck him.

Ellie had been silent, studying the pictures of the underground. She sat apart from the others, tearing into barbecued fish. A pile of bones lay next to her. Her eyes looked a bit odd, larger and more slanted than usual, and her pupils might have been slightly elongated.

"We will save the babies," Ellie said in a matter-of-fact tone. Grace jumped. Ellie's voice sounded almost like Sam's. A little deeper. She had heard that voice before, but couldn't place it. Jeremy had told her how well Ellie could mimic voices, but she wouldn't have believed it without hearing it.

Ellie's words struck Grace, reverberating inside her. Although she couldn't say exactly why, she realized that they should save the babies. That voice was compelling. She had to do what it said. As she thought about it, she realized that they would rescue those kids if it was the last thing they did.

"Sam, can you tell us where your people are?" Grace and the others studied the photos, "I can see these holes that you and other diggers have made. Are these tunnels, or are there rooms inside?"

Sam's eyes widened when he heard Ellie speak. She had the Voice and had used it to change the others' minds. Where did she get it? And whose Voice? That wasn't hers. His mind raced.

"Sam?" Grace said.

"Some are tunnels, and some are rooms." He pointed to the holes around the floor plan. "There are three people here and four here. This is two rooms with five people. I put water pipes to them from the fields. When it rains, the water flows. It comes in for the fields, and goes to them through the pipes." It hadn't rained since Sam had been gone.

"OK. Your people number fifteen, including you," Grace said. "There could be as many as thirty women. And the eleven children you've saved. That and thirty-four Bigs, makes ninety people. The shelter was built for one hundred. Could there really be that many more Bigs?"

"The Bigs could have had many children, some may already be Big. But I don't think so. The underground is dying. The fields don't make as much food. No one works, just me. Children don't grow up. The Bigs take them from the nursery and kill them."

"Why would they kill their own children?" Mel said.

Sam said it before he could stop himself. "They eat them." Eyes opened wide and people pulled away.

"They're cannibals?"

"Ay. The sheep and chickens sickened and died long ago. The fields don't yield. I tend them, but few others do. I can't make enough food." Sam held his hands up like he was holding the group off. "There's no meat. We are dying. No one wants to do it, but we must to stay alive."

"You're telling us that you've killed and eaten children?" Mel looked like he wanted to pull out a machine gun and shoot Sam.

"No. The Bigs do that. I save them. I have hidden eleven children. They're not in your pictures. No one can find them but me." He poked at the floor plan. "They're here, next to the growing fields. I built a room for them above the fields. I put water to them and I feed them when I tend the crops. The Bigs don't know. I save children; I don't kill them."

"You have *eleven* kids hidden away?"

"Yes. They are the best of the village. All the Arthurs and Sams from lines without the disease. They are good babies."

Grace stared at him. "Sam, I'll just say it. Do you and your people eat human flesh?"

"Yes, lady. The dead, only. There's no food, lady." He bent over, face contorting, begging her to understand.

"You don't kill anyone?"

"I don't, lady. That is wrong. But I wanted to live. I had to do it to live," he moaned. "If you don't want me here, I will leave. But please, save my children. They are the last of the village. The good part."

Sam stood up and went to the ladder. "I'll stay down below and you can tell me if you want me to leave." And he climbed down.

Grace looked at the group. "They're baby-eating cannibals."

"Not Sam, Mom," Jeremy said. "He saved babies and children. He kept them from being eaten. He wouldn't kill anyone."

"How do you know?" Lena barked. "You've known him for four days. Maybe he's waiting for you to fatten up."

"I don't think Sam would do that, Mother. He's the most amiable young man I've met," Henry said. "I've heard many stories of people surviving by eating the bodies of their companions. The Donner Party. Remember them, from the history books? They got stuck in the snow crossing the Sierras one winter. The survivors did so by eating those who died. It's happened many times when people face starvation."

"Sam doesn't look like he's starving," James said. "He looks pretty damned healthy."

"You should have seen him when I found him," Jeremy replied. "He looked terrible. He was gray and had fungus all over him and that eye in his stomach. It was the people from Ellie's world that made him look good. I bet all those people down there look like concentration camp victims."

"Well, they didn't eat each other in the camps around New York City," said Mel.

"Actually, they probably did," Grace said. "It's been a problem in death camps as long as they've existed. People go mad from hunger. Listen, I know Sam better than any of you. He saved my life. He put up the solar panels for us. He put the ladder down. And he's got eleven kids he cares about dying in a hole right now. Why don't we think about *them?*"

The words sounded good coming out of her mouth, but she knew it would take some time before she felt the same about Sam. Maybe forever.

27

He had seemed too good to be true, Grace thought, and he was. Her new husband was a cannibal. Would she eat human flesh to keep herself alive? She imagined biting into a nice thigh, or a liver. Tearing someone apart to eat him.

People have done worse. The general was worse. He killed but didn't eat his prey. He raped and destroyed. Is that worse than eating those he killed?

But Sam had eaten people. He *ate* people.

"Jeremy, can I look at all those images again?" She and Jeremy went into the storage container/computer lab. He pulled the pictures of the underground up and they went over them one by one. He blew them up on computer screens all over the room.

"That's just the bare suggestion, Mom," Jeremy said. "You don't get the smells or the sounds. Cut him some slack. I don't think he'd hurt anyone. Remember how scared he was when he got out?"

"Yes, I remember." I remember lying in his arms last night. I remember loving him.

"And none of us are perfect. I mean . . ."

She knew exactly what he meant. She'd fucked half the male

population. How had Sam felt about hearing that? She blushed. He had faith that she could change. Could she have faith in him?

He was sitting by the river, watching the water flow by. His head was bowed and his shoulders slumped.

"Hi," she said as she sat next to him. "How are you?"

"Not good. I'm sorry, lady. I didn't want to tell you. If you dinna want me, I will leave."

"No, you won't go anywhere. I need to ask you some questions, though."

"Yes."

"You didn't kill anyone to eat them?"

"No."

"You knew it was wrong?"

"Yes, lady. But I wanted to live."

"When did they start doing that in the underground?"

"It's always been that way, since the bad times started generations ago. Hunger is always there. There is no meat. You must see what it's like."

"I don't have to worry about your killing me or anyone else and eating us?"

"No, lady. Never."

"Have you killed anyone?"

He looked away. "No more than you."

She pulled back. She had killed the general. Was she a killer? Yes. Was he? Yes.

"Do you want to tell me about it?"

"No, lady. I could not bear it. Please." His anguish was so intense that she backed off.

"I need to ask you about something else. The children you have hidden, are they yours? Did you father them?"

He looked incredulous. "My children? They are mine because I saved them. They are the last of the Arthurs and the good Sams. I saved them."

"I'm sorry, Sam. I'm a little crazy. You don't have a pack of kids somewhere, do you? And a few other wives?"

"No. I have no children. You are my wife. I will take no other wife."

"Have you been with other women down there, Sam?"

"No, lady. I told you." He looked nonplussed. "I keep the Commands. I have no children of my own."

She laughed, suddenly relieved. "Oh, Sam. What was I thinking? Quizzing you about your sexual history given *my* past?" She slipped her arm in his. "Let's go up top and finish the meeting. I want to save those kids."

"It's OK?"

"It's OK by me. If the others have anything to say about it, I'll take my missiles and leave." He looked puzzled. "Don't worry, Sam, you did what you did and you're not going to do it again. We won't talk about it anymore."

28

"I believe Sam when he says he *and the others*, the non-Bigs, did what they did do stay alive," Grace said, looking into the eyes of each member of the reconvened group. "I ask you to give him the benefit of the doubt until you see what they were up against for yourselves. Until then, you don't have to worry. He's sleeping with me; he'll eat me first.

"Despite what I said earlier about the impossibility of our task, I want to save those kids. I also want to neutralize the Bigs. We need to vote on what we are going to do. Time is of the essence. And we need to appoint a commander. We cannot run a campaign by committee. Nominations are open."

"Grace, you're the only one who can do it," Henry said. "How can we sit here and let children die? Let's take a vote." The vote was unanimous.

"Now that you're our chief, what do we do?" Henry said.

"We contemplate. We need to marshal our resources," she said. "We need to think about every asset we've got. Stuff we have going for us that isn't guns and ammo. What skills do we have, and how can we use them now? We need to get there with supplies and weapons.

We need to break into the underground, kill the Bigs, and save the kids. We need to take care of them and get back. Sam, you know most about the place. What do we need?"

"We need to get there," he said.

"We need a bunch of trucks," James said.

"Sorry. Don't have them. Here's a bigger question: How do we get in once we're there? How many levels are there in the shelter, Jeremy?"

"Seven, with six foot-thick steel doors between them. They were strong enough to withstand the nuclear war."

"To rescue anyone from the main shelter, we'd have to fight through six impregnable doors. Down how many feet, Jeremy?"

"Two hundred and eighty feet."

They looked at each other.

"It's impossible, Mom, unless they open the doors for us. There is the hole for the canaries that they shoved Sam out. That has six locked doors, too."

"Sam, can we get the kids from the outside of the shelter?"

"Yes, lady. By digging. They are by the solar fields, but outside the shelter. They're here, in a room here." He pointed at the printouts, indicating an area outside the shelter's concrete shell. "It's much higher than the fields."

"How did you get them there, Sam? That's not in the original plan," Jeremy said.

Sam ran his finger along the photo, indicating the shelter's concrete edge. "Many generations of diggers made a tunnel from here." He pointed to a place inside the shelter.

"That's one of the cells where Sam Baahuhd thought we were going to lock up the villagers," said Jeremy.

"Yes. The cells. The villagers were locked up in them, but by each other. A digger broke through the concrete long ago. We kept digging, secretly. We made the tunnel go up, toward the outside."

"Why do the diggers dig, Sam?"

"To keep from going crazy. To do something against the pain here." Sam rubbed his chest. "Sam Baahuhd was the first digger.

Some said he was crazy, he dug so hard. I know he was not. It was all he could do."

Grace blanched, thinking of her dear friend locked in a cement dungeon. "Oh, Sam. That's so awful."

"Yes," he said without inflection. "The tunnel went outside the wall around the fields, and up. We were going to escape through it. We could have dug all the way out many years ago, but we didn't because the computers said the radiation would kill us. What they said never changed." A tiny smile curved his lips.

"Now I know the computers were wrong. But as time went on, fewer of us were strong enough to dig. I am the only one now." He shrugged. "The water for my children comes from the big pipes at the top that go to the main tanks. It flows down to the children's room.

"I thought I could finish the tunnel in my life, dig all the way out, so that we could escape, even if it meant dying from the radiation outside. But when the Bigs took over, I needed to save the children. I made a room for them at the end of the tunnel. I used wood and things I could find to hold up the roof and walls."

"So you dragged those kids through the tunnel and left them there?"

"Yes. In the dark. Alone." His voice broke. "Oh, please. We have to save them."

"We will save the children," Ellie said in that man's voice so like Sam's.

Sam stared at her, mouth a little open.

"We will save them, Ellie, don't worry," Grace said. "And then you brought food and water to them?"

"Yes. I put in a pipe for water and brought them food. I stayed with them as much as I could." Sam's shoulders drooped and his face screwed up into a mask of pain. He looked like he'd dug the whole tunnel himself that afternoon. "Please . . . I can't talk of this."

"OK, Sam. One more question. Any idea how close you were to the surface?" Jeremy asked.

"Close. At the beginning, the tunnel is mostly rock. Now, it's much easier to dig. But the dirt is very heavy in winter. And slippery."

"Take a break, Sam. We'll work on it," Jeremy said. "It sounds like he's digging through clay. The field where the shelter is was once a river valley. There's a deep layer of clay over the bedrock, then lots of topsoil. That's why the estate's garden was so great. Might be easy to dig out the rest of the way. On the other hand, clay can be very unstable. The roof could cave in."

Sam groaned. "Aye."

"So we bring shovels," Grace remarked.

James mumbled, "And a backhoe." He smirked, shaking his head.

"Cynicism doesn't help, James. Though if you can find a backhoe, that would be great."

"Mom! I may know where one is! Remember that I told you on my first night here, I found the equipment barn and slept there? It was underground, totally covered with dirt. I found a pipe sticking out of the ground and dug down to the barn's roof. I pulled a piece of the tin roof up and got in. There was equipment in it—tons of equipment. And barrels of stuff, maybe fuel. The plastic fuel we use wouldn't explode."

"Would the equipment still work? We don't know how long it's been there."

"I don't know."

"Anybody?

"Car batteries die when they sit less than six months," Henry said. "The vehicles are probably frozen solid with rust. The rubber hoses will need replacing. The crud in the fuel is probably solid in the bottom of the tanks . . . "

"Do we have any mechanics among us?"

"I can change a car's batteries," Mel volunteered.

"I watched my granddad do any number of things with the equipment on our farm," Lena said. "I watched him real good."

"OK, these are assets we didn't know we had. This is what I wanted to get out," Grace said. "The barn is near the shelter. It has water.

I think we should use that location as our headquarters. We'll spend the first night there. We can check out the machine barn and see what's in it. If we could get there tonight, that would be best."

"Only thing, Mom. I couldn't find the pipe the second night when I came back with Sam."

"But you're sure you were somewhere near it?"

"Yeah."

"OK. That's good enough. Sam, what are they afraid of in the shelter? What will make them stay inside?"

"The hant, lady. They are afraid of the hant, Shack."

Grace thought back to the story Lena had told her about the dog that had killed itself to protect Eliana and had been a powerful protector of the village in its last days. Grace had thought the story was nonsense. "The little dog that died to protect Ellie is protecting the village *now?*"

"The village of Sam Baahuhd, lady. The hant knows that what is inside is not what Sam wanted. It sends terrible thunder and lightning storms. Even the Bigs lie on the ground and scream when they come."

"They think thunderstorms are caused by the ghost? If we could get a thunderstorm going, we could scare the crap out of them. And keep them inside. Do you know how to contact the haunt, Sam?"

"No, lady." His eyes widened talking about it. He shot a look at Eliana, who was stuffing down roast fish with a sharp expression on her face. "Only the angel could reach him. He became a hant to save her."

"How can she do that?"

"I don't know. He lives by the village. We are here."

"We'll work on that." Grace glanced at Ellie, who seemed oddly irritable. Like she might bite. Why was she eating so much? And fish? She was a vegetarian. She'd found all sorts of plants to eat by the river. "Ellie, if you can think of any way of contacting Shaq, go for it. Tell him our plans and that we need to keep the Bigs inside."

"Rain will also make the water flow to my people," Sam said. "More will live if it rains."

Ellie kept eating. She hummed, an unpleasant vibration. She didn't answer.

"What we really could use is a couple dozen well-trained horses. They would be our greatest asset, aside from the weapons. Can you train them fast, Lena?"

"I can try. Do you have a lariat?"

"What's a lariat?"

"It's a stiff rope with a loop at one end. You throw it to catch horses or cattle. Or anything that needs catching," Lena explained.

"I don't think we have a lariat, but we've got halters and lead ropes." Grace looked hopeful. "Will those work?"

"If I can get a wild horse to stand still long enough for me to put it on." Lena frowned. "This isn't going to be so easy. We don't have any corrals or places to snub them down so we can sack them out. I don't have Grandpa here to help me. I guarantee you, they're not going to be happy when I put saddles on them, assuming I can get that far. And riding them will be another matter. I think I might go 'splat' if I go off now."

The wild horses had been milling around below the cliff since they'd been there. They'd take off for a while, then return. They didn't seem all that wild, other than moving away when a human approached them.

"Just because they look tame, doesn't mean they are tame," Lena warned. The group peered glumly over the rock face.

"Mom, I'm going to search the satellites. Maybe there's something there that will help us."

"Do what you can." Grace thought his search silly, but if anyone could find something useful with a computer, Jeremy could. "Do you have a computer to take with us that can relay between the shelter and our field location? And to the satellites?"

"Sure. Let me work on it."

"Let's start getting ready to go. I'll work on ordnance. We have special clothing, courtesy of the general. Commando suits with all the trimmings. I've got the most advanced bulletproof everything on the planet. We'll look like medieval knights—actually, not too much. It's all very lightweight. But we have helmets. Night glasses. I'll go looking for them. And start packing the weapons."

"What if they don't shoot, lady?" Sam asked. "What if they fight us, hand-to-hand? They are very fast. I can show you. What if the weapons get in the way?"

They turned to him. How could a wrestler stop an armed warrior in Russian commando clothing?

"OK, show us, Sam. I'll be the warrior. Take me down. Let me go get dressed first." Grace slipped into the munitions container.

"I'm here," she said, emerging in the circle. No one had seen her. Her face and head were covered with a black sock-like mask. It flowed smoothly into a black suit that covered her completely. Her molded cloth shoes were soundless and supple gloves disguised her hands. She was like a black shadow.

"Grace! How did you get here?" Henry asked, followed by exclamations from the others.

"You'd better wonder about that, because if this were a battle situation, you'd be dead. There's a rear entrance to the container. I used it. *Always look for the rear entrance. Expect the unexpected.*" She began stretching her legs prior to the contest. "I'm sloppy now. Let's put some mats out so no one gets hurt."

They got their bed mats and arranged them in a square.

Grace and Sam stood on the mats, facing each other. She feinted. He dropped into a wrestler's stance with a fluid, graceful motion that was almost feminine, an alert, soft look on his face. She took a step toward him, hands raised in a karate position.

He grabbed a hand, spun her toward him, and had her on her back in an instant, his elbow to her throat. He made sure that everyone saw she was completely helpless, then he let her go.

"I am sorry, lady, if I hurt you."

She was surprised more than anything. "I have a black belt, Sam. How did you do that?"

"I am fast, lady. I used to wrestle with them."

"Are they faster than you?"

"No, but stronger. I cannot beat them now."

"Holy shit," said Mel. "He could make mincemeat out of us. And there's only one of him."

"Should we even try this?" Henry asked.

"I don't know," Grace said. "The general's solution is looking better to me again. If we could aim a pinpoint strike and miss where the children are—you said they're outside the shelter, Sam?"

"Yes."

"But can anyone really do a pinpoint that's that well aimed? Isn't a 'surgical strike' sort of point and splatter?" Mel asked.

"It would be hard. Especially with equipment that's been sitting as long as ours has. That's another factor we need to consider. The farm equipment's hoses are sure to be shot. What about the missiles' wiring?"

"That is not the worst, lady," Sam looked dejected. "Sam Big has the Voice. All the Bigs have the Voice."

"What is the voice?" James asked.

"What is the Voice?" he replied in a voice so similar to James's that it could have been his. "Everyone in the underground has the Voice. We can sound like other people, and make noises like things. We can make people do what we want with it. But Sam Big has the Big Voice. He can make you think your ma is calling you. Or your love. Or that they're hurt and screaming for help. He can use the Voice to make you come out, even if you know he's there and will kill you. The Voice is his most terrible weapon."

"SAM OF EMILY, COME HERE, YOU FILTHY RUTTIN' PIG. GET BACK HERE OR I'LL PULL YER GUTS OUT YER ASS."

The words cut through them like a lash. They turned toward their source. Ellie sat, vibrating with energy, holding another fish. She smiled. Her teeth seemed very sharp.

"That was his Voice," Sam said, wild-eyed. "Sam Big's Voice. He will do that if he catches me. I don't know how he sent his Voice here."

Ellie smiled. "Me," she squeaked. "I have Voice."

"How did you get the Voice, Ellie?" Grace asked. She knew all about the Voice, having heard Sam Baahuhd use it to bend people's wills back in the old days.

"From Sam Baahuhd. Meet Sam when I on Earth first time. We hold hands. Hearts open up. I know all him; he know all me. He give me Voice." Ellie frowned. "Voice no work on gold planet, only here, Sam's home."

"*That's* whose voice that was!" Grace exclaimed. "Sam Baahuhd's. I knew I recognized it." Grace was thrilled. "Did you use it earlier?"

"We will save the children," she said in that masculine tone. "It does not matter if I use Voice. *We will save the babies.*"

"Well, of course we're going to save the children." Grace smiled, "I think we just found a powerful new asset. Henry, keep that girl in fish."

29

"Mom! Everybody! I think I've got something that will help us tame the horses." Jeremy called them into his computer lab/storage container. He had the same images coming up on all his screens. "These are feeds. They're footage sent by a television network from one station to another. It's a way of moving data.

"This wasn't a network program; it was a privately produced program, and this is really raw footage. They were probably sending it somewhere for editing. This was faster than shipping it if they were behind schedule.

"I searched for ways to train horses fast and found this. 'How to Train a Wild Horse in an Hour.'"

"No one can do that," Lena said. The group agreed.

"*He* can." A figure appeared on the screen, a tall man with long braids and hat with a high crown and wide brim. He wore a western shirt, and long jeans that showed only the toes of his cowboy boots. He had the suggestion of a belly. He stood in front of a fancy two-story barn. Tall pines surrounded that. Corrals filled in the corners of the screen.

"He's an American Indian," Jeremy said. The group focused on the screen. None of them had seen an Indian. Before Earth's end, the

Indians had claimed their own country, which ran from Canada to Mexico down the center of the United States. It was a kingdom, really; they controlled cross-country shipping. "Listen."

"Hi, there, y'all, I'm Bud Creeman, the Horse Manager. I'm here at Will Duane's ranch in Montana with some of my friends. We're doing this film as a benefit for the Wild Horse Rescue Network." The camera focused on his face. His brown face was not too good-looking, but good-looking enough. His expression was earnest and kind.

"First off, I want to tell you that you're out of your friggin' mind if you do any of the stuff I'm going to show by yourself . . ."

"Cut." A voice spoke from outside the screen. "Mr. Creeman, please stick to the script. We're trying to increase wild horse adoptions, remember?" The screen went blank for a second, and then came back on. Bud was there, looking exasperated.

"I think the people should know that what I'm doing is very dangerous and only professionals should attempt it. Training a wild horse is not a do-it-yourself project."

"Cut." Blank screen.

"Look, you send this film anywhere you want and edit it however you want. I'm going to tell it like it is. Horses are dangerous, folks, and if you think you can train them by yourself, you're nuts, unless you're a professional or pretty damn good amateur.

"Having said that, let's go to the round pen."

"Jeremy, can you stop the recording. How will this help us?" Grace said. "He says we can't do it."

"Watch him, Mom. He shows how, exactly. There's more you have to see. Plus, you won't believe when this was made."

"When?"

"2015. Way before the Second Revolution."

"My God, how did you find it?"

"It's been floating out there all this time, bouncing off satellites. I sent out a search on horse training and got it. This guy was famous back then. He's called the Horse Manager. He trains executives how to be better managers by working with horses. He works for someone named Will Duane, who's the richest man in the world. Or he was. That's his ranch." He turned on the player.

A camera in a helicopter panned over a vast forest interspersed with meadows. It showed a log mansion to rival any estate Grace's family ever owned. The mansion was surrounded by lawns and gardens and had a pool in back. Just a glimpse of it was given, then the camera moved to the perfectly groomed barnyard and ranch buildings.

"It's a palace, Mom."

"It's beautiful, Jeremy. The estate here didn't come close to it." Grace was captivated. "Let's watch."

A tall man with white hair walked across the stable yard toward the barn, gesturing at the camera to get away from him. A voice on the film said, "Will Duane. That's as close to him as we'll get. He's a hermit."

The camera settled on a big corral with a bunch of horses milling around in it. Next to it was a round corral with solid walls that looked about eight feet high. They were tilted out a little.

Bud stood outside the pen and said, "OK. You need a round pen to do this. This is the best, safest way to put a horse under saddle. Forget breaking . . . and don't use that word in the title," he said to someone off screen.

"I'm just going to go do this thing; you can watch me. First off, if you want to train a wild horse, you need to have a wild horse. We've got about thirty of them here, brought in from the herd." He walked over to the corral and picked up a lariat that was hanging on a post.

"Since they want me to do this in an hour, I'm going to rope a horse." He walked around the herd, looking at the animals. "I like this mare, that bay one. I like a dark horse, but what I like about her is the depth through her heart. Gives the heart and lungs room."

The horses were watching him carefully. He took one step toward the mare, did something with his hands, and the loop of the lariat was around her neck. She pulled back and he ran with her, ending up next to her against the corral wall. The other horses moved away, and he started talking to her, speaking a language none of them understood. An Indian language, they realized.

She dropped her head and he touched her, whispering to her. She seemed to be mesmerized. "I'm just going to scoot her right over to the round pen before she realizes she's caught."

The mare was in the round pen running around the outer edge with the lariat removed from her neck. "I'm just letting her blow off a little steam." She stopped and he backed away. The horse moved toward him, head down. Then he was touching her all over, talking to her.

"When you step into the round pen, you step into horse time. I'll give this mare all the time she needs. You need to be able to touch every part of a horse. Otherwise, you throw the saddle on and it hits somewhere that ain't been touched before, you got a rodeo."

He enchanted the group. "He knows so much. Look at that," Jeremy said. Bud moved in a smooth, almost slinky way. He was riding the mare in thirty minutes, walking around the round pen.

"I'm riding her with just the halter. She needs to learn how to stop and turn, how to pay attention to me." He was turning her as he talked, from one direction in the pen to the other. "OK, boys, open the gates." The pen opened. "She's gonna get a little silly when I walk through the gates. That's because she can't see what's out there. A lion could be behind that gate, according to her."

He walked her in and out a few times until she did it with no nervousness, and then walked down the driveway and around the yard.

Jeremy stopped the player. "See what I mean?"

"He made it look so easy," Mel said in awe.

"He's an expert," Lena added. "*We* couldn't do that. And besides, we don't have a round pen, or any of that. We don't even have a lariat."

"I've got saddles, Lena," Grace said. "We brought eight. The general thought we'd have to ride across Mongolia. We have a basic horse setup, halters, everything we'd need. But I agree with you. We don't know how to do that.

"I don't see how this helps us, Jeremy."

"Lady. I would like to try to tame a horse," Sam said. "Did you see how he touched the horse? I can do that. I can calm people. I have not touched animals, but I would like to try."

"I'd like you to, too, Sam. But in the right place with the right equipment and facilities. We don't have anything. Besides, where are the horses?"

"Right below the cliff," James said. "Ellie drove them here. They're just standing there."

"Ellie did that? How?"

"Beats me. They're down there and they're not moving."

"What do we do now?"

"Get the saddles out and see what we can do," Grace said. "Lena, you and Henry and Sam are the horse detail. I have to get all the medical stuff and ordnance ready. I can't do horses, too."

Lena, Sam, and Henry looked doubtful.

"There's more, you guys. You have to see the rest," Jeremy started the broadcast again. "He can do way more than train horses."

The screen showed the same scene of the mountain ranch. A motorcycle drove up to the barnyard and a lean man got off. He pulled off his helmet and looked at the camera.

"Oh, my God," said Grace, Lena, and James. "He is *gorgeous*. Who is he?"

Bud was speaking on the screen again: "Well lookee here, folks, it's my ol' buddy Wes Silverhorse straight from shootin' his latest movie. How did we lure you out here in the woods, my ol' friend?" Bud sauntered over to him.

"Cut the crap, Bud. You know we're shooting a film on the other side of the ranch. I'm getting paid more than the Queen of England to be here."

"I'm glad to see you, too, Wes. It's been a while."

"Cut." The screen when blank.

"Hi, Wes. Great to see you." Bud shook Wes's hand. He turned to the camera. "Here's the world's favorite Indian actor."

"Not just Indian, Bud. I'm bigger than that."

"Cut." Blank.

"Hi. This is the man who used to be my best friend until he went to Hollywood and got a swelled head." Bud's hat flew off. No one saw what knocked it off. "He's also the sweetest tempered darlin' . . . " Bud flew back about five feet. "Knock it off, Wes, or I'll pop you one."

Jeremy stopped the images. "Did you see that? He knocked his hat off without moving. And he shoved him the same way. Keep watching."

"Go ahead and pop me, Bud. I'd love if you tried."

"Are you in the role now, Wes?"

"Yes, Bud. I won't come down 'til we're done shooting."

"What are you playing, a psychopathological maniac?"

"A serial killer. An out-of-his-mind, raving, covert ops, military anti-terrorist gone bad. I just finished six months of guerilla training with the Special Forces and a couple martial arts experts so I could do the part. I'm finally in role and, thanks to you, I have come over here and can train horses the nice way."

"He's got guerilla and martial arts training! And he's in shape!" Jeremy practically shouted. "And they can fight, watch . . ."

"Oh, good." Bud shouted over to the corral, "Run hard, you poor creatures."

"Shut up, Bud." Wes looked at him and Bud slid back a few feet.

"One more time, Wesley, I'm going to pop you good. I couldn't do it when Grandfather was around, but he's gone. So you got no protection, buddy boy."

"Hey, Bud. Do you know what my face is insured for?" Wes stuck his face out. "Millions and millions."

"You know, Wes, I really liked you before you got famous. You used to be a nice guy."

"When I was a nice guy, I lived on a broken-down ranch using equipment that should have hit the junk pile before I was born. Our bulldozer came from the dump. I rebuilt it."

"But you don't have to do that anymore, Wes. You went to school. If you weren't an actor, you're still an architect."

"Yeah, right. Sit in an office and take orders . . ."

"See," Jeremy broke in. "He knows about farm equipment."

"But our kind of equipment?" asked Henry.

"Look, could any of us rebuild *any* kind of a bulldozer? And he's an architect. Does anyone know how to build anything?"

"Let's see the rest."

"Hello, boys," Bud and Wes stepped back as a third man entered. They recognized the tall, white-haired man as Will Duane. He was old, but stood erect and had a commanding presence. "Having a friendly discussion, boys?" He smiled into the camera, looking like a white-haired grizzly.

"Whoa, Mom, Look at him," Jeremy said.

"I *am*, Jeremy. He reminds me of myself in a previous life."

"Keep listening, Mom."

"Well, boys, philosophical discussions are nice, but it's my nickel," Will said on the screen. "It's my ranch, my film, my TV station, and my movie. You're both on my salary. Are you getting the drift? Finish the job and get out of here." Will disappeared off camera.

"He does have a way about him, doesn't he?" Bud said. "So what are you going to do, Wesley? We're trying to increase the adoptions of wild horses and raise money ... "

"I thought I'd break a few of those horses, Bud." He indicated the milling herd.

"We don't break them, Wes. We put them under saddle."

"I break them, Bud. I break their hearts."

He walked over to the horse corral and vaulted over the six-foot fence as though it was nothing. He approached a horse in the pen. Blue sparks flew off him. He touched the horse's nose with his hand and it moved away from the group. He had his hands all over it. The horse looked like it was covered with a shining blue blanket. Then he was up on it riding it around.

And on to the next horse. And the next. Throughout the herd. The camera kept rolling.

Only the herd stallion was left. "I saved him for last, since he has an attitude," Wesley said into the mike. The stud reared and pawed the air. Wesley did something, and the horse was on the ground with Wesley sitting on his head. Blue stuff came off his hands like blue gel shaving cream. He got off and the horse stood, shaking its head. Wes leapt on top of him. The horse made a couple of little bucks and began trotting around the corral at Wes's direction. It stopped and turned, bucked. Began to gallop in one direction, then the other, and then started doing complicated maneuvers.

Grace was enthralled. "He's the best horseman I've ever seen. He's got that wild horse doing dressage. Play the rest of it."

"Yeah. You gotta see what happens," Jeremy said.

"Let's see if he can jump." Wes pointed the horse at a six-foot corral fence. The horse flew over it, but Bud went ballistic.

"That horse wasn't ready for that," Bud snapped. "You would *never* do a stunt like that when you were a spirit warrior."

Wes turned red, then white. He spun around like a bull looking for something to charge. A golf cart was in front of him. Jumping off the horse, Wes picked it up and hurled it at Bud. Bud caught it and set it down.

"Hey, Wes, I'm sorry. I shouldn't have said that." Bud lifted his hat and ran his fingers through his hair. "What happened to you wasn't your fault."

Wes deflated, shoulders hunching.

"But you sure can pitch a cart . . ." Bud laughed and Wes finally joined him.

"What was that all about?" Grace asked.

"I just found hints about what they are on the 'net. They're 'spirit warriors' trained by a great shaman named Grandfather. He taught them to do all that stuff. Wesley had some kind of falling out with him and got kicked out. It was a very secret Native American movement.

"But look what he can do, even kicked out," Jeremy said. "They could fight the Bigs!"

"We need them," Grace exclaimed. "We need them *now*."

30

"But they're in 2015," Henry said.

"How can we get them here?" Grace mused. Her mind immediately went to the people of the golden planet. They could do it. She looked around. Everyone else seemed to have the same idea.

"You *can't* be thinking that," Jeremy shouted. "You can't trust them."

"That's true," said Grace. "But they're the only way I can think of to get Bud and Wesley here. Can anyone think of any other way?" They shook their heads. "Do you think we can win without them?" The collective answer was no. "So that leaves us with: Can we control the goldies somehow? Can we keep the upper hand?"

"I don't think so, Mom. Look at what they were going to do to Ellie. Look what they *did* do to her by not sending her food and medicine. They almost killed her. You can't trust them."

"But they didn't actually do anything to Ellie. I mean with . . ." she petered out, looking dismayed.

"We know what you mean, Grace," Henry said. "With James, Mel and me. Once we laid the law down, they backed off and sent us home."

"And they sent doctors for Ellie when she was so sick," Grace added. "Of course, I had to let them know that the whole universe was listening in and could see their cruelty before they did anything."

"So we can control them some. We have already," Mel summarized.

"We can say no to them. We can shame them. What else can we do to control them? Can we bribe them into helping us? What cookies can we offer? What do they like?"

"They like pets. They like stuff. Minerals. Jewelry. Gold. They all wear jewelry all over." said Mel.

"They like style. Fancy hairdos, golden robes, and things like that," James added.

"They like to watch *anything*, the more private the better," Jeremy said.

"That's true," Henry said. "They like watching people live and on their screens. Every single one of them has a screen. They're supposed to be for watching the stars, but they watch anything they can. There's no programming, so they spy on their neighbors. They'd go crazy over a good soap opera."

"Maybe we should give them something different: a dose of violence," Grace said. "Wesley Silverhorse was playing some sort of criminal in the movie he was shooting. A sociopath."

"In that movie, he was the *good* guy," Jeremy responded. "I sampled his films. He made close to a hundred movies, including those he directed. They're brilliant, but so brutal I could barely watch them."

"Ah," said Grace. "How about if we sent some of those movies, and the video we just watched, to the golden planet? Kind of like a teaser? And Bud's horse-training videos, too. What if we offered them exclusive coverage of Bud and Wes and the rest of us saving the children? Material that we control completely. They would have to play our way or get nothing." She looked around. People nodded.

"Do we have anyone who's good with a video camera?"

"I am, Mom."

"You'll be busy. Anyone else?"

"Well, my videos of the NYC Hair Show won awards," James offered. "And I've filmed the major designers' collections, too. I'd be glad to film us." He tilted his head a bit, looking apologetic. "I want to save the children, too."

"OK. You've got a job filming, James.

"Shall we offer exclusive coverage of our entire adventure? They bring us Bud and Wes here from 2015. We film what happens and broadcast it to them at the end. They have to do their part before we can start. No double-crosses possible." Grace was getting excited. "What do you think?"

"I don't think you're asking for enough." Jeremy scowled. "You don't realize that moving people around the universe is no big deal to the goldies. They can do it with a *thought*. With the *shadow* of a thought. They're so advanced it's pitiful. It's not like you're asking anything that will cost them anything or even be hard. And you ought to get everything in writing and still not trust them. Because if there's a way to screw us, they'll do it." Jeremy got up and stalked away.

"But we can't get the Indians here without them, Jeremy," Grace called after him. "Send that entire show to Ellie's planet. And send everything you can about Bud Creeman and Wesley Silverhorse. Then set me up to broadcast."

31

Jeremy was in the computer container downloading Wes Silverhorse movies and sending them to the golden planet when Ellie came to the door.

"We talk, Jeremy?" she said. Her eyes looked huge. Something was wrong.

"Sure, babe. I've got everything set up on automatic. What's the matter?"

"We go our house." She turned and walked toward their ruined adobe casita.

"Sit next me, Jeremy." She sat on their bed and patted the place next to her. Jeremy did as she wished, feeling puzzled. She looked up, through the non-existent ceiling. "This nice house."

"Oh, yeah, baby. Wait until you see how I'm going to fix this place up. I'm going to use part of a space station in the junk pile to make a roof. I'm..."

She held his hand and put it to her cheek. "Jeremy good person."

"Is there something the matter, Ellie?" Her eyes looked weird. Her pupils were long, like a cat's. "Are you OK? Should I get my mom to call that doctor again?"

"No, Jeremy. I fine. I want say I love you. I want you know." Her eyes filled with moisture. Tears were poised to spill over her lower lids.

"I know you love me, Ellie. I love you. I'll always love you. I'll never love anyone else. What's the matter? You're freaking me out."

"Nothing matter, Jeremy. Everything fine. No problem."

"Well, good. I know—you're worried about the battle. Don't worry. We'll be fine. We've got munitions that can . . ."

"No worry, Jeremy." She touched his face with her fingers, tracing the outline of his eyebrows and jaw. "I no worry." The tears breached the ramparts of her lids and flowed down her cheeks. "I never love any person but Jeremy. Never."

"God, El, you're scaring me. What's the matter?"

"No is matter, Jeremy. Is me. How I am."

"What's going on?"

"I want baby *so* bad. You know how much? Bigger than sky. Bigger than ocean. So big." She stroked his head and let her hand flow down his neck to his shoulder. Her eyes remained fixed on his. "I want baby, Jeremy. Save Sam's babies."

"We'll save them. We'll adopt Sam's babies, El. All eleven of them, if you want."

She smiled. "Good. You take care of babies, Jeremy. You good father."

He started to protest, but she kissed him, a kiss that might have said I will love you for eternity or this is as much rapture as a human being can stand. She pulled him down on the bed and his control disappeared. He could never say no to Ellie, could never do anything but please her. He had no defenses against her sweetness and joy. He pressed her to him.

"I love you, El. I love you." He began to undo her clothes, but she stopped him.

"Not now, Jeremy. No can do now."

"Oh, yeah. I'm supposed to be getting ready for that broadcast. Tonight, El? Let's love each other tonight? OK?"

She nodded, yes, but her eyes looked so sad. It was like she was leaving him forever.

"El, are things OK? You're not mad at me, are you?"

"Never mad Jeremy. Love Jeremy." She stroked his face and got up.

Mel's voice intruded, "Hey, Jeremy! Where are you? Your mom's ready to broadcast. Let's go."

He looked at Ellie. "Tonight?"

"*Always*, Jeremy. Always Jeremy and Ellie."

32

The doctor stroked his chin with his long fingers. His eyes narrowed. She was broadcasting again. He stood in the hall of the elders with his fellows, watching the great screen. The other elders grumbled even before she began to communicate.

He felt strangely excited. She looked different than she had before. He liked the smooth curve of her hairless skull. She was clean and sparkling and her features appeared to be augmented in some way. A shiny garment accentuated the protuberances on her chest. Jewels glittered on her neck and ears. He fingered the jeweled collar around his own neck, smiling. His rings reflected the light. She was more like them this time.

"Hello, everyone, Lady Grace here." She waved into the camera. "Lots of news. I've had a personal rebirth. Sam helped me get over the trauma of my early life. I feel like a new person. I cut my hair to mark the change; you might have noticed."

Noticed? He tuned into the current of his people's psyches that was always available to him. The intuitive abilities of his kind were magnified in the elders—he was in direct contact with the essence of every one of his people. He could stand in the great hall and know what each individual felt.

The entire planet was delighted.

Since the elders had taken to broadcasting Mrs. Edgarton's high volume rebukes or pleas for help, everyone had upgraded their screening systems and lived in hope that the soft dong of the chimes would let them know that she was at it again.

The elders had broadcast her messages as a cautionary note: Stray from our calm and contemplative culture and look what happens. In so doing, they created the planet's first superstar.

And today! Oh, great ball of golden substance, before her broadcast, she (or Jeremy, whom they detested when he was on planet, but who had grown so much more appealing millions of miles away) sent a TV series on training, not breaking, horses. They had never seen horses before, but all agreed that they had to have some to go with the dogs. That show was the most exciting thing to hit the planet since the humans arrived with Ellie and the Lhasa Apsos. Maybe the most exciting thing ever.

After the program about horses, the people were glued to their sets, a term Jeremy taught them, hoping she would appear. And she did. The buzz about her hair rocketed around the planet and its moons. The doctor's smile broadened. This suited his plans.

"And Sam and I are married." She blushed. "I'm so happy. I didn't know I could be so ecstatic. He's *wonderful*."

The tall doctor scowled. She married an Earthling? Since touching her hand, he'd been captivated. Her warm flesh was part of it. Solid flesh beating with life.

Unlike the other elders, he was aware of the mesmerizing effect that Mrs. Edgarton—now Lady Grace—had on everyone on the planet but the elders. (He really liked her new name, Lady Grace.)

The planet was changing. Ellie and that scruffy brat, Jeremy, had left thousands of half-human offspring, saving them from dying out but posing new challenges. People were finding their adopted little mutts hard to handle. They didn't obey.

The doctor had watched the material about the two Indian horse trainers and thought it very interesting. Maybe if they imported Bud Creeman and Wesley Silverhorse to their planet, they'd be able to control their little ruffians. But the men were violent; the film showed that. A trial of their abilities somewhere farther away from the home planet would be best. He continued stroking his chin, contemplating what good might come to his people as a result of the broadcast.

"We're going to march against the underground tonight," Lady Grace said. "We have to train some of the horses before we go. There's a new wrinkle at the underground. Aside from the monsters that would annihilate and enslave us . . ." she turned off camera, "Jeremy, can you send those images of the Bigs?" She paused a moment. "You should be getting the images now. It's turns out that my husband, Sam of Emily, has built a secret hide-away and hidden eleven children in it. These are the best of the village, kids who don't have the genetic diseases shown so clearly in the photos. So, in addition to destroying those beasts before they get us, we need to rescue the children.

"That's what makes our mission imperative. And that's why I contacted you. We must save the children. We are committed to it. Sam says they will die in just a few days. We're running against time . . . "

And then she gave a run-through of the futility of their plan. "We don't know how to train horses. We aren't in shape to carry arms. We need a backhoe and a tractor. The children are forty feet underground; the shelter is hundreds of feet down. We need people to drive the equipment. I don't even know how to drive a car. I don't think anyone does.

"But, we are determined to save those babies. We're leaving at dusk. We'll probably all be killed. The odds are vastly against us. But we cannot let those children die."

"Hey, Mom, there's a big thunderstorm over the village." Jeremy shouted from off camera. "It just showed up. It's a monster."

"Well that's one problem down!" She beamed. "The Bigs are afraid of thunder. Ellie must have contacted the haunt somehow. She's a real asset, though she is acting oddly. She's been eating fish nonstop since she heard about the captive children. Is that a problem?"

The doctor's eyes widened. A problem? Oh, celestial spheres. Did they know what they were unleashing?

"I hate to ask for anything more, but if we could have Bud Creeman and Wesley Silverhorse for a day or so, I think our problems could be solved. They know how to fight, apparently without weapons, and Wesley knows about farm equipment. They train horses. We could be ready to go in an hour if we had them. I don't know how much trouble it would be to get them here, but we would have a real chance of saving the children and not getting killed, plus eliminating the monsters. They live in the year 2015. Hope that's not too difficult for you.

"Jeremy is here with me. He's sending you more Wes Silverhorse movies; he's an amazing actor. And some videos of the Horse Manager. Plus coordinates for where they are.

"It would be so nice if you could help us again. We'd be so grateful. And—we're going to film the action as it happens. We would be delighted to send you an exclusive copy of the images, with my commentary, if you help us.

"Well, all the best from the planet Earth. You have my love and good wishes.

"This is Lady Grace."

She blew kisses at the camera.

The doctor could feel the planet swoon. Oh, she was divine. Marching to sure death. Sure death? She couldn't die. If she died, they couldn't watch her any more. They had to save her. And the children. And stop Ellie before . . .

The elders reviewed the data as well as the millions of intuitive calls to action that were barraging their consciousnesses. After flashing through several Silverhorse films, they were horrified. "He's violent. He's a monster," the elders said. And so sexual, they didn't say.

"He's just in role," said the tall doctor. "Look up Method Acting. Here," he split their screen. "Lee Strasburg started it in New York before the Second Revolution. See, the actor *steps into* the role, *becoming* the character temporarily. See, there's Strasburg on 'Inside the Actors Studio.'" They watched for a while.

"Wes is really a healer and holy man. He's very gentle. Here's his teacher," The image of an elderly man with white braids and a blissful face covered the screen. He looked directly at the elders and his portion of the screen blanked out with a hint of a rebuke. "A very *powerful* teacher."

"And besides," said the doctor, "they'll be fighting *monsters*. What could be better?"

"We'll give her no help. We will not import the Indians."

The doctor crossed his arms over his chest and bided his time.

In the first popular uprising in the history of the planet, the people massed in front of their screens and hummed. Someone was jostled in the hallway in front of the wall of the elders. He or she did not lose his or her footing, but did get an elbow in the ribs. The perpetrator apologized profusely. The violence was shocking.

"Our society is at a breaking point," the doctor said to the elders. "She's a cult heroine. We'll have trouble with the people if we don't go along with this."

Then he sprang his idea of importing the two horse trainers to the cliff and seeing what happened as a test run before bringing them and some horses to the planet.

"The hybrids," as Ellie and Jeremy's children were known, "are getting out of control. Those two humans could keep them in line, if they don't prove too dangerous themselves."

The elders saw the wisdom in this, and injected some more. "Maybe we could do something about *her* in this military action they're planning. An accident or something. Then we wouldn't get any more calls from her."

The doctor sputtered, "But the people love her. If she dies, they'll be heartbroken. The hybrids are much calmer when she's on. Maybe we could give her an hour a day program, about life down there."

They thought that an interesting idea.

"If we need to kill someone, we could kill her husband," the doctor added. "Everyone thinks he's an idiot."

The elders decided to send the horse trainers to the cliff, and hold on the other concepts until they saw some results. The doctor wanted to survey the populace about their feelings toward Sam. And the others. Maybe they could do a cleanup. Get rid of Jeremy. And Ellie. The humans obviously didn't know what she was turning into.

Lady Grace, he shoved his way in front of the transmitting device so he could be the one who sent the good news. He used his new skill, *thinking* to her in English. Next, he would master speaking out loud. *I'm very pleased to tell you that the elders have granted your request regarding Wesley Silverhorse and Bud Creeman. They should be arriving momentarily. We advise you to take precautions with Wesley Silverhorse. We have data indicating that he can be volatile.*

You have our best wishes for the completion of your mission. We look forward to receiving your reports. He smiled as enticingly as he could into the transmission device.

Lady Grace heard him speaking words into her mind. Silent words, but not the intuitions he'd used earlier. She responded right away, "Oh, you're the doctor who treated Ellie. How good to see you again. I'm *thrilled* that you'll be helping us with Bud and Wesley. We may have a chance with their help. And with you as our contact, we may have a more cordial relationship in the future. Many thanks," she put her hands together in the prayer position of her people and bowed to him.

"Oh, one thing," she added. "What's the matter with Ellie? She seems to be turning into . . ."

He cut the transmission. They'd find out soon enough.

33

Sam looked over his shoulder as he walked away from the container where the lady was talking to the goldies. James had shaved off all of her hair. He put paint on her face around her eyes and on her cheeks. She wore a blue gown of soft stuff cut so low that he didn't want any other man to see her.

The others had said, "Oh, you look beautiful."

She did. Too beautiful. When he had been near the goldies when Ellie was sick, Sam didn't like them. Part of it was that he had not been out of the underground very long. Part of it was *them*. He experienced them the way he did everything, from the inside. He knew all of them. Nuances and subtle shadings. They were too powerful. He couldn't understand their thinking or the way their souls worked. He didn't think it possible to make a good bargain with them, but his new family needed their help.

He didn't want to listen to what the lady said or see her shining in front of the cameras, so he walked to the end of the cliff. He stood, looking toward the underground shelter. The storm continued to rage. The Bigs hadn't gotten the general's weapons out. Yet.

After a while, he sat down with his legs crossed, a safe distance from the ledge. It still felt dangerous to him. It was dangerous. Sam picked up pebbles and threw them over the edge, listening to them bounce when they hit the rock below.

"Sam?"

He jumped at the soft voice. Ellie could walk even more quietly than he did.

"Yeah, Ellie?"

"Talk, Sam?"

"Sure, Ellie. What about?" He knew Ellie from holding her when she was sick. Which was to say, he knew her as well as another person possibly could. She was good and kind and fine all the way through.

"Tell about babies, Sam. What their names? How old? Any sick?" She came around and sat in front of him, her back so close to the edge that it made his stomach churn. She was unconcerned.

"OK, Ellie, ah'll tell ye." He immediately went into the village dialect. Ellie was the only one who'd asked about the children specifically, as individuals. And she'd used the Voice to make sure that the others saved them. She cared about them most.

"Bobby's th' oldest. He's this many." He held his fingers out once, and then held up just two.

"Twelve."

"Yeah. He's the biggest. He's an Arthur and has some . . ." He recited Bobby's genealogy, as would be proper in any discussion of children among those underground, or in the village in the old days. Sam went through all the other kids, describing them and giving their names and lineages. "Th' youngest is Winnie. She's . . ." He held up one finger. "One." He smiled. He knew that number. "She's a bonny thing, and smart. She looks small, Ellie. They're all wha' ye'd call sick, Ellie. Ev'ry one of 'em. But it's na' sumthin' to stew over. They need this," he waved his arm, indicating the outdoors and air. "They need food and a place to play. They'll be fine. Fair an' fine."

She laid her hand on his knee. "No is problem, Sam. Babies can be sick, no care. Want babies. They want mother?"

"They want a mother more 'n anythin', Ellie. Tha's wha' they need. Bein' held and loved. They need you."

Strangely, Ellie's eyes filled with tears. They weren't tears of happiness. Something was going on with her. She looked different; her eyes were larger. She seemed sharper, too, as though she might attack.

"You good man, Sam. You take care babies." She was silent for a while. "You want to know me like Sam Baahuhd? Hold hands and know?"

"All right," he replied cautiously. She had known his ancestor and touched him. What would she think when she knew that Sam Baahuhd was alive in him, along with 105 generations of Baahuhds? He was the keeper of the ancestors.

Ellie stretched her hands out and took Sam's.

He touched her and they joined. She was different than the Ellie he had held when she was sick. Foreign. Getting more foreign. Losing the vestiges of humanity she bore. Becoming something else. But still totally good.

And then he knew. Ellie was saying good-bye.

Sam Baahuhd reared up inside him and grasped Ellie's hands. "Yer a fair an' fine lass," he said. "As fine as a butterfly or a humming bee. Ye'll be remembered, lass. For generations, they'll sing yer name. Ah'm so glad ah knew ye."

The rest was beyond words. He knew Ellie and Ellie knew him, more than the lady did, maybe.

He sat in a trance.

"Good-bye, good Sam. I go now. You take care babies. Take care Jeremy. Use Voice, Sam. No be afraid."

When he opened his eyes, she was gone.

34

"OK, Wes. We'll do the shot as rehearsed," Kim Rogers, the director, sat beside the camera, an umbrella shading her command chair, bullhorn in hand. The rest of the crew stood where their jobs put them. "The crane with the camera is on the hill. It will catch you from above. The copters are in place. The logging truck is rolling in this direction."

The shot took place in a particularly scenic area of Will Duane's ranch. A hill sloped down from Wes's right. Out of sight, the logging road curved around it and sloped downward. The knoll was thick with timber, which broke into meadowlands below the road. Sunlight illuminated the scene.

"You're going to do exactly as we discussed, Wes. You'll hit the curve at fifty, no more, and pull to your right out of sight. We'll do the rest with a computer. No adding thrills or speed. You are too valuable to risk. This is a tough shot, as you know."

Wes knew the scene. His character rode around the corner with the bad guy in hot pursuit. A logging truck was coming up the other way. In the film, he was supposed to swerve, throw the bike sideways, slide under the truck, and escape. The bad guy got creamed by the truck. Bad guy number one. There were dozens of them in the film. The actual shot simply required him to ride the bike around the curve. The stunt would be completed in the computer lab.

"I promise, strictly to contract, no changes," Wes said to Kim. No fun. The director's assistant yelled, "Action." Wes put on his helmet. He was in a form-fitting black biker's suit with a black racing helmet. He was riding a hot bike. Hell of a hot bike. This shot was a total waste of a bike like that.

Wes gunned it. OK, he had an attitude problem. The speedometer said seventy, and he was still putting on speed. He knew they were filming, because Kim wouldn't waste the shot. She'd scream at him afterward. So what?

He shot over the hill. There was the logging truck. He was exactly where he was supposed to be. He swerved to the left, swinging the cycle's rear tire toward the truck. Gravel spun from under its wheels. He leaned to the right, gunning it.

Wesley found himself flying through the air, bent forward in the same position he'd had on the racing bike, hands out in front like they were on the handlebars. But the bike was gone. He tipped forward and skidded on the top of his helmet, then his helmet and the backs of his gloved wrists. The smell of burning plastic and leather filled the air. He stopped when he hit a stone wall, upside down. He didn't move.

Bud Creeman walked into the men's room of the main barn at Will's Montana ranch. He hated being filmed. Wes gloried in it, but Bud knew he'd spend a half-hour sitting on the can afterward, until his guts settled down. He loved the bathroom in the barn. Like everything on Will's estate, it was oversized and over the top. He could live in this bathroom very happily. He pulled out the latest issue of *Reined Horse Journal* and lightened up.

Moments later and much refreshed, he opened the door and stepped into brilliant sunlight. He looked around. He was standing on a rock ledge, with no barn in sight. No ranch anywhere. Just rock.

"Bud," Wesley ran up to him and whispered, "where are we?"

He looked around and saw a bald woman in a black commando outfit advancing on them with an automatic machine gun.

He raised a hand. "Hi, there. We're just . . . standing here."

"Certainly, no problem. I'm packing the ordnance. *Jeremy*, can you get Bud a saddle?" She called toward a storage container sitting a short distance from them. "He'll be out in a minute. I'll leave you with my son, Mr. Creeman." She walked away.

"How did she know your name?" Wes whispered.

"I don't know. Where are we?" Bud asked.

"I don't know. I was on a motorcycle doing a shot at Will's. Look at my wrists." Wes held them out. They were badly abraded. "Good thing I had gloves on. Shit."

Bud put his hands on Wes's wrists, healing them. "There, is that better? Good thing you got me around."

"Yeah, but where is this?" They were huddled at one end of a massive rock shelf. More rock formed a vast dome overhead. Two huge cargo containers sat a few yards away. A gigantic pile of pieces of metal and other junk sat in the middle. The hunks looked like they came off a space station.

"This cave could be the Cliff Palace at Mesa Verde in Colorado," Wes continued. "Or the Gila Cliff Dwellings. And that valley out there looks like Santa Ynez Valley in California. I just bought a weekend place there. That over there, where that thunderstorm is . . . I don't know where that is. I've never seen a thunderstorm centered on a particular spot. And there's a herd of wild horses beneath us."

Bud looked over the cliff edge. "Sure is. Who is *that*?"

A bad-ass little girl, who looked about half wasp, sat on the edge of the cliff, glaring at them. A pile of raw fish was next to her.

"Hi, there! We're just stopping by."

She jumped off the edge and buzzed away. She could fly.

"Did you see that?"

"Yes. Why does that woman have a machine gun?" He turned around and watched the woman who had met them.

She handed some guns to a couple of guys and then walked over to them, "I'm Lady Grace. Welcome to our home."

"Howdy. I'm Elmer Fudd and this is Hopalong Cassidy." Wesley looked at her through narrowed eyes. "What is this? Why are we here? What are you doing? And put down that gun."

Bud also stared. "That goes for me, too. I think it's time for us to go home. My wife's making pot roast tonight."

"Yes, we definitely need to go," she said. "We're behind schedule. Would you mind breaking those horses for us? We have several beginners, so we need them to be very gentle."

"I don't break horses," Bud said.

"I know, you put them under saddle. We'll explain the whole thing as we travel. Come now, go down the ladder and get to work."

"Look, I'm under contract. I can't work for anyone but Will Duane. That's it."

She leveled the gun at them. "Get down the ladder and start with the horses. We need to leave before dark."

"How many do you want trained?"

"All of them. We have to bring supplies and may have wounded to care for and take home. We need to load all of that." She pointed to an enormous pile of stuff at the bottom of the cliff.

"Are you crazy? We can't possibly load all that on green-broke horses. That's like a whole movie set you've got out there," Wes squawked.

She came closer. "I don't need to get this close. I can render you null and void a hundred yards away. Not to mention your contract with Will Duane."

Bud and Wes climbed down the ladder.

"Do you need any help?" Lena ran to the edge. "I used to help my grandpa with horses and mules."

"No, ma'am. We're used to doing it alone. Thank you, though." Bud tipped his hat.

"It's one of those reality TV shows," Wes whispered to Bud as they were working with the horses. "That's what it's got to be. They kidnap people and put them in some weird location. There are teams. One team wins and another loses. Lots of money in it. People get really intense. Usually they don't use celebrities as famous as me in the middle of a shoot . . . "

"Wes, you are the biggest pain in the ass. You think the world begins and ends with you."

"Well, you're a celebrity, too, Bud. They probably wanted you, too. This might be Indians against white guys, or take over the bitchin' lady commando. We'll probably have to do all sorts of tests, like rescue team members and like that. Sometimes you have to eat bugs or play paintball."

"That's what those are, paintball guns? You're out of your mind, Silverhorse. We're fucked. And Bert is making pot roast tonight."

"Do you have your cell phone?"

"Yeah. Good idea." Bud opened it up. "Nothing. No signal at all."

"It's because of the cliff. Why don't we get into that valley, and call Will to rescue us? He'll send in helicopters."

"Let's get this show on the road. The faster we train these horses, the faster we get rescued."

"Hey, look at that guy!" Wes broke into a grin when he saw Sam. "The really big one with the red stubble? He was in *Vision of Blood* with me. He was the captain of the stunt team. He's a great guy. See, they didn't think I could remember. Let's get him over here and recruit him to our side."

Sam was surprised when the Indians beckoned him over. Wesley, the good-looking one, acted like he knew him.

"Hey, my man. Your name is Gunnar Helvik, isn't it? You were in *Vision of Blood*, weren't you? You were captain of the stunt team." He did the high-five handshake.

Sam was glad that he knew how to do it. Lady Grace had given them very strict orders: "Do or say *anything* to get them to go along with us. Lie if you have to."

"Yes. I was the stunt captain."

"Oh, cool accent, Gunnar. Are you in role?"

"Yes. I am in role."

"What is this? Is this a reality show? A contest or something? Where's the other team?"

"Yes. This is a reality show. The other team is over there," he pointed to the underground, identifiable by the vast thunderclouds over it. "We need to go there very fast."

"When we get there, can we go home? My wife made pot roast. I hate to miss it."

"Not tonight, maybe tomorrow."

"We have to, like play games and things, yeah?"

"Yes. We have to do that."

"Why are we taking all the guns?"

"To use. Can you show me how to shoot a gun?"

"You were good at it in *Vision of Blood*."

"Yes, but these are real guns."

"What do you mean, real guns?"

"Real guns."

"But this is a reality show. I thought you used paint guns."

"We have those. But this is a real reality show. We use real guns."

"Fuck. I don't get it, Gunnar. If this is a show, why real guns? Is this, like, some feud that Will Duane and his worst enemy got into and are playing to the death?'

"Yes, it's like that. Can you teach me how to tame a horse? I need to know. My children are dying."

'What? Your children are dying?"

"Yes. The Bigs have them trapped under the ground. We need to rescue them before they die. We have very little time."

"What are you talking about? They took kids and put them underground and we have to rescue them? That's the game? That's terrible."

"Yes, it's terrible. *I* put them there so the Bigs wouldn't eat them."

Wes began dancing up and down, the small initial steps of a war dance.

"Oh. I see." Bud pulled the tall man aside. He didn't like the way Wes looked. "Gunnar, Wesley is a really famous movie star. He's basically a nice guy, but he's had some adjustment issues, coming off the ranch and becoming so famous and rich so fast. Do you have any Xanax? Or tranquilizers?"

"My wife might. Do you want me to find out?"

Wes heard him and came over. "No, no! I'm fine, Bud. It's fine. Every day, in every way, things are getting better and better. I'm *great*. If my probation officer doesn't find out I've skipped town, I'll even have a life again. If we get out of this, I'm going to build a guest cottage at my place in Santa Ynez and I'm going to hire a shrink to live in it and never leave home."

Wes began doing war yells. The horses looked around nervously.

"This is good, Gunnar, he's doing much better now."

"We must finish the horses and go. Can you teach me how to ride? Jeremy said you give riding lessons."

35

Sam stood in the field watching the Indians tame the horses. They worked together, putting their hands all over them. The animals dropped their heads and seemed to fall asleep. When they did that, Bud slipped a saddle on and Wesley mounted, slowly guiding them around. When they "woke up," they were trained.

Wes and Bud went from one to another, working quickly. Sam thought he could do what they were doing—making the horses fall asleep by touching them, at least.

He was about to offer to help when he heard an unfamiliar noise, a loud buzzing coming from farther out in the meadow.

"What's that?" Bud said. "Sounds like a helicopter."

"Will sent a helicopter!" Wes faced the noise and waved his arms over his head. "Over here! We're over here!"

Whatever it was was coming their way. The thunder of hooves drowned out the whirring noise. Sam could see something zigzagging behind a group of new horses, driving them toward the cliff—and them.

"Holy shit! What is that?" Wes dropped his hands, holding them around his eyes to see better.

It was dark and had a huge belly. Wings whizzed above it. Their speed made them almost invisible. Light glittered off the thing.

"Run! Those horses are gonna stampede!" Bud took off toward the cliff with Wes and Sam right behind him. The herd almost doubled in size when the new animals ran into the existing livestock. The horses milled around, raising dust. Whatever had been chasing them hovered above them.

Sam reached the cliff and turned back to look at the thing. Its belly was more than twice as long as he was, bulging and covered with horizontal plates. The top half was shiny and blue-black, glistening with a pink-purple luster. Some of the crawling bugs in the underground shone like that, like oily water.

The scales of the creature's abdomen were pale pinkish lavender mottled with black markings like one of the lady's fancy dresses. Lace, she had told him it was. The whole thing shimmered in the light, flashes reflecting from its hard plates. The wings were almost transparent, held together by silver veins and iridescent membranes. Each wing was much taller than him.

The creature had six black legs, which it extended when it got close to the cliff. The back legs were shapely; each bore a tiny hoof. He'd seen those legs and hooves before.

His jaw loosened and his mouth opened; he was unable to speak or move. The flying thing moved slowly, compelling him to follow it with his eyes. Nothing he had seen was so beautiful—or terrifying. It could be a winged forest bogey from the snake men's tales.

The thing turned so that he could see its face. Huge silver eyes regarded him through slit pupils. Their expression bore no vestige of human feeling. Silver curls covered the creature's head. Little furry antennae poked through her locks. It was Ellie. Sam's knees buckled and he staggered, almost falling.

"Holy shit! It's a giant wasp!" Wesley cried, running for the ladder.

Jeremy was a little way up the ladder, guiding a load of camping equipment that Mel and Henry were lowering with a rope. He saw the monster's face and gasped, clattering down the rest of the rungs. He landed unsteadily, bumping into Wes.

Sam grabbed him, putting a hand over Jeremy's mouth. The creature hovered above them, displaying herself. Her wings created a hurricane of dust and grit. Sam held Jeremy, turning toward the cliff to escape the dirt.

"It's all right, Jeremy," Sam said, using the Voice. He felt as though Ellie were telling him what to say.

"She loves you, Jeremy. She did it to save the babies." Sam clutched Jeremy, keeping him from falling to the ground. Jeremy screamed, clawing at him, trying to run.

"Stop," Sam said, making his Voice more powerful. He had hesitated to use it, even now that he was free. Ellie had been right. He needed to use his Voice, and he needed to be a more powerful leader than he had ever been.

"We must save the children," he took over, using the Voice. "We will start now. Finish training the horses, Bud and Wes." He gave everyone jobs, including the lady. Then he sat with Jeremy. Ellie had flown off in the direction of the underground shelter. They could hear the thunder from the huge storm hovering over it. Ellie's doing, undoubtedly.

"She's a wasp, Sam! Ellie turned into a wasp! I knew she wasn't human, but I didn't know she could change like that. Oh, God!" Jeremy sat with his forearms on his knees, tears flowing. "She came to me earlier. She sounded like she was leaving me. I didn't get what she meant." He wept, shaking his head.

"It must have been the fucking fish!" Jeremy sat up, suddenly furious. "I bet the goldies knew. They must have known. Son of a bitch!"

Sam put his arm around him. "She came to me, too, Jeremy. I didn't understand, either. But now she's gone. We need to mourn her," he used the Voice harder than he knew he could, "and we need to get going. We need to save the children."

Jeremy stood up and wiped his face with his sleeve. "Yes, we must save the children."

36

"You guys doin' OK?" Bud rode up and down the line, seeing how the new riders were handling the long trek, as well as how the newly under-saddle horses were holding up. They'd done the horses as well as they could and set out. All Grace had was a bunch of very high tech English saddles. Bud hated English saddles.

"What if we have to rope something?" he said.

Grace shrugged. "We don't. These are Russian cavalry saddles. This is how they ride. I agree. Western saddles would have been better. But I didn't have any say in what went. The general organized this."

Bud liked her a lot. She was one hell of a rider, though she didn't know how to do anything with horses. That was how the rich folks were on that boutique ranch outside Dallas where he used to work. Trophy ranch. Trophy horses that won every time they stepped into a show arena. The ranch owners never rode their horses in shows. The staff rode them. The owners never saddled, bridled, shoveled, or did a damn thing but show up for parties. He got a clear image that Grace was used to a staff, and a big one.

The two of them went up and down the line, encouraging the others and keeping the horses together. The trees were too close now to try leading the packhorses. They let them pick their way by themselves, counting on the animals' herd instincts to keep them going. That and the darkness. Some moonlight filtered through the trees, but it was a hard ride at night.

They had nine riders; all but Grace, Wes, Lena, and Bud were rank beginners. Henry was like the executives who'd been to one of Bud's seminars. He knew enough to stay on, most likely, but he didn't know enough to realize his limitations. Lena looked like she'd been a good hand, but now she was a rusty hand. The party consisted of nine riders and that wasp thing that flitted above them like Tinker Bell on meth. Jeremy's wife, he understood. Wes should look at her. He'd stop complaining about his wife.

They let the extra horses follow along. Grace had said they'd need them for the wounded and sick. Bud was getting a little sick of this reality show bullshit. He didn't see any of it as real. When they stopped at "the base camp," he was going to confront Grace on the whole stupid thing. Or maybe he'd do it right now.

"Grace, where are we?" he asked. "These are eastern forest trees, green, close together, and skinny. Back by the cliff, that was California oak savannah. The cliff dwelling is New Mexico. Where are we? Is this just some big set for the show?"

"Bud, I don't know where we are. We need to have a meeting and bring you and Wes into the picture better. You need to know some things. But we need to keep going. This isn't what you think."

He didn't know what he thought. The quality and amount of firearms on the packhorses and the quantity of medical supplies she'd loaded said this was the most bad-ass reality show ever attempted. Unless it wasn't that.

"What is this, Grace? Tell me. Am I going to get killed out here?"

He could hear her mind grinding away as she decided what to tell him. "Bud, I'm going to tell you, and then I'm going to let you tell Wesley. I think it will work better that way.

"I don't think you'll get killed, especially if you can fight like you and Wesley did on that demo movie about taming the wild horses."

"That we shot this afternoon?"

"I guess it was this afternoon for you. When you threw the golf cart at each other and were covered with blue lights?"

"They were supposed to deep six that. I told them to put it where the sun don't shine."

"They did. Jeremy, my son, the guy with the dreads down to his waist?" Bud nodded. The husband of the stinging death mutant flying above them. "Jer picked up the show's signal floating in outer space. We have technical abilities that are beyond your time."

"What do you mean, 'our time'?"

"I mean *your* time. We aren't in your time. You know that, don't you?"

Bud got the willies right up his back, the way he did when he felt a ghost around. "Not our time?"

"No. We don't know what time this is. We know that the Second Revolution was in 2097."

"What?"

"Let me talk; then you can ask questions." She told him about the Second Russian Revolution and Tsar Yuri's supposedly getting rid of the atomics. "Before the nuclear holocaust, we had martial law all over the planet, prison camps, and genocide."

"Are you making this up?"

"Bud, I wish I were."

"Stop right there. I need to take a break . . ."

"Why don't you ride up and down the line and check people? I'll tell you the rest when you come back. Don't tell Wes."

"Don't worry."

"OK, from what you just told me, it's about 3,000 years after my time, give or take," Bud said a few minutes after returning from his circuit. "The reason that there's no development around here or people is that everything got blown up by a nuclear war. Except you guys. We're on our way to rescue some more survivors."

"Yes. The children."
"I'm going to ride the line again."

"So where were you when it all blew up?"
She told him about being in the bunker with the general, how the others escaped to the golden planet, Ellie, the whole story.
"How did you get to Connecticut? Take the Trans-Siberia-Atlantic Express?"
"It was through the goldies. The only one who's from around here is my husband, Sam . . . "
"You mean Gunnar?"
"He said his name was Gunnar?"
Bud thought, "No, he agreed with Wes, who said his name was Gunnar."
"His name is Sam. He came from the bomb shelter we're going to be attacking. Under the lawn of the old estate."
Bud nodded. Right. Ellie chose that moment to make a high speed pass above their heads. Her multifaceted eyes glowed in the night. "Yeah, I'd say that she's an extra-terrestrial. She's as close to a little green man as I've seen."
"Oh, Bud, you should have seen her before. She was beautiful."
"She is on our side, isn't she?" Bud asked.
"I think so. She rounded up the horses for us, and I think she's responsible for the thunderstorm over the village. The hant who lives there loves her."
"Hant, like *haunt*? Now wait a minute, you didn't say anything about a *ghost*." It wasn't that he and Wes were afraid of ghosts. They just didn't like to be around them, or dead people, much. And a lot of their People agreed with them.
So she filled him in about the vicious Shaq.
"OK. It's a *dog* ghost. I'm going to make another circuit, Grace. We'll talk more when I get back from checking the horses and riders."

"OK, Grace. Sam was in the bomb shelter for a few thousand years."

"His ancestors were. One hundred five generations have lived and died down there, Sam says. We forgot one thing in planning the shelter, Bud."

"What was that?"

"The people. The villagers who went into the shelter were closely related to start with. They produced mutations. Do you know about them, Bud?"

"Yeah, from horse breeding. Mutations either make things better or worse."

"Or much, much worse." He could barely see her face in the dark. "They're monsters down there, Bud, in every sense.

"That's why we asked the people of the golden planet to bring you and Wes to help us.

"Will you help us, Bud?"

He could sense how beautiful she was, even in the dark. And hear how much she needed help.

"Grace, I've never shot anyone in my life. Neither has Wes. We're trained to fight, but it was just as an exercise. Grandfather, our shaman, said that the inner state of the warrior was the reward. We've never been on any mission. I've only been in one fight and that was in high school. Wes's got more experience on that score. That's why he's on probation. He got drunk and mixed it up in a bar in Beverly Hills.

"We're spirit warriors, not killers. We've never done anything like this. And we don't have permission from Grandfather to use our Powers, so they may not even work."

"Oh."

"I'd like to go home, ma'am. If you don't mind. How about we take you to wherever you're going and say good-bye?"

"I don't know if that will work, Bud. Jeremy told me that he found a bunch of bugs—surveillance devices, not insects—in our things. We planned on doing an exclusive video and sending it to the golden planet in return for their bringing you here, but it looks like they circumvented that plan. I rather expect that they're watching us on

Ellie's planet. And I expect they'll want a good show before they'll let any of us go anywhere. I don't think your wife's pot roast dinner will satisfy them as a reason you have to go home."

"Oh."

Bud rode up front to where Wes and Sam were talking.

"Hey, Bud, you gotta get to know Gunnar. He's amazing."

"Yeah, Grace and I have been talking about him a lot. I expect being shoved out that hole with a surveillance eye in your gut was quite an experience," Bud said sardonically.

"You didn't tell me about that one, Gunnar," Wes was enthralled. "He's been telling me about a sci-fi movie that they're in where there was a nuclear war and Ellie, that big wasp flying around, took them up to her planet . . ."

"Hold it, Wes. I want to tell you something. You know your idea that we're on a reality show?"

"Yeah."

"We are on a reality show, a real reality show, like your friend told you. We don't get to go home until we liberate his village," he pointed at Sam. "And that isn't . . ."

"Wesley, I told you a bad thing," Sam broke in. "My name is not Gunnar. It is," he said it with the full village brogue, "Sam, o' th' line o' Sam Baahuhd, ou' a' Em'ly. I'm the last of the Em'lies. I as' for yer aid and arms to fight for my fam'ly and kin."

Wesley looked at him. "Wow. That's a really cool name, especially with the accent. Much better than Gunnar. Don't worry about the name switch. I got it. A lot of guys don't get their professional iden-tity down until they're mid-career.

"But, what did you say?"

Sam started over. "I am Sam o' … "

"No. I got that part." Wes turned to Bud. "This is real?"

"It's worse than real. Remember how Grandfather never let things get out of control? Safeties on and all that?"

"Yeah."

"This isn't like that. This is fucking shoot to kill. This is war, Wes. We can't go home until we win."

Wes slid his horse to a stop. "It's *real*? We get to kill people?" Bud nodded. Wes let out a series of war cries that had the horses spooking all the way to the end of the line. "This is just what I need. Fuck *therapy*. I want to kill."

"I think we should get Grandfather's permission. We can't just go into some other time and kill people. That's not the warrior's way."

"Bud, Grandfather left us. He's either dead, like half the people say, or he's traveling the world and doesn't give a shit about us. I say, kill the fuckers."

"I can't believe how you've changed, Wes."

37

Sam put up their tent. They had reached the approximate location of the buried equipment barn very late at night. Dawn wasn't breaking, but it couldn't have been more than an hour or two away.

The lady had entered the tent first. When he walked through the opening, something tripped him. He ended up on his back with her on top of him, kissing him furiously.

"Lady? Now?"

"Oh, yes, Sam, now. I'm going to jump your bones."

"What does that mean, lady?"

He figured it out when she straddled him and began pulling at his belt.

"I think we're going to win, Sam. Last night, I thought we were doomed, but with Wes and Bud, I think we're going to do it. Let's celebrate." She leaned down and kissed him. "Have I told you I love you recently?"

"No."

"I love you, Sam."

They were getting into the bone-jumping process when Jeremy whispered at the tent flap, "Mom? Can I come in?"

"Wait. Just a minute . . ." They frantically pulled themselves together. "Come in, dear. What's the matter?"

"Mom, Ellie *stung* me."

"What!" Grace crawled to the tent flap to open it. "What happened?"

"She was sitting in a tree. I touched her, and she stung me. Her stinger's in her hoof."

"Is it bad? Sam, do we have a flashlight?"

Jeremy crawled in and exposed his hand. It was reddened, but not grossly swollen.

"I can't believe she did that to you."

"Neither can I, Mom. You saw her, didn't you? She's an *insect*. My beautiful Ellie. She's not human at all. I don't know what happened."

"I don't know either, Jeremy. But I bet the elders of the golden planet do. I bet they could have told us about this. And that we shouldn't have allowed her to eat meat, ever."

Jeremy crouched on the sleeping bags, wiping his cheeks with his hand. "I can't believe it, Mom. It was the children that Sam hid. When she heard about them, she went nuts. She wanted a baby so bad. That doctor told her she couldn't have any more kids, so she did what she did."

"Sam, could you get Jeremy's sleeping bag? You can sleep with us, dear. Like we did those first nights. Tell me, have you found any more surveillance devices?"

"They're all over everything. It would take me a week to debug our stuff. I think we're *their* reality show. I told you we couldn't make a deal with them. 'Exclusive coverage in return for sending Bud and Wesley.' They have exclusive coverage with their bugs. Forget controlling them . . .

"The whole planet is probably getting off on us. They probably saw Ellie sting me and laughed." He whispered fiercely toward the sky, "Assholes!"

"I think we need to pray to the Great One before we go any further," Bud said. He and Wes had staked a camp a little way from the others. Everyone else was snoring away, but he and Wesley couldn't go to sleep without getting straight with their ancestors and their own heads.

"You know what, Wes? I'm not sure if we shouldn't get back on our horses and ride out of here."

"Fuck them and their reality show?"

"Yeah. Let's see what happens when we pray. If we don't get a clear signal, let's head back to the cliff and try to call Will."

Bud didn't have a ceremonial pipe, which he always used for serious prayer. However, the remains of a cigar were jammed in his back pocket. Tobacco was the sacred herb of his People—the cigar was good enough.

"There's some issues here," Bud spoke to the night sky around them. "You can't just go in and start shooting people because someone says they're monsters. I'd say that flying thing is a monster, but she's a good guy because she's married to Jeremy."

They lit the cigar. Not having matches, Wes snapped his fingers until he got a light. "This place is like the Mogollon Bowl," he said. "The Power is strong here."

"The whole story sounds fishy to me. I mean, what if we're being waylaid for a bad purpose?"

"Saving children?"

"That's a good purpose. But what if it isn't their real purpose?"

"They seem nice."

"Yeah, but do you just meet strangers that seem nice and go kill for them?"

"You're nervous because you've never killed anyone before."

"Neither have you."

"You're right." Wes began singing the song to welcome the Great One. His voice wavered as he tried to remember the words. It had been a long time.

Bud stood and raised the cigar to the four directions, chanting with Wes. He sat down.

"You talk, Bud," Wes whispered.

"Dear Great One, and Grandfather, if you're listening, we got ourselves in this *deal* an' we sure could use some guidance. These people want us to help them dig up some kids and kill monsters. The kids part is OK, but the monsters is a relativistic situation, morally speaking. What if these are just people who were underground for two thousand years and got a little gnarly? Being able to tell the difference between a demon and someone with bad manners is important.

"We need a sign. Should we go back to the cliff? Or if we stay, is it OK to shoot with the safeties off? Can we use our Powers? Grandfather didn't let us use them unless we had permission from him. But he's not here, so we need permission."

"And also, make our Powers big enough to do the job," Wesley added. "This may take some Power, real POWER, not just what I used blowing up rocks. If that wasp-girl is a good guy, I'm worried about the bad guys."

They had a moment of silent contemplation.

Bud prayed, "I hope that we save the kids tomorrow. An' that things come out right. A lot of people saw us as bad because we looked different and wore feathers and so on. I don't want this to be like that.

"Grandfather, if you're around, I'd sure like to hear from you. Can you send a sign as to what we should do? Make it real clear."

Bud was distracted by the thunder booming a mile or so way. The storm had not let up one bit since they left the cliff. It occurred to him that digging the kids out of the bomb shelter was going to be really hard if the clay was soaked all forty feet down. So he added, "It sure would be nice if where the kids are was dry and easy to dig, but the rain kept fallin' on the other side."

They settled in to sit quietly, as Grandfather taught was appropriate after prayer.

"Ahhh!" Wes and Bud screamed when they opened their eyes. A lion-like monster filled the horizon. Its face—flowing hair, wild eyes and vicious fangs—seemed to smile at them. It snapped its teeth before their faces.

"The hant!" They leapt up and ran back to the campground. Their tent seemed pitifully small. They turned around and headed for the biggest tent. "To Sam's!"

38

"I was taking a dump when I saw it," Jeremy instructed the group. "You can only see it when you're squatting."

Wesley waddled around the area, approximating the point of view needed to reveal the tube. They were searching for the flue sticking out of the earth that indicated the buried barn.

"Here it is," shouted Mel. The pipe protruded only a few inches from the soil. The hole Jeremy made to enter the machine barn was visible when they got close.

"You got down through *that* hole?" Mel said. It looked too small to admit an adult.

"Wolves were after me. Motivated me a lot. I left some skin on the roof," Jeremy explained. "And all I had to dig with was a branch."

Wes stared into the hole. "If you could step back and give me a little privacy," he said to the others.

Bud pulled them away. "Wes likes to work alone. We'll go over here."

Once he was sure no one was looking, Wesley pointed the palm of his hand at the hole. A beam of blue light emerged from his palm and cut through the dirt. Whatever he and Bud did in their ceremony last night had worked! His Powers were active. A pile of dirt appeared beside the original hole. And then the hole was five feet across and a circle of rusted tin roof was exposed.

The others stood gawking. Wes glared at them. "Don't you have something else to do? Like getting ready to rescue those kids?" His peevishness hadn't disappeared. "I need some shovels and tools."

Soon he was tapping the roof to determine its soundness. Then he jumped down and pulled up the corner that Jeremy had pried up earlier. Moments later, he'd disappeared inside the building.

"Need a flashlight, Wes?" Bud asked.

"No. This is fine." Wes held up his palm. Blue light illuminated the barn. The barn was a good-sized workspace: about twenty feet by sixty feet with a peaked roof maybe fifteen feet high at the center. The pipe was by the northeast corner, the barn's low side, so he didn't have to drop too far when he eased himself through the opening. The barn held everything a decent-sized farm would need. He gazed at it in wonder.

Beautiful equipment filled the building. It wasn't brand new, but it was a hundred times better than anything he'd had at his family's ranch. He couldn't imagine anyone calling the machines old junk. Though a little dented and dirty, these were way better than anything he'd ever seen, even at Will Duane's.

The machinery drove home a point their hosts' words couldn't. These were better machines than any that *existed* in his time. This was more advanced technology. Which meant that whenever this barn got covered up was already in the future from his time. That's what they had said. Wesley shuddered.

Maybe their story was true. If that were so, those were real kids over there, buried under forty feet of dirt, and dying.

He moved around the space rapidly. Steel drums were stacked in one corner. Some of the drums were empty, but most were full. Probably full of liquid plastic fuel; that's what Jeremy said vehicles used back before everything blew up. That wouldn't go up in the blasts. The belts and hoses on the tractors and backhoe loader, on all the machines, were rotten. As were the replacements in the boxes around the carefully organized barn. Whoever set this up knew what he was doing.

Wesley was getting frustrated because nothing was usable. When he laid a hand on one of the rotted hoses, it softened and became pliable. He was able to mold it into something that was, if not new, at least serviceable. The various kinds of motor fluids were thickened and grotty at the bottom of their tanks, but he laid his hand on them, hoping the same thing would work. He thought it did. If so, the bulldozer could run. He laid his hands on all the equipment, not knowing exactly what he'd need to dig out the kids. He was glad no one could see him, because he was working so fast his limbs were a blur. He could barely see himself.

He had to get fuel into the machines. He assumed that was what was in the metal barrels. How? That's when reality caught up with him. The uppermost part of the barn was buried under three feet of dirt. What about the sides? Who knew how much dirt blocked the building's front end? Would he have to dig a trench ten feet wide and eighteen feet deep to get the machinery out? He'd have to excavate a driveway, the whole nine yards.

So far, his Power had held up, but how long would it last? When he did a martial arts exhibit for Grandfather, he was totally exhausted afterward. He usually had to sleep for twenty-four hours. And that was just blowing up some rocks. This was much harder.

"You idiot," he said to himself. "Why not just dig the kids out of the shelter with the blue light?" They didn't need the equipment at all. He'd been wasting his time.

Wes clambered out the hole in the ceiling and said, "This isn't the way to do it. Come on, Bud, let's go get those kids."

They grabbed Sam and marched toward the underground shelter. "OK, show us where the kids are buried."

Sam was able to pinpoint the location precisely. He showed them how the underground growing fields had glassed-in solar panels covered with heavy metal shutters over them. Sam explained that metal shutters had allowed them to weather the nuclear blast. They retracted, allowing the glass panels to collect sunlight, which powered the underground's electrical systems. The sunlight also was redirected to the farm.

"I grow mostly soybeans, but the Bigs grow weed that will leave you seein' hants for days and mushrooms that will make your eyeballs shake in your head. They're against the Commands, but there's naught I can say about 'em.

"This is the edge of the solar field," Sam said. The panels were depressed a few feet from the surface, but were not blocked by dirt or refuse. "A wind comes up from inside and blows it clean, like it does for the canary hole." He paced off a few feet from one corner.

"The room I built is right here, next to the fields. It is outside the shelter, on the other side of its concrete wall. The fields are far below, but the room is not too deep. Its walls are dirt. I had only a little wood to reinforce them, or the ceiling." His wary expression said what Wes feared.

"So if we don't dig it just right, the ceiling will collapse?" he said. "Yes."

Wes gave the orders. "I want everyone to keep away. What I do is private." He turned to Bud. "I need you to help me, Bud. I know you don't think you can do this, but I need help."

Bud and Wes approached the job surgically, paring away a layer of dirt at a time. Bud quickly picked up the technique for moving earth. A pyramid grew off to the side. They scooped deeper and closer to where they thought the children were.

Wes stepped back and wiped his face, feeling heartened. It was working. He was in one of those half-in-one-world, half-in-another states that went with spiritual experience. He always had felt that way when Grandfather was present, but he hadn't felt so blessed since leaving the old shaman's side. Now he could feel the power of grace, along with gratitude. He felt like the man he had been. He liked that man.

Wes couldn't help notice that the thundershowers had continued at the front of the shelter, and that the earth they were moving was easy to cut and moist. Not soaked. He shivered.

And then they were there.

"Don't step on the ceiling," Sam said. They'd made a trench down to the room, leaving a wide passage to the surface behind them. They could lift the children out and carry them to the field hospital that way. When they saw how flimsy the ceiling was, it stopped them cold. Who was light enough to pull the children out?

A buzzing from the sky behind them caused them to turn around. Ellie droned insistently. They understood her. She could weigh nothing by hovering. She could fit through the hole, and her eyes let her see in the dark. She could find the children and bring them out one at a time. She wasn't tired at all.

"Let the wee girl try. I think she can do it. We need to hurry, lass," Sam said to Ellie. "The Bigs know we're here. They may burst through the wall. Do ye hear them?"

They heard them all right. Grunts and sounds of sledgehammers striking the cement wall from the inside assaulted them. The Bigs were real, and they were right beyond the concrete. Something like a pick or shovel made a higher-pitched reverberation. Guttural voices rose and fell, growling beyond the wall.

Wes jumped back as Ellie brought the first youngster out. The child was a shapeless thing with long, floppy arms and legs. Gray. Ghastly. Unmoving.

"It's Bobby," Sam cried, trying to pick the boy up. Ellie buzzed menacingly, driving Sam back. "What we' ye doing?' he shouted. "Stop, ye'll kill him."

Ellie positioned her rear feet over the lifeless child's chest. Her hoofed foot reached out, and a hidden stinger lowered from it. She stung Bobby's chest and he jerked off the tarp. She stung him again, and he began to cry, then move.

"Ellie! You brought him back."

After that, they let her do what she wished. Some she stung, others she massaged. Others she fed a liquid from her mouth.

Ten children lived. She brought out an eleventh, but the girl had died days before. Elllie put the child down and buzzed out of sight.

"We must get outta here," Sam cried. So many Bigs were beating on the concrete outer wall of the shelter that the ceiling of the little room shuddered. Pebbles and crumbles of dirt hit the floor. The ceiling split, part falling into the space where the children had been. The cement wall cracked under the Bigs' assault, but it held. The clang and thud of tools striking concrete grew frenzied.

"Hey, ye . . ." The Bigs' Voices were muffled just enough to keep them from compelling obedience. The walls of the excavation collapsed and the dark hole where the children had lived disappeared.

Sam and the others ran up the passageway to the surface.

"Get out of the way," Wesley shouted. He and Bud rolled back all the dirt they'd removed, sealing the Bigs inside the shelter.

They went back to the campground. The children were lying under a large tent with the sides rolled up. Grace had set up pediatric IVs of saline solution for several. Others sucked at bottles of formula or water.

"Just a little at a time," she said. They stood around, looking at the newest members of their community. Gray skin, yellowed teeth. Red-rimmed eyes, oozing sores. Patches of hair stuck out of filthy scalps. Fungus and mold mottled their bodies. The biggest one, Bobby, couldn't sit up or walk. The littlest one was supposed to be a year old. She looked three months and couldn't roll over. Lena cried outright, holding onto Henry. James and Mel stood silently with grave faces. Wes and Bud stared at the fruit of their labor in horror.

Only Sam beamed.

"Oh, thank ye so. Ah will take such care of these babies."

The others didn't see how they'd last the night.

39

"Oh, no!" Jeremy exclaimed. He had set up a field computer lab in a tent. The first thing he did was turn on all the surveillance equipment in the underground and have images broadcast to his screen. About a third of the cameras worked. They were enough. The access to the general's munitions stash was through his computer lab in the shelter. His lab was tightly secured; the Bigs couldn't break into it. But the computers in Arthur's old room were very available. You could get into the lab using them. He could see two Bigs bent over workstations there. "Get Sam here. How much do they know about computers?"

Grace stood behind Jeremy, hacking at his hair. She had gotten through his reluctance to part with his dreadlocks by saying, "Jeremy, I know you love your dreads. I do, too, but those monsters can grab your hair and pull you down in a second. You know what that would mean."

"Shit. They're trying to get into the munitions vaults." Their previous photos showed that the outermost chamber had been breached and resealed years ago, without weapons being removed.

"Damn! They're really smart," Jeremy exclaimed. "My face and voice are the security codes for unlocking the doors to the general's weapons. They're pulling my face and voice off the broadcast we did when we first got here, when I was trying to scare them into staying put."

He focused on a computer inside the lab in Arthur's room. Its screen bore his wild-eyed face taken from the earlier broadcast. One of the Bigs was working on the image, making it look like a normal face. "They'll do the same with my voice. They must have a recording of that broadcast. They'll have all that stuff ready in minutes. Then all they have to do is figure out the password."

"What's the password?" The group gathered around.

"Jeremy Edgarton . . ." he said. They gasped. Jeremy continued, "Prisoner of Hermitage Academy. Life sucks, dinna ye kin?' I didn't make it that easy. But it's not that hard, either. We need to get over to the other side of the shelter. I need my computers there, too.

"Do they know any more, Sam? Do they have computer specialists?" Jeremy asked.

"I don't know—I was not allowed near. They closed the library and kept the books for themselves. And Arthur's computer lab. Not all the Bigs are like Sam Big. He rules by right of blood and by his might. The Voice, and his," Sam searched for a word. "Power. He can do things with his mind. Others are not so ..."

"Intuitive?" Henry suggested.

"Yes, or ..."

"Vicious?"

"They are all vicious. Some of the Bigs are just a little taller than me, and they don't have the faces," he indicated the distorted facial structure of the most obvious Bigs, "but they are as bad as the worst. They can fool you into thinking they are good. They are not. Look at the pictures and see what they are doing. Don't be fooled if you meet one."

Jeremy's computer showed one holding up a printout of his image to the security system's viewer. They heard a voice that sounded like Jeremy's coming out of the speaker.

"They don't have the password." Jeremy chuckled. "And they don't know that they get three tries and the thing locks up tight. They won't be able to get in. Only I will. But we need to get over there. There are three entrances to the shelter: the canary hole, the back entrance in the lawn, and the big entrance from where the ballroom was."

"There's another entrance," Sam said. "Where we dug the babies out."

"But we filled that up again."

"That's loose dirt. Easy for a Big to dig through. They were breaking through the cement. If they want out that way, they will come."

"Oh, good." Jeremy said. "There are thirty-four of them for sure and nine of us, ten with Ellie. How do we cover all these fronts?"

"And take care of the babies," Sam added.

"I'd like to stay with the babies," Lena said. "I love babies. Plus I'm so sore from that ride I can hardly move. I could remember how to ride just fine; it's just that my muscles haven't caught up." She put her hands on her lower back and stretched. Jeremy heard a crack. "I'm best off staying here."

"That's a good idea, Lena," Grace said. "But have you ever handled guns? If they get past us and find out the children are here, they'll come for you."

Lena smiled. "Grandpa taught me how to shoot. I was quite the sharpshooter. If you're eating squirrel for dinner, you learn to hit your target."

"We're not leaving before we've suited up," Grace said. "We have eight suits. Wes, you and Bud should wear them, too. They offer full body coverage, including hands, feet, and face. They're bulletproof and highly fire-resistant. If a missile hits you, they won't help, but pretty near anything else, you'll be OK. We will use the whole night kit underground: suits, night glasses, facemasks, boots. I'll show you."

Grace disappeared into her tent. They waited.

"Boo!" she said, creeping up behind them. "The boots are more or less silent." They looked around in surprise. She was almost invisible, even when they knew where she was. "We're reaping the benefit of the Russian army's research. They found that 100 percent black *is* invisible. Every army wants invisible warriors, so they worked hard to make these suits as black as possible. And they succeeded. These will make our chances of survival in the underground much greater."

They ran off to get suited up.

40

The oak-studded meadow was so quiet after everyone left. Lena turned to the children. She loved babies, but these were so weak. The task of caring for them was almost as scary as being by herself. What if one died while she was on duty?

Lena looked up and noticed something else: The thunderstorm around the front of the shelter was gone. Totally. She looked into the heavens, "Shaq, my good little dog. I know you fell in love with Ellie, but please don't forget your first mama. I might need your help today. Please watch for me along with the others."

Turning to the kids, she set about determining what each needed. Grace had unhooked the few that had IVs. That was good, because Lena had no idea how to change the IV bags or do anything with them.

They lay in two rows, five each row, on a tarp on the floor of a tent with rolled up sides. The first thing she did was lower the sides. The children were squinting and turning their faces away from the sun. They'd never seen daylight, poor things. After closing the tent except for the front flap, she got heavier mats for them to lie on and put towels on top of the mats. The fluids they'd given the children had gotten their systems going. Some of the little boys resembled fountains. She realized that diaper duty was going to take up much of her time. Except they didn't have diapers. Towels under them would have to do. She'd wash them in the pond later.

In the darkened tent, they began to look around. And she studied them. She thought of the children as babies because they were so stunted and small. Sam said the oldest, the floppy-legged boy named Bobby, was twelve. He looked maybe six. He looked like one of those kids they showed in the newspaper every once in a while whose crazy parents had locked him in a cellar and fed him once a week. He couldn't stand up. She doubted he could roll over—none of them could. His legs and arms were so rickety she wondered if he'd ever stand.

The others ranged in age down to what? The littlest ones looked like babies. She realized what Sam had done: He'd created the burrow for them and put them in it. He had no access to it from inside the growing fields, and however he fed and watered them must have been invisible to anyone passing by the cement wall.

Why did Sam need to rescue them? He had said that these were the best of the village, the only ones not polluted by the genetic weaknesses and mutations of Sam Baahuhd's first wife. Who would destroy their best? Why did Sam *need* to save the children?

Lena got it all at once. Sam said they were cannibals. The photos they'd seen showed the men running wild in the women's pen. With no birth control, they must have had many babies, from all the bloodlines. What did they do with them?

Eat them. Lena blanched. God in heaven, no. A newborn wouldn't make much of a meal to a full-grown Big. They must raise them somewhere that the cameras didn't show, and when they were big enough, eat them.

Oh, God. She sat down heavily on the tent floor. A stupid thing to do; she needed to be vigilant and watch the perimeter of the camp. But the realization of the depravity in the shelter stunned her. Sam's tall form came to her. He was so good and kind. Or was he? How could he be, coming from there? Did he have rages like the others that hadn't appeared yet? He'd told them to kill the Bigs without listening to them, that all of them were evil. Were they? Or was he?

But Grace had taken to Sam, had married him after one night. He had healed her; that was obvious. Lena trusted Grace. Sam must be OK. He *had* to be OK, or what they were doing was murder.

She looked at the "babies." They lay there, naked, filthy, and looking at her. Totally helpless, except for something lovely coming from them. She could feel their souls.

"Well, children, we're here together. We should get to know each other."

At the sound of her voice, ten sets of eyes focused on her. Their eyes were mostly greenish blue. A few had brilliant blue eyes, while others were a muddy blue; still others had hazel eyes. No dark brown eyes. Their eyes were huge, probably looking larger because of their emaciated bodies. Their whites gleamed silvery in the semi-darkness. They lay absolutely still, staring at her.

"Do you like Sam? *Sam*?" she said.

"Sam," said Bobby. "Sam?" The others tried to say the name, some doing it well.

"Sam. Does Sam take care of you?"

The repetition of his name was a mistake. They stared at the crack in the tent, searching for Sam.

"Sam." "Sam." "Saaam," became a wail. They were calling for Sam.

"Shh!" she said. "He'll be here soon enough. He's taking care of some bizness over yonder. He'll be here."

They loved him; she could see that. Their anxious looking for him continued. And she kept watching. They didn't like lying apart from each other. They weren't people from the normal world, who wanted space. She arranged them in two rows, side to side. Once they were in contact with each other, they relaxed. After she touched the children, Lena noticed a crawly feeling moving up her hands. Parasites.

Those filthy babies bothered her. She got some more towels and a bucket of water they'd brought up for washing. She also got a cup of cooking oil. Might as well try to loosen up that dry skin. She also brought all her guns inside, just to be careful.

"Hi, Bobby. It's Lena again. I'm going to give you a little wash off. We'll do better later. This is just for now. I had two daughters, so I know how to wash kids just fine." She soaped him carefully, looking at his scaled, wrinkled skin.

Bobby pooped and demonstrated that his innards were riddled with worms. They'd have to worm them all. And delouse everyone, including herself. Why didn't the stories talk about parasites? Fiction was so nice and clean. That's why it's fiction, she thought.

"Bobby," she cooed. He was so sweet. The corners of his mouth turned up in a smile. He had little bowed lips so that he looked like a doll. His eyes were wide and trusting, despite all that had happened to him. He held his arms out to her. He looked like—Arthur! Jeremy's driver, Arthur, had come home for dinner with Henry many times. "Do you know Arthur?"

"Art'ur. Bobby o' Art'ur." Bobby waved his arm, attempting to indicate himself.

"You're an Arthur," she said, amazed. "You look just like him. I knew your . . . grandfather, Bobby. He was a nice man. A good man." Who made the wrong choice by going underground. But who knew it before the war?

She moved quickly to wash the other children. They loved to be touched. Their faces glowed when she washed them, even those that seemed almost in a stupor. Sensation was the key in their world. When she was finished, they were cleaner and oiled. Their towels were changed. And her hands were filthy. The crawling sensation had climbed up her arms and reached her body.

Picking up the sharpshooter rifle, she made the rounds of their meadow, eyes searching for anything unusual. All was quiet. She brought formula and water to the babies, which they devoured this time, knowing what it was. They were stronger, she could see that.

She went outside and waited. Only the chirps of birds and rustling of small animals disturbed the peace.

Until the explosions came. She counted three of them. Two were from the front of the shelter and one originated where the canary hole must have been. The children started crying. She picked up her rifle and went in to them.

"Shh," she said. "Shh. Be quiet."

She opened the tent flap and walked out.

He grabbed her before she could raise her gun. She never saw where he came from. The rifle flew out of her hands, useless. He held her by the throat at arm's length, studying her.

He looked somewhat like Sam. Taller than he was, and heavier. His features were coarser, but not gross like the monsters they'd seen in the pictures. Bright blue eyes, gray skin, gray teeth. Something moved on his skin, worse than the children's.

"I never saw a darky," he said in a pleasant way. His speech had a hint of the village brogue, but less pronounced than Sam's. "Such a pretty. Pretty face, pretty teeth. White." He chuckled at the wonder of her teeth. A vision flashed through Lena's mind: Her face bloodied with her teeth broken and splattered down her chin. She had to do something.

"Have you been here long?" she said, smiling. Surprisingly, she wasn't shaking.

"Long enough to know you have babies in there." His hand tightened on her throat.

"Did the explosions make a hole so you could escape?"

"Wha' differ'nce does it make?"

"I was just wondering if you heard the explosions."

"Aye," he looked at her shrewdly.

"What's your name?" She managed another smile.

"Why?"

"Just curious." She wasn't thinking at all, babbling, trying to keep him talking. He was naked, like everyone in the underground. His body told her exactly what he intended to do to her.

"We'll get down to names later, darky. Right now, I need to take care of this," he indicated his erection. "I never had one fresh as you.

When the rest get here, sure you won't look the way you do now. When I'm done, I'll stomp the heads of those brats."

He pulled at her bulletproof vest. The vest was a poncho. To put it on, she'd slipped her head through a hole in the middle. It dropped down to cover her torso, front and back. It had a wide tab that ran between her legs, fastening at her waist in front. It fastened with the highest tech Russian hardware. He couldn't get the vest off.

After trying to undo it, he yanked hard, pulling her off balance. She fell, and managed to roll away from the tent before he was on top of her. She had never seen anyone move the way he did. He was as fast as Sam had been in his wrestling demo with Grace. She realized her disadvantage on the ground; she could not get away from him.

"How d'ya get it off?" he whispered savagely. His Voice reverberated inside of her. She couldn't resist him.

"Here," she started to undo one catch. Some part of her screamed silently: Help me. Please help me. Please.

He raised his torso, trying to undo the straps. He held himself up with one arm, and fumbled with the other hand, his legs spread on each side of hers. She couldn't get away. She wasn't fast enough. Help, help me, she thought nonstop. She wouldn't cry out, wouldn't make a noise. Maybe the babies would be safe.

He swore fiercely, splattering her face with his spittle.

And then he was gone. She watched him flying through the sky, gripped by teeth whiter and sharper than her own. Something huge had grabbed the Big. Long white hair fanned out from the creature's jaws, flowing from a rounded head like a mane. It was Shaq, her dear little dog. She knew it absolutely, even though he was huge and filled the sky. She heard the crunch of bones as Shaq consumed the Big. The dog's face and bright black eyes hovered over her.

"Thank you, Shaq. Thank you, baby dog. If you were your old self, I'd give you a rib roast all for your own."

Lena picked up her gun and stood in front of the tent. She wanted to be hysterical, but there was no time. Everything Sam had said was true. That was one of the smaller Bigs. He didn't look so awful, but he was. He messed with her mind. She couldn't resist him. She was showing him how to undo her vest! Lena shuddered.

"Hell, I made it easy for him. Now I'm gonna make it hard for the rest." She covered the babies with bulletproof vests, saying, "You be quiet while I'm gone. I'm gonna do a little hunting. Make the world a safer place."

She looked around for a place to set up. Somewhere she could be hidden and have a vantage of the openings to the underground and their camp. She found what she wanted, a little rise several hundred yards away with a few scrub oaks for cover and a view of everything.

She settled down in the dried leaves, becoming part of the landscape. "OK, you little squirrelies, come to Mama."

41

"Let's put it over here." Jeremy selected a location for his computer lab/mission control center that was close enough to what they thought was the underground's rear entrance to be convenient, but not so close that a horde of Bigs would run into it as they stormed out of the shelter.

The group followed him and the packhorses. The field where the mansion and its gardens had been gave no evidence that the shelter existed—or that the estate had ever existed. The meadow was peaceful: bright sun, a sweet breeze, the crash of the surf, and delightful bird sounds. A bucolic scene overshadowed by a grating sense of foreboding.

This place was wrong. Something wicked lurked here. Grace felt it as a grinding in her belly and a sensation like grit in her mouth.

"Do you feel weird?" she said. The others nodded.

Sam put his finger to his mouth and Grace understood. The Bigs knew they were there. How, she couldn't imagine. They were hundreds of feet down, separated by a series of impermeable metal gates and cement. But they knew the group was there.

Motioning with his hands, Sam pulled them together and pointed toward the shelter, shaking his head with his finger to his mouth.

Grace understood immediately. They needed some way of protecting themselves from the psychic intrusions of their enemy. They needed protection now, and they would need it all the time they were engaged with the Bigs.

Wes and Bud looked at each other and smiled. They dropped into a crouching position and began a dance, singing in a language Grace had never heard. Their native tongue, she realized. They danced in a wide circle, around the tent housing the computers, around the grassy area, including the grassy dome she thought was the shelter's rear door.

Their dance became wilder; they spun and leapt, acting out a war party's attack. They bent to the ground, stalking, and then thrust with invisible spears and lances. Both men whooped and screamed to announce victory.

And the meadow was full. People were there; she could see their shadowy outlines the way she had seen Shaq up in the clouds. The way she saw her Rinpoche when she needed his help. They were bonneted Indians. War chiefs. Bud and Wesley's ancestors had come. Of course!

She leapt into the circle, her hands in the namaste position, folded over her heart as if in prayer. Namaste, the Sanskrit word meaning, "I bow to the divine in you." She began to chant her mantra, slowly at first and then faster. Her voice rose, higher and louder. She danced wildly, becoming a warrior woman.

Shri Rinpoche appeared before her. Shri Rinpoche filled the meadow, the sea, and the forest. Her teacher was present, along with an ancient American Indian shaman—Grandfather. She knew who he was, though she had never met him. Grandfather and the Ancestors, warriors of all eternity.

The rest of the party entered the circle and called to whatever gave them strength. And the invisible world came.

"OK, now we can talk," Grace said. The presence of the holy ones enclosed them safely. "If we didn't have their help," she nodded toward the invisible beings surrounding them, "we'd be lost. I didn't realize what Sam meant about the Bigs."

"They will attack your mind," he said. "You will think I'm bad. You may think your friends are bad. They may try to make you want to join them, to kill for them. They are very strong."

"Well, we'll have to take responsibility for our own minds. Bud and Wes, you have spiritual guides and support. I have my Rinpoche. I don't know what the rest of you believe in, but now's the time to call on it for help. So, what should we do?"

"Why do anything?" Mel said. "It's going to cost us dearly to get down there. *If* we can get into the shelter, we'll be at a disadvantage. They know the place. They have all these powers. There are seven levels, and they'll undoubtedly make us go all the way down to get them. What is it that we want down there?"

"We want to keep them from getting the general's weapons," Jeremy said. "That's the number one priority. If they get them, they can blow us out of the water. They can send one rocket where we came from and there'll be no more cliff. No more babies or us if they reach the arms. I don't need to say anything about what will happen to us if we end up their prisoners.

"Which brings up another topic," Jeremy said. "When I landed here from Ellie's planet by myself, I got pretty depressed. I went over to that cliff and looked over. If you're about to be taken, if you can make it to that cliff and jump over—that's a solution. You will die, and they won't get you."

"I have a more portable solution of the same sort," Grace said. "I have suicide capsules. Bite one and you'll be dead in seconds. I would rather be dead than end up in that pit. I've got enough for all of us."

"Lady!" Sam said.

"I will not end up in the pit. That's the end of the discussion," she said. "So, what *are* we doing?"

"We don't need to go down there," Jeremy said. "We *do* need to stop their acquisition of the big weapons." He went back in the tent to check his computers.

"Holy fucking shit!" He was glued to the screen. "They've got two thirds of the password." Everyone ran into the tent.

Grace looked into the computer screen. A Big was holding a better version of Jeremy's face up to the monitor. He said, "Jeremy Edgarton, prisoner of Hermitage Academy." Grace could have mistaken his voice for her son's.

"How did they get that?" she gasped.

"I don't know. I've only said it out loud twice in my life, once when I programmed it and the second time was back in the tent. We were all there." He looked bewildered.

Grace glanced at the others. "It couldn't have been one of us. None of us knows how to use the computer to contact the Bigs. And none of us has been down there to visit and tell them directly. I see what you mean, Sam, about planting doubt."

"That is just regular doubt, lady. What the Bigs will do is much worse."

"Great. What now?"

"Well, they have one strike left. If they don't get the password on the next try, the system will lock tight and I'll be the only one who can get in."

Jeremy picked up an electronic device that looked like a wand and waved it around the seams of the tent. Lights lit up on the tent corner and the computer.

"Son of a bitch!" he exclaimed. "The goldies laced every single thing they moved here with bugs. The Bigs picked up the goldies' transmissions of what we're saying." He spoke into the bug. "Hi, guys! Having fun spying? You may have killed us, assholes." He pulled the bug off the tent, twisted something in the back and tossed it in a bucket. "I've been doing that for days. You disable them by twisting the back. See?" He held the wand to the bucket and no light appeared.

"They're broadcasting us on their networks. We're the Late Night Comedy Show. The Bigs must have figured out how to pick up the signals. *That's* how they knew the password. Our 'friends' from Ellie's world gave them what they needed to decipher it. Shit. Now they just have to get the rest, and they'll be able to fry us."

"How can they do that?" Henry asked.

"How else would they get that code? I used to broadcast from that lab all the time. If you can broadcast, you can receive. They picked up the signals going to Ellie's planet and deciphered them. Man, I never would have believed they were that smart."

"Some are not smart," Sam said. "Those are strong and have the Voice."

"This is great," Jeremy ran his hands over the stubs of his dreads. "OK, I say, blow them up. I brought lots of plastic explosive."

"There's another issue," Grace tossed in. "Sam's people that are still down there. We've started this conversation, but we haven't finished it. Sam, how many of your people can take care of themselves? If we brought them out, how many could survive without taking the able-bodied people away from productive work?"

He pulled his lips together as though trying to swallow them and grimaced. "Lady, they need to be fed and cleaned. They would need to be dressed if they had clothes."

"Can they be taught? Can they speak?"

"Some can speak a little. They don't think like you or me, but they are people, lady. They are alive here," he touched his heart.

"The thing is, we don't know about winter in this place. We may be starving very soon. Can we take care of disabled people? I'm being the devil's advocate. I'd like to take care of all of them."

"Well, I'll tell you how to make it through the winter," Bud said. "Shoot the horses and eat them. You got enough horseflesh there to get you through just culling out the old ones. If you want to take the disabled people and kids back to the cliff, we can use the horses and make travois. Those are horse-drawn rigs made out of long poles. We can rig them up and train the horses to pull them. And Wes and I can show you things that our people did to survive. We're survival experts."

"Well, that's good. One problem down. What's next?"

"Well, we need Jeremy to blow up the underground computer lab and the entrance to the munitions storage so that it can never be breached—without blowing up all the general's explosives and killing us."

"Yes," they said.

"And once that's done?" she said. "What are they likely to do, Sam?"

"They will either stay inside or come out." He thought. "If they are frightened by the blast, they will use the guns they have from Arthur's room and Sam Baahuhd's and shoot out the glass of the solar fields." He gestured in the direction they had come.

"That's where Lena is!" Henry exclaimed.

"Yes," Sam said.

"We'd better go help her!"

"Can you shoot like her?" Sam asked.

"No."

"Then stay away. She's stronger alone." Sam was very definite. "If they get her and you, they'll stomp the children's heads."

Grace recoiled. "No."

"That is how they kill children." He shrugged. "Some of the Bigs, who want to make a new," he searched for a word, "tribe, will go out the back.

"Some—Sam Big and the biggest Bigs—will stay below and wait for us. Some will come out after us, out the front or other ways they find. Those are the ones who have the disease and rage. They will not be afraid of us, and they will not be able to wait below when they start to get angry. They will kill everything they see."

"OK, I'm going to blow the computer lab," Jeremy said. "Should I do the canary hole and the back door? Will that lock them in?"

"They will get out," Sam said. "I am not the only digger. They have tunnels. Not so many, because they can't fit through my tunnels. And not so many tunnels, because the dirt from digging is hard to," ... he searched for a word ... "put somewhere. But they will get out."

Jeremy looked a little crazed. "I'm supposed to blow stuff up without killing the good guys, as soon as I figure out where the openings are."

"I know where they are," Sam said. "I will show you."

"One problem down. I'll get my kit and the plastic and wire them up. I need everyone else to find the bugs the goldies planted and pull them down. Mel, James, Mom, everyone, find those lights and defuse them. They're everywhere.

"I will not be *entertainment*." He shouted at the tent and all of its surveillance devices. "Those assholes may get us killed, just because they're bored with their stupid lives."

Sam and Jeremy stood on the grassy areas placing the explosive charges.

"This is the back door," Sam said, standing in the grass and indicating a point by his foot.

"I thought it was that mound," Jeremy said, pointing at something a few feet away.

"No, it's here. I can feel it."

Jeremy brought a large hand drill and cut through the turf easily. About three feet down, he heard a metallic clank. "You're right." He set a charge there.

They went on to locate the lab and the area where the main entrance to the shelter had been, the mezzanine that led to the mansion's ballroom.

"This will blow up half the meadow," he said after setting the fuses.

And on to the canary hole.

"I guarantee, no one will ever go through this again," Jeremy said. He set the third charge like a pro.

The rest was a matter of pushing a button.

42

Everyone on the planet who had a space big enough to permit a screen sat in front of it. Most of the monitors had been recently upgraded and enlarged. Those who did not have room for a private screen clustered in public areas. Public viewing equipment had also been enhanced.

The space before the great screen of the elders was so jammed that some people expressed irritation when others came late and blocked their views or stepped on them as they found a seat. Unheard of, but true. Everyone on the planet watched as Lady Grace and her people approached the battle.

The tall doctor knew that the entire population was watching, because he had organized the plan. He was behind the upgrading of the screens. As the show began, he sat beside equipment that monitored who was watching and how much of a gratuity they'd paid for the privilege.

That was his innovation: After viewing the Wesley Silverhorse and Bud Creeman broadcasts, he had tuned in to a soap opera from the planet Earth. It was disgusting, but enthralling. Now his systems allowed him to watch an infinite number of programs, as well as receive instruction in merchandising and sales, which the Earth channels broadcast endlessly. He came up with the idea of making the same programming available to his people, for a small charge.

The council of elders had been hesitant about his idea of charging for the privilege of watching one's screen, because the concept of charging for anything intangible was foreign to their culture.

"Don't call it a charge!" he explained, "Call it a gratuity. A gift of gratitude for the joy their civilization gives them. For the privilege of having a private screen, a newer, bigger, full-sound screen in each—well, almost each—place.

The elders readily took to that concept. And the people were grateful. The programming available was wildly exciting. Not only could they receive all the television programs that had been produced on Earth and most of the galaxies, they could also watch Lady Grace and her friends.

When that programming became indispensable to their existence, the doctor planned to increase the suggested gratuities. They would later become charges for services that could be cut off if they weren't paid. Such tactics were foreign to his soul, but his soul was becoming increasingly perplexing to him. Ever since he had touched her. He could still feel that touch.

It wasn't all her; he also knew that his people needed things. Not just screens, but things like new sources of nourishment and energy. Theirs was an old planet, with old people. That's why they'd tried the hybrid project, which was a great risk. It did bring them new people, who now needed more things. Their systems—transportation, energy, and food production—were wearing down. They *needed* things for the first time and had to learn how to pay for them. His plan with the screens was the first of his new concepts for saving the planet. The council of elders didn't know the rest yet.

The surveillance devices he'd sent to the humans fed into a central control where their technical people sifted through the multitudinous views of the humans' reality and picked out the best strands. Those they combined into a show, the highlights of the day on Earth. He might direct the technical people to show the whole day. Those who were grateful enough could watch it around the clock.

The evening's episode was beginning. He turned to his more than life-sized screen—and why shouldn't he have such a screen? He was behind everything. There she was, going into her tent. Ten cameras caught her telling the others that she was changing into commando garb. Inside the tent, she stripped off her clothes and stood facing one of the surveillance devices. It picked up every color and nuance.

Enormous cones of flesh protruded from her chest. They were tipped with large burgundy-tinged circles, flat with lovely little dimples in the middle. The camera focused on them and zoomed in. Lovely soft skin. The flesh sagged just the tiniest bit and swayed as she picked through her clothes. She found a wide black band and wrapped it around those amazing globes, tightening it so that they were compressed and covered, no longer jiggling in that lovely way. He could barely breathe and froze the image of the pressure of that band around her unbelievable . . . things. He wanted to grab them.

The cameras glided over her body, replaying on small screens. Everyone on the planet saw her hips and thighs. No one turned off a screen. He knew this dressing interval would be played and replayed. She was a star, and a moneymaker. He'd up the gratuities for the replays.

After she put on the rest of her military gear, she walked out of the tent, disappearing from the screens. She became invisible when dressed, because her uniform was so close to absolute black.

He replayed the dressing scene the minute it was over. He was a man; he knew that. He had begun a medical program that should yield tangible evidence of his manhood soon. The program was his own invention, which he shared with no one.

He felt a little different, due to the procedures and medications. Hormones. Maybe they influenced his thinking. Maybe the change from an intuitive, peace-loving healer and intellectual to the way he felt now was due to the drugs. Who cared?

He'd be able to mate with her soon, he knew. Why not create two superstars—she would be the female and he would be the male? With so many hybrids, they would be the models for the new society. His network would have no censors; nothing would be forbidden.

He stopped daydreaming when Jeremy blew up his targets.

"Good boy!" he cried. That troublemaker was a hero on the screen. Jeremy created more viewers, even as he cursed the doctor and his people over the bugs. The doctor liked that.

He watched them moving around the meadow, planning their next step. They were going to *fight* the monsters.

This was so exciting. He'd given the process a little nudge. The Bigs had been casting about with their computer broadcasts in a clumsy and ineffective way. He'd contacted them and given the Bigs a snatch of information in exchange for a peek at the underground. It was only two thirds of the password, but the exchange certainly livened up the human's activities. In exchange, the viewers on the golden planet were able to access the underground's cameras.

He leaned forward as the shelter's seven levels appeared in the dim lights. On the big screen, it was more disgusting than Jeremy's pictures could convey. They were going to *fight* in that hideous place.

The women's pit appeared, with its unhappy occupants. The Bigs were using the howling creatures, even as their security was being breached.

He sat up, horrified. *She* was going down there! What if they captured *her*?

43

"Shit! I've got to get better with plastics!" Jeremy said. The explosions had hurled debris across the pasture. Chunks of cement and metal flew and bounced, settling to the ground moments before they made their inspection.

Sam thought Jeremy had done a great job. The canary hole was a mass of twisted metal, concrete, and dirt. No one would ever go through it again. The area forming the entrance to the shelter and the computer lab was a crater. What hadn't been blown up collapsed upon itself. The Bigs who had been working at the computers were gone—buried or blown to bits. They could see two of the doorways leading deeper into the underground. They were fused shut.

That part of the operation was a total success: No one would go in or out either way. The powerful weapons were sealed off, but not blown up, and the Bigs had no computers.

Only the "back door" didn't turn out the way Jeremy wanted. He hoped to seal the exit. The blast blew off its heavy metal lid and left a gaping hole in the earth. Sam took a fast look down the shaft. The entrances to the underground consisted of a series of round metal doors going down to the lowest level of the shelter. Between the locked entries, passages were cement-lined shafts with steel stairs or ladders going up and down. The accesses widened at lower levels of the shelter.

The back door itself had been a steel pipe three feet across. The blast made the opening twice as wide. Sam could see that the metal ladder inside was bent and twisted, but was still usable. He could see all the way down to the fourth level of the shelter. The blast gave the Bigs a much larger exit. They could swarm out easily.

"What do we do? Wait until they come out, or go after them?" Henry said. He stood with the others in front of the tent containing Jeremy's computers. Clad in black commando suits, they looked pretty impressive. "I've never done anything like this before."

"None of us have," Mel said. "Shouldn't we have a plan?"

"There's a military adage about planning," said Grace. "'No plan survives contact with the enemy.' Because the unforeseen *always* happens.

"We need an *intention*. The military works on the Commander's Intent. The CI. Even if the enemy screws up our plans, the CI can operate. Like: We intend to make our land a safe, good place. Our immediate intent is: Clear and secure the underground. That's a CI. If we had a Commander."

"You're it, Grace," Mel said.

"I'm not qualified," she replied. "I've never done any of this for real, either." Her head turned toward the hole, catching something moving. Sam's eyes followed her glance. The muzzle of an automatic rifle was sticking out of the back door. It disappeared inside.

Grace motioned to Wes and Bud. They nodded and moved noiselessly to the hole. Picking up her machine gun, she waved at the others to get out of sight and followed Bud and Wesley. Sam followed them. They positioned themselves behind the hole.

The machine gun's muzzle appeared again. Soon the Big carrying it was crawling out. He stayed low, surveying the meadow in front of him, but not looking behind him. When he got up on all fours in preparation for standing, Grace nodded. Bud waved his hand as he had earlier. A blue light came out of his palm. The Big's head rolled to one side, taking a turn on the grass while his body twitched.

After a short while, someone whispered from the hole, "Hey, Billy. Wher' r' ya?"

"Ah'm o'tside, nuthin' here," Sam said in a voice that was pure village. "C'mon out. They musta run awa."

The next one climbed out and made it all the way out, far enough to see Billy's headless form. Wes cut him in half.

The third was more cautious. "We're'ya? Billy? Russ? Ah canna see ya."

"W're lookin' a' th' ocean, Johnny. An' it's a sight. Come on—straight ahead." Sam's voice mimicked the downed Big, even sounding like he was a distance away from the opening. He knew the Bigs by voice. "C'mon."

Number three got half as far as number two before being cut in two by the blue beams from Wes and Bud's hands.

No more approached the opening.

Grace motioned for them to back off. The next one came up shooting. Bullets sprayed out of the hole. The shooter was too far inside to do anything but shoot a circle in the air. It wasn't even a circle. Sam knew he'd never shot a weapon before. He'd played with one, pointed it, pretended, but he didn't know what it felt like when the machine came alive. Sam watched carefully. Grace had told them that bullets from an automatic weapon such as the shooter held shot high. It was true. The Big came out slowly, not looking behind him, spraying bullets over his head. He was standing on the rim of the hole when he finally turned around.

Wes got him. He fell backward, feet sticking into the opening. Sam ran and pulled him away, so they couldn't see him from inside. "Hey!" he yelled into the hole, "We got th' Egerton bitch! I got her b'tween th' tits."

Laughter erupted from below.

"C'mon!" Sam mimicked. "Me'n Billy an' Russ'r gonna have 'er! She's daid, bu' wha's th' diff'rence?"

Two more came out, placing their guns on the ground outside the hole before pulling themselves out of the opening; they looked around, apparently not seeing the black-clad warriors. Either the absolute black of their uniforms or the unaccustomed brilliance of daylight blinded them. Or perhaps the prospect of having a dead woman was too enticing.

"Where she?" one yelled. They stood side by side looking toward the ocean's crashing surf.

"I'm here," Grace said softly, feet spread and crouching slightly, her gun ready. When they turned, she cut them down. Sam pulled their bodies away from the opening. The warriors stepped back and waited.

Sam took a quick inventory. They'd killed six. At least two more were in the computer lab. He counted eight on his fingers. How many were left? He thought there were thirty-four. Sam opened and closed both hands three times and added four more fingers, then closed his fingers one at a time until he'd taken away eight. Twenty-six. Plus how many more that he didn't know about? They had two hands of fingers: ten people. He didn't think that the next Bigs would be as easy.

They stepped back and waited. He felt something grabbing at his mind, trying to pull him under. He knew how to counter it, repeating the Commands to himself, and thinking of the Book. He beckoned to the others, retreating toward the computer tent.

"I felt something awful trying to enter my mind," Grace said. "Shri Rinpoche came to protect me. I could see him and feel him, and I repeated my mantra. Did you feel that awful pull?"

"Aye, lady. They will try to win our minds now. They saw that we will not be easy to kill, so they will try something else. Destroying us from in here." He pointed to his head. "I think of the Book, and I think of the Commands. I live by those. I think of things that the first

Sam said about God. How God wasn't what people thought. God was what made things turn out right. That you couldn't see God, but only know when God was there.

"The Bigs are not as powerful as these thoughts. You must fill your mind with them, no space for anything else, and they will not poison you."

"I don't believe in God," Mel said. "The concept causes more harm than good."

Sam nodded. "I'm sorry. They will probably get you. You need something stronger than your doubt to hold them off."

"OK, everyone," Grace said. "I offer my mantra." She explained to them. "It's used by a number of traditions, some of which don't believe in God. Use it happily, Mel. But you have to concentrate."

"Listen, think about Grandfather and the ancestors," Bud said. "That's easy. Call to Grandfather and he'll come. You can see him around you. He'll bring the Great One. You don't have to believe in anything."

"Yes," Wes said. "That will get you through anything. I remember . . . "

"Before you really get into this chat about theology," Jeremy interrupted, "has anyone seen Ellie?"

"She was sitting in a tree back by the camp before we came over here," Mel said.

"Sitting in a tree?"

"Yes. She appeared to be making an egg sack."

"Really?"

"Yes. It was about three feet across when I saw it," Mel added. "I would have told you, but I didn't know what to say. I couldn't believe it. And then we got busy."

"Wow," Bud said, putting his hand to his mouth. "They've been having some real bad problems with Africanized bees in the Southwest. This could be really . . ."

Jeremy stared blankly. "I thought she would help us."

Explosions of machine gun fire from the rear of the underground jolted them into the present. They could hear glass shattering.

"What are they doing?" Henry cried.

"They are shooting out the solar panels covering the growing fields," Sam said. "They will escape that way."

"But that's where Lena is!" Henry jumped in that direction.

Sam stopped him. "If they catch you, they will make her surrender by torturing you. Trust her. We must watch this hole."

The rat-a-tat of gunfire coming from the backdoor brought them back to their job. Grace, Sam, and the two Indians moved toward the hole.

"Watch your mind," Mel whispered. "Think of Grandfather."

44

Three gray figures rose out of the field in front of her. They crouched, getting their bearings and adjusting to the light. Lena could see that they were the smaller Bigs, like the one who wanted to rape her.

She had expected them since she heard the three explosions. Whatever her compatriots did up front would scare them out the back. Bursts of machine gun fire and breaking glass as they shot out the solar panels above the growing fields told her she was exactly right. And then the ghastly forms appeared.

Once moving, they followed each other, bending low, beelining it for the children. She waited until they were into the open before firing, wanting to make sure no one could see what happened to them from where they'd emerged. She picked them off, one, two, three. They dropped when hit, with no further movement. The gun's silencer made their deaths anticlimactic; they just disappeared into the pasture.

She hoped she'd get a few more before they wised up. Another Big poked his head out of the shelter. He looked in the direction the others had taken and pulled back.

She felt something tugging at her mind, searching for her. Their invisible intelligence probed the area. They were looking for her, and they found her. That fast. She felt sullied by their touch. And dizzy. She had to protect herself. They were calling to her. She felt an urge to get up and walk over there.

Help, she thought. Help me. She needed the greatest protection she could get or she would be lost. Her mind grabbed on Him lickety-split. Jesus, I need your help now, she prayed. Protect me. Jesus, stay with me. When the Bigs' probing became more intense, she dropped the extra words and repeated His name over and over, clinging to Him.

The disgusting, invisible touch didn't come near her again. It felt all around her, maybe, but it didn't reach her.

What would they do now, knowing that she was watching the hole in the solar panels? If they had other exits, they'd use them. Sam had said that other tunnels and burrows existed. Where? Where would they emerge? Could be anywhere. Even underneath her. How many years had they been digging? But Sam said they had trouble getting rid of the diggings. Where could they put the soil from their tunnels, other than in their living areas? So the tunnels most likely wouldn't be too long. Would they?

Lena wished she could change position, but hers was the only hill around. She thought of dragging her arsenal up a tree and shooting from there. She'd have a change of position, but it would only fool them for one volley of shots. Then she'd be treed, like the raccoons her grandfather had hunted. Treed by some very nasty hounds. She knew what happened to those 'coons.

How many of them were there? She did a little trick, praying as hard as she could and then thinking, Now, Jesus, I need to think for a little while. You stand guard while I figure out what to do. The sense of the Bigs reaching for her was more intense and disgusting than she could have imagined. Cut me a little slack now, Jesus. I need to plan.

Sam had said there was a minimum of thirty-four Bigs, maybe many more than that. She'd shot three of the smaller kind and Shaq ate one. How many more were there? There were the monstrous big Bigs with the distorted faces, the faster ones that she'd encountered, and others. What had Sam said? Some of them had to be chained up because they had rages.

She expected the ragers would stay underground, to be unleashed when Grace, Sam, and the others went down. What use were ragers, anyway? They had no protection against guns and could only run screaming straight ahead. Rage doesn't allow for strategy and thought. The rest would come after her.

The Bigs she'd shot didn't have weapons. Someone shot glass out for them, and they came out with no guns. Why? Because they were low status? Or because they didn't expect her to be waiting for them? Or was it because they didn't have that many guns that worked and what they had were needed for the big standoff?

Were the ones that came out the cowards? Or the smart, brave ones who were supposed to capture the outside, securing it for the big Bigs after they killed the people underground? Would they keep their children inside to be safe, or send them out through the tunnels? It was too much to think about.

She sank deeper into the leaves and debris under the tree. If they got her, they'd get her weapons and kill the babies. She hadn't taken one of those suicide capsules Grace showed her. She would not take that way out.

Up in the sky, a few clouds drifted in a balmy blue dome. It looked like heaven, if she didn't feel that repulsive pull tugging in her mind. Where are you, my Shaq? Don't forget about us, Shaq. Don't go away, baby dog, she thought. I need you, Shaq.

What bothered her most was that the canary hole was at the far left of her vision. The growing fields were a few hundred yards in front of her. She could make out Jeremy's tent through the scope on her rifle on the other side of the underground shelter. She saw them moving around over there, her people. She could see very well in front of her and in an arc to the right, but not to the left. The hill obscured it.

She heard something and spun around, keeping as low as possible. A funny-looking dog stood there. A female obviously: her belly hung with swollen teats. She had pups. The dog hit the ground, groveling when Lena fixed the gun on her. What was she doing there? She had ears that were halfway between pricked and floppy hound dog. Her coat was a nondescript, mottled color. She was as much a mutt as Shaq had been a purebred.

Lena remembered Jeremy telling them that a dog had come out the first night, a bitch that had puppies. She took him to her burrow and saved his life. "Are you here to save my life, girl?' Lena whispered. The dog crept forward, groveling and wagging her tail.

"Tell you what, sweetie . . . ," Jeremy had given her a name. What was it? Flossie. That's what he'd called her, after old Sam Baahuhd's hound dog. "Flossie, you watch my back, all right. You keep watch for me. They'll likely rush me all at once, from all directions." The little hound nestled in the leaves by Lena's feet, watching Lena's rear.

A growl rattled in Flossie's throat. Lena spun around and plugged a Big trying to sneak up behind her. And then they came. They were ranged along the side of the hill out of her sight, doing just what she expected. A pincers move, classic strategy. She didn't know how many tunnels they had or where they'd come from exactly. Lena's heart beat hard. She might die in the next few minutes.

But it didn't work out the way the Bigs had planned. She heard them screaming from behind the hill. The snarling of many dogs was intermingled with curses and shrieks. A Big ran across the field in front of her, pursued by a half-dozen wild dogs. She shot him. The dogs gutted him where he fell.

She crept closer to the edge of the rise to see better. Dogs were on their bellies, searching the grass for more of the easy new quarry. Bigs began rising out of the ground without any idea of what awaited them. The dogs crept closer, silent, eyes on their prey.

A Big walked stealthily past the place where she lay hidden in the grass. She didn't drop him. He moved cautiously into the field. A bit farther, and then he stood up and walked away. Three Bigs shuffled behind him, looking every which way.

The dogs did what the Bigs had wanted to do to her: ambushed them and cut them down. Bigs ran with dogs snapping at their flanks. They were pulled down by the dogs or shot by her.

The dogs' pack behavior took over. The animals hunted as a team, stalking one after the other, crisscrossing the field, searching for strays. They entered the woods and chased out two more. She dropped them and the dogs tore into their bodies. Only a couple of the Bigs had weapons, and they couldn't hit a thing with them.

She and the dogs killed eleven, and the dogs might have pulled down a few more that she didn't see. Listening to the ferocious animals savage the Bigs' bodies brought her no joy. She'd won, but she was a killer now. Lena sat up, tears glistening on her cheeks. She'd killed people.

The dogs in the meadow noticed her move. Every head popped up, all eyes fixed on her. They forgot their feast instantly. They lifted their muzzles, sampling her scent. The dogs soundlessly assembled at the base of the hill. The pack leader dropped his head and stared into her eyes. The others followed him.

Lena leapt to her feet and picked up her machine gun for the first time that day. "You mess with me, dog, you'll be dead." She aimed at the pack leader. "You wanna see *bad*? I'll show you bad."

She stepped carefully down the hill, eyes on the leader. He dropped back, keeping his head down and ears back. She got on the flat, looking at him. "Well, what are you going to do? Do it!"

He broke eye contact and moved away, slinking sideways but keeping his head pointed toward her. She'd bested him. But not the number two dog. A smaller, grizzled dog leapt at her, teeth flashing. She shot him, remembering Grace's admonition that automatics shoot high. The dog collapsed mid-leap and fell in a heap, twitching. The others began to melt into the grass, disappearing the way they'd come.

"Wait!" She didn't want them to leave. She wanted them to help her. She'd blown that by killing their pal. "I don't want to kill you."

The sky roiled and darkened. She looked up and saw Shaq's face across the meadow. "I'm sorry, Shaq. I know you sent them to help. I didn't want them to kill me." Had she destroyed his trust? She stood there, afraid of her own dog. Of course, he had weighed twelve pounds when he was her boy.

"I need to make sure no more of them get out. I can't do that alone. And I've got to get back to the children."

Shaq was in his rollicking puppy mood. Playing, he bounced over the field away from her, and then spun in circles on his hind end before coming to a stop in front of her, front end down and tail wagging. Dust and leaves flew. His passage caused small whirlwinds to flurry around the meadow.

"Oh, good, Shaq. You're not mad at me. Would you make them obey me? I need guards. They can eat the Bigs later."

"Woof!" resounded over the grasslands. The thunderous sound caused the dog pack to drop flat on the ground. After wagging his tail and barking again, Shaq bounded off.

"All right, you hounds, follow me," Lena walked boldly in the direction the Bigs had come. She wished she had a whip like her grandfather used with his hounds. He never hit the dogs, but the snap of the whip told them where they should go. Those were hunting dogs, not ladies' pets, and ferocious. All of them were killers, though they loved and served Grandpa.

The Bigs' trail was easy to follow. They knew nothing about hiding their tracks and probably didn't think it would be necessary. Lena identified three fresh tunnels that they must have used to get out. No more Bigs were visible as she passed. She also located the detonated canary hole. "That's one down." No need to fear attack from that direction.

After completing her survey, she returned the way she had come. One of the Bigs was emerging from a tunnel as she approached. He looked at her, his blue eyes locked on her brown ones.

"Darky," he said, smiling. Her aim was off. She shot him in the right arm. He kept coming. She shot him in the left shoulder. He slid back into the hole, either pulled by his compatriots or backpedaling hard with his feet.

When the opening was clear, Lena pointed the muzzle of her gun down the hole and fired a few rounds. Screams told her that she'd hit paydirt.

She fired down the other holes, even though she didn't see Bigs. Muffled groans and shuffling from underground said they'd gotten the message. But not all of it.

She looked at the lead dog and pointed at the burrow nearest her. Making a downward movement with her hand, she said, "Stay here. Kill anything that comes out." She swept her arm to the other holes and looked at the leader. "Cover them all for me, and cover my retreat."

The dog looked at her, seeming to understand. Other members of the pack trotted off to the other holes. "You can have all you can eat. If we stay friends, we'll hunt together. You'll get more food than you ever would without me." She knew that the dog couldn't understand her, but it made her feel better to talk to him. "I'm sorry I shot your friend, but you can't attack me."

She had to get back to the kids. They needed her. Lena climbed back up the hill, got her sharp-shooting guns and ammunition. Her water. She found that the Russian bulletproof vest was very well-designed. It had tabs and pockets to allow her to carry her gear efficiently. She set off across the field to their camp and the kids.

It was a long, hard trek. She was exhausted before she even started out. As she walked, Lena wished that she had worked out every day she'd spent in Ellie's world, and every day of her life before that. Then she'd be up for this.

The only nice thing about the hike was Flossie's trotting along next to her. "You're a good girl, aren't you, Flossie?" She was a different type of dog than the hounds. More of a housedog or companion than a hound with a blood lust.

Lena kept trudging. She was so tired when she got to the children's tent that her hands trembled as she unloaded her guns. She wanted to flop on the ground, but they were so quiet inside.

"Are you all right?" she unzipped the tent flap as fast as she could and stuck her head in. The smell of feces and urine assailed her, but nothing moved under the bulletproof vests. She piled into the tent and lifted one of the vests. "Bobby! Are you . . .?" His blue eyes looked into hers. "Oh, my God. You were so quiet. I thought . . ." She slumped. "Well, you are good children. I told you to be quiet and you were."

What to do? She shouldn't leave her guns out there. She should be out front herself, watching. But she couldn't leave the children in there, stinking and lying in shit. Maybe they'd done that all their lives, but she couldn't allow it. She decided to take a chance and tend to the kids.

Flossie was gone when she came out to get towels and water to clean the children. Lena looked around. She saw Ellie sitting in a tree behind the camp. She'd been there all day. A huge gray ball like a wasp's nest hung from the branch. It must have been four feet across. An egg sack, Lena thought, having seen Ellie's other "babies." This one was many times larger than the others, though. Lena thought Ellie would help the others, but apparently her maternal duties had deep-sixed her involvement in the battle.

Lena felt better tending to the children. They loved to be touched and talked to. "Everything's gonna be fine. Don't you worry. We're gonna be fine. I'll take care of you the rest of your lives. We're gonna get out of here and you babies are going to run across that pasture havin' fun.

She knew some of their names. Bobby. Patrick. Ellen. James. Billy. All she had to do to know a child's name was look at him or her, and the name came to her. They had the Bigs' intuitive abilities, but theirs had kindness behind them. She knew how the new food was agreeing with them, and who wanted water and who needed formula. They were wonderful to be around—and very alert, now that their fluid levels were up.

"All right, children, I have to cover you up again. I'll be right outside, but don't make any noise."

Shadows lengthened. She had a bad feeling about what was happening to the others. She hadn't heard a thing, but the oppressive quality of the Bigs' presence weighed upon the camp. It was much worse than what she'd experienced with the smaller Bigs. She had the feeling that Sam Big and all the others were working on her friends' minds. She repeated Jesus's name, hoping that she could withstand the urge to leave her post and march directly into the underground. Flossie and her pups curled up underneath her, as though she could provide them with protection from the darkness.

Lena heard a whirring sound and looked up to see Ellie flying toward the main battlefield. Light glittered off her faceted body plates, shooting flashing beams around the meadow. Her wings moved faster than the eye could follow, beautiful iridescent things like flying knife blades. Ellie looked at Lena. Her eyes were brilliant silver orbs devoid of feeling or expression.

She shuddered. Ellie reminded her of the exhibition of military planes she and Henry had seen at the air base. Streamlined fighter jets rose high into the air in tight formation, swooping down and over the field where they stood. They thrilled and terrified at once. Ellie was like that, beautiful and horrible. She streaked toward the field where the others were massed.

45

"Ah, 'tis the beautiful Mrs. Egerton," Sam Big's voice emerged from the hole in the ground like an oily balm. He sounded like a gracious host welcoming his guests, "The dear friend of my ancestor, Sam Baahuhd." He spoke normal English, tinged with the village's burr. "Ah welcome ye with all the love in dear Sam Baahuhd's heart. For ah am his true son and heir."

They stood in the lawn area between Jeremy's computer center and the blown open rear entry to the underground. Jeremy had pushed a wand-like periscope over the edge to see what was going on down below and found all seven levels to the underground were wide open.

As Jeremy withdrew the scope, Sam Big began his courtship of the group—and that was what his words amounted to. He had perceived the subtle movement of the periscope from the shelter's depths. Grace was surprised; either Sam Big's eyes were very sharp or he had highly responsive computerized sensors functioning.

"How lovely to have you and your friends. Jeremy, the great Tek himself, is here. And Henry, whose drinking powers Sam Baahuhd could not best." He seemed to know some of those who were present, but not all. He missed the two Indians and Mel and James. And he didn't speak to Sam.

Grace looked at her friends and found them spellbound, focused on the opening and the voice coming from it. The man was charming. They drifted closer to the hole as they listened. Sam beckoned them back from the edge. Grace moved away, along with the others. She sensed that it would be harder to resist that voice the closer they got.

Gathering them in front of the tent, Sam whispered, "It is the Voice. Do not believe anything he says. He welcomes you to your deaths. You *will* go down there if you listen to him."

Grace shook her head to clear it. She *did* want to go down the stairs. Worse, she felt a throb of desire deep in her body. Sam Big was magnetic and knew her weaknesses. "What can we do, Sam?" she implored.

"What ye did before, say your holy words and remember Him who made all this world. This is the easy part. It will get worse. He will change."

Jeremy ran into the computer center and came out of the tent wearing big, padded headphones from his computer. He pulled them off in disgust. "I thought they'd cut the sound, but they make his voice louder."

"You have to call on what power you have. He will call you until he dies. Or you do."

The Voice continued and they withstood it using the means Sam had suggested. Sam Big's tone changed when no one marched down the stairs.

"Ye're a whore to beat the best, you lil' cunnie. *Lady Grace.*" Sam Big's laugh rolled over the lawn, almost toxic enough to poison the grass. "Named yerself a new name, but it can't hide the bitch beneath. Veronica Egerton. That's a proper whore's name. Ah'd take care o' ye so ye'd stay put, ye and yer nice little quim . . ."

Grace felt herself pulled forward, wanting to run straight to the beast. The malevolence in his voice throbbed through the air. And through her. She wanted him, though she would have died before admitting it. What he said seemed the absolute truth.

"Ye'll never change, hell-bitch. Come down to me and get what ye want. I'll give ye what's yers. Com'ere, hell's wart!"

She moved forward three steps. Sam grabbed her and pulled her back.

"Ah, me Sammy," the voice recognized Sam's presence for the first time. "Me love. Do yer friends know that you and I been rammin' it home since we was lads? Y' were fourteen when ye let me have ye, body and soul. Th' bitch thinks she's got you, but we know, don't we?

"Ah *own* ye, Sammy. Get down here, now!" The Voice became ferocious. For the first time, they could feel Sam Big's power and rage. "I *want* you! The bitch will na' steal ye from me."

Sam backed off in horror, but couldn't turn away.

"Ah, Sam, did I tell yer secret? Those jolly boys w' ye ain't nuthin' 'pared to you and me. Ah'm *embarrassin'* ye? Ah'm so sorry …"

Sam covered his ears and bent over. They couldn't see his expression.

"We had such great times. 'Member the way ye squealed?" Sam Big laughed uproariously.

Sam dropped to his knees, holding his head in his hands, groaning, "No, no …"

"Ah is embarassin' ye w' yer new lady, the cunnie from hell? Aw. I'm sorry, but yer *my* pretty. An' ye love me, na' her." He paused artfully.

"That ain't what really bothers ye, is it? It's the *punishment* ye got. Ye're a very bad man, Sam of Emily. I had to punish ye. So I took yer sister. Ah know ye remember wha' happen t' her. A fine piece a' flesh, she was. Didn' need legs for what we did. Didn' last long, though.

"And that girl ye fancied? Th' skinny one? Jennie? Ah—she hardly lasted a day when my boys had a' 'er. Ah know ye fancied 'er, Sam, but ye don' allus get wa' ye want.

"Ye got *me*, luv. Ye love me, an' ah love ye. Think yer new friends will want ye now they know about ye?

"C'mon down, Sammy boy. *Ye know ye want to.*"

Grace could hardly bear to hear it. She covered her ears, but it didn't do any good. The words covered her like filth. She turned to Sam.

He leapt up in anguish, tearing open his bulletproof suit and exposing his chest to the others. He screamed, "KILL ME! KILL ME!" He turned to each of them, offering his chest. "SHOOT ME! I WANT TO DIE! *Kill* me or ah will go down there . . ."

When no one would kill him, he pointed his gun at himself. Wesley grabbed the weapon.

"Excuse me, Sam. I need to reach over here for a second." Bud spread his hand wide, touching Sam's chest. Sam collapsed. Bud softened his fall and laid him on the ground, squatting next to him with his hand remaining over Sam's heart. Sam Big's voice continued to belch out of the hole. Bud turned to Wes. "Would you shut him up?"

Wesley stood facing the opening and raised his hands above his head, eyes closed, apparently in prayer. A spray of blue sparkles appeared from his fingers, becoming a fountain that eclipsed the sun. A column of light arose from his head, spreading out, filling the area over the underground. It covered the meadow and went all the way to the sea. Inside that dome, peace reigned.

Bud laughed at his companions' reactions to Wesley's display. "You ain't see ol' Wes in his glory. He's been known to sprout a giant over his head that would do in Sam Big and all of his dogs without no trouble at all. Unfortunately, he's only done that in the Mogollon Bowl with Grandfather there.

"But let's get to work; I don't know how long Wes can keep that goin'." Bud focused on his hand and his connection to Sam, who was passed out. "I needed to do this to get a little control here." He closed his eyes and might have been thinking, or calling upon something unseen.

"OK, we know what happened to Sam down below," Bud said. He kept his hand on Sam's chest, squatting as he talked. Sam remained insensible. "And we know just how mean that sumbitch is, and how he plans to destroy us." He looked up at Grace, who was white-faced and shaken. "Grace, ma'am, I don't believe what he said about you."

"It's true, Bud, Absolutely true. I used my body to gain influence and power, not because I loved anyone. I was a whore . . ."

"Mom, that's not true. You did some bad stuff, but you made up for it," Jeremy stepped forward, appalled by what Sam Big had said about his mother and the effect it had on her. She looked shrunken.

"No, he's right, Jeremy. I could feel myself wanting him as he was talking. I almost went down there. I'm no good." She was distraught.

"OK, Grace, we know how he works now. He tears you down. Everybody here's got stuff they want to hide. Bad stuff, maybe. I was a fallin' down drunk. Spent so many nights in the gutter, only Grandfather and the Great One could pick me up.

"I had such a low opinion of myself that Grandfather had to send me out to save some dyin' people lost in the desert. That's how I met Will Duane and them. Only when I healed them an' brought them home did I believe I could do anything.

"But that low down part of me's still there. If Sam Big tuned into that, he'd probably have me down those stairs and drinkin' all the hooch he's got. That's how he works. The way you look now is how he works.

"That SOB needs killing. All of them down there, 'cept maybe a few of Sam's friends, need killing.

"And Sam needs to do it. I got my hand on his heart. This is a good man. If he's ever going to be 100% right with himself, he needs to kill Sam Big and do it quick."

"Hurry up," Wesley called. He stood in the field, blue lights coming from his hands, blocking out Sam Big's voice. "I don't know how long I can do this."

"OK. Jeremy, you got that stuff you told me about?" Bud asked him.

"Yeah," he handed out some architectural drawings. "They're the original plans for the underground. The metal and concrete parts should be the same.

"People live on the lowest level, the seventh level. There are two more levels that can be inhabited. See level five and six . . ." Jeremy showed them catwalks that circled the three floors on the plans. "These are for maintenance. We can get to above where Sam Big is sitting, if the structure is still good.

"They Bigs are used to darkness. I'm going to zap them with light when we go in. That will be from the shelter's lighting system. I can control it from my computer. I'm going to alternate bright light and darkness. Blind them.

"We have night vision glasses and..." Jeremy passed out black goggle things to everyone. "Gas masks. So we can use these," he continued as he distributed canisters of tear gas. "I wish you'd had nerve gas, Mom."

"We did, Jeremy. The people of Ellie's planet took it out when they moved the containers."

"Grace, come over here," Bud said before they got going. He put his hand on her chest above her heart and closed his eyes. His face was relaxed but intent. She gasped and then smiled at him.

"Bud. What did you do?"

"I just messed with your energy, Grace. An' you know what? I found out you're a good woman. I hope you know it, too."

"I do, Bud. I feel fine."

Sam sat up, and stood slowly.

"How do you feel, Sam?" Bud asked.

"Good." He closed up his commando suit. "What did you do?"

"Oh, I just reestablished the truth in you. You're a good man, Sam."

"OK, folks, we got a job to do. It's show time."

46

Wes slid through the first doorway and into the underground. Light from a fixture in the ceiling flooded the space beyond the portal. Jeremy had turned the shelter's lighting system up as bright as it would go. He had set the lights to alternate between on and off. The Bigs' eyes wouldn't be able to adjust. Wes adjusted the light filter on his facemask. He was set for light or dark.

The plan was for him to go down first and scope the place out. He would relay information to Bud via their psychic connection. They were as hooked up mentally as they had been when Grandfather had led them.

When he slipped through the first doorway, Wes stood perfectly still, scouting the battlefield. The underground was a world of concrete and steel. The stairway into its heart passed through a series of foot-thick round metal doors that screwed shut. They were set in steel housings surrounded by cement. Every door had a generous landing on both sides. The landings were heavy steel mesh with welded staircases going down to the next level. Even though the doorways were only three feet in diameter, the tunnels leading to them allowed plenty of room to stand.

Standing at the top and looking through the first doorway, Wes could see all the way to the seventh, and lowest, level of the shelter. The Bigs had opened their home to them. Wesley's jaw clenched.

Jeremy had blown the first four levels open. The first two landings were wrecks, doors blown off and lying in the rubble below. Their landings and stairways were twisted and hanging, an impediment to getting in or out. Rescuing Sam's people would be hard if anyone was chasing them.

In the next two levels, the doors and surrounding steel framing were blown open, but the landings and walls around the stairways weren't so damaged. This made the doorways much more dangerous. A dozen Bigs could be hiding out of sight on the platform behind the walls.

Wes realized something was wrong right away. The lights were alternating light and dark, as he knew they would. When they first went on, the Bigs howled, but then they fell silent and stayed that way. The lights kept cycling. Why were they silent?

He used a tiny periscope to check what was on the other side of the fourth doorway. The first of two maintenance walkways were supposed to be on the other side. Another maintenance scaffold circled the floor below. The plan was that he should use the walkway to make his way around the perimeter until he was above Sam Big's chair. There were openings in the ventilation system there; he could go through one and reach the main floor. If he could kill Sam Big and his chiefs, he would. Then he'd call the others down to rescue people.

Sam Big's Voice rolled past Wes and out the top of the stairs. He could imagine it covering the grassy field like a lethal toxin. Sam Big found each person's weak spots and hammered them, but he didn't seem to notice Wesley or the fact that he was in the underground. Why?

Wes paused, listening before going through the doorway. Sound was reverberating incorrectly. He had become an architect because he loved building things and also because he was acutely aware of space and volume, and the physical world around him. The vibration of the landing and rail beneath his hand was wrong for a solid space.

When Jeremy handed out the plans to the underground shelter, Wesley had inhaled them. He could read plans like others read comic books. He knew the layout of each of the levels, where the mechanical, electrical, and other systems were. He knew the shelter, as Jeremy had designed it.

The place below him wasn't what Jeremy had constructed. In the original plans, the three lowest levels were *floors* with eight-foot ceilings at most. Above the main hall were two floors of rooms accessible from the levels below. Jeremy said that he had built the extra floors to give the inhabitants of the shelter more space as the radiation cleared. When the instruments said it was safe, they could open a door in the ceiling and have more legroom.

Using the periscope, he took a careful look at the other side. A vast space greeted him. The second and third floors of the underground had been removed, creating a huge cavern three stories high. Its ceiling was supported by a lacy confection of metal rods that the most sophisticated engineer would have admired.

What was going on?

This had to be the work of some advanced civilization. Sam had said that at one point in the shelter's long history, everyone could read and use computers. Then that died out. Made sense. Only an advanced society could accomplish the engineering feat the ceiling supports represented.

How did they make that open space? Where did they get the steel framing? Where did they put the dirt? He could hear the sound of the ocean. How could that be?

Wes couldn't figure it out, but he had to move.

He stuck his periscope through the doorway again. Whoever had removed the floors had left the doorways and their cement supports up. The metal stairways connected the landings, swinging almost whimsically across space. The maintenance corridor was a steel catwalk attached to the cavern's outer wall, not a hallway within a building.

The lights went off again. His night vision glasses gave him better vision than he would have without them, but not much. He could see Sam Big and a dozen or so of his henchmen sitting against the far wall. They sat like they were holding court. Sam occupied a throne of a chair with a few others arrayed along the wall with him. Still more were seated on the floor like loyal subjects. The pit where they kept the women lay in front of them and to the left. He could see moving forms within it, but nothing clearly. Black holes in the far walls must be passages to other chambers, or tunnels that Sam dug.

Bud, he thought furiously, sending Bud a thought message, there's something wrong. Ask Sam how high the highest part of the main hall is.

As high as two Bigs, Sam's answer came via Bud's thoughts. Most of it is the height of just one Big.

Wesley realized that the excavation must have happened after Sam left. He thought one more question, Are there levels lower than the main floor?

Again, Bud relayed the answer from Sam, No.

Wes slipped through the opening and onto the catwalk. He was on red alert the instant his foot hit the metal. He knew how a suspended metal corridor of the type that he was standing on should feel if he were the only person on it. He knew how the sound of his movement and breath would echo in an empty chamber. This place was not empty. The Bigs were not its only occupants.

He ran as fast as he could toward the Bigs. Out of the corners of his eyes, he saw bulbous white forms swarming over the railings, heading for him. Multi-faceted red eyes reflected his form. Enormous split mandibles snapped like the blades on hedge clippers.

Wes shot energy beams from his hands at the creatures. They dropped, to be replaced by others. He aimed his palms at Sam Big and the others. Light sliced the Bigs in two. He sliced them again, and again. They were motionless, as though nothing had happened. He realized that they were paralyzed. Or dead.

He looked across the hall. The white creatures were dropping from the scaffolding on silken cables, swarming over women in the pit. The women didn't resist, acting as though they were drugged.

They were spiders! White spiders with bodies five feet long and legs extending twice that span filled the hall. They raced toward him, dropping down the scaffoldings, crossing the vast space, swarming.

Silken threads fell around him. Wes slashed with his bright blue lights, striking as hard and as fast as he could. A curtain of silk fibers dropped around him.

Something bit him at the back of the neck. Everything went black.

47

"They got Wes." Bud stood with his feet spread, fingers on his temples. "We got to get down there, fast." Everyone jumped. Bud kept fingering his forehead. "Grace, you got flame throwers? We need them, and as much gun power as you got. And explosives."

"I have an incendiary device—what used to be called a flame-thrower," Grace said.

"You know how to use it?" Bud said.

"Yes."

"And I've got plastics and what I need to use them," Jeremy added.

"Those might get us in and out of there alive. Let's go, they're killing him." Bud ran toward the opening. Mel, Henry, and James followed him. "No. Only me, Jeremy, Grace, and Sam are going. If you don't hear from us in ten minutes, go back and get Lena and get as many of those kids as you can carry. Run back to the cliff and be prepared to defend it with your lives."

"There are that many Bigs?"

"It's not Bigs. I don't know what they are. I been trying to reach Wes all the time he was in there. Nothing. Then *they* tell me they've got him."

"It's a setup," Henry said.

"Yeah. But they don't know what I can do when I'm mad. And they don't know about them," Bud waved his hand in the air. Outlines of warriors in war paint and bonnets appeared. "I will not let them kill a spirit warrior."

They saw what Wes had seen when he went in, the two ruined landings that would make rescue or retreat hard. They saw the opened doorways and went through them until they reached the landing of the fourth level.

When he stepped on the platform, Sam froze. "This is not right. Let me do something." He stood by the side of the door and made a deep noise, something like Grace's throat-singing Buddhist monks might have made. It was very brief.

Sam stood there. Finally he said, "It's not safe."

"We know that," Bud said pulling out his periscope in preparation for going through the door.

"No. We must not do what they want." Sam looked at the cement wall of the passageway behind them, tapping it with his fingers. "Jeremy, can you make a small explosion here?" He pointed to a specific spot. "Like this?" He indicated about three feet square.

"The air vent. You knew it was there." Jeremy grinned.

"Yes, by the sound in the wall. My people have found it, but we couldn't get to it through this."

"Well, I can."

"Not too much, Jeremy," Sam entreated. "My people are not far behind the wall."

Jeremy blew a hole into the vent and they made their way on their bellies through the duct system, traveling in a large circle around the hall.

After what seemed like miles, they came to an arm of the duct system poking toward the center of the hall. Grace dragged herself into it. She was the smallest and lightest. She left her weapons behind: no room for them in the pipe. At the first vent aperture, she peered through the slatted opening into the room below. She was about a fourth of the way over a huge hall, which was at least three stories high. The ceiling was held up by an elaborate metal frame. The walkway was a bridge draped between the doorways. Everything else had been removed.

The floor looked as it had in Jeremy's photo composites and floor plans: a living area, the pit with the women, the Bigs' court at the back of the room. All was exactly as she expected, except that everything was hung with gauzy ropes as thick as her thumb. She could see forms moving under the gauze.

And then she saw them: Hundreds of huge spiders massed around the opening of the fourth door, ready to attack when they came through.

Sam Big was still caterwauling, but his Voice had a pleading quality, as though he were singing to save his life. Her eyes went to the source of the sound, an opening on the far side of the hall next to the Bigs' court. She saw the human figures sitting on chairs, draped with spider silk. Red bled through it. They were dead. Wesley must have shot them while they were alive, or they wouldn't have bled. How long did they sit there alive?

Sam Big's voice came from the wide opening next to the dead bodies. She could see a ramp going down.

The shelter had an eighth level! She could see daylight coming from it and had the crazy idea that she heard the ocean. Sam Big was down there, lobbing halfhearted insults at them. That's where Wesley was!

Grace backed out of the vent as quietly as she could. She knew that spiders didn't have ears, but were acutely aware of vibrations. If they knew she and the others were there, they'd mass around the vent where they'd have to exit, the one above the dead Bigs.

"No, is not so!" Sam whispered into his radio mic when she told them what she'd found. "The hall is the height of two Bigs in the middle. The rest is just above the Bigs' heads. Some of them hit the ceiling. It's not high. This is not the underground."

"What else is it? How'd the ceiling get so high?" Bud asked.

"I don't know. When I left, the ceiling was low. Rooms were above it, but sealed off. It's where we put the dirt from our tunneling. And there is no other level below the seventh. There is not."

"I was tryin' to get ahold of Wes all the time he was gone," Bud said. "I couldn't reach him. It was like his mind was turned off. He would have noticed that the ceiling wasn't what was in your plans— he's an architect. He would 'a' sent me a message asking about it. I didn't get any."

"They did something to him."

"Yeah." Bud's eyebrows pulled in and down. His face reddened. He looked like he wanted to bite. "They tricked him."

"We have to be careful they don't trick us." Grace said. "The simplest thing would be to go over to the exit, firebomb the place, and wipe out everything in it, then rappel down into the hall and find Wes."

"But that would kill the women and my people in burrows," Sam said.

"Do you think they're still alive?" Bud asked.

"They could be," Jeremy said. "Some spiders inject their food with venom, then wrap it up to eat later. They only eat live food."

"We need to get out of here," Grace said. "The spiders will find us. They can go out through the hole Jeremy blew. Let's head for the vent on the other side and see what happens."

The spiders were in the tube when the group got to the vent above the dead Bigs. They could feel the spiders' legs skittering inside the vent and see them traveling along the scaffolding of the hall. They finally reached the opening above Sam Big's throne.

"Fasten your line here, on the post, balance yourself on the wall with your feet and drop." Grace rappelled into the room. Jeremy followed her. Both had rappelled down everything from boulders to mountain faces with the general. Sam was slower, but made it down.

"Wait just a minute, I want to send a message." Bud crouched inside the vent tube, set to back off the edge. He let out a scream of defiance that echoed down the pipe and around the hall. Bud Creeman had declared war. Something came out of his palms. Whereas his Power usually displayed as cool blue beams, this was explosive and hot. A firebomb flew back up the tube they'd just exited. Shrieks followed. The tapping and sliding of spiders' limbs on the vent's interior ceased. The spiders behind him were dead. Bud leapt off the hot vent and slid down to the main floor.

The spiders attacked, coming from under the scaffolding, their perches around the fifth doorway. From all around the hall. Even from under the silken mantel covering the women's pit.

Bud shot flames everywhere. None of the rest did anything for fear of getting in his way. Dead arachnids piled up, twitching and scratching their pointed legs on the floor.

"Get down there and get Wesley," Bud said, pointing at the opening to the lower level. "Look sharp. These boys are fast." He intercepted some about to head off the group. The minute they moved toward the opening, the spiders leapt in that direction, abandoning their fight with Bud.

"Watch it. There's somethin' real important to them down there." He sidled over and scorched them as they crowded into the opening. He blasted, and kept blasting, turning around as intuition or his ancestors prompted him. The hall boiled with Bud's rage. He kept firing, and whatever energy was coming off him kept coming.

And so did the spiders. They kept coming, climbing over the bodies of their friends. There seemed to be no end to them.

Grace, Sam, and Jeremy slid down the incline to the lower level. It wasn't made of cement and steel like the rest of the underground. The ramp was newly excavated earth. It looked like a gigantic bulldozer had created it only hours before.

When they raised their eyes, they stopped abruptly. She sat on the opposite side of the grotto on a silky throne, her enormous pearly abdomen hanging over the edge. Jagged hairs ran along its ridges. She looked at them with multifaceted red eyes, a white queen.

Spiked arms and legs ferried the lower portion of a human leg to her mouth. Her split mandible clicked as it scissored open and shut. Her bulk filled half of the thirty-foot wide tunnel. Far beyond her, the surf crashed and blue sky glistened. The tunnel extended under the meadow and opened to the sea.

Spiders skittered down the ramp into the queen's chamber. Why, was easy to discern . . . her egg sack was bigger than she was. Eggs squeezed out of her abdomen as they watched.

To her right, in the corner of the freshly excavated cavern, long cocoons hung. People were in them, the Bigs by the size of them. One was darker, indicating something black inside. Wesley in his commando suit was packaged for later consumption.

Sam Big was hanging from the ceiling, spider web holding him up. His body swung freely, exposed. His eyes bulged and sweat poured off his face. He squawked in the Voice, now just a wail. Both of his hands were cleanly nipped off. The stubs didn't bleed; the queen's venom must have stopped it.

"Oh, Sam! Kill me! Kill me if y' can find it in yer heart. If y' ever loved me, kill me. She's eatin' me piece by piece."

His freshly cut lower leg dribbled a bit. The queen held the leg to her mouth for a suspended instant.

Sam raised his gun and raked Sam Big up the trunk, and then across. And then he turned the gun on the queen.

"Get back, Sam, this is better." Grace fired up the flamethrower. The queen leapt at her, screaming. Grace stood her ground. Jeremy tossed a bit of plastic explosive at her and they all ran for the hanging bodies. The queen caught what Jeremy threw in her mouth. When the plastic exploded, she splattered the walls of the cave and everything in it.

The spiders shrieked. Bud took them on, while Grace cooked the remains of the queen and her egg sack.

Jeremy tried to cut through Wesley's sac with a knife. He couldn't. The spiders rushed him.

"Mom! Bud!" he cried, not wanting to use his machine gun for fear of hitting Wesley.

Bud turned and sliced the spiders in half with the blue beams, leaving Wesley unharmed. Grace and Sam covered his back. The grotto rang with shots and surging flames, and then it seemed to be over. Sam and Grace stood down, backs to Jeremy and Bud who stood by Wes.

"Can you cut through the cocoon?" Jeremy said, "I couldn't."

Bud narrowed the beams coming from his palms and sliced Wesley's cocoon top to bottom. Jeremy pulled his feet out and he slipped to the ground.

He looked dead. Bud leaned over him and pushed on his chest, breathing into his mouth. "Come on, Wes. This is not a good day to die."

Bud did more with his hands, and the small cave roiled with spirits. "Come on, Wes."

Wes's eyes opened. He blinked. He rolled over on his side and threw up. "Oh, God, I feel so sick." He saw Bud. "Spiders, Bud!"

"We found them, buddy. We need to get you out of here." Wesley's eyes rolled back and he lost consciousness again.

"Come on, Jeremy, let's get him out of here. We'll tell the others to get ready to go." Bud looked at Sam. "Are any of your people left alive? We can get them out."

"Yes, they are alive. I can find them."

"OK, we'll get Wes up top, and bring the others down to help. I'll get the horses ready to pull them with travois. We'll be right back."

Jeremy and Bud lifted Wes and headed up the stairs.

Grace pulled up her facemask and looked around. "We did it, Sam. We won."

He opened his mask and smiled at her. "Yes. We won."

"Let's get out of here, Sam," Grace said.

"We must finish." He turned his gun on the web-shrouded forms hanging from the ceiling. They were Bigs. If they escaped, they'd kill them in a minute. And if they were left there, they'd die a slow death of spider venom and suffocation.

They moved methodically over the hall, killing the surviving spiders. Finally, they stood in the middle of the hall, the stairs to the surface in front of them. They pulled their masks up again.

"I love you, Sam. I will love you forever."

He smiled. "I love thee, my Lady Grace." He kissed her. Then he put her gloved hand on his heart. He wrapped her in his arms. They could have stayed there a long time, but the scaffolding creaked ominously.

"I need to get my people, lady." He looked upward. "Will ye be all right?" he asked.

"I'll be fine, Sam. I doubt there's anything down here that I can't handle with a flamethrower and a machine gun.

He waved at her and made his way to a shadowy opening she hadn't seen.

Grace watched him go, wanting to get out of there, yet unwilling to leave until Sam was back.

The scaffolding groaned again.

48

Grace waited for Sam, looking around the hall. Splattered and singed hunks of the spiders and mounds of the white guck inside them were everywhere, along with segmented white legs and sharp pointed feet, and spider hide with lines of spiky hair. Some of the remains were blood-streaked. Those must have been spiders that had fed on the Bigs' blood or the women's.

Looking up at the lofty ceiling with its steel armatures laced with webs, she marveled. They fought *spiders*, not Bigs. It was crazy. She caught a movement from the women's pit. A spider? A surviving person? That was unlikely; the women were encased in cocoons and full of venom. But some might be alive.

The lights were still on, but were much dimmer than they had been during the fighting. Grace was surprised when the air a few feet from her began to glow. The glow took on a lovely golden hue. It grew brighter and a figure materialized inside it. She shouldered her gun and picked up her flamethrower. The figure became more solid.

"Oh, it's you!" she said, smiling widely. It was the tall doctor who had saved Ellie's life. "What a surprise."

His eyes were fixed on her. He needed to be very skilled and very compassionate. He also needed to be fast. No telling how long that ceiling would hold up. He could survive the collapse, but she couldn't.

He smiled at her. "I want to congratulate you."

"You speak English."

"Yes, I've learned all of Earth's languages since we last talked. Congratulations are in order."

"Oh, well, yes. It was quite a battle, but my friends and I worked together."

"I wasn't referring to that, though it was a very clever piece of work." He needed to weave a bit of magic around her so she could absorb his message. Her arms relaxed and she lowered her weapons.

"You've been singled out for a rare honor, my dear." She listened. "I need to tell you more about my people before explaining it.

"My world is close to perfect. We have no crime, no war, and no hunger. We are ancient and intuitive. These gifts have come at a cost; our ability to engage in carnal reproduction disappeared many ages ago."

She gazed steadily at him. He could have dressed her in a ball gown and feasted on her opulence, but he liked to look at her in the singed commando suit splattered with white guck. She was so exciting.

He noted her compacted chest and knew her breasts were bound. He wanted her to open her suit a little, so he could see the swell of that constrained bosom. Something subtle. She raised her hand to her throat and undid her suit just enough. Wonderful. She was following his directions without words. He gave her the maximum level of sedation as he reached the most delicate part of his message.

"We need to be frank about your future, my dear. You will die if you stay on Earth. If you manage to stave off starvation or disease, you'll get *old* and ugly. That would be a tragedy."

He peered into her eyes, hoping to see that she was agreeing with him. He couldn't tell; her eyes were slits and her pupils had rolled up in her head. He'd made the spell too strong. Well, it would wear off.

"The good news is that you have *charmed* our world. Every household in our world has its monitors turned to you."

He paused a moment, wanting to see her reaction, wanting to set the stage for his great announcement.

"I *also* won a great victory today. I am the new chairman of the council of elders." She was silent, so he elaborated. "I have unlimited powers. I have made myself the first of our kind to begin live breeding with humans. Our experimentation with Ellie and Jeremy's children made it possible." He lowered his voice, imparting the wonderful secret. "Grace, I am whole, as nature once made my sex."

Her eyes opened wide and she struggled to speak. She couldn't.

"I am the first male in the live breeding program, and you will become the first female. That is the real honor you won today." He smiled at her.

"Do you know what really made our being together possible? The show today—the battle. I worked so hard to make sure it had the effect I wanted.

"I carved out this huge space. I had to, how would we get the wide-angle shots? The result was electrifying! Shocking! Exciting.

"I dug the queen's lower level and dumped the dirt in the ocean. What a surprise for the viewers—a grand underground vista instead of a cramped little pit. It was a lot of work, as was bringing the spiders. Hard work, even for me." He beamed at her.

"The spiders were what gave you your ratings. You are a superstar, Grace—our first and only. I got on the screen at the first commercial break during the battle and asked my people if they would like me to live with you on our own moon, and to share our life together on screen. The response was incredible. The data gatherers couldn't hold the information, so many people voted yes! They want us to be together, now!"

"I won't go with you. I'm married to Sam. I love him, not you," she choked out.

His eyes narrowed. "You'll come with me if I have to paralyze you and carry you off. And you'll do whatever I want. Do you understand?" He grabbed her shoulder. She glared at him, but couldn't move.

"We're going now, Grace. Give me your hand."

She grabbed her machine gun and leveled it at him, pouring bullets into him. They passed through him, making his body jerk, but not hurting him at all. When the gun was empty, she pulled up the flamethrower and attempted to burn him. The flames did nothing.

"*Nothing* from your planet can harm me, Grace. But I can harm *you*." He didn't touch her, just looked at her. "You must learn that. I can hurt you. And I will hurt you, whenever I wish."

She doubled over in pain, gasping. "I won't go. I'm married to Sam. I love him. I'll never love you."

"That idiot!" He raised his hand the way he had seen Bud and Wes do. He thought of flames coming out of it, searing, scorching flames that would destroy anything, especially Sam. They shot forth from his palm, boiling golden flames, a hundred times hotter than the Indians' and a thousand times worse than her flamethrower's. "*I love Sam,*" he mimicked her voice. "*I'm married to Sam.* Not anymore."

He blasted the entire hall, his fire filling the space, all but the area where they stood. The two of them stayed cool and safe, but the flames ripped around the chamber, incinerating everything, burning the dead spiders and women to ash.

Flames sought the tunnel that Sam had taken. He heard cries from behind the wall, but they ended in moments. He laughed.

Grace cried out. "You killed Sam." She stood, staring in the direction of the tunnel he'd taken. "You killed him, and all his people. And the women."

"You'll come to love me more than him. I'm a doctor. I can make you love anything. You'll feel more pleasure than you can imagine. Forget him."

Grace moved her hand quickly. He knew what she was trying to do, but he was quicker. Her suicide capsule was hidden in her glove.

He grabbed the capsule. Putting it in his mouth, he bit down. The poison did nothing to him.

"There's nothing you can do." His eyes glowed. "You have too much spirit; you need to learn to obey. You will do whatever I want, and you will be grateful." He slapped her face, hard. Blood appeared on the corner of her mouth. He wiped it off, healing her instantly, but leaving the pain.

"You don't appreciate how hard I worked today. I carved out tons of rock, blew that tunnel to the sea. Made the scaffolding so the roof wouldn't fall in." His voice was petulant. "Tell me you appreciate it."

Her jaw clenched. She stood defiantly.

"Tell me you appreciate it, or I will rip out Jeremy's right eye."

"I appreciate your efforts very much. Thank you," she said.

"Now, put your arms around me. We're going."

She hesitated.

"Do it or I'll cut off both of his hands."

She stepped closer and put her arms around him, tears in her eyes. "Please don't hurt anyone. I'll do what you want."

He chuckled. "I think I will bring your people with us. You obey so nicely when I threaten them. Hold on, we're leaving." He put his arm around her to draw her away.

A powerful blast of air almost knocked him off his feet. Ash and cinders flew in fiery cyclones, zigzagging around the hall. He put his hand out to steady himself. Buzzing filled his ears. Something whirred above his head. Before he could turn, it settled on his back.

Grace leapt away, half propelled by the gust of wind. Ellie's iridescent wings appeared on each side of the doctor's head. They created a hurricane of moving air. She could barely kept standing. Grace put her hands over her ears, trying to mute the sound. Flashes from Ellie's scales shot around the cavern, mingling with the flying cinders and ash.

Grace watched in horror as Ellie's curls and slit silver eyes appeared over the doctor. Ellie leaned over his head and the lower part of her face split vertically. Her mandible closed on his skull.

While her spiked front legs pierced his eyes, Ellie's other legs clung to him. He screamed and lunged backward. Ellie's wings moved tirelessly, preventing the doctor from flinging himself over and pinning her down.

The stingers on Ellie's hind legs appeared. She stung him again and again and again, all along his spine. He choked and gasped, face swelling.

"No . . ." he said. He fell on the floor, golden light emanating from his corpse. His outline softened and he dissolved into a puddle. Fumes arose from it, making Grace's eyes sting. The puddle disappeared into the floor.

"Oh, Ellie, you saved me. Thank you," Grace choked out.

Ellie buzzed at her, shrieking. She was telling her to get out of here, to run. And then Ellie took off, flying straight into the hole where Sam had disappeared.

Grace grabbed her weapons and ran up the staircase.

49

As she climbed, the stairs became steeper; the distance between landings, endless. She dragged her weapons, fearing to leave them. When Grace reached the severely damaged second doorway, she didn't know if she could make her way across the rubble and up the twisted wreck of the staircase. She left the flamethrower and machine gun below the door and pulled herself up.

Hanging in the chunks of blasted cement, she collapsed, weeping. He killed Sam.

"Jeremy . . . Help me, help me . . . someone." She called over the rubble. "Help me . . ."

"Mom?" Jeremy was standing in the meadow, peering down the hole he'd blasted. He turned to the others. "Did anyone hear a voice?"

"Jeremy . . . Help . . ."

He jumped into the opening. He saw his mother hanging over what was left of the second doorway. "Mom?"

"Help me, Jeremy. I can't . . ." She was crying.

"Bud, Henry, help me get Mom." Jeremy clawed his way to her. "Mom, what happened?"

"He killed Sam." She went limp.

"Get her guns; they're back there," Jeremy directed, picking her up beneath the arms. Bud took her legs. They carried her out and laid her on the pasture. She didn't move.

Mel, James, and Henry stood by. They were ready to pull out and go back to their base camp where Lena waited with the babies—hopefully. The packhorses were laden with the computers and the tent. The other horses were saddled and ready to ride. Wes sat in the grass with his commando suit peeled down to his waist. His skin was tinged gray, but he was alive and pretty alert.

Jeremy and Bud moved Grace over to the trees and put her down. She sat, staring, her face frozen. No one talked to her, not knowing what to say. After sitting rigidly for a few minutes, she put her head to her knees and began to sob. Her naked, wrenching sobs conveyed what words couldn't. Sam was dead.

After a while, Jeremy asked, "Mom, what happened?"

She looked up. He'd never seen her so desolate. "It was the doctor who came to help Ellie. He developed a fixation on me. He's been filming us and selling it on his planet. We're cult figures there. *I'm* a cult figure there.

"He dug out that entire hall and brought the spiders in *to get better ratings.*" She started to laugh, semi-hysterical. "He did it for *ratings.* We were fighting for our lives, and he wanted *ratings.*

"He wanted *me.*" She shuddered. "He wanted to take me to a moon of his planet and film us *fucking* for their TV." She raised her face, furious. "He wanted me to marry him. When I told him that I was married to Sam and didn't want him, he burned up the hall.

"Everything is ashes down there. Before the doctor arrived, Sam went into a tunnel to find his people. I saw the fire race after him, down the hole he'd used."

"Did you see Ellie? She flew down there."

"Oh, yes! She saved my life."

They gathered around her.

"Ellie saved Wes, too," Mel broke the silence. "The spider poison was killing him. She stung him in the chest, and he came to."

Wes smiled ruefully and waved his hand.

"Look at that!" Bud said. Ellie burst out of the underground, wings smoking, carrying something close to her body. She landed lightly and set down her load. It was a charred figure. She took off again immediately, shrieking something at them in a high-pitched buzz. They were to get Sam's clothes off. Now! And then she disappeared back down the hole.

Jeremy jumped toward the motionless form. He tried to unzip Sam's suit, but the fasteners were melted closed. He pulled out a pocketknife, which did nothing. Sam's suit was smoking like Ellie had been, but the suit had a toxic smell. They knew it would kill him if his burns didn't.

"Let me try," Bud said. He closed his eyes in prayer and mumbled something. When he opened his eyes, he ran his finger down Sam's torso. The suit opened. Bud sliced his helmet and goggles off. They were fused together. Then he ran his finger the length of his arms and legs. The others peeled the suit off as soon as Bud loosened it. Wesley crawled forward and helped with the small pieces that Bud had missed. Sam was unconscious. He might be alive, though they couldn't see him breathing or feel a pulse.

They continued to peel off his clothes. Something fell out of his suit. A couple of somethings. One was a book. Bud picked it up. The pages opened and glittering letters appeared. The pages turned by themselves, light flashing from the interior.

"It's the Book," Jeremy said. "He went in there to get it." Jeremy picked it up. "This is part of Ellie's notebook from the golden world. It wrote down all the stuff I said at the end, the Commands. It's Sam's Bible."

He felt tears on his face. Sam died for this? The other thing that fell out of his suit was a satin jewelry bag. It was his mother's; he recognized it. It must contain some of her jewels. Sam died to bring her a gift?

Bud and Wes continued to slice pieces off Sam's suit. Their system worked until they got to his lower legs and feet. There, the suit had fused to Sam's flesh. Bud and Wes worked carefully, separating Sam from the fabric. Their faces became grave when they saw the burns. His lower legs were charred. The skin was gone in places, with muscles and tendons exposed. They couldn't get his shoes off without taking too much of him.

The commando suit was smoking. They dumped the pieces at the far end of the pasture by the cliff that overlooked the sea. It looked like it might go up in flames. And so did Sam's shoes, but they were still on him.

Ellie reappeared, her legs wrapped around another person. He was obviously alive: His eyes rolled in terror. She set the newcomer down and went to work on Sam. Her stingers came out and she zapped Sam twice, then a third time, over the heart. Sam's eyes fluttered. She waved her wings over him, and he woke up, making a horrible sobbing groan.

Ellie landed and sat next to his legs. She bent over the burnt areas. Something came out of her mouth, a foamy, frothy white stuff. She coated his legs, sealing them. Then she worked very carefully to remove the boots. His feet looked like barbecued meat. She squealed and they got what she meant—get those boots out of here, pronto.

Bud threw them onto the pile and the whole thing ignited. The fumes were horrible. Ellie stopped working for a minute and flew to the fire, sweeping the toxic smoke to sea with her wings. Bud followed her, raising his arms. The burning uniform shot over the cliff and into the ocean.

Cooing softly, Ellie treated Sam's feet. When she was done, he was wearing hard boots of the white stuff on his feet and legs. She told them by squeaks and squeals to cover him and keep him warm.

She turned to the second person she'd rescued, and looked him over. He required a shock to the heart and some white stuff on his feet and lower body. He was conscious and very surprised.

Ellie rose from the field and reentered the underground.

The group looked at the newcomer. He was a little person, a dwarf. Gray, like the others. He sat up and looked at them, dumbfounded, but alive and alert.

"I'm Jeremy Edgarton," Jeremy said, extending his hand. "Welcome to our community."

"I'm Jim Bob." The little person shook back, ducking his head and looking awed.

Their meeting was cut short. "I think we're going to have to get going very soon," Jeremy said. A shimmering golden mist appeared in the area over the underground's main hall. It rose, forming a tall column of yellow smoke with a pointed top. The earth quivered.

"Let's get going."

"Not without Ellie!" Jeremy cried.

"You guys go," Bud said. "We'll pack up Sam and . . . Jim Bob."

They tried to figure out how to transport Sam. They finally laid him over a bareback horse with Bud riding in back. The little person sat on Wes's horse with Wes riding behind him. He looked as terrified as he had flying out of the underground in Ellie's grip.

Jeremy wouldn't depart until Ellie came out, even through what was happening over the meadow told him he should leave. The golden column of smoke was beautiful. It rose majestically, creating circular ripples along the ground. The middle of it formed concentric circles, so that it looked like Jupiter with rings around a tall central spire. He had no doubt it would blow.

Ellie wobbled out of the hole, her entire body smoking and singed. She carried two bodies with her, both in worse shape than the others. She chided him in her insect talk, telling him to leave. She flew toward their camp with the survivors.

He ran to follow her. They headed to their camp, where the children and Lena waited. The golden column and the ground under it rumbled. Finally, he heard a crack!

"Run!" Jeremy screamed as he caught up with the others. "It's going to blow!"

They ran, passing the body of a Big splattered with gunfire. It must have been Lena's work. They passed another, and another.

Lena was standing in front of the tent, her machine gun in her hands.

"Oh, Lord! I thought I'd never see you again." A stampede of horses and people ran toward her. She stood up and raised her hands, shouting, "Thank you, Jesus! Thank you for takin' care of us!" And then she hugged Henry.

"Get down!" Jeremy shouted.

They could see the gold column in the distance. It dropped to the ground, exploded, and then rose into the air, a perfect mushroom cloud.

Jeremy watched it. Was it radioactive? He ran into the tent, almost stumbling on the kids who were covered in the bulletproof suits. "Hi, kids," he said, grabbing a Geiger counter. Given the way his life had gone, Jeremy always kept one handy.

He went out in the meadow by their camp and set the instrument up. He moved toward the meadow over the underground. That's where the radioactive readings would be strongest. He backtracked sufficiently to see the site of the old mansion and the shelter. The entire area had sunk as the underground's main hall collapsed, forming a deep, flat depression. The underground was sealed forever. They would have died if they'd remained where they were. Ellie got them to leave in time. His instruments didn't register any radioactivity. Whatever it was that blew up, it wasn't radioactive.

He turned back to the camp and found Ellie ministering to the newest members of their clan, the two she'd rescued before everything blew up. One was a boy with perfectly developed arms and trunk, but stubs of legs. The third might have been a boy or a girl. The child was draped; Jeremy couldn't see. It was very small and its eyes were milky. It must be blind.

When Jeremy came close, the blind child said, "Jeremy," in a perfectly understandable voice.

"You know I'm here?"

"We all knew you were here."

Jeremy bit his lip, shaking. "I'm really sorry."

The child, or whatever he or she was, asked, "Why should you be sorry?"

"Because I didn't save all of you."

"You saved the ones you were meant to save. My name is Martin. Jack is with me." He held out his hand, pointing it directly at Jeremy, and nodding his head at the legless boy.

Wes and Bud began clean-up duty, incinerating what was left of the Bigs' bodies after the dogs ravaged them. They worked fast. Jeremy could see Grandfather and the ancestors moving with them, giving them strength.

Jeremy flopped on the ground. He heard Ellie humming, tending to the sick. Tending to the children. Humming and buzzing.

He knew he'd never touch her again, but they could have a life together. They could sit together by her tree. It didn't have to be a regular life like everyone had. He was one of the most open-minded people in the world. He didn't care what she was. She was Ellie.

He closed his eyes.

PART THREE

50

Jeremy stood, blinking the sleep out of his eyes, then looked around the burnt-out campfire. His muscles hurt more than he thought possible. Every step reminded him of the battle the day before. He moved stiffly, but as quietly as he could. The sack Ellie had made—whatever it was—hung from the oak a hundred yards behind the camp.

It was larger than when he'd seen it last. Its gray, papery exterior looked like the wasps' nests he'd seen in the olden times, but this one was four feet across. It almost looked like a cabbage, attached to the oak's limb by a heavy stalk. Broad, flat leaves were wrapped around a mass inside. Eggs? How could that be? Ellie carried her babies internally.

He wanted to find Ellie and thank her for everything that she'd done. But she wasn't perched on the limb above her sack as she had been before the battle.

Jeremy poked around, circling farther from their camp. He walked past a massive oak and stopped.

Ellie lay on the ground, fallen on her side. It looked like a chunk of her abdomen had broken in; a piece maybe eight inches square was gone from one of the plates of her belly. He could see inside her.

She was hollow. Nothing inside. No bug guck. No white stuff. She was empty.

"Ellie," he said. She didn't answer. She would never answer, not even with an angry buzz. She was hollow because the white stuff she'd spread over everyone's injuries was her. She'd killed herself saving the others.

Jeremy's eyes stung. His chest froze. He felt saliva at the edges of his mouth. He couldn't move. This couldn't happen. Nothing like this could happen.

"Ellie?" he bent forward and touched her. Her bulging belly disintegrated, shattering into hundreds of pieces. He bent and picked up a hunk, wanting to stop the terrible falling apart. The little chunk became dust in his hand.

The wind came, just a gust. Ellie's wings caught it. They detached from her body soundlessly, not even making a pop. They tumbled along the ground. He ran after them.

Jeremy caught one wing, stuffed it under his arm, and chased the other one. He caught it and held them both to his chest. The wings' front edge, a sturdy spine, was still intact, but some of the lovely iridescent material that held her aloft had shattered. No matter. He'd keep them. He put the wings under his arm and went back to where her body had been.

"Ellie!" he called, looking round. "Where are you?" He spun. "Where are you? You can't *die*, Ellie. You're not allowed to die."

Nothing comforted him. Nothing spoke to him. No Commands or God or Great One. No Native American shaman or Buddhist monk appeared. Nothing came to him to wipe away his tears. That's what he always got: nothing.

Ellie, you can't leave me! What am I supposed to *do*? His soul screamed. He looked down and saw the most enduring part of her. Those little hooves. He had thought they were adorable when he first saw them. They made her seem like a little pony and let her dance en pointe without distorting her feet. They let her dance the way she had through the days and nights of their life together. Through love, and storms.

His mouth opened and he almost screamed. He stopped himself and picked up her hooves. The stingers were retracted. He put them in his pocket and ran.

He would never come back. He would never love anyone again. He never wanted to see anyone in this shitty world.

51

"I'll keep an eye on him. You go back and get the others ready to break camp," Bud said, sitting easily astride his horse. Wes and his mount were next to him, watching Jeremy run across the plain. He was heading toward the river. At least he'd get home going that way.

They stood on the rise where Lena had done her shooting.

Bud and Wes had done an early morning patrol, looking for dead bodies they'd missed the day before and any new spiders and Bigs. It looked like Lena had picked off everything that ran out the back way, but they wanted to make sure that nothing needing killing reared up anywhere. They got up at the break of dawn before anyone and saw Ellie's body before Jeremy did. They debated telling him, but decided he'd find out soon enough. They had to reconnoiter.

The group had agreed that going back to the cliff by the river was the best bet. Too many bad things had happened where they were. Not to mention the view being ruined by the smoking pit of the underground.

"You watch Jeremy and I'll try to get the camp going," Wes said, wheeled his mount, and headed back to the impromptu encampment.

"May take a couple days though. Those horses have never pulled a travois."

Bud rode down the hill in the direction Jeremy had gone. He wanted to give him privacy to grieve, but make sure he didn't do anything stupid. Once he got on the flat, he followed the tips of Ellie's wings. He'd let Jeremy run until he slowed down by himself.

"I'm not going back, so don't try to make me," Jeremy shouted over his shoulder. "I knew you were following me." They'd gone a fair stretch when Bud closed the distance between them.

"I'm not trying to take you back. I'm going to get poles for the travois," Bud replied. "We got the little kids and the new people and Sam to get back to the cliff. They can't walk."

"Oh." Jeremy slowed down.

"You can go your own way. The rattlesnakes are done hunting for the morning. You'll be pretty safe."

Jeremy slowed further.

"I did see some bear scat back there. Grizzlies were a real problem in California in the old days. They'd rear up twelve feet out of the grass. Real bad dispositions, too."

"This isn't California; it's Connecticut."

"Bullshit, Jeremy. You know as well as I do that this place is no place. This here grassland with the big oaks is *California*. I'll tell you exactly where it is in California, too. It's the Santa Ynez Valley, down by Santa Barbara before any humans got there."

"I know. My mom had a ranch near there. It looked just like this."

"So what do you think?"

"What do you mean?" Jeremy was walking very slowly, but still didn't turn around.

"This place is bogus, Jeremy. It's made up. Somebody made it up, and they're keeping it going."

"What do you mean?"

"Well, what if Ellie's people—and I want to tell you I'm sorry about her, Jeremy. She was a really good . . . *person*. And son, you're losing a lot of her wings holding them like that. Why don't you let me see if I can make them stronger?"

Jeremy stopped and turned toward Bud, holding the wings to his chest. He looked at them. They were eight feet long and did look ragged after his treatment of them. "What can you do to them?"

"I don't know. I been doin' so much magic lately, I thought something might come to me." Bud swung off his horse, which didn't take too kindly to the wings being waved around. The mare snorted loudly and pulled away. Bud handed Jeremy the reins. "Here, you hold her. I'll see what I can do."

When he put his hands on the wings, that Power that had been with him so much came over him. It came over the wings, too. For a moment, they were enveloped in blue light. Bud stood with his eyes closed. He opened them, and touched the wings.

"That's better. They're just as light and pretty, but I don't think they'll break."

Jeremy took them back, squeezing his lips tight and holding Ellie's remains hard against his chest.

"We might as well just walk along together. Boy, I sure am worried," Bud said congenially. "I'll be damned if I know how to get forty tree trunks back to the camp by myself with just this one horse. We need those for the travois poles. If I do get them back, I don't know how we're going to get all those kids and people back to the cliff through the woods. We could barely ride through on horses. The travois will be too wide. And if we walk along this oak savannah, what about the bears and wolves?

"If we make it through that, I don't know how we'll get them up the cliff to where we live. How will we lift *Sam*, for instance?"

"We have a big pulley," Jeremy said. "It's in the equipment container with the weapons."

"OK. We just have to set a pulley in the rock and drag 'em up. I don't know how to do that. What's going to happen when those kids start walking? They will, you know. Some good food and room to move, they'll be walking. They'll fall off the cliff. And how is that guy with no legs going to get around? I don't know how to make a rig for him. You'd need wheels and who knows what."

Jeremy stopped. "Did you really see bearshit?"

"Swear to God. A big mound."

"Why are we walking around with bears here? We need to get out of here."

"Well, it wasn't that fresh. About thirteen hours, I'd say. I got a gun. One thing this useless saddle has is a scabbard for a rifle. I could also blue-beam 'em. I'm getting really good at that."

"What are you talking about? There are bears here!" Jeremy stood with his eyes bulging and feet spread.

"Yeah. And rattlesnakes. But when it gets hot, they get out of the sun. And the mountain lions are probably closer to the cliff area, though they live in California, too. Around Lake Cachuma, lots of cats. Illegal to hunt them in my time. Probably OK now."

"What are you doing? Trying to scare me?"

"Yeah. You shouldn't be walking around unarmed here, Jeremy. And we need you. There's lots needs doing and you're the best one to do it."

He stopped and glared at Bud, "Well what am *I* supposed to do? My wife turned into an *insect*, saved all sorts of people, and then *died*. What am I supposed to do?"

Jeremy turned his back to Bud again and clutched the wings. He stood there and Bud wondered if he'd explode or implode. He could see Jeremy's body shaking from his feet to the stubs of his dreads. He was holding the wings so tightly, they must be strong as steel, because they would have broken in his grasp.

"Just leave me alone. OK. Leave me alone for a while."

Bud rode on ahead. He turned back and Jeremy had slumped to the ground. He was holding the wings like you would a baby.

And then his head fell forward. Bud rode on and kept watch. If he heard Jeremy crying, or if he heard anything at all, he'd never tell.

"It's not an egg sack," Jeremy said when they took up walking again. "The goldie doctor told Ellie she couldn't have kids any more. And we haven't done anything to make a baby, anyway. "

"What is it?"

"I don't know. Some wasp thing. I don't know what it is." Jeremy sent a pointed look to Bud. "I do know that it stays here. When we leave, it stays where Ellie left it. She made it, and it stays where she put it."

"That's fine, son," Bud said. He sent a thought message to Wes that no one should disturb the thing in the tree, period.

They hit the forest. Finding the tall, skinny trees wasn't hard. Bud blue-beamed more than forty of them down and then stripped the branches off. All they had to do was get them back to the base camp.

"I wish we both had horses," Jeremy said. "We could each pull twenty back. I could use the top half of my commando suit and put it around the horse's chest, wrapping the arms like a girth." In seconds, Jeremy outlined how to make a travois and haul the trunks back.

"We can do it with this one horse and walk next to her," Bud said.

"You can't just whistle and call another one?"

"Sorry. I do blue beams and healing. And don't tell anyone about the blue beams. Many traditional people wouldn't like that."

"Talking about them, or having them?"

"Both. Most folks, even my People, can't imagine stuff like what happens around Grandfather. They think it's sci-fi. But it's not. Holy men and women like him are rare, but they exist. I can't do anything like what he could do. And usually, stuff like you've seen happens in the Mogollon Bowl with Grandfather present only. Must be a really big reason for us to succeed here, or we'd be dead."

Jeremy looked at him. "I'm glad I know you, Bud."

"Put those wings down, son. I need a hug more than you do." He put his arms around Jeremy without waiting for his answer. They both needed a hug.

"What about this being a bogus world, Bud?" Jeremy asked after they'd continued a while.

"Wait a second. We're being tailed." He pulled the rifle out of the scabbard and handed it to Jeremy. "Don't miss."

The bear stood there, roaring, five-inch long claws pawing the air. Jeremy sensed he had one second to shoot it before it charged.

He used two shots. Its heart was where he thought it was.

The animal dropped with a thud that caused dust and bits of grass to fly.

The mare, heavily tranquilized by Bud's touch, and way stronger than Jeremy thought she was, pulled the travois, the poles, the hide, head, paws, and the choicer bear cuts into the camp way after dark.

"Come on, folks, we got bear steak tonight. We got bear liver, and we got a new warrior here. Jeremy, the bear killer!" Bud called out as they entered the site.

Everyone rose and cheered.

52

"Gi' me the heart, Bud," Sam said, leaning toward the hunks of bear meat from his chair. Bud handed the raw heart to him. Sam called Jeremy over to the campfire where everyone sat.

"Hail, Jeremy the bear killer." He held up the heart and wiped its bloody surface down Jeremy's forehead and nose and across both cheeks. Then he smiled at him. "Ye make me proud."

Nothing his real father had ever said or done made Jeremy feel so good.

"Take a bite," Sam said, offering the raw heart.

"Sorry, boys," Bud interceded, "not a good idea. My People used to eat the bear's heart raw for symbolic reasons. But in modern days, we know that bears carry roundworms, which no one wants. I'll throw it on the barbecue and then you can eat it. I'm cookin' everything lightly cremated tonight."

Everyone laughed. Jeremy felt relieved to be spared from roundworms. But Sam holding that hunk of raw meat gave him a start. They used to be cannibals. Seeing him with that bloody chunk was pretty freaky. He realized that none of the people from the underground had eaten cooked meat. He wondered about celebrations in the underground and the significance of rubbing the bloody heart on his face.

Then he stopped wondering, because he was having fun.

"Tell us how you killed the bear, Jeremy," Sam's brows rose and his mouth opened a little; his face was a study in expectation.

"Yes! Yes! Yes!" the village people chanted, looking at him as a hero.

Nobody had ever wanted to know how he did something so much. He was going to underplay it, but they wanted more than that, so he acted a little.

When he was done, everyone applauded as if he were a superstar. The people of the village were especially appreciative and noisy, making an ululating noise.

"Hail to Jeremy, the bear killer!" James said. "Now, can we eat? I'm starving."

They laughed and ululated. Pretty near anything made them start that howling.

Soon, they were eating well-done bear heart and liver, then well-done bear steaks. Jeremy got the first slices of the heart.

"What do you think of bear, Jeremy?" Bud asked.

He made a face. "Might be better if our chef from New York cooked it."

"I never liked bear myself," Bud replied. "Never stopped me from eating it if I was hungry."

The song started at the campfire after dinner. Sam held an overturned bucket between his knees and beat on it as though he'd been a drummer all his life. His skin shone and teeth flashed as he leaned into the rhythm. Everyone was playing some improvised instrument. His mom shook a can full of nails, rattling in time with Sam.

Sam raised his hand, and the racket stopped. He looked different from the way Jeremy had seen him. More—more everything: bigger, stronger, and more confident. Better-looking. His head with its reddish stubble of beard and hair, his face with its planes and angles and wide cheekbones, were beautiful.

Jeremy didn't like to use that word for a man. His father, Chaz Edgarton, had been called beautiful, but all Jeremy saw when he looked at him were his flaws. When he looked at Sam, he saw his strengths.

Sam began to speak.

"I want to thank everyone for what they did yesterday to help me and my people." Sam sat tall in his chair and easily captured the assembly's attention and affection. "We fought a great battle. We fought to save ourselves and the village," he waved to the three survivors and the babies. "We fought like a people who belong together.

"We need to remember what we did and who we lost. Ellie gave more than anyone. She saved Grace and me. And brought us these good friends," the three sitting at his feet and the babies. "She saved us from death. And then she died. Hers was a noble death, and I thank her."

Jeremy sat up and listened. Sam was doing something to them as he talked. His voice enthralled them.

"I thank Lena for her shooting, and I thank Bud and Wes for their power and bravery. I thank Henry and James and Mel. And Grace and Jeremy.

"I thank the unseen world. We would not have won without its help. I thank God for making things come out right.

"Having given proper thanks, I call for a change: Our world has been all wrong for a long time. *It's time for the village to be right!*"

Whistles and ululation danced around the circle. Sam raised his hands, and all the noise stopped. His voice resonated, pulling them in, making him seem many times his size.

"I am Sam of the line of Emily, direct descendent of Sam Baahuhd, head man of the village before we went underground. I am the oldest man in the line of Sam Baahuhd. I claim my birthright and my legacy: I am headman of the village, the village here," he waved his arm to take in the entire area of the old estate. "And the village by the river and the cliff," he waved his other arm to take in their other home, and all the territory in between, encompassing an area four or five times larger than the original manor.

The people of the village cheered, ululated, and made clicking noises that none outside the underground had heard before. Jeremy found himself standing up and clapping like a madman, tears in his eyes.

"Sam Baahuhd!" "Sam Baahuhd!" "Sam Baahuhd!" The cries went up from the village people. Jeremy found himself calling out the name of his old friend and sometime foe, Sam's ancestor of long ago.

Sam raised his hands and stopped the cheering. "It is my right to call m'self Sam Baahuhd and to have you call me that. With all respect to my ancestor, I say—I will never be known by that name. I reject and denounce the name Baahuhd!

"In the language of the village, baahuhd means 'bad.' I am not bad, and neither are any of my ancestors, or any that are here. I am a Good Man. I take that for my name from now on. I am Sam Good Man.

"I will run the village from the Book," and he pulled it out from his suit, where he'd held it close to his heart. Its light sparkled and illuminated Sam and everything around him. "I live by the Book, and I will run the village by the Book. No changes. No excuses.

"*We will never have what happened to us in the underground again! We are good people, and we will live as good people! I swear that I will lead you on the good road!*" He put his hand on his heart, and then closed it into a fist, and touched his heart again.

Jeremy watched him, transfixed. Sam sat up straight, his feet and legs encased in the white boots Ellie had put around them. If they hurt, nothing in Sam's face or demeanor indicated it. Sam was earnest as an angel. As earnest as anyone he'd ever seen. As good, and trustworthy, and kind. He glowed in the firelight. Sam Good Man— that was a perfect name for him.

"I tell you by my word and my bond, that I will work for you as long as I live. Do you accept my leadership of the village? Do you accept my hereditary right?"

Jeremy shouted, "Yes! Yes! Yes!" And so did everyone else. The children, the newcomers, Lena, Henry, James, Mel, and his mother.

"You accept me as your leader from this time forward?"

Roars of approval arose.

Sam smiled a funny little smile. "OK. I'll lead ye. I been working on it all my life, might as well take what's given to me.

"I claim a few more things." He turned to Grace, "I claim you, Veronica Piermont Edgarton, Lady Grace, for my wife, for all my life. You will be my only wife. I know we are already wed, but this is official, before the village.

"Will you be my wife, Lady Grace? I will love you as much as a man can love a woman. I will care for you and provide for you and make you the queen of my heart."

His mother looked like a girl. Tears streaked her face and she moved closer to him. "Oh, Sam, I already am your wife. I belong to you, like you belong to me. And I will spend the rest of my life loving you."

Sam's eyes glistened in the firelight. He was so good-looking, Jeremy thought. Like the old Sam Baahuhd, but better and kinder.

"Good, lady, for I have a gift for you. I've already given you my heart and soul, but here is all I own." He pulled out the jewelry bag that he'd rescued from the underground. He pulled something out of it, and then gave the bag to Grace. "These are some trinkets I found diggin' my way through paradise down there. They're probably yours a'ready, but they're yours again. My jewels."

She took the bag. "Thank you, Sam."

"But this is not yours. This comes through the line of Emily. Emily came to the village that last morning, naked except for some boots from Jamaya. And this." He held an impressive sapphire ring surrounded by diamonds out to her. Its blue stones flashed in the light. "This was Emily's ring. I give it to you. I am the only living descendent of Emily, and you are my wife."

Everyone saw the flash of light when he touched her to put the ring on her finger. She jumped, as though shocked.

Sam pulled her over and kissed her.

"And I claim ye," he pointed at Jeremy. "Ye, Jeremy the bear killer, Jeremy the Great Tek, as my son. Will ye be my son, Jeremy?"

Jeremy stood up, staring at Sam. Sam wasn't that much older than him, but he seemed decades older. Eons older. The ache of loneliness that haunted Jeremy reared up and pointed out the impossibility of Sam being his father. It was an insult to the memory of his highly flawed biological father. What was happening was impossible. They were in the middle of a tribal ritual; a new chieftain was claiming authority. He was part of it. Jeremy felt himself slide into acquiescence.

"Yeah, I'll take you for my father, Sam. I'll do my best to be a good son."

Sam smiled. "Good. I will be a good father as long as I live."

Jeremy ran around the circle and kneeled by the big auburn-haired man. And then Sam's arms were around him, pulling him in to the fire of his heart. Jeremy hugged Sam back. He felt like a lost son coming home.

"We are a *good* family," Sam said, eyes misty and glowing at the same time.

Sam turned back to everyone. "I claim ye as my people. I will lead ye well for all time. Do ye accept my claim?"

They did, with the same enthusiasm they'd accepted everything. Jeremy couldn't stop his eyes from blinking. His chest rose hard and convulsively. He had a father and a mother. He had a family.

53

Sam claimed the village the way Sam Baahuhd would have: fast, before another leader came forward. If he used the Voice to do it, so what? He planned on governing just as his ancestor had. He would be a strong and confident chieftain, fearless and immune to pain.

The problem came with the morning.

"Are you all right, Sam?" Grace said. He'd winced. He couldn't hide anything from her sharp eyes. "You look feverish." She put her hand on his forehead. "You don't have a fever."

"I'm fine, lady," he lied, lowering himself back on their mat. She pulled the bucket of his slops away. His face burned as she opened the tent and went out to dump it. Jeremy and Bud came in to lift him onto his chair outside. He hoped they hadn't seen the bucket. Being weak embarrassed him.

He couldn't stand; his legs and feet hurt too much. He'd awakened after the battle the day before to find them wrapped in hard white boots. He remembered being in the underground and suffocating heat. They told him the skin on his feet and legs was burned off. He didn't remember.

"You're lucky you're alive, Sam," the lady had said when he came out of the blackness.

Aye, he was. He remembered the buzzing of wings and Ellie, but they were lost in darkness. He couldn't remember what happened, other than that Ellie had saved him.

He sat up straight in his chair, trying to act like Sam Baahuhd in a chair with his feet burned off. The rest sat around the fire drinking coffee. Henry brought him breakfast.

"Leftovers," he said. "Barbequed bear." Henry bent down and said, "I sure liked what you said last night, Sam. I'm glad you're our leader."

All of them repeated those words. He smiled. He'd be able to keep smiling if the pain didn't get any worse.

She put a hand on his forehead again. "You're a little feverish, Sam. I think you should take antibiotics. I've got painkillers, too."

"I feel fine, lady. Are you wantin' to kill me like before?"

"No, Sam. I brought medications that you're not allergic to," she looked at him, her expression saying, don't fight with me, Sam. I'm afraid.

"I'm all right, lady. I'm fine." He smiled. Why did he need to pretend? Sam Baahuhd looked out through his eyes. *He* would never need pills or counsel.

"Well, if you're all right, I'll leave you for a while and go look in the machine barn with everyone."

They left, all of them, and climbed down the hole Jeremy and Wes had made in the roof of the old equipment barn. He wanted to go with them but he couldn't.

He sat there in his chair, coming to enjoy the sunshine and birds. He continued to marvel at their hoping and twittering and the feel of sun and wind on his skin. His legs hung down from his chair.

As time passed, they felt like they were expanding. Like they would burst their wrappings. He could feel the beating of his heart in them, throbbing. His cheeks felt hot. He'd take her pills when she came back, even though Sam Baahuhd would never be so weak.

When they came back, it was like an invasion. He was dozing. Their voices and excitement roused him. He jerked awake and struggled to listen.

"You won't believe what's down there," Mel said, face alight. "I don't know what all that stuff is, but there's *lots!*"

"We should be back to the cliff in no time," Henry added. They clustered around him, crackling with excitement. "Wes says we'll be able to go back right away."

"You've got a complete setup for a ranch in that barn." Wesley provided the most information. "You've got better machinery in there than I ever had. You should be able to grow food—if we can find seeds. You should at least get a crop of wild oats with it. You've got a backhoe loader, a couple of tractors. Some quads—4WD utility vehicles. Harrows, an auger. Even a big plow for breaking up sod. And a truck!

"There's everything you need for a *sawmill* crated up. You'll be able to make boards and posts—you can build a real ranch. There's tons of tools and hardware. You should take it all."

"The only problem is that it's buried," Bud added sardonically. "Some of it's eighteen feet down. But Wes and I can dig it out the way we dug out the babies."

"That is good news," Sam said, trying to imitate Sam Baahuhd by ignoring the pain in his legs. "Dig it out. We will take it all home."

They trooped off to watch Wesley and Bud work, but he caught Grace's eye. She came over to him.

"I'll take yer medicine, lady." He smiled. "I reckon you don't want to kill me."

She put her hand on his forehead. "You're burning up, Sam. You're really sick."

When they had him back in bed, she examined the white covers Ellie had put on him, sniffing under them and looking for streaks up his legs. "You seem fine, Sam."

Bud remained after putting Sam on his mat. He squatted next to him and remained there silently for a few seconds, as though sensing something. He put his hand on Sam's shoulder and said. "I've done some healing in my time, Sam. Call me when you need me. I'll come to you." He left, looking troubled.

Sam drifted the rest of the day, hearing the others coming and going. He saw flashes of blue light coming from the direction where Bud and Wesley were working. The medicines made the pain less, but they made him sleepy. He kept dreaming, bad dreams.

Something was pulling him inside, into darkness shot with golden light. It captured him and held him. When it held him, he didn't care that he was being weak. Who he was supposed to be faded and strands of a golden web held him fast.

He could see the doctor from Ellie's world standing by Lady Grace. He could see the big hall covered with spider silk before the fire came.

54

The next day, Jeremy and Bud brought Sam out into the fresh air.

"You'll be able to watch us dig out the equipment barn," Wes said. He was in high spirits. "I think everything should start right up."

The barn was invisible from ground level; Bud and Wes set about excavating, blue beams flying out of their hands. The others stood back. Seeing them work like that seemed almost commonplace. Mounds of earth grew on each side of the door to the barn. When they were finished, a driveway sloped down eighteen feet with the fill piled on each side. Bud and Wes were exhausted and filthy.

Everyone shouted when the barn doors were exposed.

"OK, open the doors," Jeremy said. James and Mel knocked a few rocks and hunks of dirt back. Wesley sliced through the padlocks and the doors were thrown wide.

The barn contained a rancher's dream. A tractor, backhoe, utility tractor, barrels of fuel, and every kind of tool. More vehicles.

Wesley examined the treasure trove. "If we'd had one tenth of this on our ranch, we could have . . . made some money. Maybe even survived. Look at that tractor."

Bud didn't have Wes's mechanical skill, but he could see that the machines were wonderful and in fantastic shape.

'It's great, Wes. Only one problem, how the hell do we get it all back?"

"We drive it back, Bud. Straight shot home."

"Yeah," Bud agreed. He shook his head. "Thing is, you need a barn for it. Can't have the equipment and tools out in the rain, assuming we get rain. And you can't be running up and down the ladder every time you want a wrench. "

Jeremy added his input. "I could blow a hole in the cliff face, maybe off to the side. We could make a rock grotto there for a barn."

Bud looked cautious. "Jeremy, how do you know the whole overhang wouldn't collapse?"

"Well, yeah. You're right. I'm not so hot with explosives." Jeremy acknowledged. "Can you blue-beam a cave big enough for a barn?"

"Into solid rock?"

"OK. But we could take the doors off this barn and hang them on it. That would be cool."

Bud and Wes looked at each other and shrugged.

"Maybe. I'll feel better when I get all this equipment working," Wes answered.

"I can't get a damn thing to start," Wesley said after a couple of hours of intense labor. "I remade the hoses and belts. I thought everything would turn over the minute I tried it." He stood in front of the machine barn. "I guess I'll have to drain all the fluids and clean out the tanks. Go over the entire engines. God, this drives me crazy."

Sam watched and saw everything, despite his illness. He kept an eye on Wesley. Even though Wes worked very hard and had helped so much saving the babies and fighting in the battle, Sam had a bad feeling about him.

He'd never seen a man with a body like Wes's. A body where every muscle stood out, defined by light and shadow. A body with no fat on it, all smooth brown skin like a piece of art. A moving, living sculpture like those he'd seen in the books before they closed the library. Such a body must be very exciting to a woman.

Sam wondered why Wesley's shirt was always off whenever Grace was around. Grace took water to the machine barn, and Wes walked back with her, his shirt tied around his waist, muscles smooth and sleek, smile flashing.

If Lena was there, Wes's shirt stayed on.

55

After watching Wes get nowhere with the engines, Bud took stock. "I'm going for Plan B. That's the 'horses only' plan. I'll start gentling enough horses to get what we can home without the vehicles. I'll make a trip to the forest to get more travois poles right now."

He turned to the group. "Henry, do you want to help me?" He would have asked Grace since she was the best rider of the bunch, but she was too worried about Sam to go anywhere. And Lena was busy with the babies. "I want to get the poles now so we have everything we need to get out of here. We'll bring enough packhorses to get poles for every horse we've got. If we go right away, we won't have to stay overnight."

Henry agreed. They were heading out when Wesley shouted, "What's a *Duo/Duo?*"

"Probably it's a dual engine, electric and plastic fuel. Our fuels aren't flammable, which explains the barrels not going up," Mel replied. "All of our engines are Duos, or plain electric. Most of our vehicles hover instead of rolling on the ground, but some hover and have wheels, and even tracks, like a tank. You'd need wheels or tracks for farm work. They have more traction. That's where you get the Duo/Duo."

"What an idiot I am!" Wes hit himself on the forehead with the heel of his hand. "There's this thing in the middle of the engine. I didn't know what it was. It's an auxiliary electric motor. *They* aren't charged. That's why nothing starts. And I don't have anything to charge them with. Shit!"

Bud raised his brows and shrugged. He'd get the poles and start gentling horses anyway. Part of him had always expected the "Horses only" option to be the one they used. At least *horses* couldn't go dead, unless they died.

"Henry, get your stuff. Before we go, I want to stop by Sam and make a couple of social calls. I'll be fast."

When he got to Sam's tent, Bud looked in. Sam was asleep. Bud bent over him, listening and observing. Something was wrong with Sam, and it wasn't his feet. He didn't have a handle on what it was yet, but he knew what he had to do in the meantime.

"Sam, buddy," he whispered, "call me when you need me."

He left and went to the babies' tent. They'd set up all the tents they'd brought: one for the computer lab, one for Sam and Grace because Sam was sick. One for the babies and the last for the three new people. The babies and the new people were having a hard time.

"Hey, kids, how're you doin'?"

"Bud," they said, turning to him. Every one of them knew his name.

"You guys hangin' out OK?" He went from child to child, touching them, talking to them. Using what Grandfather had taught him on them. "Bobby, my man, what do you say?" Bud had taught Bobby the high-five, and he had taught the other kids. Bobby could roll over and almost get up on his knees now. "You kids are gonna be racing around here soon, causing trouble." He went down the rows. "I'm going to be gone a while, getting some wood with Henry. We'll be back probably late tonight; you guys keep everybody in line."

Bud left the tent. Despite his cheerfulness when he was with the children, he feared that a couple of those kids weren't going to make it. He could feel them drifting away. Bud could heal, but only if the Great One wanted it. Only where and when the time was right. Oh, let me heal those babies, please.

His eyes stung as he stood outside the tent for the adult newcomers. He couldn't help the sadness he felt. He missed his own kids so much. And Bert. What were they doing without him? What did they think? He hoped that Bert didn't think he'd run off with some other woman. There was no other woman for him. How long had they been gone? The days blurred together. It felt as if they'd been gone weeks.

Getting ahold of himself, Bud said, "Hey, you guys? Can I come in?"

"Yes, Bud." That was Jim Bob, the little person.

"Yeah. Come in!" from Jack, the guy with no legs.

Martin welcomed him silently, an expectant smile on his face. Martin was the blind one and the one Bud had come to see. He was the strangest person Bud could imagine. Very small, five feet tall at most, and skinny and gray and gray-toothed, like the rest of them.

Bud didn't realize how extraordinary Martin was until he had been around him for a couple days. The man was entrancing. He was a seer, a prophet, and infinitely valuable in this fragile community. Martin moved with a grace that Bud had only seen in Ellie, before she changed, and in Grandfather. He reminded him of Grandfather in a way that tugged at the hole inside Bud where Grandfather had been.

"I gotta make it brief today. I'm going off with Henry to get some more poles for the travois. You guys doin' OK?"

They nodded and looked at him, knowing the real reason he had come.

"Good. Listen, Martin, keep an eye on Sam. Something's got him. His legs are bad, but that isn't it. I'm worried about him. Call me if you need me. I'm goin' now before things get worse. I'll be back before we need to make a move."

Martin "looked" at him silently. He was in a rapture, Bud knew, like Grandfather. Living in a place that most people had no knowledge of and would scoff at if anyone tried to tell them about it.

Long hours later, he and Henry rode horses back into the camp. Each led a horse on both sides of his own, riding one and ponying two, as they would say on any ranch. All of the horses pulled as many poles to make travois as they could handle.

They'd had an adventure. Midway through cutting the trees, Bud's blue beam quit, so they had to chop and trim the trees the old-fashioned way with axes and saws.

Bud had a feeling that he and Wes were on borrowed time with the beams and showier supernatural manifestations. When Grandfather used such tools at the Meeting or any of the "warriors only" events, they were the frosting, not the cake. Here, the Great One seemed to have given them more slack, probably because of the enormity of the task in front of them.

Bud felt edgy riding back. He kept hoping he and Wes would be allowed to go home "when they were finished." But it was turning out that when they got one task done, more arose. "That's the nature of life," he said absentmindedly.

"What?" Henry responded.

"Oh, I'm just talking to myself. Seems like we do one thing, and more comes up."

"That is the nature of life," Henry replied. "Bud, what's wrong with Sam?"

"His burns, for sure. But something else, too," Bud said. "Lord, I wish I had Grandfather here. He always knew what to do. But, we'll have to watch and see what happens.

"More than that," Henry added. "I don't like the feeling I'm getting around the camp, do you? Not between us, but with the place."

"Yeah, I feel it, too," Bud replied. "It's like fallout, but I don't think radioactive. Remember that explosion at the end of the battle? And the yellow cloud? I don't know what caused those, but I think they're part of this creeping crud that's getting me down. And I don't know about that cloud at all."

"Me neither. But let's not mention it around the camp. Let's not make people nervous."

56

"I think it was that doctor," Lena said. "What do you think, Henry?"

"What are you talking about?" he said, straggling over to the campfire.

"What Jeremy found out this afternoon," Lena explained. "He's trying to charge up the batteries so the equipment will run. The solar power he's got for the computer isn't enough. He went over to the underground to see if any of the solar units could be used. They weren't . . ."

"There's this yellow powder all over everything," Mel cut in. "I went over there with him. It's toxic—both of us were nauseous in a few minutes. It's not radioactive—he had his Geiger counter with him and checked it. But it's harmful."

"I bet it's from the yellow cloud," Henry said.

"That's what we think," Mel said. "Jeremy doesn't know what it is, but we think that doctor did it."

"Or *is* it," Jeremy walked up and sat down. "Mom, didn't you say that he seemed to melt after he died?"

"I don't remember, Jeremy. All I remember is the fire coming out of his hand and Ellie stinging him. I'm going to check Sam."

Grace left, but the discussion started up immediately afterward.

"What do you mean, *is* the doctor, Jeremy?" Henry asked.

"I think the explosion was him, maybe the reaction of an alien chemistry with our atmosphere, or maybe it was just what they do when they die."

Bud joined them and sat down. He'd finished with the horses. He was staggering slightly with exhaustion. "Thought is very powerful, and will is more powerful. Grandfather used to say that. Whether it would make you melt and explode after dying and leave a poisonous mess, I don't know.

"I do know that I'm more bushed than I've been in a long time and I have to start gentling horses for the travois tomorrow. I need help. My blue beam went dead while I was cutting trees. I need help in stripping the poles and everything else."

"Well, I almost got my battery going this afternoon," Jeremy said. "Tomorrow we'll have to christen it."

"What battery are you making, Jeremy?" Bud asked.

"It's a urine-powered battery. They've been around for ages. I've got copper piping. Magnesium is in the fertilizer. I should be able to work something out tomorrow. Piss on it, bingo! Electricity."

"A pee-powered battery?" Bud laughed.

"Sure. All you need for electricity is the interaction of acid and base. We've got 'em. I'll figure a way to harness the power," Jeremy said. "Though it would be a lot easier if we could find where the extra solar panels were stored.

"The equipment barn we dug out isn't the only one. The place was a village—a hundred people lived here. They had the stables, sheds, and warehouses. Houses. When I built the underground, I ordered extra solar panels. We were going to make the main house solar, too. But that didn't happen . . ."

"I tried to find other barns, Jeremy," Wesley said. He looked as bushed as everyone else. "I dug everywhere you said. I couldn't find any other buildings. And I think my blue beam's about to quit, too."

"Well, we should go to bed. We're just depressing ourselves," Lena said. "I want to take a look at the babies and then pass out." She got up. "You know, at my grandparents' farm, the big barn had storage sheds on each side. Did you think of that?"

Jeremy looked thunderstruck. "Of course! We'll check tomorrow morning. But the pee battery will work though, I'm sure."

57

First thing in the morning, Bud and Wes hopped on horses and rode over to the place where the battle had been. All that was left of the shelter was a flat crater; the whole thing had sunk into the earth. A stinking, yellow powder covered everything. It seemed to be heading directly toward their camp: An arm protruded from it as though the doctor was clawing his way over.

"We'll have to keep an eye on this," Bud said.

"It's moving. Look!" Wes nodded his head in the direction of the arm. They could see it move. Wes shot his blue beams at the powder until he came up empty. "My blue beam just died."

He had succeeded in blasting the arm's edge back a couple of feet. It started moving again as they watched. Soon, it was farther than where it had started. It was only a twenty-minute walk from the underground to where they were camped. The crud was moving slowly, but inevitably. It was as though it had their scent.

Bud felt ill sitting on his horse. He could see that it targeted the people from the underground, Sam first and hardest, and then the others, babies first. It made everyone sick. Nauseated. Weak. Shaky. They needed to stop it.

But how? Wes's blue beams had just slowed it down—and neither of them had that kind of Power any more.

That was what he'd been working on in his head all day. He had a plan that needed to be followed to the letter. And it would, he hoped.

"Let's get back to the others," Bud said, wheeling his mount.

"The storage sheds *are* here! On both sides!" Jeremy shouted as he tore boards off the inside of the barn. "Look at this stuff!"

Sure enough, the extra solar panels were stored there. They had enough panels to light a small city, had one still existed. Bud was impressed.

"I'm going to turn the vehicles into straight solar power when we get to the cliff," Jeremy said. "We'll fill them up with fuel here and take all the barrels of fuel we can, but we won't need it much once we get there. I'll start on the conversion right away."

Sam never got off his chair. Most of the time he lay on a pad watching them. His fever was so high that you could practically see heat waves rise from him. The worse Sam got, the harder Jeremy worked. He felt what they all did: Sam might not make it.

It was funny what got to people. Bud had never seen Grace show anything but bravery and fortitude until they found a stash of her furniture in one of the sheds. It must have been stuff that was discarded from the house. He could see a broken table leg, torn upholstery, a chipped glass tabletop. She touched a settee—he knew it was a settee and not a sofa or couch because his wife had been redecorating and introduced him to the vocabulary of furniture. The settee was upholstered in brocade; he knew that, too.

Grace ran her hand over the curve of one arm. The fabric was so old; it would probably crumble if anyone sat on it. But the raw, sad look on her face touched him. He realized that she'd lost a glamorous life like Will Duane lived. Estates all over, designer clothes, fabulous trips, everything. Prestige. Power.

He'd see to it that they took most of the furniture, as well as everything else that was potentially useful. The flatbed trailer would help a lot.

Bud had been sure Wes would get the farm equipment going in no time once the solar panels charged the batteries for the duos. But it didn't work that way. After a week of more drudgery and disappointment than anyone anticipated, they were packed up and ready to go—without the machines or solar panels. None of the engines would turn over.

Bud had spent his time gentling horses and getting them used to the travois. Everyone had pulled the stuff they could pull with the horses out of the barn and packed it. It was backbreaking work. They couldn't fit everything they wanted to take on the travois and had to leave some of the most important things. Tempers were frayed from the work and the inescapable stench of the yellow powder. Several days passed. It seemed too much trouble to count them.

Bud and Wes rode out every evening, keeping track of the yellow crud. It *was* worse, and closer.

Finally, they were leaving. Everyone who could ride was mounted. A fleet of travois was attached to horses and loaded for the trip. The kids were strapped into horse-drawn drays, as were the three disabled people.

Bud stood next to Sam's chair with a travois. Sam refused to be lifted into it. Bud held the horse, turning from side to side as though he were looking for somewhere to disappear. "I have sat here while ye slaved," Sam said. "I have done nothin' to help. How can I be yer chief, riding like a baby? I canna, and I will na'. Bud, get ma horse!"

"Sam, I know the last two weeks have been hard for you." Grace bent over him. "No one thinks you were shirking. You have to stay off your feet. You don't have any skin on your feet and legs. Bacteria can enter your wounds and you can't stop it. People *die* of injuries like yours."

"It dinna hurt, lady. I am fine."

"You are not fine. And you do hurt. You're taking antibiotics and pain medication."

Bud's calm voice cut through the tension. "Sam, if you ride a horse, you'll have to get on and off a bunch of times in a day, not just once. You'll have to hop on one foot getting on and land on one foot getting off. Your legs will rub on the stirrups and the leathers. The horse could fall down or buck you off. Please get in the travois . . ."

The sound of an engine coughing drowned out Bud's voice. They looked in the direction of the machine barn.

Wes was so pissed off. He *intended* to get the fucking motors going, and they weren't helping a bit. His head and arms were jammed into the center well of one of the AWD vehicles. He had the cover on the Duo-duo-duo-*stupid* battery open and was trying to uncouple the solar connection that had been charging it up, or so they thought. He and Jeremy had no real indication that the solar was doing anything. None of the dials on the instrument panel moved. Getting the jury-rigged contraption hooked up to the solar panels had been hell; uncoupling it was double hell.

"I think you should let it charge a little longer, Wes," Jeremy said.

"A little longer and everyone will have left without us. We uncovered all this stuff, and we're *going* to take it back to the cliff. We don't have time to *let it charge*," Wes snarled. The stench of the yellow powder had made him explosive.

"It won't do any good to unhook it if it's not charged, *Wes*."

"But you said you didn't know if it was charging. So who the fuck cares if I unhook it?"

"I care, Wes. I want to take everything as much as you do. Look. Give it ten more minutes." Jeremy pointed at the clock on the vehicle's dashboard, which *was* working. "I'll see if I can crank up the solar power." He walked to a system of linked panels and cable that fed into the engine. He fiddled with the cables, then turned a knob on a control board. "Tell me if anything happens."

Wes felt a buzz in the AWD's battery immediately. He quickly rehooked the connections that he'd been trying to unhook. "Now we got something." The buzz was steady. "Why didn't you do that to start with?"

"I was afraid the engine might blow up."

Wes jumped back. "Why didn't you tell me?"

"I just did."

"You stinking son of a bitch!"

"You better be careful that my mother doesn't hear you talking like that."

Wes felt like lighting into Jeremy, but didn't. "OK. I take it back. God save the queen."

"What did you say?" Jeremy's fists clenched and he took a step toward Wes.

"Hey, hey. I'm sorry. I'm just fucked up . . . a little nervous. I didn't mean anything about your mother."

"OK. What does it look like now?"

"What?"

"The meter on the electrical adapter. The thing that shows whether or not the battery is charging."

"Oh." Wes looked into the well in front of him. "It's charging! I can see the needle rise!"

"Ten minutes and we'll give it a try."

They gave it a try. Wes turned the key in the ignition. Nothing. Wes *and* Jeremy swore.

"The only thing it can be is the computer. There's gotta be a loose chip or some bad code." Jeremy whipped out one of his mini-computers and hooked it up to the center panel of the duo. "I've already tested everything, but not with the batteries charged. I'll do it again. Come on, come on."

Jeremy launched himself at the machine. He reminded Wes of one of the cow dogs on his family ranch. Once one of them locked onto a job, the only way to stop the animal was to shoot it.

Jeremy finally pulled away. "Try it now. There was a glitch in the code and a loose connection."

Wes was almost afraid to turn the key. He shot a look at Jeremy.

"Go on. Try it." Jeremy urged him, moving his hands like he was scooting Wes along.

Sucking in a breath, Wes hit the ignition. He could see Jeremy's tense face next to him. The vehicle belched, then bucked, and settled into a rumbling purr.

"Yahoo! We got it!" Wesley shouted. "We're on our way out of here!" Jeremy launched himself on Wes, giving him a bear hug. Wes recoiled. "Hey, man, that's enough." Then he just grinned. The engine ran rough, but it was running.

He drove the vehicle out of the sunken barn and into the open. Jeremy hung on the back. The two of them grinned widely. They drove up to Sam and Bud and Grace, honking the horn until they saw the effect it was having on the horses.

"Hey you guys, it works!" Wes shouted. "We can get them all going."

Sam drifted in and out of a haze, feeling people moving around him, seeing the equipment being loaded and then moving. Two days had passed since Wesley and Jeremy had started the machines. Sam could see the fleet of farm vehicles in the center of a herd of loaded horses. The lady had told him they had a special conveyance for him.

"You'll be safe, Sam," she said. He had drifted too far away to hear the concern in her voice. And then what they'd rigged up to carry him heaved up in front of him.

"Hey, Sam! Climb in!" Wesley waved from the driver's seat of the largest machine. Exhaust fumes and engine noise belched from it. The machine had a huge scooper on the front with a smaller scooper like a hand and arm on the back. It pulled a huge disked drag with the blades pulled up. On that, drums of fuel and as much hardware from the barn as they could pack were strapped down tight.

Wes drove to where Sam sat with Grace, the machine's front bucket raised triumphantly. He stopped near Sam and lowered the bucket until it rested on the ground.

"Sam, get in." Wes grinned. "Best seat in the house. I'll be your chauffeur."

Sam, wan and pale, gazed at the machine.

"It's a backhoe loader," Wesley shouted. "The bucket in front is balanced by all the stuff I'm pulling behind. I can keep you up there the whole way. C'mon. It beats a travois."

"It's a good idea, Sam," Grace said. "I'll put the pads inside and cover you with a tarp. You can rest while we're traveling."

Sam acquiesced. He hadn't slept well for days, falling into black dreams. He shivered and could feel his cheeks flaming. He allowed Jeremy and Henry to lift him into the bucket.

"Here are your antibiotics. And the pain pills and water," Grace said.

"I'm fine, lady. Dinna worry." His face felt leaden. He hurt all over. He wouldn't let them know. He would not be a burden.

Wes raised the bucket and they were off.

Sam grabbed at the sides of the bucket when the vehicle rumbled forward. The machine looked huge when he first saw it, and it seemed more enormous when he rode in it. The sound it made running and the feel of it moving rattled his bones and made his feet ache. He pulled himself up and looked over the edge. The others spread out before him.

The lady had told him the names of all the vehicles. Lena and James drove the two tractors. They pulled trailers full of things he didn't have words for. There was a truck. Its back was covered with something like a small house. That must hold the babies and the three people from the village. The truck pulled a trailer jammed with more things. Jeremy drove something like a car, which pulled a vehicle similar to itself. A mule, Jeremy had called it. Both were loaded. Bud, Henry, and Grace rode horses while leading horses with travois. A bunch of horses pulling drays ran along with them, loose.

Sam lay back, dizzy. He felt the way he had when he had first gotten out of the underground when he'd wanted to scream and throw himself on the ground. His body felt hot. The sun bore down. They had covered him with a tarp, but it magnified the sun's heat.

He tried to look backward at Wesley, but could only see the roof of the machine behind him. Wesley couldn't see him, and he couldn't see Wesley. Sam didn't trust Wesley. Would he drop the bucket and throw Sam out?

He shivered as the hours passed and the sun baked him under the tarp. He drifted in and out, thinking and being awake, and then being fuzzy. Not knowing where he was or why. He needed water, but was too weak to get it. His legs flamed like the fire was still burning them.

His eyes closed. He was in the spider queen's chamber. Sam Big hung there, his lower legs nipped off, screaming for Sam to kill him. And then *he* was hanging there, legs cut off below the knee, screaming like Sam. The queen ate his legs silently.

He was tunneled deep into the earth, smiling. He'd recovered the Book and his packet of jewels. Emily's ring. He put them into his suit, fastening it up. And then flames and heat enveloped him. His goggles fused to his suit. He was dying, burning up. He struggled to breathe, fighting to live. No air. He could hear himself choking, his throat closing.

Then he didn't remember anything.

58

Where the hell was Wesley going? Bud looked out ahead of the caravan. Wes was just a speck on the horizon. Bud lifted his hat and held its brim in his teeth, wiping his forehead with the back of his arm and then replacing his hat. They were in danger of liquefying out in the sun. He looked around the struggling caravan. The vehicles weren't quite road-worthy. Jeremy had to stop every ten minutes to fix something.

His job was no picnic, either. Ponying two horses and riding the one he was on with a stupid English saddle wasn't easy. Lead ropes and reins filled his hands. The saddle had no horn to dally a lead line around, nothing to tie anything to. They'd been traveling for hours. His horse kept turning toward the horse on its right, ears pinned back, mouth opened to bite.

"Settle down, buddy," he said. "We're all a little testy." Some worse than others, he thought. It was hard to lose sight of a gigantic machine on a flat plain studded with oak trees, but Wes had nearly pulled it off. He was so far ahead of the slow-moving horses and farm vehicles that he'd almost disappeared.

What was he thinking? Wes was supposed to keep them in sight and keep his mind on Sam's condition every minute. The backhoe loader was so much more powerful than the other vehicles that it pulled ahead of them with no trouble. It reminded Bud of the famous race that Secretariat had won; he was so far ahead that the pack was only a memory.

"We better be more than a memory, Wes," Bud whispered. "You're playing with Sam's life."

The plain became utterly still and clear. No movement, no birdsong. Golden meadows, big oaks dotted around like gnarled-up giants. Blue sky. Sun. The little dot carrying Wes and Sam in the far distance. Flat and eerie. The scene stilled and sharpened again, becoming a super-real vision of meadow and oak.

The center of the scene ripped open the way it sometimes did when Grandfather was with him. The shaman pulled you into his reality, a reality that showed you the truth of everything, no matter how far away it was, and no matter how dense the cloud of lies around it. Bud found himself in that mystical state. He knew what was in Wes's mind more clearly than he knew his own thoughts. It was like the old days in the Mogollon Bowl, when the spirit warriors were so close they practically were each other. He couldn't believe what Wes was thinking.

Wesley drove straight ahead, punching it. At first, the drone of the engine and the machine's jolting absorbed all his attention. After a while, the monotony of the rough ride blocked out the world and his mind roamed.

How did I end up here? he thought. I'm an *international* movie star. I'm booked for the next seven years. No Indian has *ever* made what I make. *Tribes* don't make what I make, even with casinos. If I don't get back soon, no one will hire me again. I'll lose it all.

My life has been shit since I was born. I was a squalling brown brat on a dirt ranch. We worked our asses off, for what? So I can get yanked out here to rescue freaks?

Why do things like this always happen to me? Wouldn't you think I'd get some slack once in a while? On one lousy thing? I was a spirit warrior, for Christ's sake. That should count for something.

He looked at the bucket in front of him. The tarp prevented him from seeing his passenger. Even without the cover, he wouldn't have seen Sam. He was nestled in the bottom of the deep bucket. If Sam needed him, he'd have to move enough to get Wes's attention. Wesley had vowed to keep an eye out for movement down there. He had seen Sam's terrible condition when they put him in the bucket.

The guy was going to die. Anyone could see that. Why were they pretending they could save him? He was probably dead already. And there was not one lousy thing anyone could do about it.

Fuck, Wes thought, jerking as he hit every rock and gully. His brown arms were spread, gripping the steering wheel. He felt as powerful as he ever had been, lean and spare.

The one good thing about all the work and the lousy food was that his water weight was down and his muscles even better defined. He looked the way he had back on the set, with no dietician telling him what to eat. He didn't need that bullshit. Wes knew how to keep himself fit.

The forest was up in front of them somewhere. They'd turn left, north, and head along it until they could see the cliff. How stupid all this was. He was busting his ass to get home, when *home* was a stone-age dwelling that his ancestors had built a million years before and abandoned.

He punched it, driving harder than he had all day. Anything to get out of there. The others could catch up.

"Damn it to hell, Wes!" Bud cursed. "You're a tragedy queen!" Wesley had been the purest man Bud had ever known, a shaman of shamans, sure to be Grandfather's successor. Now he was Wesley, the superstar who drove back to the cliff with a dying man in his bucket—and didn't care.

Bud leaned over and tied up the lead lines of the horses he was ponying "Henry, watch these two," he shouted. Not waiting to hear Henry's answer, Bud galloped to the truck carrying the children and rescued people. Martin had the side window open and was screaming out of it, milky blind eyes reflecting the sunlight.

"He's dyin'. Sam's dyin'. Ye gotta get to him."

"That's right, Martin, we gotta go."

Mel stopped the truck and stuck his head out the window. "What's the matter?" He was red-faced and sweaty.

"Sam's in big trouble and Wes don't seem to know it. We gotta get up there." Bud waved in Wesley's direction. "I need Martin for the healin' an' I need Jeremy." He looked around frantically. "There he is. You get him an' Martin up to Wesley as fast as you can."

"It's rough ground. I might break an axle."

"You get 'em there, or I'll break *you*." Bud glared at Mel.

"OK. I'll punch it."

Bud pulled his hat off his head and whacked his only partly civilized horse in the flank with it. The horse leapt forward like it had been waiting for the chance. That mustang was made to run, which is why Bud picked him.

Bud shoved his heels down and took a deep seat in the saddle. Ground flew past him as the cayuse stormed across the pasture. The three-beat cadence of the gallop filled his ears. The horse's legs moved like scissors, reaching out and pulling the ground in. Bud sat like a Native Buddha as the powerful animal beneath him heaved and blew. Sensations and sounds merged as he flew.

And then he heard nothing but his ancestors' prayers, blessing his way. Would they be enough?

Wes jumped when Bud came galloping up alongside him, gesturing at the bucket. He rattled to a stop.

"What's the matter?" he shouted.

"Sam's in trouble. Drop the bucket. We have to get him out of there." Bud swung off his horse and pulled the tarp off the bucket. "Oh, no. Help me, Wes. Get him on the ground over here, and some of those mats under him."

Wes froze when he saw Sam. He was as gray as the people who had just escaped the underground. His arms were pulled up on his chest, crossed over with his hands like claws. Wes had seen people who were almost dead in that position.

"I'm sorry, Bud. I didn't know."

Bud looked at him carefully. Wes quailed. They both knew that at one time, Wes could feel what was going on with anyone around him as well as Grandfather could. This wouldn't have happened if Wes was who he had been.

"I'm sorry. I couldn't tell." His voice was a wail.

"I know, Wes," Bud said with all the kindness he could muster. "But I got to help him fast or I won't be able to. You make sure the rest get to the cliff safely. That's your job. I've given everyone orders. Jeremy and Martin will stay with me."

Grace rode up. She looked at Sam on the ground and her face went white. She started to swing off her mount.

"No, Grace," Bud said. "He won't heal if you're here. You've got to go . . .

"Henry, take her away. I got to get to work. You all have your assignments. Now do them."

59

The minute Bud stood next to Sam, the Power hit him so hard he couldn't think. He sat down on Sam's left side. A gray cloud came up around them, straight out of the earth. He couldn't see any of the others outside or even hear what they were doing. The outside world might have ceased entirely for all he knew. He'd seen Grandfather surrounded by such a cloud and knew that you couldn't see in if you were outside.

Jeremy led Martin through the gray wall. Only those who were supposed to be there could enter. Jeremy sat cross-legged by Sam's right shoulder and Martin sat next to him, by Sam's hip. They leaned over him, stricken by his terrible condition.

Bud's eyes closed and the Power took over. He spread his hands over Sam and said, "Oh Great One, You know we've got a sick man here. Please heal him. We'll do whatever we have to do to see Your will done. We're waiting on You. Please release this good man from whatever's put him like this."

Bud opened his eyes. He was back in the Bigs' chamber with the battle against the spiders raging. Then he and the others were in the lower level, beneath the main hall. The air around them glowed too white for actual reality. Everything but what mattered was bleached out. He had been pulled into a very powerful vision.

The spider queen's pearly white abdomen pulsed as she squeezed out eggs. Her mandible was split in the middle, opening like a nutcracker. Her spiky feet aimed a human's lower leg at her jaws. A red trickle ran down her opalescent belly.

"Oh, Sam! Kill me! Kill me if y' can find it in yer heart. If y' ever loved me, kill me. She's eatin' me piece by piece." Sam Big's voice grabbed Bud's attention.

Suspended from the ceiling by spider silk, Sam Big's malformed head shone in the vision's surreal brilliance. Terror lit his eyes. With his severed hands and missing lower leg, Sam Big looked like a freshly killed steer hung to bleed out. His eyes locked on Sam's.

That moment froze. Sam looked at his tormenter, transfixed.

"If y' ever loved me, kill me." The words filled the space, filled their minds.

"If y' ever *loved* me, kill me."

Sam came to life, leveling his machine gun and ripping Sam Big with bullets. He tore him apart.

"If y' *ever* loved me, kill me."

Bud sat quietly, the words rattling around their private world within the gray mist shroud. Bud wanted to ask Sam something, but he couldn't speak.

Abruptly, the scene changed. Bud was in a darkened underground chamber. Sam Big was lying next to him, facing him. He must have been lying down, too, because Big's misshapen face with its heavy brows and cheekbones was right before his eyes. Bud realized he was in Sam's body, lying with Sam Big.

The other man looked at him, eyes soft and wondering, feelings flickering over his face. Awe, fear, and love. Definitely love. Sam Big reached out and stroked him, whispering something in the language of the village. An endearment. He continued to caress Sam, looking at him in amazement.

Bud heard Sam's voice, not a true voice; Sam was too close to death to speak with a physical voice. Still his voice filled Bud's mind.

"I saw him when he was naked." The words came out slowly. "I saw him when there was just him and me."

The vision continued. It was a scene of love.

"Aye, I loved him,'" Sam's voice continued. "I saw who he was without the sickness and his friends to make him bad.

"He watched out for me. The others would have killed me. He kept them away. He knew I was saving the babies, and he didn't stop me.

"I loved him."

The truth of that filled them as completely as Sam Big's desperate plea had earlier.

Sam lay still for a moment, and then his jaw clenched and his hands formed fists. His fury erupted like the Bigs' rage.

"*And I hated him!*" Sam exploded, words charged with everything he'd suffered.

"He loved me, and he . . ." Sam threw his hands in the air, face contorted. "He killed my sister . . .

"He put the eye in me. He knew it would kill me. He knew how it would hurt . . ."

Sam drew up his hands and howled, expressing the misery of living in a place where love promised betrayal, nothing was sacred, and love and pain and sex and filth were intertwined. An unmoored universe with no escape. His cry beat against them.

"Oh, Sam!" Jeremy leaned over Sam, grabbing his shoulders. "I'm *so* sorry." He peered into Sam's tightly closed eyes. "When I made the shelter, I wanted to make a place where good people could grow and live. I wanted to make a *better* world, not one where *that* happened.

"I wanted things to be nice, Sam." Jeremy opened and closed his eyes furiously. "I'm sorry, Sam. I didn't want what happened down there."

Sam opened his eyes and looked into Jeremy's. "Aye, lad. I know what ye wanted. It's in the Book. But it wasn't what happened." Cascades of tears ran down Sam's cheeks.

"Ah know that he loved me, and ah loved him. It wasn't what ah wanted, but it happened. And he did what he did, knowing it would kill me. Like love was nothing. Like it was a lie."

"It's not a lie, Sam," Jeremy grabbed him again. "You said you wanted me for your son. You wanted me because you love me. I can feel it. Don't die, Sam. Don't take that away!" Jeremy's voice approached a wail.

"Don't die, Sam!" He pulled so hard on Sam's shoulders that he hauled him to a half-sitting position. Sam put his arms around Jeremy.

"Ah won't leave thee, son. Not if ah can help . . . "

"Don't leave us, either," Martin piped up. "Sam—we need you. An' we love you." He pitched himself at Sam, grabbing him around the midsection, the only area he could reach.

"I love you, Sam," Jeremy and Martin said at once. Sam's long arms reached around both of them.

"And we don't care what happened in the underground. It's *over*, Sam. I don't care what happened to you or what Sam Big did or what you did. *It's over*."

"*Now* is the time we get out and make a better world, Sam," Martin said. "That's what the Book says. *We're* the good people. *We're* supposed to make a good place. All of us, with you leading us." Martin was insistent.

"Do you want to live, Sam Good Man?" Bud wasn't aware of what he was doing. The Power blotted out everything. He bent over Sam, who had his arms wrapped around Jeremy and Martin. "*Do you want to live, Sam?*" He put his face in Sam's.

"Yes," Sam cried. "Ah want to live with all m' heart. Ah want to be here and live."

"Good." Bud rose onto his knees and turned toward Sam's legs. He grabbed the coverings Ellie had put on them with both hands. The casts let out a loud Crack! and split from top to bottom down the front, falling open like halves of shells.

Bud looked at Sam's legs. Spots of green and streaks of red indicated gangrene and blood poisoning. Sam would be dead within hours because of his legs, but they weren't the real problem. Yellow vapor and a vile odor rose from Sam's calves when the casts let loose. The yellow powder creeping toward them from the shelter had smelled the same. Golden swirls peppered with darkness rose from his lower legs and eddied above them. Sam's legs had black tracings over them, like colonies of mildew reaching out to touch each other. He was shot with rot.

"You're cursed, Sam. This is a black curse."

The vapors rising over him compressed into a figure. The doctor's golden form appeared in the mist, eyes a bit larger than they had been in life, his body sticklike. He had long limbs that moved stiffly at knobby joints. He looked less human than he had before. The doctor rose ten feet above Sam, staring down at him with loathing.

"*I am going to kill you,*" he hissed. He pointed at Sam's face. "*You are dead.*" Sam stared back, aghast. The doctor turned to Jeremy. "I am going to kill *you*, and *you*." He pointed to Martin.

"No, you're not," Bud's voice was calm.

The creature turned to him. "Why not?"

"Because I won't let you." Bud found himself standing face-to-face with the doctor, far above the other men.

"I will kill you." The doctor pushed Bud's chest, growing taller, filling the sky above the meadow.

"No, you won't." Bud pushed back, hard. He grew just as big as his opponent.

The doctor screamed at him, enraged. He kept growing, and Bud rose with him. They soared above the meadows, feet scrambling for a toehold. They fought, grappling and tearing, punching and gouging.

Bud didn't look down; he just kept giving what the Power gave him to dish out. The doctor seemed to know how to fight better than you'd think a peace-loving alien would. He grabbed Bud by the short and curlies. Bud bent forward and started to yell, but rage overtook him. He rammed the doctor in the belly with his head. It was like ramming a Gummy Bear, those disgusting jelled candies his kids loved. Bud tore after his opponent with his teeth, which caused the doc to loosen his grip. Bud took advantage by kneeing the doctor in the groin, giving back what he'd been given. The doctor screamed, apparently not knowing what it felt like to have his new equipment assaulted.

That put some life in the yellow boy, who came after Bud, swinging wildly. Bud kept his elbows in and watched where he punched. Gumby could be hurt, but it tended to hurt Bud just as much. The doctor leapt at him, and Bud gave him a one-two punch in the face. That stopped him, but only for a minute. The doc was back, slugging better, learning from Bud.

He swung away, not knowing how much time had passed. His knuckles were bloody and he was past winded. The doctor was equally spent, looking at Bud with surprise. The doctor held up his hand, indicating he needed a break. Bud stepped back, catching his breath and staring at his opponent. Something occurred to him. The problem and the solution.

"You're all *wrong*," he bellowed.

The doctor pulled the punch he was getting ready to throw. "What?"

"You *can't* win. Everything about you is wrong. Look at you. Anyone in your world saw you, they'd laugh. What the hell is that hanging down to your knees? What did you do to get *that*?" Bud pointed between the doctor's legs.

"You call *that* natural? There's nothin' natural about that at all. You couldn't make babies with that. *What did you do to yourself?*" Bud was outraged. "And why?"

The doctor looked at Bud proudly. "It's magnificent."

"What did you do to get that stupid thing?" Bud jeered. "Have surgery? Eat pills? Take hormones?"

The doctor was taken aback. "I went through a series of treatments . . ."

"Well, there's where you went wrong. If you were supposed to look like that, you would already. But you have to go messing with what you're given and what's right for your kind. You're against the Law!"

"What law?"

"*The* Law, the Natural Law. The Law of the Great One that created this universe and keeps it going. God's Law. You're outside all of that, and what you did is outside of that. You are an abomination, that's why you stink." Bud stood outraged. "I *rebuke* you in the name of the One that created and upholds the universe.

"Look at what you did and why you did it. Every bit of it was outside the Law. You lusted after a woman who didn't want you and did all sorts of unnatural things to yourself in hopes she would. And she didn't, did she?"

"No." The doctor blanched.

"She told you she was married to another man, didn't she? You were lusting after another man's wife! That's *really* against the Law, buddy.

"So you tried to kill *him*. You're *still* trying to kill him. Now you're trying to kill me and everyone else on this planet. All because she didn't want you.

"But you did more than that. You destroyed your own planet's goodness, getting them hooked on smut TV. That's evil. And you got hooked yourself, grabbing on to impure thoughts? You did, didn't you? So all you want now is more and more filth.

"You will stop now!" Bud waved his hands as though he was sweeping away dirt.

The doctor opened his mouth and disappeared. Poof! Gone. Bud looked down. It looked like he was on top of a huge skyscraper, like the world below was a toy. As the doctor vanished, he could see the yellow stain over the meadow whisked away.

"You scare me so much. You scare me to *death*." Bud was normal-sized, kneeling by Sam. He hid his face in his hands and trembled. The other three men stared at him.

His chest heaved as he tried to figure out what had happened. He put one hand on his heart. "Oh, Great One, You scare me so much. You are *mighty*. You are *good*. But You are so *big*.

"I'm an ordinary man. I'm not big like You. I seen You make Wesley and Grandfather huge like that, but I'm just ordin-- . . ." Something like thunder rolled around them and Bud gasped, "OK, I'm whatever You want me to be. You want me to be big, I'll be big. Whatever You want."

Bud's eyes fell on Sam's exposed lower legs. They were riddled with disease. He began speaking in a voice that was more exaggerated than his normal country diction and sing-song in its cadence.

"What kind of a mess is this? My, my. This is a' infected mess. We can't have that. Take this, you disease, get out of here." He scooped out gangrene and bacteria, throwing them in a pile near Sam's feet.

"I just *hate* this mess. Look at this mess, Great One. All green and cruddy. Clear out, you mess." Bud looked up and saw Sam staring at him. "Sam, you might want to lie back now. Shouldn't hurt a bit." Sam flopped back on the mat and didn't move. Bud's hands sunk into his legs and pulled out internal decay.

"Oh, dear. This man needs *skin* on his legs, Lord. Let's have some skin here, and all around here. Look at those feet! They don't have any covering at all. He needs a *resole*. A good, thick resole. Double resole. Make this man fit to run a marathon in his bare feet. Cover those pinkies!"

He grabbed Sam's feet, which had only suggestions of new skin growing on them. "Skin. We need *skin*. All up and down here." His hands moved up and down Sam's calves.

"Now that's better! That's what I like to see: lots of skin. Oh, Lord, now make it match the rest. That color don't match. Don't want to scare anyone if ol' Sam goes wadin'. Now watch out here, y'see. Little too much skin here.

"Kinda overdid it between the toes, Lord. Ol' Sam's feet look like Sea World. Like a web-footed creature. Le' me do this," Bud sculpted Sam's feet, pushing the edge of his hand between his toes. "There, that's better. I must say, I love this Power. I love it when You come to me, Lord. I'll do whatever You want for You to come to me." He took a good look at Sam's injuries. "Well, you look pretty good, Sam."

Bud sat back like he might be finished, but he looked over at Martin and frowned. "Oh, lookee here. Here's a man who can't see. That's a shame." He leapt up, just like he wasn't verging on middle-aged with creaky knees, and stood behind Martin. Bud put his hands over Martin's eyes.

"Oh, you can't see, you poor thing." Bud considered, hands resting lightly on Martin's face. "Except you *can* see." He experienced what Martin did. "You can see things others don't know. You can see the truth, and the other world. Spirit World, my people call it. You can see, but not like other people." He was silent a moment.

"Martin," Bud leaned around to speak to his face, hands still over the other man's eyes, "would you like to see like the rest of us? Would you like to see Sam's handsome face—or Jeremy's pretty brown skin? Would you like to see them *and* the world you're used to?"

"Yes. Ah would like to see." No hesitation from Martin.

"OK. I can do somethin' about that." Bud's fingers slipped into Martin's skull. "Oh, yeah, we got a bad connection here. A bad connection. Let's pull this out and move this around. Put these together. And these aren't even formed yet. Let's see about this."

Sam and Jeremy stared at Bud, astonished. His fingers were inside Martin's skull, tinkering. Martin sat still, a blissed-out look on his face. Bud felt around, then twisted something.

"OK. That should do 'er. Look over there, Martin. Sam's right there." He pulled his hands out of Martin's eye sockets and turned his face toward Sam.

Martin opened his eyes, blinking in the light. "Is that you, Sam?" He squinted. "I can't see much."

"That's because your nerves don't know what they're seein', you being blind for so long. Here, let me adjust 'em." Bud gave him a good whack across the back of his head. "How's that?"

"Sam!" Martin shouted, embracing Sam. "You look … You look … like Sam." He turned to Jeremy, examining his face and skin. "You're darker than us."

"Yeah, my father was an African-American. Black, they used to call us. That's where I got my hair." Jeremy rubbed the stubs of his dreads.

Martin looked around, marveling. "What's this?" he indicated the gray cloud around them.

"Darned if I know. I've seen Grandfather pull one up when he was doing something most folks wouldn't understand. It just came. We needed some privacy." Bud turned to Jeremy. "Oh, we're not done yet. Not by a long shot. Son, what is that sadness over you? What is that grief?" He focused on Jeremy, moving behind him.

Jeremy fell forward, landing on Sam's chest.

Bud dropped to his knees, leaning over Jeremy's back and sticking his hands into his brain. "Oh, Great One. Look at this boy's grief. Look at this." Images from Jeremy's life began to appear above them. A little child, wandering alone and bewildered, surrounded by plenty and nothingness. Faces, scenes. The Hermitage Academy. Hiding in his basement apartment. The nerd. The forgotten heir. His emptiness until he discovered the joy of creating. The electronic world. The computer world.

Bud found what had happened when Jeremy was nine years old. His father sat dead in his chair, a rubber tube around his arm and a needle in his vein. Jeremy could remember every little thing, frozen solid in his mind, like a specimen you could slice and examine under the microscope.

"Oh, you poor thing," Bud kept up a steady flow of commiseration and love. "You were just a child alone."

Until Ellie. They could see her image floating in the air. Ellie when he first saw her at the Hermitage Academy. Loving each other, jumping onto the "space ship," and living uncountable years on her planet in love, but in misery, too. And then Ellie turned into a wasp and died, saving most of them before she did.

"Now son, stay here with me. We can work it out. Oh, Lord, come down here now! We need a miracle." Bud didn't know if he'd opened up something he couldn't handle.

That's when Ellie came, as graceful and lovely as she had been when she and Jeremy met. Long dancers' limbs, lovely musculature, elegant movement. She wasn't a vision—she was totally real, except that she floated two feet off the ground.

She smiled at Jeremy, reaching for him. They touched. "I love you," she said. "I would never leave you." And she was gone.

Jeremy stared at the air where she had been, wonder on his face. "It was her species' life cycle," he said. "The meat she ate started her changing, but wasn't all of it. It was being here, on this planet. She couldn't stop it." He sat, struggling with what she'd imparted. "She'd never leave me on her own. She had no choice."

Bud staggered around the circle and plopped where he had been, gazing at Jeremy with the same pole-axed expression that Jeremy wore.

"Oh, Lordy Lord." He pulled out his handkerchief. "I guess I need some healing, too." He told them about Bert and his kids and how he was so scared that she'd think he ran off with someone. "I want to go home so bad . . ."

60

"Martin, you might want to tone it down a little." Bud waved his hand at Martin and his horse. They were making good progress catching up with the others on the mounts that had been left for them. With one problem: Martin kept yelling and ululating every time he saw something new, which was everything he looked at. The horses spooked in every direction.

"What is *that*, Bud?" Martin whooped.

"That's a tree."

"What is *that*?'

"Another tree."

"They look *different*," Martin shrieked.

"Yes," Bud explained. "That's a sycamore; the other one was an oak."

"*Two* kinds of trees!" Martin exploded with joy, causing the horses to spin.

"There's lots more kinds of tree than that, Martin. You'll see. Now all of you, keep those heels down. You gotta keep the heels down or your feet will run right through these English stirrups. If your horse runs off, you could get dragged. Look here . . ." Bud rode around the others, giving them an extended riding lesson.

"We're gonna pick it up now. We don't want to be out here all night. To ride a trot, just stand in the stirrups and grab the front of the saddle with your hand. Lean on your hand. Like this . . ." Bud's demonstration proved impossible for the others to copy.

"OK. You can also post." He showed them how to rise to the trot, with similar results. "Well, since you can't do that, just sit. You'll either figure it out or have the sorest balls in the world tomorrow. Let's go."

"What's that?" Martin asked. The light was fading but the pale rock face stood out in the dusk.

"That's the cliff where we live. We're home." They'd ridden longer than Sam ever cared to do again.

The place looked like a war zone. Loaded travois littered the ground. Sam could see the motorized vehicles parked against the cliff with their trailers still hitched up and heaps of stuff all over, but he didn't see any people.

Bud rode to the cliff and then back toward the river. The others followed him. "They're over here!" he called.

Sam jolted to a stop when he saw the lady walking up from the river with Wesley. He had his arm around her and was leaning over her, whispering. She wore one of Sam's big shirts. It was dripping wet, its fabric plastered to her body. She covered her face with her hands.

"Get away from her!" The Voice burst out of him before he could think.

Wes shot back ten feet. "She's upset!" he squalled. "I was taking care of her."

Sam rode forward and saw that his wife was really upset. Tears streaked her face and she trembled. He stepped off his horse and went to her.

"Oh, Sam! I didn't know if I'd ever see you again." She clung to him, quaking. "I need to get ahold of myself. I'm really having a moment." She wiped her eyes with the tails of the shirt. "We were washing the babies and treating them for the itches, and all of a sudden they seemed so fragile and helpless. I didn't know how we'd ever raise them. Or how we'd put all this stuff away. Or if we'd survive." She waved her hands helplessly. "You and Jeremy were gone . . .

"Oh, Sam. I thought you were going to die." Her voice rose and she embraced him again, tearful. "I'm so glad you're back. Let me see you. How are your feet?"

"I'm fine, lady. Bud healed us. Martin can see now."

"Oh, Martin," she called to him. "That's wonderful. Bud, how did you do that?"

Bud scratched his neck. "We can talk about that later, Grace. I think the first order of business is for us to use whatever you put on the babies. We're crawling."

When night fell, everyone gathered at the base of the cliff for a homecoming barbecue that turned into a bonfire. Sparks flew into the air, and the people from the underground whooped and hollered.

"We made it home," Henry cheered. "I never thought we would." The others clapped and ululated. The party was on.

For everyone but Sam. His eyes narrowed. Now that he wasn't hurt, he could see what Wesley was doing clearly. He laughed and joked with the lady, passing hunks of barbecued fish. Sam's hatred grew as he watched Wesley's flashing eyes and brilliant smiles on the other side of the circle. They were all for the lady. Why was she over there?

She finally walked around and sat beside him. "Sam, I can't tell you how glad I am to see you." Her eyes filled and he pulled her to his chest. She snuggled into him as though that was the only place she wanted to be, and held on. She held on so tight that the others went silent and then quietly moved to campsites scattered around the base of the cliff.

"Lady," Sam whispered, "let's go to our room." She agreed.

He pulled the ladder down and helped her climb up. When they were home in their cave, he felt better.

But he'd seen Wesley's eyes glisten as she walked by. Sam shivered. His hands closed into fists. He would kill him if he touched her. The lady was looking at him.

"Don't be jealous of Wesley, Sam." She put her hand on his forearm. "He's a pathetic little man.

"He's no competition for you." She looked at him with those bottomless blue eyes. He looked into them and saw as far down into her as she went. She loved him. She was true.

Her eyes filled again. "I can't seem to get ahold of myself." She dabbed at them with a hankie. "I don't know what I'd do without you. Nothing would make sense.

"Oh. I had such different plans for this evening. Our homecoming was going to be so joyous. Well, maybe we can still make it that way.

"I found something in the piles of stuff." She picked up a slender cylinder. "Do you know what this is?" He shook his head. "It's a candle. I could have brought an electric lantern in here, but this makes a nicer light. See?" She lit the candle and pressed it into a holder sitting by their bed. "See how the light moves?" She stirred the air around the flame and it flickered. "Beautiful isn't it? The way it lights up our bedroom? Sort of a blush."

She began unbuttoning her shirt. "We can see each other this way. I thought that would be nice." She opened the shirt. "Would you like to look at me, Sam? I'd like it. I'd like to welcome you home."

The candlelight glowed on her skin. He watched her undress. Voluptuous curves, shadowed recesses. A darkness that enfolded him and held him past any hope of escape. He couldn't look away.

She opened her arms and he lay next to her, studying the perfect features that the candle revealed. He ran his fingers along her face and shoulder, over her hair.

"I love you, Sam."

He bent over her and covered her mouth with his. Something took over inside him, stopping time, replacing pain with pleasure, and then more pleasure than either could hold.

She lay face down on the bed, head turned to one side, sleeping. Sam sat next to her, watching, unable to sleep. He belonged to her so completely that he would die if he lost her.

But she was true. He knew that as surely as he knew Wesley was a snake.

61

"Just when everythin' seems t' be workin' out, I have a meltdown," Bud said to Grace. "I don't know how much longer I can keep on goin'. I just gotta let my hair down." Bud was seated on a rock by the river, elbows propped on his knees, hands dangling. His long braids were unkempt, and his hat's brim was torn and coming loose from the crown on one side.

The air was nippy again; their second cold season was on its way. The first winter was one of those piddly California deals where it rained a few times and got down to forty degrees. None of the people from the East Coast even noticed it and no one was worried about it this go-round.

"Grace, I never imagined this happenin'. I thought we come here to do a job—help you all with the underground and savin' the kids. But we done that.

"We done that an' more, and *more*. We got the sawmill going by the river, cleared a logging road, built corrals an' sheds. Wesley built a whole barn an' got all the equipment going perfect. We taught you how to slaughter and dry meat, how to plant and harvest. Everything we know we taught you, Wesley and me both. You all worked like demons, too. But how much more can we do? I don't think we're ever goin' to get to go home."

"Oh, Bud. I'm so sorry. When I asked the people of the golden planet to bring you here, I never imagined they wouldn't send you back."

"Yeah, well, things didn't turn out the way anyone expected, that doctor going crazy an' all. But it's been almost two years! All I can think about is what's goin' on with my Bert. An' the kids? She'll think I ran out on her. Or got killed somewhere and she'll never know what happened to me."

He pulled his hat off and struck it against his knee. "Lord, I wish I could go home. I'm beyond goin' crazy. I'm completely off my gourd." His shoulders slumped and began to heave. "I'm gonna sit here cryin' until I die."

"Oh, Bud. Don't cry." Grace put her arms around him. "I'd call the goldies up and ask them to send you back . . ."

"You *would*?"

"I would, but for what happened the last time I talked to them. Their planet is in a shambles because of me. That doctor wanted to set me up as a porn star. Who knows how many of them still want that? I won't contact them again."

"I see what you mean." He slipped farther into melancholy. "Don't you think there's anything can be done? I been thinkin' of all sorts of things in my misery, Grace. You know how bogus this place is, don't you? It's part California, part New Mexico, part Montana. Maybe some Connecticut. This place is made-up. That's what I've been thinking."

"I've thought that from the very beginning," she answered.

"This is what else I've been thinking. This place is made up out of your mind, and Jeremy's, too. Places you've been. It's like someone reached into your head and pulled out a bunch of memories and then used them to make a place—here—for us to land."

"Who would do that?"

"The goldies. Could they do that?"

"Why would that doctor go to all the trouble to dig out the underground and make that movie set with the spiders if he could just think up something without the work?"

"So it's not likely that the goldies did it?"

"No, I don't think so."

"OK. When you sent out those messages to outer space, or when Jeremy did and they sent Ellie, did you send them just to the golden planet, or did you send them all over space?"

She looked at him, blinking. "All over, Bud. Later, we tuned into the golden planet, but still, we both sent wide band messages."

"So any other world in the universe could have picked them up?"

"Yes, if they had sufficient technology."

"And an interest in you, Jeremy, and our little band of outlaws."

"Yes."

"Say they were interested. Say they made this world for you, and hauled you out of wherever you were and put you here, then did the same with Jeremy and the underground, all at once."

"But the underground was ancient. People had been there forever."

"If this other world could create all this—this phony paradise— they could stick the underground in it, and whatever else they wanted. Not only that, this whole deal might not be real." He indicated the riverbed around him. "This could be somebody's imagination. It could disappear the minute they forget about us."

"Don't tell me that. I worry enough."

He pulled something out of his pocket.

"I've been wanting to show you this. I've been carryin' it in my jeans since I got here. We call this a flash drive where I come from. It goes in a computer. You can store stuff on it. Pictures or whatever you want. I've got pictures of my family on this one, an' my world. I'd like so much if Jeremy could play it.

"I didn't pull it out before because I wasn't sure that I could handle seein' Bert an' the kids. Now, I can't handle *not* seein' 'em.

"An' I got some ideas. Here's the deal. I think this place could break apart at any time. I think we need a Plan B, right now."

"What can we do? We don't have any other options."

"I think I've got one. It's from my time, 2015." Bud dropped his voice, "I get the shakes any time I talk about Will Duane. He's so private that to work for him, you gotta sign an inch-thick contract saying you won't talk about him or anything he's got, including his cat, if he had one. I feel funny talking about this, but I need to.

"There's a famous physicist, Dr. Vanessa Schierman. She's got a PhD from Berkeley an' she was in on developin' the Cyclotron and who knows what else. She's an older lady, a tad strange. Dr. Schierman is a good friend of Will's an' has an estate up on Skyline Road above Woodside. In California. I heard tell that Dr. Schierman is doing experiments with a time machine." He dropped his voice still further.

"Actually, what I heard is that she *has* one and uses it. Will Duane an' Willy Fish an' Dr. Schierman are workin' on a commercial application of it. They're working on something about *time travel*. Willy Fish is Will's tech genius, by th' way. Sort of a Jeremy in my time.

"I was thinking if Wes and me could get home, I could tell Will about you folks, an' maybe he and Willy Fish and Dr. Schierman could figure out a way to pick you up. All of you.

"If Will had Jeremy and Willy Fish working for him, he'd dominate the tech field worldwide, hands down. He'll figure that out right away. And Sam could be the super manager of the universe with that Voice and his Power. Will would want to do it, I know."

"So there's some possibility that we may be able to escape to the year 2015?"

"Yes, if we can figure out where and when we are now so we can tell Will and them where to find you. And if they can develop the technology to do it before this place rips apart."

"It's a very slim possibility."

"Very."

"That's a lot to think about, Bud. I'll get this," she held up the flash drive, "to Jeremy. I don't know that we'll even be able to use it with our computers. I've never seen anything like this.

"Let's go back to the others. Bud, I'm so sorry you're having such a bad time. But we love you. You've done more than anyone could, healing Sam and working so hard. You've saved our lives. Come on . . ." She held out her hand to him and pulled him up.

"Can I hug you? I need a hug," Bud said.

She nodded and they embraced. He kissed her cheek, just as Sam walked down the path.

62

"Oh, Sam, I'm not gettin' fresh with your wife." Bud let go of Grace and turned away. "I'm just havin' a nervous breakdown." He pulled out a hankie and wiped his eyes. "I miss my family so much and I don't know how I'll get home."

Sam hugged him. If he had found Wesley with his arms around the lady, he would have attacked him. Wes had been chasing after Grace almost the entire time they had been back. Bud was a different story.

"I don't know how you can get home, Bud," he said. "I'm sorry."

"Thank you, Sam. I appreciate th' sympathy. I think I'm going to take the equine therapy approach to going plum out of my mind. I'm going to go for a ride. Want to ride with me? I've got that stallion I been training ready for you to try."

"OK."

"I'm going to give this to Jeremy," Grace held up the flash drive, "and see if he can do anything with it. Bud, why don't you tell Sam what you told me?"

"Sure. An' you tell Jeremy. I think we should keep it at that, just the four of us. It's too chancy to get people's hopes up."

"I agree. Let's see if Jeremy can get a show ready for us this evening. We can broadcast your photos against the rock wall above the cliff."

Sam sat at one side of the circle where he could watch everyone. By the time Jeremy got everything set up, the moon glowed over the plains. Wolves and coyotes howled, but no one on the ledge paid much attention to them. Sam searched people's faces, while the others concentrated on Bud and his picture show.

The lady was sitting next to Lena, chatting away. Wesley walked over to her, smiling like a rabid coyote. He started to sit down next to her, but she got up and moved next to Sam. He patted her knee as she sat down on her log and tossed Wesley a triumphant glare. Wes glowered. Sam felt his breathing quicken. When would he call him out? He'd taken more than any husband should.

His ancestors rose inside him, roiling and roaring, warning him day and night. Telling him to keep sharp. Sam knew what happened with the first Sam Baahuhd and his wife Emily. Theirs was a love story for the ages, but it wasn't perfect love. He knew the danger other men could pose in a small group of people. The strain made him sharp and anxious. He felt like he did when he drank the coffee and the caffeine made him shake. He couldn't get away from the feelings. Or Wesley. Or her.

Sam had watched Wesley stalking her for almost two years. She did nothing to encourage him. But she didn't slap him or yell at him or tell Sam to kill him. Suspicion nipped at him, clawing its way through his soul. First, over Wesley. Then it spread to Henry. And even James. She was good friends with James. He was gay. Sam was getting crazy.

If he could get rid of Wesley, things would be much better. He'd call him out. The two of them, someplace quiet and out of the way. Down by the sawmill maybe. The supernatural Indian warrior might discover that the underground held a few secrets of its own. If he was soundly beaten, Wesley would leave.

"Sam, pay attention to what Bud's saying," Grace whispered, nudging him. He turned to the picture show.

"This is my wife, Bert. That's short for Roberta," Bud stood up as Jeremy projected images he'd taken from the flash drive on the wall of the big cave. Everyone stared, enthralled. "Isn't Bert just the cutest thing? I love that little space between her front teeth. That knocked me for a loop when I met her." The image of a round-faced, brown woman with the warmest smile covered the wall.

"An' here are my kids, Buddy, Les, and Allie." In the next photo, the woman was joined by three adorable brown kids, two teenagers and a girl about six. All had the little space between their front teeth. "It's a good thing I like that space, because the orthodontist wanted a lot of money to get rid of it." More images filled the wall: the older kids playing baseball. The little girl dancing in a tutu. All of them playing in the snow. Riding horses.

Wesley got up and moved to the other side of the lady. "I can see better here," he stage-whispered. Sam felt like belting him. He was pushing too hard. The lady pulled toward Sam.

"Sam, watch," she whispered. "Take a good look."

"OK. Here I get into shaky ground. When you work for Will, you gotta sign a contract saying you won't mention his name outside of your closet. But I took some pictures, takin' my life in my hands. This here is Will Duane's Montana ranch house." Many more images appeared, showing posh log interiors and spectacular decoration. Paintings fit for museums. Garlands of greenery. A Christmas tree.

"It was Christmas then. The house is twenty-five thousand feet, not including the guesthouses, of which there are plenty. He built the ranch before his financial disaster. This and his Woodside house are the only two he's got left. He picked the two best ones, I'll say. He hires the best architects in the world to build for him, or he did."

"Sam, that's where we would live," she whispered in his ear, so quietly that only he could hear.

Sam squinted at the picture. The house was beautiful. Living there would be better than on a rock ledge. But it was impossible . . .

"Will's real edgy about people, because with all that's happened to him..."

"Can you tell us what happened, Bud?" Grace asked.

"About everything that can happen." He gave them a brief rundown.

"That's awful," Grace said. "That poor man."

"Yeah, really. The final blow was the financial crash of 2001 and the big one in 2008. But he's recovered some, and realized that half of the fifty billion he once had is still a lot of money."

When the show was over, people gathered around Bud. "I wish we could get you home, Bud." "Those kids sure are cute." "Something will come up, somehow."

Grace and Sam got up to go to their cave. Wesley lurched forward and caught himself by grabbing the lady.

"I'm sorry. I'm a klutz. I apologize." He stroked her clothing, smoothing it. He ran his hand over her breast, more than a little too slowly.

"Take yer filthy hands off o' her," Sam said, the Voice and the village speech bursting out of him. "Ne'er let me see ye near her. Y' ken?" He stepped forward so he was inches from Wesley.

"Well, sure, Sam. I just tripped is all." Wesley looked him straight in the eye.

Sam took the lady's arm and headed for bed. He'd call Wesley out the next day.

63

Grace slipped down the cliff face. It was late afternoon. Mel was giving a math class to Sam and the others. Everyone else was busy or napping. This was a perfect time to ride the lovely mare Bud had trained for her. It was also an opportunity to get through something that plagued her about Belle. She never stumbled, reared, bucked, shied, or ran away. She was sure footed and had plenty of go, but she was easily controlled. The perfect horse, except for one thing.

Grace looked at the bruise on her forearm. Being bitten by a horse felt like being hit by a hammer. Pain and shock bundled together. Belle only did it when being bridled. She never did it when Wes or Bud was around. Only with Grace. She unrolled her sleeves and secured them around her wrists. The fabric might take up some of the force if the animal snapped.

"She's got you buffaloed," Bud had said. "Approach her like a warrior. An' every horse got somethin'. Weren't this, it'd be somethin' else. Maybe worse."

She was a warrior. Why couldn't she master this horse? She caught Belle and tied her halter rope to a fence post. A post, not a rail. "A horse can break a rail if it pulls back, but ain't likely to pull out a post," Bud had told her. He was the guru of horses.

She groomed and saddled the mare expertly. Grace unbuckled the horse's halter and slipped her nose out of it, buckling the halter around her neck so she could bridle her.

Grace pulled in a deep breath as she picked up the bridle. OK. Showtime.

"That's a girl," Grace stood erect, projecting as much authority as she could. "We're going to do this."

Belle's teeth snapped as they closed on her shirt's arm. That good old Russian commando fabric didn't tear. It didn't shield her much, however.

"OK. That's it. I'm putting this on you if it's the last thing I do." She clenched her jaw in determination, taking the top of the bridle in her right hand and raising it up the front of the horse's head. She held it in front of Belle's ears. She'd slip the strap behind her ears once she got the bit in her mouth.

Grace held the bit by the left shank. "Open up. Come on, Belle. Don't do this." The mare clamped her teeth shut and refused to open her mouth. Grace tried pushing the bit into the crack where her lips met in front, and then using her fingers to push on the side of her mouth behind her front teeth. That's where the bit would rest; horses had no teeth there. She was furious. All she could say was that Belle's current tactic was better than being bitten.

"Need some help?' Wes had approached silently, startling her.

"Yes. She won't open her mouth."

"You're doing OK. The saddle's on fine." He tightened the girth. "We'll check it again before you get on.

"Just keep going. If you don't quit, you won't fail." He stood to her left and behind her, close to Belle's head. "Push against her cheek where she doesn't have teeth."

"I already did that." She did it again and the mare merely tossed her head. Grace stood awkwardly, the top of the bridle in her right hand, her arm stretched to the horse's ears. Her left hand hovered in front of Belle's mouth, holding the bit.

Wes stepped closer. She could feel his body heat and the energy that he had used to do all those amazing things coursing through him. She felt a little dizzy. She turned and saw his white teeth as he smiled and the precise sculpting of his face. She felt his charisma. He was irresistible.

"Keep going; you've almost got it. Take your thumb and put it in her mouth, right there by the corner."

"I can't. She won't open her mouth."

"OK, I'll help you, but *you* have to do it," Wesley stepped behind her, reaching around her back with both arms. He put his right hand over hers on the top of the bridle. His left hand covered her left over the bit. Wes guided her thumb and forefinger to a place where she could push against the horse's teeth. The mare opened her mouth. Wesley pulled Grace's right hand up so that the bridle went over Belle's ears and the bit slipped into her mouth.

His arms were spread around her and his body was plastered against her back. Neither of them moved.

She couldn't breathe or think. She had that melting feeling, that "Here we go" feeling, that dissolving of will she knew so well.

She leaned back against him, feeling his hard, compact frame quivering. Feeling more than that. She felt his bulge. She was light-headed. Her face turned toward his without any conscious thought. His lips were soft and lustrous. An instant more and their mouths would . . .

"NO!" she shrieked, darting under Wesley's arm. A dozen heads appeared at the top of the cliff, looking for what was wrong. Grace tore up the ladder.

She ran into their room and threw herself on their bed, curling up on her knees, wrapping her arms over her head.

"Oh, no. Oh, no." She rocked and keened, tears dropping on their bedcover.

"What did he do, lady?" Sam's voice startled her. "Did he hurt you?"

"Oh, Sam. Oh, God. I can't believe it." She pulled away. "I'm so sorry. I never want to do anything to come between us."

"What did *you* do?"

She told him.

"You didn't kiss him, or touch him?"

"No, but I felt that *feeling*. Oh, God. I never wanted to feel that again for anyone but you. I'm so happy with you, and then out of nowhere, I'm feeling . . .

"I thought I wasn't like that any more."

"You didn't do anything, lady."

"I don't want to be the way I used to be. Oh, Sam." She threw herself at him and hugged him. "I was an immoral woman, Sam. I was a terrible person."

He sat next to her. "Did you go looking for him?"

"No. I didn't see him at all."

"Do you think about him?"

"No. He's pathetic."

"You're not in love with him?"

"No! I'm in love with you. When I felt *that*, that's why . . . I'm so terrified. What if I destroy everything? Us!

"Oh, Sam. Tie me up so I don't do bad things. Tie me up!"

He petted her and stroked her hair, kissing her streaked cheeks. "You're afraid."

"I'm terrified—of myself."

Sam picked up the Book from his side of the bed. "Lady, don't be afraid. Ye said 'No!' so loud it frightened the kiddies. And ye ran to me and told me. A person can feel things, but doesn't mean you have to do anything." He smiled at her.

"Who knows, maybe some day, some lass will make me," he made a gesture indicating an erection.

"Oh, no!" she cried. "I never want any other women around you. I couldn't bear it."

"Lady, I don't want anyone else. Only you. You have not done anything bad; that is what I wanted to say."

She turned around and saw Jeremy in the doorway.

"Mom, are you OK?"

"Yes, I just got scared, that's all."

"What happened?' He came over to her.

"I thought I'd ruined everything. I thought things were going to be like they were with your father. I don't want to raise a baby in that kind of a marriage." She turned to Sam.

Sam and Jeremy stared at her.

"I just thought that . . . with the baby coming . . ." she explained.

"The *baby* coming?" both men said at once.

"I didn't want to tell anyone until I knew for sure, but I'm almost three months late and I think . . . I want everything to be perfect"

Sam hugged her. "Ah, lady. I'm so happy." He kissed her, and then looked up at Jeremy. "Jeremy, could you get Lena to stay with her? I need to do something. I need your help."

64

"Look, Sam, I'm sorry. I need to get laid, that's all," Wes backed away. He was still by the horse corrals.

"You must leave," Sam said, towering over Wes. He didn't yell at him, punch him, or blow up. Didn't use the Voice or his Power, either. "You must leave, now."

"I'd love to leave. Nothing would make me happier than leaving. But how?"

"*You* will talk to the golden planet. *You* will ask them to take you and Bud."

"OK. I'm all set up and ready to broadcast." Jeremy had a computer out with a powerful camera and heavy-duty lights. "We're live to the goldies whenever you're ready."

"I can't possibly go on camera," Wesley objected. "I'm not dressed. My hair isn't right. I don't have any makeup . . ."

"I'll handle that," James stepped forward.

A bit later, Wes was combed and jelled. His lips were even more lustrous than usual. His hair gleamed. His eyes were softly outlined.

His pectorals and rock-hard abdominal muscles glistened with oil and James's special ointments.

Wes stepped in front of the camera and took over the golden planet. He was shirtless, glistening, and unbelievably attractive.

"Hi. This is Wesley Silverhorse. It's great to connect with you folks from the golden planet. I haven't had the chance to talk to you directly. I understand some of you are fans of my work.

"Boy, I love that. Everything I do is for my fans. You guys," he touched his fist to his chest and teared up, "really give meaning to my life.

"I'd like to tell you about a jam I'm in—well, Bud's in it, too. You know, we came here to help our friends out here on the cliff. We fought and won the battle for the underground. You got terrific footage of that, I'm sure.

"We did the job, and now we're stuck. We could live here forever, happily, with our friends, but I got to thinking of my fans.

"In Hollywood, if you miss four days of shooting—well, three, really—you're toast. No one will hire you again. Poof! There goes your career.

"That's the situation I'm in, folks. I've been gone a long time. Almost two years. You're probably noticing that you can't get some of those Wes Silverhorse movies you used to love any more. That's because I didn't make them. I got waylaid out here and never got back to finish my life. All the movies I would have made from the time I left until I die don't exist.

"I'm asking for your help. Can you send me back to Will Duane's Montana ranch, where we were shooting when you picked us up? Just take me back there, and I'll kick butt and make you more exciting movies than you can imagine." He smiled seductively.

"Oh, and one thing," he leaned forward and stroked the side of his head. "I've got some gray hair and a few wrinkles. Maybe you could handle those, too? For my fans. And here, too . . ." He grabbed the skin under his chin. "It's a little loose."

Bud shoved into picture, hair sticking out wildly and looking desperate. "I'm Bud Creeman, the Horse Manager. You probably have seen some of my tapes from workshops and seminars, telling you how to handle your horse.

"My tips work on other animals, too. Like báslikays and those big Lhasa Apsos I understand you all have. My techniques will shape 'em up fast. I'd like to go back with Wes so I can make some more of those tapes for you. I got some great ideas for new seminars, like teaching beauty queens and movie stars about horses. You'll love 'em." He was sweating.

"Please, I really miss my family, and by the way, could you bring all these people," he turned around and made a sweep with his arm, indicating the community, "with us . . ."

"They're gone," Grace said, "just like that."
They stood on the ledge, looking at each other.

"What do we do now?" asked Henry.
"We go on living until something else happens," Grace replied.

Part Four

65

The seedpod's cabbage-like leaves were storm-torn and tattered. Mildew streaks had formed on their cracks, along with lichen and moss. Something inside the pod struggled, causing it to rock. The thick stem that attached it to the oak's limb held firm. The sack's interior movement halted, and then began again. Paused and continued, surging with ever greater urgency.

The tree from which the sack hung was unconcerned. It spread its branches as it had for hundreds of years. Flooded with light, the oak forest around the tree seemed timeless. Leafy crowns rose high and wide, as majestic as living gods. Swaths of golden grass filled the meadow between the trees. Insects hummed. Squirrels darted. Nothing indicated that a struggle for life was underway.

The pod kept swaying. Jerking. Convulsing. Then it became still. Time passed. A sharp object pierced the pod's shell from the inside, close to where it joined the stem. The object cut down the pod, creating a slit that could have been made by a knife.

A hoof protruded from the bottom of the slash, and the stinger that had made the cut retracted into it. A slender leg followed, then another hoof and leg. The sack wobbled, and a creature fell from it and lay panting on the ground.

Whatever it was curled into a ball, its too-long legs curved to its chest. Waxy and not completely formed, it might have been a larval form of a giant insect. The creature lay on its side, resting. After a pause, its head rose and looked around. A somewhat human face regarded the meadow with huge silver eyes.

"Jer'my," it chirped. "Jer'my," and began the laborious task of standing. It rolled up and propped its legs under itself after many tries. The creature pushed itself erect. And fell. Fell and stood. Kept trying to stand like a newborn horse. Eventually, it remained erect, revealing its gender.

"Jer'my, Jer'my," she chattered. Her voice sounded like a cricket's. Her skin gradually turned from waxy gray to rosy flesh. The hair on her head curled as it dried, showing its streaked silver coloration. She looked around and then fastened on a direction.

She began walking. As she walked, her legs grew straighter and more human-looking. Her torso, belly, arms, and head formed up quickly. Someone who didn't know Ellie well would have thought the creature was she.

"Jer'my? Jer'my?" She headed straight for the community on the cliff.

66

Henry climbed the embankment from the river carrying his fishing gear and four big trout. She was lying in the middle of the path.

"Oh, no! My God!" he cried. "Ellie? Ellie, is that you?" Thin, dirty, and naked, she lay face down in the sand. Her hooves were worn and cracked. Her feet and lower legs looked like she'd trudged through sawgrass for miles.

"Ellie? Are you OK?" He turned her over. She obviously wasn't OK; she was unconscious.

"Hey, everyone! I need help. Ellie's down here!" He cupped his hands around his mouth and yelled toward the cliff.

Heads appeared over the fence.

"Ellie? What are you talking about?" shouted Mel.

"Get down here! I need help."

They milled around her when they got her up to the top. Grace shooed them away. "Take her into the container where the medical supplies are. I need to examine her. Get me some water and rags."

Grace carefully examined the unconscious girl. Or whatever she was. She looked like Ellie. Peachy skin, silver streaked curly hair. Hooves. Beautiful proportions. She took her blood pressure and listened to her heart. Perfectly normal for a human. Grace pinched a fold of her skin and let go. The girl was badly dehydrated.

"Thanks, Mel," she said as he delivered drinking water. "Can you hold up her shoulders? I'll try to get her to drink." The minute Mel touched her, the girl's eyes shot open.

"Jer'my?" she squeaked. "Jer'my?"

"He's not here now. He and Sam are at the sawmill. Do you want Jeremy?"

"Jer'my?" the girl said, blinking her eyes at Grace and Mel. Her eyes were even larger than Eliana's, which was saying something. Shot with more silver, too. She showed no recognition of Mel or her. "Jer'my?"

"Jeremy will be back in a while. Try some water." Grace could smell the barbecue and hear the sizzle of cooking fish. "For God's sake, Mel, tell Henry to keep those fish away from her. Get some greens from the garden. Soybeans . . ."

"Well, I can tell you one thing: She's not Ellie." Grace had gotten some beans into the girl and she had fallen asleep in the container. Grace went out to the campfire to report to the others.

"She's whatever was in that egg sack thing, isn't she?" Lena said.

"I think so, but we'd have to inspect the sack to know for sure." Grace replied. "All I know is that she's not Ellie. I examined her completely and can tell you that she's built exactly like a normal female human. Ellie wasn't."

They stared at her.

"She also has bigger eyes and she didn't recognize either Mel or me. All she says—maybe *can* say—is Jeremy."

"And not even that, Grace. She says 'Jer'my,'" said Mel.

They nodded.

"Do you think she's Ellie's baby?" Henry asked.

"I don't think so, Hen," Lena answered. "We know what her babies were like. She delivered big pods with hundreds or thousands of babies inside. There's just one of her."

"Unless the rest show up tomorrow," Mel said.

The group gasped and looked toward the edge of the ledge.

"She doesn't seem dangerous."

"She's been unconscious. And neither did Ellie."

"But Ellie never hurt us, even when she changed," Mel reminded them.

"Do you think she's a clone?" James's eyes were wide.

"That might be, but she's not an exact copy of Ellie," said Grace. "The anatomical differences are very clear. And she doesn't know anything. I'm not even certain that she's speaking. 'Jer'my' may be her natural chirp. She doesn't seem as intelligent as Ellie was. We'll have to wait and see."

"One thing's for sure," Mel said. "We need to keep those," he pointed at the fish on the grill, "the hell away from her."

"Absolutely! Vegetables only." Grace's forehead contracted. "There's someone else we'll have to keep away from her."

"Who?"

"Jeremy. Can you imagine the shock of loving Ellie, having her turn into a monster, die, and then having whatever is sleeping in that container show up?"

They caught their breath again. "What will we do?"

"I don't know, but the elevator just started moving. Sam and Jeremy are coming up."

"Jeremy, I have to tell you something," Grace approached him the minute he and Sam stepped off the elevator.

"Sure, Mom. Let me put my stuff away." He was at the computer container/medical facility before she could stop him.

"No, Jeremy! Don't go in there. I have to tell you something."

He swung the door wide and stood, staring.

"WHAT IS THAT!?" He put his hands up to fend her off, then backed away from the container as fast as he could. The naked girl stepped out quickly; she was even more agile than Ellie had been.

"Jer'my? Jer'my?" She chirped, looking at him without recognition. But she held her arms out.

"Get her away from me!" Jeremy shrieked. The girl came closer. "Get away!" He turned and ran to the elevator and disappeared over the edge.

"It's her or me, Mom. That's how it is. I will not live on the cliff if she's there."

Grace stroked his shoulder. They were by the equipment barn at the base of the rock face. They'd gone there to talk. "Jeremy, I know it's a shock. It's a shock to everyone. But we can't just toss her out. She'll die."

"Maa-aahm," he said in the tone he'd used as a kid. "She's the larval form of a predatory insect. She can live anywhere, places where we'd croak in a day. Give her a chance and she'll eat all the fish in the river. And the horses. Maybe us."

"Jeremy, Ellie never did that."

"You said she's not Ellie."

"No, she's not. I think she's something like a clone, but more adapted to Earth. She looks like a normal woman, Jeremy. Not like Ellie. But I don't think she's as smart."

"Oh, great. You want a *mentally deficient*, mutant clone of a giant wasp to live with us. That sounds terrific. What about the kids? Huh? Did you think of them? What if Ellie-poo eats them?"

"Ellie loved the kids. That's why she sacrificed herself, so they could live. I don't think that's a problem."

"Well, I'm living right here at the bottom of the cliff as long as she's here. I don't want to see her. And I'm carrying a firearm, no matter what you say."

"I think that's a good idea. There are grizzly bears and wolves and all sorts of things down here. I understand what you must be going through . . ."

"No you don't. None of you understand. You can't possibly understand. Now leave me alone."

67

"We don't know how much the goldies taught Ellie," Mel explained at a group meeting. "She might have been just like this before they sent her to school. Ellie said that they had taught her for many years. We all know that Ellie was somewhat . . . limited in her intellectual development. Jeremy told me that she was two hundred years old when they met. Think of the maturing and learning that must have happened in those years. This one is just hatched, so to speak. We need to make allowances and be patient."

"Jer'my. Jer'my. Jer'my," the clone chirped endlessly, hopping about the edge of the circle.

"Let me see what I can do with her. Maybe I can teach her a few words. She'll be my project," Mel concluded.

"Teach her a few words and shut up that damn, 'Jer'my, Jer'my, Jer'my,'" groused James.

"Amen."

"I'll start tomorrow. No, I'll start now. And the rest of you," Mel turned around quickly and caught the kids trying to sneak away, "it's a school day. Just because you did chores doesn't mean you can get out of learning to read." He turned to Sam, "That means you, too.

You're writing a book, remember? You won't get it done unless you do it. Over to the classroom." They'd turned one of the little caves into a schoolroom.

"Come on everyone. Time to get to work. Ellie, you, too," Mel extended his hand to her.

She pulled away and put her hand to her chest. "Ellie?" She obviously had no idea who Ellie was. "Ellie? Ellie? Ellie? Ellie?"

"Oh, God, no," James cried. "She's changed channels."

"Ellie, honey," Mel took her hand. "Come over here. I'm going to teach you some words." He put his hand to his chest. "I'm Mel. Can you say *Mel?*"

"Mel, Mel, Mel, Mel."

He held up his hand. "No, just one Mel."

"Just one Mel." Her voice sounded exactly like his.

"Mel." He held his hand up to stop her.

"Mel."

"Yes! That's it."

She smiled. A real smile.

"Oh, Ellie, honey, you're going to do fine." Lena beamed. "Ellie, honey, go with . . ."

The girl touched her chest again. "Ellie honey. Just one. Ellie honey." She smiled widely. "Ellie Honey. Ellie Honey." Eyes widening as she caught her mistake, she said, "Just one Ellie Honey."

"Do you want that to be your name? Ellie Honey?" Lena and Mel crowded in. "Ellie Honey?"

"Ellie Honey!" She threw her arms over her head and danced around the ledge, coming so close to the edge that everyone cringed. "Ellie Honey!" she cried.

68

"Jer, we miss you," Mel and Jeremy sat outside the shack by the sawmill. Jeremy had been living there since Ellie Honey got her feet under her and began careening up and down the ladder like it was her own private jungle gym.

The sawmill was a couple of miles down the river from the cliff where the community lived. They put it there because the river narrowed at the mill's site, increasing the water's speed to drive the wheel. The area around the mill, and the route there, had been forested. Harvesting the timber to make the corrals and barns and the rest of the ranch buildings had pushed back the tree line a couple hundred yards. The back of the rock mountain housing the cliff where they lived rose above the trees. A few ravines emptied out near the mill site, but other than that, only one path led to the mill, the logging road that Mel had taken to reach Jeremy.

"Everyone wants you to come back. Talk to me about it, at least."

Jeremy drew in a huge breath and released it slowly. "OK. I'll tell you. I couldn't talk to my mom about this, but I'll tell you." He struggled, playing with the fabric of his pants. "You and James have been together a thousand years. You know how it is . . ."

Mel looked at him quizzically.

"Ellie and I did it like, five million times. Not fucking, either. Loving each other. Though we did lots of fucking, too." Jeremy waved his hands in the air. "I'm trying to say that I was inside her and she was in me. No, she is, not was. She is in me. I can't forget her.

"She turned from a soft, sweet girl into a monster with a hard shell. I made love to a monster with antennae and stingers and wings that didn't even recognize me, I don't think. I mean, I didn't really have sex with that, but it's all mixed up for me. Ellie and monster."

"Oh."

"It's more than that, Mel. That thing, the new one, makes me sick. When she came out of that container and headed for me, I wanted to jump off the cliff."

"You practically did."

"Yeah. I feel like *vomiting* when I think about her; she creeps me out so much." He shuddered. "I loved Ellie and she died. Bud did a healing on me. I saw that it was her life cycle; she didn't want to leave me. I've made peace with that.

"But I can't deal with another one." He looked wildly at Mel. "You know she'll change. A couple of fish, and it's buzz and sting time all over again. I can't handle another bait and switch. Falling in love and then . . .

"I *will* fall in love with her. Ellie's in my mind; she's in my body. I don't have any resistance to her."

Mel regarded him. "You feel like you don't have any control . . ."

"Not feel like, I *don't* have any control. Ellie and that monster and sex and love. I can feel El around me, and I can hear her *buzzing*. It's making me crazy."

"You're scared," Mel said.

"I'm scared *shitless*, Mel."

"OK. I get your point."

"I won't go back. Don't try to convince me. If people want to see me, they can come here like they already do. And leave that *thing* behind."

"Your mom really misses you, Jeremy. She can't bring the baby out here easily. He's getting big."

"She brought him down once. She can come again." Jeremy dug in.

"The truck doesn't work any more, Jeremy. If she comes, she'll have to pack him on her back."

"She can ride a horse."

"She won't ride a horse. She's afraid of falling off with the baby."

"Sam can carry him."

Mel sighed. "Yes, Sam could carry him, except that he works all the time already. Your brother is growing like crazy. You'll never get to see him as a baby again. He looks so much like Sam."

"With my mom's blue eyes. I know, I've *seen* him." Jeremy sulked. "OK. If you get *it* out of the way, I'll come and fix the truck."

"I guess we can do that, if you'll come."

"Just to fix the truck."

"And tune up the computers. They're all getting wonky without you to maintain them."

"You have to get rid of *it* before I'll come."

Mel changed tactics. "Jeremy, one thing the computers *are* keeping track of is the calendar. It's going to be Christmas in a couple of months. That really matters to your mom and Lena. They've got a big dinner planned. They've been making presents for everyone. For you, especially. Your mom and Sam—everyone—has been making gifts for you."

"Sorry. Can't make it." He turned away.

"Jeremy, it's been more than a year since you left . . ." Mel looked at him hopelessly. Jer's beard had grown down his chest. He looked like he was working on dreadlocks as spectacular as the ones he'd had in the golden world. "You can't stay here forever, Jeremy."

"Try me." He swung around and glared at his former teacher. "Get it, Mel. I will never, ever get involved with something that can potentially, in any way, turn into a monster and die.

"I *know* what you're thinking at the camp, 'Maybe they'll fall in love . . .' Forget it. Never. Never. Never. I'm not going near her."

Mel ducked his head, as though Jer had guessed exactly what everyone was thinking. Then his face became guarded.

"Look," Mel continued, "she's not Ellie. She's *amazing*. She's the best student I've ever had, including you. She's been my student for just over a year, and there's nothing left for me to teach her. She has to use the tapes and materials in the library. She's way past college level in everything."

Jeremy sniffed. "Great, Mel. She's a *brilliant* mutant monster."

"That's not fair, Jeremy. She's very pretty. And you're not safe here." The fresh hide of a mountain lion was nailed to the side of the wooden shack. "What if one of those gets you next time? There's snakes. We can't save you way out here."

"*Never*, Mel. I will not come back if that thing is there."

"Is it because she's your daughter?" Mel asked softly.

"What!" Jeremy yelped. He jumped to his feet and stood in front of Mel. "You sat there listening to me spill my guts about sex and everything, thinking that I was talking about my own *daughter*?" Mel didn't say anything, which caused Jeremy to become more agitated. "What kind of sick asshole are you?"

Jeremy fought to stay in control. He didn't have screaming fits any more. He wouldn't have one. "That *thing* is not my child. Jesus Christ, Mel. Ellie couldn't have any more kids. Remember that? We didn't do anything to make one, either. We *lost* a baby right before the battle. We were still grieving." He paced, staring at Mel.

"Is that what you guys think? I'm in love with my own kid and won't come back because of it?" Jeremy stepped closer to Mel, towering over him. "I don't know what that thing is. I don't know a lot about Ellie's species, Mel. I didn't know she would turn into a wasp. *That* was a big surprise.

"There were probably *lots* of things I didn't know about her. Maybe she cloned herself, or morphed into something adapted to Earth. Maybe she could do even more than that. You could ask Ellie, except she's dead." Jeremy clenched his fists. "Whatever it is, that *thing* isn't my baby.

"Get out of here, Mel."

"I'm sorry, Jer. There's been some speculation around the camp that maybe that's the reason you won't come back."

"I spent the last half hour telling you the reason, *Mel*. I'm afraid to get involved with her. And now *you* better be afraid." He darted into the shack and came back with a shotgun. "If you don't get out of here right now, I'll shoot you."

Mel raised his hands and backed away from the cabin. "I didn't mean to cause offense, Jer."

"You did cause offense, Mel. SHE IS NOT MY DAUGHTER. Don't come back here. I don't want to see any of you." Jeremy emptied both barrels of his shotgun into the air.

Mel took off at a run.

69

"Oh, pardon me," she was standing in the middle of a canyon near the mill. She stood up on her little hooves with her long pretty legs, wearing a short dress with a tight bodice and frilly skirt. A dancer's dress. It looked like it had been sewn from a floral sheet. Her eyes were bigger and shinier than Ellie's. Her face wasn't exactly like Ellie's, either. She was a bit taller. One hand held a bunch of tattered weeds. The other hand went to her mouth when she saw him.

Jeremy glared at her. "What are you doing here? You're not supposed to be here." He looked around, ready to bolt.

She looked at him solemnly. "I apologize. I have become disoriented. I was gathering medicinal herbs at the top of the cliff. I scrambled down this ravine, thinking it would circle back to the area beneath the elevator where everyone disembarks," she said in English more precise and perfectly formed than that of any English teacher he'd ever had. Her voice was chirpy and sweet.

"I apologize for intruding on your privacy. Is this the way back?"

"Yes. Follow the path," he growled, pointing behind him.

She moved toward him, heading along the trail.

"My name is Ellie Honey," she held out her hand when she passed. He ignored it. She gazed at the hand dangling by his side. "I was taught that proper etiquette requires people greeting each other to clasp right hands and to say 'How do you do?' Is this not a custom among your people?"

"Yeah, it is. Unless you don't want to meet the person."

"Oh," she said, blinking hard. "You do not wish to meet me. Well, my name is still Ellie Honey." Her lips compressed. "When I first came, everyone called me Ellie. I don't know why; I don't know any Ellie. But Honey is a sweet viscous liquid produced by . . ."

"I know what honey is."

"I must be in the vicinity of the sawmill." She looked around. "That means you must be Jeremy Edgarton. They said that Jeremy Edgarton lived at the mill. I have been warned that you do not wish to be disturbed. I will not come this way again. I am sorry."

"I'm Jeremy. What else do they say about me?"

"They said that I should stay away from you." Big wide eyes. Guileless. Like a child. "Something in the way they spoke of you intimated that you were a danger to me." The silver eyes got bigger. "But you don't look dangerous, Mr. Edgarton."

"I'm not."

"Oh." She seemed to realize something. "You live out here because you don't want to see me. You left the community when I came."

"That's it." He stared at her, hoping the hostility in his gaze would hurry her along.

"Well, I won't return." She studied him, tilting her head from one side to another. "I must say that your face is intriguing. Your skin is not as dark as that of Henry and Lena, yet you are darker than Sam and Lady Grace and the others."

"Uh-huh."

"That's because your ancestor, Chaz Edgarton, was of African origin. They told me that. Lady Grace has photographs of your ancestor. He was her first husband. Oh. That makes him your father."

His dander started to rise. He didn't like anyone talking about his father.

"That's a very close ancestor. I don't know my ancestors. I suppose that I look like them."

"Do you remember anything of your mother or father?"

"No. I remember falling out of a tree."

A snort of laughter escaped Jeremy. He covered it with a frown.

"I was very young and didn't know what had happened to me. It wasn't until I reached the community at the cliff and began to learn words that I was able to verbalize the experience."

"I fell out of a tree. That's how I was born." She was utterly serious. "I must have had a mother and father, though, because I have studied sexual reproduction and parents are required for the reproduction of advanced life forms. I am a higher life form, though I am not human."

Jeremy could hardly believe her. She was hysterically funny, and very serious. "Can you remember anything before that? Your mother?"

"No. Just the tree. It was a long way down. I lay on the ground for some time, stunned. You're really lucky to know your ancestors, Mr. Edgarton. Not knowing is very confusing."

She skipped topics without waiting for his response. "You're very interesting in that you have hair on your face. None of the other men do. Every morning, I see them put lather on their faces and scrape them with razors. Your face shows what would happen if they didn't. Is it comfortable? It looks as though it would itch."

"It's fine. I'm fine."

"I'll go now. I'm sorry to have bothered you." She turned and headed down the trail.

His eyes followed her. She wasn't Eliana. Ellie Honey. What a stupid name. She walked lightly, the way Ellie had. Beautiful legs swinging. She was so sweet. Didn't have any meanness in her. Stop it, Edgarton. Remember what she is. An insect.

"Hey!" he yelled after her. "You need warmer clothes. You'll get sick." Her legs were dappled with goose bumps. His mother must have something she could wear. They shouldn't let her run around like that.

70

"Why did you come back?" Jeremy growled as she approached the shack. Weeks had passed. She wore one of his mother's sweaters, some leggings, and soft boots that let her walk on her hooves. He could still see the lovely curves of her legs.

"You don't have your beard!" She beamed at him.

"No, I shaved it off. Why are you here?"

"You look very nice without a beard. I can see your face. Why is the hair on your head like that? Sticking out in ropey protuberances?"

"They're called dreadlocks. It's the way my hair grows if I let it. What are you doing here?" He put his fists on his hips and scowled, but he wasn't *too* unhappy to see her. Though she certainly wasn't the reason he had asked Henry to bring him a razor.

Henry had come out to talk to him after his blow-up with Mel. "I never thought she was your child, Jeremy. Most of us didn't."

"Who did?"

Henry hadn't wanted to tell him, but Jeremy had wheedled it out of him. "James. He talked about it in the camp. Some people listened. Mel, mostly."

"James didn't want to fight for the children, either." Jeremy's eyes had narrowed.

"No, he didn't."

Jeremy's attention was pulled back to the girl. She was talking at record-breaking speed.

"I know that I promised that I wouldn't come again, but Mel said that you could teach me about computers. He said that no one knows as much about computers as you."

"Why do you want to know about computers?"

"Because I've exhausted the learning resources at the camp and Mel wants me to continue my technological education. He said that he wouldn't ask you, but that I might." Her pronunciation and diction were perfect, if a little prissy.

"Who taught you to talk like that?" Jeremy asked.

"I learned to speak from Mel and the others. They taught me English as it is commonly used, and colloquialisms. But recently, the recorded English lessons that Grace took from your computer have been most useful."

"My computer?"

"Yes. Long ago, Grace did something called 'hacking into it.' She said you were very angry at her for doing it." Wide eyes. "But I'm sure she didn't mean anything bad by what she did.

"Anyway, you recorded lessons in many languages for the use of the people in the underground shelter. I've heard about that, from Sam Good Man, by the way. I have mastered all the lessons in English through the PhD level. I particularly like the vocabulary sections and the dictionary. I've almost memorized those. I listen at night."

"You learned to talk like that from the lessons on my computer?"

"Yes. I am sure you will forgive your mother for hacking into your computer when you see the level of understanding and practice that having those lessons has allowed me to attain."

"Yeah. I totally forgive her. Listening to you makes it all OK." He could barely keep from laughing.

"Please, would you teach me about computers? I'm so bored."

"I'll have to think about it. I'm doing a lot of computer work out here. I need quiet."

"Oh, certainly. Working at your level of proficiency would certainly require seclusion and intense concentration." Those clear, ingenuous eyes. "At any rate, I think I'd best go home now. The sun is dropping toward the horizon. The predatory animals will begin hunting soon."

"Do you want me to walk you home, Ellie Honey?"

She shook her head. "No. I am very fast."

"Faster than a mountain lion or pack of wolves?"

"Yes. I can outrun both. My reflexes are very quick and I have great endurance." Her brows knitted. "Would you please let me know as soon as possible when you have made up your mind about teaching me? I'm eager to learn. And I need to talk to you of other things."

"Yeah, sure." He waved at her and she headed down the trail.

She disappeared, but his eyes followed her. Cursing, Jeremy spun and went into the shack. He would not worry about her. If she said she was faster than a charging cougar, he'd believe her. He sat down at his console and pecked at the keys. Shit. He turned and looked in the direction she'd gone.

Never. Never. Never. He lost himself in algorithms.

The howls jarred him into the present. A pack of wolves was raging in the direction of the cliff. They must be after her. Jeremy grabbed his rifle. He ran down the trail. What if he were too late? What if they got her? Tore her apart? Images of Ellie's bloody body and savaged form flooded him. He ran toward the howls.

"Ellie! Ellie!" he sobbed. He ran through the dark woods almost to the base of the cliff, almost to the camp. She wasn't there. She had escaped, as she said she could. He stood in the path for a moment, gasping, and then walked back to his shack.

He sat on one of his sofas, a rough thing made of planks and a cushion. Clutching the rifle, he rocked back and forth. The wolves could have killed Ellie. Torn her limb from limb. His knees jumped and shook. He couldn't stop shaking. He wiped his eyes.

When it was pitch black, he lay down with the rifle on the floor next to him. He stared into the darkness. What if they'd gotten Ellie?

It wasn't Ellie; it was someone else entirely. But his heart couldn't tell the difference.

71

When she came the next time, he was standing in the shack's doorway. She wore a too-large coat, a knitted cap, and mittens. Something inside him felt better seeing that she was dressed for the cold. But he wouldn't relent. He had decided not to teach her computers. Chicken on his part, but he didn't care.

She was out of breath. "I hope you don't mind my coming. I couldn't stand waiting for your decision any longer."

"No problem." He'd tell her in a moment.

"I've been working all day. I didn't know if I'd have time to get here before dark. I take care of the children, which I like very much. I also take care of Sammy some of the time. He is Sam and Grace's baby. Oh, he's your half-brother. He's very charming."

Jeremy found himself wishing he'd seen his brother more than once. He frowned. "Does my mom pawn him off on you?" The way she'd dumped him with nannies and maids?

"Oh, no. She is devoted to Sammy. It is only when she has some dangerous task to do that she asks me to help."

"Dangerous?"

"Well, they are redoing the elevator, making it larger and stronger."

"Oh." He should be overseeing that. He scowled. She didn't notice, having changed topics. You could almost see her mind jump from one subject to another.

"Taking care of children is not as satisfying as learning. Not if you do it all the time," she explained. "When I finished reading the encyclopedia, things slowed down for me."

"You read the entire encyclopedia?"

"Yes. And many of the texts in your library. Some are tedious, especially those written before the seventeenth century."

Jeremy turned away to hide a smile. She made him laugh, the way Ellie had. He felt good around her, even though he didn't want to.

"But if you don't want to teach me computers, I'll understand. If you won't teach me, I can still learn. I can finish learning Russian. And there are other languages as well, French, Spanish. German. Lots of Asian languages. I've studied the globe. Asia is on the other side of the world."

"Yes, I know."

She frowned and then made one of those shifts in topic that indicated she was thinking of several things simultaneously. "Do you think it probable that the *entire* world was destroyed in the nuclear holocaust years ago? I think it highly improbable. Only if the nuclear installations were rearranged all over the world could the then-existing stock of nuclear weapons incinerate the globe and wipe out all life. Doing that would require an enormous investment of time and resources . . ."

"Wait a minute, Ellie Honey. You're going too fast." He studied her. She was very smart. Maybe smarter than him.

"Oh. Mel says I do that."

"Would you like some something to eat, Ellie Honey? I made soy bread. I've got water, too. Can you drink that?"

"Of course, I can drink water." She looked at him as though he'd said something odd. She wasn't Ellie, Jeremy reminded himself. "All right, I'll stay. Though I must insist that you don't have me in unless you really want to. I know your aversion to me."

She noticed everything. Wanted to know how the sawmill worked. Spotted a weak spot in the supports. Noticed the mountain lion skin on the wall right away. A couple of wolf hides had joined it.

"Oh, Mr. Edgarton, you must be very careful. Catamounts are very dangerous to humans. They hunt in pairs. The mate could be stalking . . ."

"Catamount?"

"That's what they called them in an 18th century text I retrieved from the reader. It's most interesting to read of the settlement of the United States from the words of the settlers. I would bet that the country looked very much like it does now."

"Probably, Ellie Honey. Can I call you Honey? It's easier."

She pulled in a breath. "Well, that is not a proper person's name, but I suppose that being called the sweet product of a bumble bee is nice. You may call me Honey."

"And you may call me Jeremy."

"Oh." Her gleaming eyes grew round as marigolds. Or mari-silvers, he thought, smiling inside. She pulled up to her full height, looking as though the thought of calling him by his first name shocked her. "Well, that is very nice indeed, Mr. . . . Jeremy." She blinked several times.

He brought her into his cabin. They sat on his sofas and ate soy bread and drank herb tea. She kept chattering about catamounts and the mill and the state of the elevator. Chattering nervously, when she really wanted to know what he'd decided.

"Honey." She looked at him expectantly, wide shiny eyes like mirrors reflecting the sky. "I hate to disappoint you, but I can't teach you about computers."

Her shoulders dropped. She seemed to get smaller. "Oh."

"I'm just too busy. I'm working on a special project and can't spare the time."

"Perhaps I could help you, I'm very quick."

"I'm sorry. I can't do it." He felt like such a heel telling her no. But she was taking it OK.

"All right. I can continue with the computers at home. And I'll accelerate my Chinese."

"I thought you were learning Russian."

"I finished almost all of the materials that were available. Now I need to converse with those fluent in Russian," she said in perfectly accented Russian. "I'm on to Chinese." That was in perfect Mandarin.

"Oh. Well, good. So you're all set."

Her shoulders still drooped. "As 'all set' as I can be, given that you will not be teaching me. I do so wish that you hadn't such antipathy toward me. I don't know what I have done to make you hate me so much." Her eyes misted.

Jeremy's stomach lurched. Not the tear treatment. "I don't hate you. I've got some really important projects going and need space."

"And I wanted to speak to you of some vitally important things." She sighed.

"Well, you still can."

"It makes no sense if we are not to have a collegial relationship. I will proceed on my own." She stood up. "I might as well go back. Grace wanted me to help with Sammy. And it is growing dark." She headed for the door.

"No, wait, Honey. I'll walk with you." He picked up his rifle and put on his gun belt with two pistols. He refused to suffer the way he had the last time she walked home by herself.

The area around the mill had been logged out, so he and Honey walked across an open stretch at the start of their journey. The trail meandered through the stumps. Pine trees grew at this end of the mountain, another anomaly of the landscape. Pines were OK for construction, but not as durable or fire-resistant as redwoods. The redwoods were way upstream. They cut the pines because they were easier to get to. The forest smelled nice, especially in the crisp air.

Jeremy's breath made puffs as he walked. The sky was clear, which it usually was unless it was raining. Winter hadn't really come on yet. Stars were starting to emerge above them. Not much of a moon that night, so it would be dark, but the setting would have been beautiful if he'd been with Ellie. Or if he'd been less nervous about getting Honey home. Jeremy hustled her along the trail, holding her elbow.

"You do not need to be solicitous of me, Jeremy. I do not require your assistance. I can get home quite safely by myself."

Jeremy's lips compressed. "I'm going with you."

At the end of the clearing, they entered the forest proper. They'd made sure they could drive the truck and trailer through the trees so they could get the lumber to the settlement. The logging road was wide all the way to the cliff.

The forest's rim was like something his mother's gardeners might have created on the estate—hard-edged like the manicured hedge around the maze, completely dark just inside the boundary. Still, the path was wide.

The mountain died into the forest about a half-mile from the mill. The huge rock mass seemed to collapse into itself as it hit the ground, creating ledges and crevasses that went all the way to the top. Giant shards of granite stuck up.

He'd seen Honey the first time when she made her way down one of the ravines. And he'd shot the mountain lion when it leapt at him from a ledge. That one, right there. Jeremy looked at the boulder above him. He knew that cougars mated for life. He looked up again. Was that lion's mate up there, waiting to take her revenge?

Then they had passed that danger point. They trudged along the trail. The forest was very dark. He wished he'd thought to bring an electric lantern.

Sure enough, the wolves began howling. The howls were to the west. Everything wild came from the west.

"Stay behind me, Honey." Jeremy shoved her behind him as the howls spread out. The howls came from both sides now, and from the rear. The wolves were following them, getting closer. He could see the wolves' eyes flashing in the darkness. The howling kept up. So many canine voices; he had never heard so many. And then they grew silent.

A wolfish scream would rise and fall once in a while, coming from a distance. Then closer. They were finally so close that the animals had no need to call to each other, except to bring in outliers.

"Ellie . . . *Honey*," Jeremy said. "Can you really run faster than a wolf pack?"

"Yes."

"They're all around us, except for the front. I think you'd better run home alone." The eyes flashed everywhere. He'd never seen so many. "Run home and get Sam and the others. I'll watch your back."

"I don't want to. I'm not afraid . . ."

"Well, *I* am. Get out of here now. I'll fight them off." He had his rifle ready and the safeties off of both pistols. "Go! Get Sam! Get help." He shoved her and she finally jogged away. The forest's darkness swallowed her within a few feet.

Jeremy stood, rifle raised to his cheek. The wolves' eyes were like fireflies, sparking and disappearing. He couldn't get a clear shot through the trees. Fuck! he thought. Try and do a good deed and get eaten by wolves. She couldn't be at the cliff yet. No help would come.

The pack leader walked brazenly out of the shadows. Jeremy fired off a shot, but the damn wolf spun out of the way. Wolves were slinking through the trees all around him, completely unafraid.

His heart beat so fast that he was sure the wolves could hear it. He thought about that first day when the wild dogs almost got him. But these were wolves, and he didn't have a rabbit skin to throw them. His mouth was dry; he'd been breathing through it. His shirt stuck to his back.

"OK. Come and get me," he shouted, leaping toward the place the alpha male had been. Nothing was there. He turned around. Flashing eyes told him the wolves had encircled him. They moved forward silently. They would kill him silently. Two iridescent silver orbs appeared within feet of him. The pack leader.

"Stop this immediately!" Honey's voice broke the silence. "I told you that he was my friend. You are not supposed to eat friends." She stepped in front of the big male, who backed away. "We went over this before. You do not eat me or my friends. I thought you understood." Her eyes flashed and glistened. She stamped her foot. Jeremy had never seen Honey angry. "Now go home. There are many tasty deer in this forest, as well as other prey animals. You don't need to eat people." She stamped her foot. "Go!" They went.

"How did you do that?" Jeremy stood stupidly, staring at her.

"I'm not human. They will not eat me. They understand me quite well. I used words for your benefit, but they already knew what I meant. I discussed you with them the last time I was here."

"Oh." He struggled for words. "You really are safe here."

"Yes. It is you who are not safe. I must walk you home now. I do not know what other predators might be lurking. I do not know all of them." She marched up to him and took his elbow. He shook her off.

"No. I can get home. You've taken care of the wolves. There's not much else that can hurt me. I'm armed. I can shoot. You can go home."

"No. I will not leave you."

"Yes, you will. I'm fine. They're probably hysterical up on the ledge, worrying about you. Go home."

"Come home with me. Then you'll be safe."

"I am safe."

"No, you're not." They stood facing each other, both with their feet planted and bodies rigid.

Jeremy broke the silence. "OK. I'll flip you for it."

"What is 'flip you for it'?"

"I've got this old coin," he pulled a 2012 half-dollar from his pocket, a priceless collector's item. "I carry it for luck. It's got a heads and a tails." He showed her. "I'm going to toss it. It if lands heads up, you go home and leave me alone. Tails, I'll go with you."

"That gives me a fifty percent probability of winning. I would prefer better odds. I would prefer that you came home with me and stopped this foolish wrangling."

"Fifty percent chance or no chance. I'm turning around and leaving in five seconds."

He won. "See you later, Honey. Keep out of trouble." Jeremy walked briskly up the trail, heading for his shack. It was really dark. He wondered why he was being so stubborn. No, he knew. He would not teach her about computers and didn't want any tinge of friendship or intimacy to make him feel that he should.

Though saving him from a pack of wolves was a compelling point.

He stumbled over a root. Maybe he should have gone home with her. It wasn't that far from where he'd left her. Seeing his mom and Sam would be nice. Seeing all of them would be nice. Except for James, of course. And Mel.

Suck it up, Edgarton, he thought. Soldier it through. You know you don't want to be around her. You know what will happen. You're happy living by yourself, working hard. You're doing good work.

He had reached the jumble of rocks where the mountain collapsed into the plain. It was true that she was very nice and had saved his life. And had powers that Ellie didn't. He'd never seen Ellie make friends with a wolf pack. Honey *wasn't* Ellie.

Still, she'd turn into a wasp, like Ellie, and the whole thing would begin again.

He didn't hear anything when it happened. Something huge and heavy hit his right shoulder and threw him down. He could smell the cat's rancid piss smell. She grabbed his shoulder with her teeth and raked him with her claws, but couldn't tear the Russian commando jacket. She clawed at him, trying to turn him on his belly so she could bite the back of his neck.

The death bite. Crushing the back of the skull and top of the spinal cord meant death in seconds. Predators were born knowing how to do it.

Jeremy tried to swing his rifle at her, but it was useless. She was too close to shoot or club. He pulled his legs up to shield his belly. She was doing her best to gut him with her back feet.

A snarl rose over the sounds of their battle. The cat backed off, a long, low moan escaping her throat. A similar moan hovered in the air, coming from a ledge above him. He heard a thud as something jumped off of a rock outcropping. Shit. Another cat. Jeremy looked up, but couldn't see anything.

A chorus of snarls and moans followed, the cat letting go of him and facing her adversary. He scrambled to his feet and backed away. The howls rose to a crescendo, when the cougar abruptly squatted, peed where he had lain, and walked away.

Jeremy stood mute.

"I told you that I should go with you," Honey marched up to him. "Look at you; you can't walk home without getting into trouble."

Jeremy blinked. "I guess you're right. What did you do? Are you friends with the mountain lions, too?" He rubbed his shoulder where the cat had raked him. He'd be bruised, but the skin wasn't broken.

Honey shook her head with disgust. "I did something I never do."

"What?"

"I lied to her. I told her that you were my mate and that I would kill her if she hurt you. Neither is true. You don't even like me."

He rubbed his face. "Well, I'm liking you a lot more. Thank you for saving me."

"Twice."

"Yes, twice. Thank you. I think I'd like to go home and go to bed now."

"Yes. I will accompany you." She marched off, holding Jeremy's elbow.

When they got to the shack, Jeremy shuffled from foot to foot. "Would you like to come in for some more soy bread? And water?"

"No, thank you. The others undoubtedly are quite distraught over my absence. I will go home now. And I am perfectly safe by myself."

"You could stay here. I can reach them on the wireless."

She stood up. "No. That would be improper. We are not married and should not cohabit without a chaperone. We are not friends. You won't even shake my hand."

Jeremy reached out his hand. "Ellie . . . Honey, I'd be honored to shake your hand. And be friends."

She took his hand and he felt electricity surge through him.

"Um. If you'd like me to teach you about computers, I'd be happy to."

She made a little hop, beaming. "Oh, wonderful! I will come back tomorrow and you can begin to teach me. I need to discuss something else with you, as well."

"What?"

"Quantum physics."

72

He had hauled the beefiest computers to the shack where he lived. Jeremy wasn't being lazy during his exile from the community. He was working hard trying to figure out how to let Willy Fish, Will Duane's tech guy, know where and when they were before their world fell apart. That required that he figure it out first. But now, he had to deal with Honey. Teach her, but not get involved.

"OK, Honey. This is a computer."

"Of course. I've been using one at home. This is a more advanced model than any we have. It promises much more power and computational ability. Do you turn it on like this?" She deftly powered up the machine.

Jeremy sat in his chair, bent over the keyboard and hit a few keys. "Yep, that's how you do it. OK, Honey. This is code." The black screen was covered with white writing. More writing in bright colors was interspersed with it.

"Oh. That's very interesting. The screen is black and the writing is white. That is the opposite of the computers we use. Why is this line bright pink?"

"That's because it's a command. All the colored writing tells the computer what to do."

"Show me how to write code."

"That's complicated. It takes years to learn."

"We have years."

He smiled. "You're right."

She stood next to him while he sat at the keyboard, her thigh pressing on his shoulder. She was warm. He pulled away. She didn't seem to notice. Her face was working like she wanted to tell him something important. She leaned over.

"The real reason I wanted to learn about computers has to do with something Grace told me in confidence." She dropped her voice. "She said that someone named Bud Creeman once lived here. He agreed with Grace that this place is not natural. It seems natural to me; I have never seen another world. But Grace pointed out the discrepancies in the types of flora and fauna, as well as the diverse rock formations. I realized that such phenomena were abnormal. Bud and Grace felt that this world may decompose one day. Do you think it will?"

"Yeah. I do. That's what I'm working on down here. Honey, let's sit down over here and we can talk." He motioned her over to his living area, the rough-hewn sofas with pads.

"Grace said that a person named Will Duane, who lives in the 21st century, knows a physicist who has created a time machine; she is a Dr. Schierman. She and Will Duane may be able to transport us to the 21st century, thus avoiding our being annihilated when the planet breaks apart."

"Yeah. I'm trying to figure out where we are and how we can communicate with them."

"I would like to help you."

"Thank you, but it's an advanced programming job."

"Well, I have had some thoughts about it. Programming is part of it, but we're really facing a problem in theoretical and applied physics. Post-quantum physics. We're talking about time travel. That is a tricky concept, but with the Kobayashi theorem, and the work done by the Kobayashi school ..."

"Who is that?"

"Professor Fumio Kobayashi was the leading theorist of quantum physics after a man named Alfred Einstein established the discipline. Dr. Kobayashi lived two hundred years after Dr. Einstein. Kobayashi's work, and the work of his students, was repressed by your government because he *succeeded* in finding particles that were only theoretically possible to Einstein.

"He found many particles, tachyons, for one."

"What are those?"

"They're subatomic particles that move faster than the speed of light. He also discovered and documented *photons*. You understand that Post-Einsteinian physics says that light is not a wave, but packets of particles called photons." She leaned toward him, ensnaring him with her earnestness.

"Photons originating at the same light source have an instantaneous link. No matter how far apart they might be, the same thing happens to all the particles from the same bundle. That means they have *instantaneous* communication all over the universe ..."

"Where did you learn all this, Honey?"

She ducked her head modestly. "Well, as I said, I don't sleep much. In addition to the language arts, I also worked my way through the mathematics component of your recorded lessons."

"You did all this in one year?"

"A little over. I don't sleep at all, really." She leaned forward and whispered. "I don't like the others to know because they become concerned about my health. I don't need to sleep. I study all night. One night, I was experimenting with one of the computers and managed to access one of *your* satellites with stored data from the universities of the old Earth. This was very old information, concealed in your time. Your rulers could see the implications of Dr. Kobayashi's physics."

"What are the implications, Honey?" Something deep inside Jeremy, prior to words or thoughts, stirred. She was smarter than him. He'd never known anyone smarter than him.

"But don't you see, Jeremy, photons, with their instantaneous communication, pose a real, theoretical basis for time travel. And Kobayashi's school *found* photons, physically, not theoretically." Honey beamed, waving her hands exuberantly. "There's more. Subatomic particles called *kaons* move *backward* in time."

A jolt went through him. "You're saying that we can go back? That time travel is possible? It's something we humans can do? Not just the goldies?"

"Yes! The theoretical framework for time travel exists. If Kobayashi found the particles, so can you and I. There's more. Superluminal loopholes. They can scientifically account for instantaneous time travel, backward-in-time travel and faster-than-light travel." As she spoke, she became more excited, her voice rising in pitch and her body quivering.

"We can do it, Jeremy! I can understand most of the math, but a study partner would be nice. We have so many things to do. We need to determine the time/space coordinates of the people in the 21st century and prepare on our end."

She looked down and said shyly, "I thought we could collaborate."

"You think you can duplicate what Kobayashi did?"

"It will be very hard, because we do not have a laboratory. But I think that's the only way out. That and praying that the people on the other side do work that complements ours. But if they are led by a physicist, I think she must be thinking along these lines."

Her shoulders dropped a bit and she looked wistful. "I would like to help you so much. Grace told me about New York City. I would like to see New York City, and other places. She told me about parties. I want to go to a party with many people and wear pretty clothes.

"I don't want to blow apart when the planet disintegrates, and I want to see that the children and everyone are saved. May I help you?"

He appraised her. "OK. I'll give it a try. But if you slow me down, that's it." He was just being a prick. She wouldn't slow him down. She'd be more exciting to work with than anyone he'd known. That place deep inside him registered something. He could have something with her that he'd never had. An intellectual relationship with an equal.

"That's fine. I have one last question."

"Fire away."

"I would like to invite you to have Christmas with me and the others. Apparently, I was present at the last Christmas, but I do not remember it. I had only recently arrived and did not know much. I would like you to come with me to my first Christmas that I remember.

"The others are quite excited. They have uprooted a large conifer and placed bright objects on it. The children have hung stockings and expect a being called 'Santa Claus' to come in the middle of the night in a carriage pulled by Nordic deer. He will fill the stockings with gifts. I find that improbable. More mythological than real.

"They are making a large dinner, with a wild turkey and a boar. I will not eat those. Everyone has told me that it is imperative that I not eat meat. They say something very bad will happen if I do.

"But it occurred to me that you may want to eat meat and enjoy the festivities. Grace has hung a stocking for you. I would like it very much if you came." She looked at him with her big, gleaming eyes.

He felt his insides turning over. She smelled like Ellie. Cinnamon and something musky. Shit, he thought. Shit. Shit. He shouldn't have let her near him. He should have let her go home by herself the night before. He should have been eaten by wolves so he didn't have to deal with this.

"Well, I don't know, Honey. I'm right in the middle of . . ."

"We can work the following day. One day off will not create a significant setback in our project. Besides, Christmas has a religious significance in the Christian religion. When I read the Bible . . ."

"You read the Bible?" She nodded. "You're the only person I know who's actually read it."

"I'm reading the Buddhist Sutras now, then I'll read the Koran. Sam Good Man said that the Commands tell us to read all the religious texts. I live by the Commands."

"Oh, no. Not *you*."

"Yes, Jeremy. You gave the original Commands long ago, but they're still being written. Sam showed me the Book. It has new parts that weren't there in the underground."

"What!"

"They are your words, spoken to Sam when he first met you. Sam showed me The Book and where it stopped when he was in the underground. A new Command has been added. I saw it.

"You said, 'I'll give you a COMMAND right now. Follow the Commands all you want, but if they're bullshit or make life worse, don't follow them. Do something that works.'" Her voice sounded exactly like his.

"Those are wise words." She nodded solemnly.

"They're really in the Book?" Jeremy was mind blown.

"Yes. You are the Great Tek, Jeremy, whether you want to be or not. I don't know what your life holds, but I believe it to be of great importance to the universe." Her eyes were wide and trusting. "I live by the Commands primarily because Sam Good Man is such a good person. If he's good because of them, that's how I want to be. And he and Grace are very happy. I would like to be happily married one day.

"Would you please come to Christmas?"

"Wait a minute, Ellie . . . Honey. This is too fast. When is Christmas?"

"It's tomorrow."

"I need some time by myself now. Could you leave?"

"Certainly. I didn't mean to detain you."

He stood up, looking down on her. "You're a little taller than she was."

"Who?"

"Someone. Never mind." He felt her presence, her warmth. Oh, Ellie, what you do to me. But you're not Ellie, you're Honey. You're just a little girl. He bent and brushed her lips with his.

"Oh, my! Was that a kiss?" She stepped back, blinking, and then put her fingers to her lips. Her eyes widened impossibly. "I feel extremely exhilarated. I am quite excited!"

He laughed.

"Is doing that permitted? I do not know you well."

"It's OK, Honey. You know me better than you could possibly imagine. Do you dance, Honey?"

"Oh, yes. They play many genres of music on the ledge and I dance. My favorite music is that of Chaz Edgarton, your ancestor. His music is uplifting yet extremely complex with its moody overtones."

"Let me ask you something, Honey. Would you like me to go back with you tonight?"

"Oh, yes! I would like that very much. I would enjoy walking with you and conversing more this evening. And tomorrow, there's the great feast!"

He bent over and really kissed her, feeling the soft texture of her lips, his hand supporting the back of her head. He felt himself respond. He was a sucker for Ellie. He could never let her go. Never resist her. She knew that. Did you make Honey for me, Ellie, so I wouldn't be alone?

"Oh. That is so unusual." Honey was astonished by the kiss. "I feel strange. As if I'm floating. Why is that?"

"I'll tell you later." Jeremy laughed. "I've got a question for you, Honey."

"Yes, certainly." She blinked at him.

"If I go back with you now, will you promise never to turn into a giant wasp?"

From award-winning author Sandy Nathan—

SAM & EMILY

A LOVE STORY FROM THE UNDERGROUND

TALES FROM EARTH'S END: BOOK THREE

When Sam Baahuhd carries a naked stranger into the underground bomb shelter on the Piermont estate, he has no idea she will ignite his world. Nuclear radiation traps Sam and Emily and the rest of the village's residents in an echoing cement cavern three hundred feet beneath the earth's surface. There is no escape from the underground. Not for them. Or their children, or their children's children . . .

The lovely outsider carries deadly secrets no one can imagine. Only Sam with his village headman's Power can heal her. Only Emily can make Sam the man he was meant to be.

Passion explodes between them. Passion that brings joy and pain, ecstasy and remorse. Passion that can kill.

Join the people of Earth's End for a legendary love story that will be remembered for two thousand years.

SAM & EMILY
A LOVE STORY FROM THE UNDERGROUND
TALES FROM EARTH'S END III

ISBN-13: 978-0-9762809-6-5

www.talesfromearthsend.com
www.sandynathan.com

ABOUT THE BOOK ...
LADY GRACE
AND
TALES FROM EARTH'S END

A note from author Sandy Nathan—

People ask me where I get the ideas for my books. I use a technique I call "literature through disaster." That's a cheeky way of saying that many of my books are my soul's way of making sense of my personal tragedies. The Tales from Earth's End Series exists because of a painful loss.

A few years ago, my brother died suddenly. I was heartbroken—he was my only sibling and adored baby brother. On the outside, I looked calm, but on the inside, grief fought with memories, creating a contained despair.

Perhaps three months after my brother's death, I had a dream. A shining, golden light hovered above me as I lay in bed. The light was a conscious entity radiating goodness. I would call the apparition an angel, except that she was just a hovering light. No wings or halo or so on. (But maybe those are human add-ons.)

The light lowered itself onto my body, finally merging with me. The bliss was enormous. Indescribable. For several hours, I enjoyed the state of that beatific creature.

That dream was the inspiration for the angelic Eliana in the first book of the Tales from Earth's End. My creative process turned my experience into an angelic alien sent to earth on a vitally important mission.

The rest of the book's plot was revealed to me during the next week. *The Angel & the Brown-eyed Boy* occurs hours before a nuclear war destroys the planet. The story describes the attempts of an ensemble of people to escape the conflagration. I introduce the gigantic underground bomb shelter on the Piermont estate.

When I finished the draft for *The Angel & the Brown-eyed Boy*, the characters were as real to me as people I know in daily life. My mind kept churning, turning out two sequels in record time.

The second book, *Lady Grace*, tells what happens when the radiation clears. It chronicles the attempts of the survivors to create a new world. Some of the characters come from *The Angel & the Brown-eyed Boy*; some are new. *Lady Grace* is a romance as well as a thriller, with more twists than a politician's cover story.

My mind/heart/psyche/word generator was still stoked when I finished *Lady Grace*. The character of Sam Baahuhd from *The Angel & the Brown-eyed Boy* captivated me. Sam is the headman of the village—the community composed of the staff and workers of the Piermont estate where the action in *The Angel* ends up.

Sam is huge, almost a giant, and as tough as they come. He's a seasoned fighter and defender of the estate, as well as an agricultural expert and top manager. He's been stunted by the serf-like conditions in which the villagers live.

Sam Baahuhd fascinated me so much that I wrote *Sam & Emily: A Love Story from the Underground. Sam & Emily* is a love story that takes place in the bomb shelter below the Piermont estate. It's a passionate and sometimes dangerous romance that lasts a lifetime.

A fourth book in the series is shaping up in my mind and is partially written. Book four will pick up where *Lady Grace* ends. No title yet. This book will not be released for a while.

That's because I've got two series in play. The characters in *Lady Grace* are visited—involuntarily on their parts—by Bud Creeman and Wesley Silverhorse from my other collection, the Bloodsong Series. The Bloodsong Series tells the story of the richest man in the world, Will Duane, meeting a great Native American shaman, Grandfather.

Numenon, the first book in the Bloodsong Series, takes place in 1997, as Silicon Valley billionaire Will Duane and his employees travel to New Mexico to attend Grandfather's final spiritual retreat.

When Bud and Wes drop into Lady Grace, they left their world in 2015. Eighteen years have passed since *Numenon* and much has happened in Will Duane's world. You need to know what went down.

Several Bloodsong Series books must be released before the fourth book from Tales from Earth's End can come out and make sense. When completed, The Bloodsong Series and Tales from Earth's end will cover more than half a century in our time--and span thousands of years in the world of Tales from Earth's End.

It's a spectacular journey that may take a lifetime. I invite you to make it with me.

Sandy Nathan

ABOUT THE AUTHOR . . .

SANDY NATHAN

Sandy Nathan writes to amaze and delight, uplift and inspire, as well as thrill and occasionally terrify. She is known for creating unforgettable characters and putting them in do-or-die situations.

She writes in genres ranging from visionary fiction to juvenile nonfiction to spirituality and memoir.

"I write for people who like challenging, original work. My reader isn't satisfied by a worn-out story or predictable plot. I do my best to give my readers what they want."

Ms. Nathan's books have won twenty-one national awards, including multiple awards from oldest, largest, and most prestigious contests for independent publishers. Her books have earned rave critical reviews and customer reviews of close to five-star averages on Amazon. Most are Amazon bestsellers.

Sandy was born in San Francisco, California, at the end of WWII. Her father, a first generation immigrant of Icelandic stock, created and owned one of the largest residential construction companies in the USA. Sandy grew up in the hard-driving, achievement-orientated corporate culture of Silicon Valley.

Sandy holds Master's Degrees in Economics and Marriage, Family, and Child Counseling. She was a doctoral student at Stanford's Graduate School of Business and has been an economic analyst, businesswoman, and negotiation coach, as well as author.

Mrs. Nathan lives with her husband on their California ranch. They bred Peruvian Paso horses for almost twenty years. She has three grown children and two grandchildren.

www.sandynathan.com